The Angels of Lovely Lane

Nadine Dorries

W F HOWES LTD

This large print edition published in 2016 by
W F Howes Ltd
Unit 5, St George's House, Rearsby Business Park,
Gaddesby Lane, Rearsby, Leicester LE7 4YH

1 3 5 7 9 10 8 6 4 2

First published in the United Kingdom in 2016
by Head of Zeus Ltd

A CIP catalogue record for this book is available
from the British Library

ISBN 978 1 51005 019 8

Typeset by Palimpsest Book Production Limited,
Falkirk, Stirlingshire

Printed and bound in Great Britain
by TJ International Ltd, Padstow, Cornwall

For Chris

Liverpool, December 1940

Young Emily Haycock ran like the wind along George Street towards home. She was ten minutes later than usual and her lungs filled with the Mersey mist as she covered the last few yards uphill to the back gate. She had left the munitions factory on time, but had been frustrated by the slowness of the bus, which seemed to take for ever. George Street sat at the top of a sandstone precipice from which well-trodden steps led down to the docks.

Emily knew that no sooner had she set foot inside the door than she would need to collect the food coupons and run back out again, down the road to queue with the rest of the factory workers at the corner shop at the end of Albert Street. She hoped there would be enough bacon and butter left for the family tea by the time she arrived, so that she could feed her younger brothers. Soon, it would be dark, the shop would close and everyone would prepare for the blackout.

Emily's stepfather, Alfred, had returned wounded

from fighting with the King's Own Lancaster regiment the year before. He now walked with a caliper on his leg and a stick in his hand. His constant pain was obvious to all, although he rarely complained. The day after his full medical discharge, he wasted no time in signing up for the Home Guard, which was where he spent every single night, seven days a week.

'Hello, queen,' he said, as Emily almost fell in through the back door. He was sitting on the edge of the sofa. Wooden-framed and stuffed with horsehair, it had taken all their strength that morning to drag it from the parlour to in front of the kitchen range. Here, under a darned and patched blanket, lay the pitifully thin form of Emily's sleeping mother. Earlier that morning, despite her obvious discomfort, she had insisted on being lifted out of bed and carried downstairs. The air in the kitchen smelt acrid. Of blood and sputum, of unwashed hair and vomit-laced breath.

'Shh.' Alfred placed his finger to his lips.

'How is she?' Emily whispered as she tiptoed over and gazed down at the once beautiful pale complexion, now the colour of tallow. Her mother's head was turned to one side, almost facing the back of the sofa. Beads of perspiration rested on her top lip and Emily could hear the gentle sound of her laboured and shallow breathing as she slept the deep healing sleep of the sick. Her dark hair was matted and clung to the side of her face. On one corner of her mouth remained a streak of stale blood she had wiped with her handkerchief during a bout of coughing. The thin, parchment-like skin covering her eyes appeared to have sunk deeply into her skull.

'Had a good day, love?' Alfred stroked Emily's forearm with his hand. A gesture of affection and solidarity in the midst of their shared concern. Emily could not yet answer him; she couldn't speak. Each time she walked into the house, she required a brief period of adjustment before she could step into her life as it now was, and not how it was supposed to be. She was only just sixteen and during the daytime, as she worked at her factory bench, she was able to pretend that this new situation, with an ailing mother and an injured stepfather, did not exist. She could imagine that life was still as it was, before the war, before the TB, before the days when she was forced to abandon her plans to train as a nurse at St Angelus.

'The doctor came today. He said he wants her to be admitted into the sanatorium, over the water, in West Kirby, and she promised to think about it. He said he would move hell and high water to get her a bed. He's a good man, you know.'

Emily nodded in agreement. She had met the specialist with her mother a number of times, and liked him a lot. It seemed to her as though he was kindness and concern itself.

'How do I pay for your visit?' she had heard Alfred ask, after his first call.

'You don't,' the doctor replied. 'The government

cover this under a special scheme and even if they didn't, you wouldn't have to pay.'

After he left, Emily had read his list of instructions.

Bedroom window to remain open.
Complete bed rest elevated on five pillows for at least six months.
No bathing.
Nourishing diet.
No anxiety or excitement.
One visitor at a time only wearing a face mask of quadruple tightly folded muslin.
Hands of attendants and visitors to be washed in a diluted solution of Dettol before leaving the house.
Contact the hospital should symptoms worsen.

It was at that moment Emily had known her dreams of becoming a nurse were over.

'She doesn't want to leave the house or the kids, but whatever you said to her this morning, it's had an effect,' Alfred said. 'Dr Gaskell wants her to have another X-ray and then he wants to collapse her bad lung, to rest it. He's stuck as to what else to do, because the total bed rest doesn't seem to be working. She can be so stubborn, your mam.' As he spoke, he gazed down at his wife with a look so tender, it was painful for Emily to see. Emily knew what he meant. Only that morning she had asked him to call in the doctor again. She had been concerned at what had appeared to be a rapid deterioration. Instead of coughing up blood a few times a day, it seemed as though this morning it had been every five minutes.

'At least she agreed to the total bed rest. She has stuck to that.' Emily was clutching at straws and Alfred knew it.

'She also agreed to go and visit Dr Gaskell at his St Angelus clinic tomorrow. He's a good man, coming out here to the house to see her. She trusts him, and he's the biggest man in Liverpool when it comes to this, you know. He knows what he's doing all right. I think he's going to try and persuade her, once she has had the X-ray, to be admitted straight to the sanatorium. He told me he's worried now that the second lung is badly affected. The trouble is, so many of the sanatoriums have been shut down because of the war. The waiting list could be months. There may not be anywhere for her to go.'

Alfred's voice trailed away. Both he and Emily knew that if her mother had agreed to consider leaving her young sons, she must be ill.

'We have to be at St Angelus at ten in the morning,' he said after a moment.

Emily squatted down and took her mother's hand, bony and blue-veined, like a bird's claw, and kissed the back. She hid her face. Alfred must not see her cry. He had enough to deal with and she must be his support, not a burden.

Emily's parents laboured under the impression

5

that she had no idea how bad things were. They were mistaken. She had heard them, in the dead of night, when they thought she and the younger children were asleep, talking, whispering, crying.

She had heard her mother's coughing, seen her shiver and sweat, bring up blood, collapse into a chair, swamped with fatigue. The swollen ankles and the painful chest. She had seen enough people in the same condition while she was growing up on Liverpool's dockside streets during the 1930s. She knew.

Early that morning, as Emily washed her mother and took her her morning tea, she had made her decision.

'I'm going to stop work at the factory, Mam. Rita's been great helping with the kids, but until you are better I think I had better stop here at home. After all, the doctor says you're only allowed to get up to go to the toilet once a day. I have to be here, Mam.'

There was a catch in her breath. Emily was closer to tears than she had been aware. Her mother had tried to reply, but instead began a fresh bout of coughing. Emily saw the bright red frothing deposit that her mother did her best to conceal in her handkerchief.

'I think that's best too, love,' her mother had said, grimacing through the pain, as Emily lifted her arms to wash them, gently taking the handkerchief from the thin fingers as she did so.

'That's not a good sign, I don't think, is it?' she said, inclining her head towards the crimson stain.

'Oh, I don't know, love. I think maybe it is a good sign, you know: get the badness out and then you can heal properly.' Emily's mother had no idea where the words came from as she tried to reassure her daughter. Put there by an ancient memory, or the ghost of a passed relative, or simply invented to help her in her hour of need as she struggled to reassure her family. To hold them together.

'I'll ask Da to call the doctor in, and I'll let them know at the factory that I'm needed at home. Next Friday can be my last day. We have to get this better, Mam. Will you please go into the sanatorium?'

A weak smile passed between mother and daughter. Emily bent down and kissed her mother's cheek. 'I have to get on, Mam. Can you hear the kids?'

Again, they shared a glance of understanding tinged with affectionate exasperation as the sound of breakfast squabbles wafted up through the floorboards. 'I'll drop them at Rita's on my way to work – that's unless I drop them on their heads first, mind. I have to go in half an hour or I'll be late. Alf and I are going to move the sofa into the kitchen, like you asked, and then Alf will help you down the stairs. You are right, you know: it is warmer down there, but you are not allowed to referee the boys.' Emily knew that was exactly why her mother wanted to be moved downstairs, and that there was nothing she would enjoy more.

'You go on, love, and thanks,' said her mother. She squeezed Emily's hand, but as Emily reached the door, she called her back. 'Emily, come here.'

Emily slowly turned to the bed. Through her mind ran the words, 'Don't, Mam.' She didn't want her mother to tell her what was wrong. Much better that they both went on pretending that things would soon improve. For Emily, it was easier that way.

'I know Alfred's not your real dad, but you do know he loves you, don't you? He thinks no less of you than of the boys. You have always been special to him.'

Emily let her breath go and sighed in relief. 'God, Mam, of course I know that. I love him too. Alfred is my da and I don't think of him as anything else. He's been the best. You couldn't have married a nicer person. I tell him every day he's my Alfred the Great!'

Emily grinned at her mother, who looked like a doll lying in the bed, she was now so thin. She saw the tears welling in her mother's eyes and knew that what had just passed between them was more than mere words of appreciation for the man who had provided them with a home, security and love. Her mother was looking for reassurance that Alfred would be cared for, should anything happen to her.

'Don't worry about Alfred, Mam; he will always be my number one. I will never let him down, I promise.'

Emily had lain awake the previous evening and heard the whispered exchange between her parents. 'Too far gone. Both lungs now.' Her mother sobbing, Alfred scrabbling for inadequate words of consolation. Alfred's muffled voice and her mother never once failing to comfort him.

She had wanted to run into their room, slip into their bed and beg, 'Please, tell me, what's going on, because this can't be true. I don't understand what's happening. Everything is changing and I'm so scared.' She was filled with the fear of not fully knowing what was ahead, and the dread of being aware that worse was probably yet to come.

Now, at the other end of the day, it occurred to Emily that her mother had deteriorated after just a few hours. 'She's spent most of the day lying on the sofa. She refuses go back to bed now that she's down,' said her da. 'Said she wanted to see you when you got in from work and the kids when they came home from school. You know your mam, she hates to miss anything.'

Emily smelt something that made her mouth water. Turning round, she saw that there was an earthenware pot on the kitchen table, covered by a tea towel, and instantly tears, which were never far from the surface, sprang to her eyes. She knew it was a donation from one of the neighbours; probably Mrs Simmonds, who often popped in and sat with her mother when her da did his rounds. If there was no meat to be seen she would take home with her whatever veg she could find in the Haycock kitchen, returning them hours later in a more edible state than when they left. On other days she would make double the scouse she needed for her own evening meal and then leave half on the table for Emily to heat up for the children when they arrived back from Rita's house. Rita: yet another good neighbour they depended on. Emily felt as though Rita were her confidante, her best friend. More than that even, the older sister she had never had. Only a few years older than Emily, but already with a family of her own.

Emily's mother opened her eyes and smiled at Alfred. Emily felt a twinge of jealousy. Her ma and Alfred loved each other so much that Emily often felt excluded by their private exchanges. She dropped back to her knees by the side of the sofa. 'Mam, are you all right?' She was vying for her mother's attention, dragging her away from Alfred and feeling guilty for it.

'Oh, there you are, queen,' her mother whispered, with a hint of surprise. 'I must have known you were home. I'm glad I woke up. Could you just grab the coupons, love, and go down to the shop for me before the kids come home?'

'The kids are already home, love. They've gone straight to Rita's,' Alfred said, smiling at his wife. Rita's little sons and their own were inseparable. 'They'll be back soon, queen. She took them straight from school.'

'It's like we have four little boys, or none at all,'

Emily said, extracting the ration books from the drawer in the wooden kitchen table. 'One day we'll find out which ones are ours, eh? When we can finally peel them apart.' Even her mother laughed at that, although the effort made her cough.

There had been talk about the children in Arthur Street and George Street being evacuated. Too close to the docks for their own safety, the letter had said. Many of the children had already left, mostly to North Wales, but those whose parents refused to be parted from them, or believed the war would be over sometime soon, remained. 'Our boys won't be going anywhere,' Alfred had said, when the letter arrived. 'If a bomb gets us, we'll go together.'

Emily had laughed. 'A bomb won't get us, Da, but still, it might be safer and easier for our mam if the children go. One of the women in the factory said that lots of the evacuees are being well fed. Those who have gone to North Wales are getting eggs and meat, and that's as good a reason to agree to them going as anything else.'

Many of the children in Arthur Street had been evacuated to Rhyl the previous week and the women were still crying. Alfred had seen and heard them and he was adamant that he did not want the boys to be sent away, but Emily knew that perhaps the time was right. Maybe, now that her mother wasn't coping at all any more and was no longer objecting to the idea of the sanatorium, it was time for Emily's young siblings to join their peers. The thought of life without the boys at home and her mam away in a sanatorium made her feel she was falling into a pit of loneliness.

'The war will be over before the kids even reach Wales,' Alfred had said. 'It'll be a waste of a journey and besides, I don't want no strangers looking after our kids. Yer ma wouldn't sleep at night. Worried sick she would be.'

There was some truth in what Alfred said. Emily knew that this evening the kids were at Rita's and having a great time, but she also knew that Rita was thinking of doing exactly the same thing. Her husband Jack was on the front line and he had written home weeks ago, instructing her to do just that. Rita hadn't said anything yet, but Emily had seen the woman who organized the evacuee transport leaving her friend's back yard only yesterday morning.

She had no idea how she and her da would manage without Rita. If her own children were evacuated, how could they accept her help? Rita struggled every day, but she never failed to help out, and in return Emily did what she could for her, including watching her boys while Rita did shifts down at the munitions factory at the week-ends. No doubt, if Rita's children were away, she would increase her shifts to full time, and why shouldn't she? But it would mean she would no longer be there when they needed her. These troubled thoughts had run through Emily's mind since yesterday, but now she needed to run to the shop and collect up the kids before dark fell.

'I'll run for the messages quick, Mam. I'll be back in half an hour.'

Her mother smiled weakly. 'You're a good girl, Emily, the best. I'm lucky to have you.' Emily kissed her on the brow and stood for a moment, breathing in the smell of hair that she dared not wash.

Before she left for the shop, she popped her head round Rita's back door. 'Give me your coupons, quick. The shop has butter in.'

'God, you're a love,' said Rita, taking the coupons out of a drawer. 'How's yer mam? I took her some pearl barley soup in at lunch time, but she didn't want it.' Her face was full of concern for Emily, whose two young brothers had run over and grabbed her knees as soon as she walked into the kitchen.

'We're having the best fun here, Emily. Do you want to play too? Rita says we have to listen to the radio later, because there is going to be news about the war and she wants to know where Uncle Jack is. Are you coming to listen?' Richard jumped up and down and looked up at her with eager eyes.

'I will when I've done the jobs, love,' Emily said, smiling at Rita. 'And once the tea is cleared away we can play a game ourselves tonight, at home. As long as we are not too noisy. Mam is on the sofa we moved into the kitchen this morning, and she would love that.'

'Mammy's on the sofa. Mammy's getting better,'

shouted Richard as he jumped up and down in excitement. Satisfied, he ran back off to play with the other boys.

'I was there when Dr Gaskell came, Emily,' said Rita. 'Your da asked me to sit in, when he had to pop into the club to get his rota for the blackout. He said your mam had been pretty bad this morning. The doctor gave her an injection for the pain and he left some medicine in a brown bottle on the dresser. She's to have it when the pain gets too bad. He said he wants to talk to your mam and da in the morning and they have to meet him at St Angelus. I was thinking, perhaps you might want me to go with him if you can't?' Emily was about to protest, but Rita went on, 'Maisie Tanner has offered to take the boys to school. She loves your little Richard, thinks he's a dote, and if she does that I can easily go to St Angelus. The doctor said he wants someone to be with your mam and da to listen to what he has to say and remember for them afterwards, and I said well that's not a problem, it will be Emily or me. What do you think, love? Can you go? Or shall I? I think the doctor wants yer mam to be looked after by the St Angelus nurses and I know there are none better. My own mam was in St Angelus and she loved those nurses. Angels from Lovely Lane she called them. They all live in that big white house opposite the park gates. You know the one?'

Emily nodded. She herself had seen the nurses in their long skirts and capes and frilly hats, and when she was a little girl she thought she had never seen such pretty ladies. She had confided in no one, but all she had ever wanted to do was to become one of the angels. To wear the uniform and to look after people who were sick. But the war, Alfred's being called up and then so badly wounded, her mother's illness, two little boys to care for, her nursing duties at home, had all put a stop to that.

'I'm going to leave work for good next Friday, Rita. I have to stay at home now. If Mam is taken into hospital, I can't be at the factory all day. Can you go tomorrow and I'll work out a week's notice?'

'Of course I can, love. If the doctor suggests she stays at St Angelus, I think it will be for the best. Your mam is going to need more help than we can give her soon. She will need those angels.'

Tears welled up in Emily's eyes. 'Rita, is my mam going to die?'

Rita dried her hands on her apron as she walked over to Emily. 'Die? Of course not, love.' She put her arms around the younger woman's shoulders and hugged her. 'She will be staying in St Angelus to be made better, just until there is a place in the sanatorium over the water, like Maisie Tanner's mam. Now, come on, we have no time for crying, you and me. We have too much to do. Look, I've washed yer mam's best nightie here and I've washed me own for her to take, too, for a spare. Pack those in her bag with some wash things and a headscarf to keep her hair nice. I was going to wash it for her – Alf and I, we had the range pumping out to keep the room warm, so the water was hot – but she wouldn't let me. Truth is, I don't think she could be bothered. Told us off for wasting the coke, she did. Wanted to save it until you kids got home to feel the benefit. Here's me coupons; I'll look after the kids. You go and get that bloody butter.'

She handed over the ration books and gave Emily another hug. 'Go on now. I'll have some soup ready for when you get back. Then you can crack on next door.'

When Emily reached the shop, she found Maisie Tanner in the queue in front of her. Emily knew she had been at school with Rita and was now married to Stan Tanner, who was away fighting the war, and they had a little girl who was about five or six years old. The family lived with Maisie's mam and dad, and Emily was both touched and grateful that she had offered to look after the boys.

'Hiya, Emily. How's yer mam, love?' Maisie greeted her warmly. 'I've told Rita, I can do anything you want to help, queen. It'll be no problem. Me mam was only saying tonight, she remembers the time your mam took a load of the kids to the shore at Crosby with Betty. Half a streetful they took. You remember yer mam's mate Betty? She's in Wales now, you know, sitting out the war.'

Emily did know. The Haycocks received a letter

16

from Betty once a week, telling them they were mad for remaining in Liverpool and that the sea air in Trearddur Bay would be just what was needed for her mam's chest to improve. Emily was beginning to wonder if she was right.

'They pushed five kids in each pram and took them on and off the train. I'll never know how they did it. God, it was a laugh. Our Brenda was one of the kids and she still remembers it. She's never been since. Said she'll never forget that day. I loved your mam, the poor thing.'

Emily couldn't answer. Maisie's use of the past tense was all she heard. *Loved?* It seemed to her that Maisie, who wasn't very much older than herself, was wiser than she could ever be. Maisie made Emily feel as though she knew nothing. *Is that what marriage and children do to you, make you older and wiser?*

'Rita is going with Mam to see the doctor at St Angelus tomorrow,' she said instead. 'I've decided to work out my notice at the factory. I need to be at home. I can't keep depending on others to help out.'

'Well, it's no trouble, but that's smashing for your dad,' Maisie replied. 'You're a good girl, Emily. Don't you worry about a thing. It's a great hospital, that St Angelus, you know. Some of the women on our street have started having their babies in there. My mam says they only go for the rest in bed. Seven days they make you stay, and they wash the baby and everything. You don't have to lift a finger. The Angels' Hotel, me mam calls it. She loved it in there, once she began to get better. I'd love our little Pammy to become one of those angels from Lovely Lane. God, I would be so proud I would burst if that happened. I think this one's a lad, though. Never stops kicking, he doesn't.' Maisie laughed as she rubbed her belly. 'I'm going to tell them to stop sending Stan home on leave. I don't want another until this bloody war is over. Mind you, I suppose a year without is too long for any man and I don't want our Stan getting wandering eyes, now do I?'

Emily blushed to the roots of her hair, but even as she did so it occurred to her that her street was full of angels.

The neighbours were wonderful. They took it in turns to sit with her ma, cook for her, bathe her, nurse her. The entire neighbourhood was full of angels and one of the best was Maisie Tanner.

The noise of the air-raid siren ripped through the air without any warning.

'Run,' screamed Maisie, as the sickening sound of an explosion made their ears ring as the shop window shattered and shards of glass filled the air. They had never heard or witnessed anything so terrifyingly close and for a split second everyone in the queue dropped their bags and, covering their faces with their hands, froze to the spot. A moment of silence followed as the last splinter of falling glass dropped to the floor. The shopkeeper was the first to move, yelling for everyone to leave.

'We're too close to the bloody docks here,' Maisie said breathlessly as they ran back towards the street.

'Here, into the shelter, Emily. Maisie, come on,' shouted a neighbour. It was the man who partnered up with Emily's da in the Home Guard, checking every house at night to ensure that everyone had shut their blackout curtains properly. Not a shaft of light passed either of them by. He was standing at the entrance to the communal shelter, already joking with the children as they ran in.

'I can't. I need to get back to the kids and me mam,' Emily shouted back.

'Wait, Emily.' Maisie grabbed her by her hand. 'Rita will take the kids to the shelter at the other end of Arthur Street and your da will get your mam down somehow. He'll carry her if he has to. Me mam will take our Pammy, so we're safest here. Come on, queen – it sounds really close this time, the little bastards.'

Emily looked towards the shelter and then back down the street towards home. The bombs were falling early. She knew, if she sprinted fast, she would be home in less than three minutes.

'They will all be under cover in a min. Best we do what Tom here says.' The siren continued and Emily could hardly hear Maisie above the noise, but when the older woman suddenly grabbed her by the arm again she knew that this time it was not to reason with her. The grip was too hard and urgent. Maisie Tanner's face was distorted in pain.

'Is it the baby?' asked Emily in alarm.

Maisie nodded, and Emily watched the pain fade from her face as quickly as it had come. 'It can't be, though. I'm only seven months, and I know that's right because I know when Stan was on leave. I'll be all right. It will stop.'

Emily had taken part in the street rehearsals run by the Home Guard half a dozen times. She knew that Rita and the boys would be stumbling along George Street towards the communal shelter any second now. Rita had a routine practised with the kids and they would probably already be on their way, the two younger boys piled into the pram with Richard and Henry standing on the carriage holding on to the handlebar while Rita pushed. They would be heading away from where she now stood. Rita would encourage the children to pretend that they were playing the train game. 'Choo choo,' the children's voices would whisper into the dark. 'All aboard the shelter train,' Rita's voice would ring back.

Before they ducked into the entrance Maisie and Emily turned towards the sound of another explosion and looked down towards the river's edge. The skyline was a vivid red from the flames which leapt into the air.

'Oh my God,' said Emily, clasping her hand to her mouth. 'It looks like one of the ships has been hit. The sky is on fire.'

Maisie followed her gaze down towards the Mersey and was speechless.

'Come on, girls. You coming in or what?' Tom sounded nervous and was becoming impatient.

And then came the stillness. The heavy, oppressive stillness during which no one spoke. The hairs on the back of Emily's neck rose in fear as her skin tightened, and as she looked around her she saw that everyone had stopped and was standing, dead still, waiting. Then it came. The whistling sound that pierced her ears and an explosion so loud it deafened her, as George Street took a direct hit.

It was morning, cold and misty, and the fires still burned as she walked down the street she no longer recognized. In a daze, she refused to allow panic to take hold and tried her best to remain calm as she took deep breaths, in and out, in and out. The woman who had delivered Maisie's baby girl – not the boy Maisie was convinced she was carrying – had run on ahead to Arthur Street, calling the name of Maisie's mam, just as Maisie herself had done for most of the night. She had tried her hardest not to scream out in pain as they heard the bombs continually falling. Fear had gripped Emily's heart during the long night while she sat holding Maisie's hand. 'It's bad out there,' one of the women had said.

Tom, whose duty shelter they were in, replied, 'It is, it's bad.'

Even though it was now daylight, the sky glowed a deep burnt orange through the airborne dust

21

and smoke. The noise of a solitary woman shouting and running was surreal and confusing.

'Where are the houses and the shop? Where has the shop gone?' said Emily to no one. The fire tenders blocked her way down the street and the men working on the gas main shouted to her to stop.

'Where are you going, love?' a young man called out to her as she squeezed through the barrier which had already been erected. 'Oi, stop. Are you mad or what? You can't go down there.'

'But I have to. I live there. I have to go home,' Emily replied, in a daze. 'Rita has the kids.'

'You can't do that, love. There's been a direct hit on the street. It's too dangerous.' The man took her arm, looking at her with eyes loaded with sympathy. 'Which side of the street did you live on, love?' he went on.

Emily turned to face him. 'We live on our side,' she said, confused. 'This side.' She was looking at where the houses had once stood, where now there seemed to be nothing but rubble, and that was when she saw her mother. She shook her head in disbelief. Her mind refused to accept what her eyes could see although it was there before her, as clear as the flames leaping from the pile of rubble that had once been their home. She rubbed her eyes. The dust and smoke were distorting her vision. This was a nightmare. She would wake. This could not be true. It could not be real, but it was. It was real. It was her mother.

'Oh, God, no, no,' Emily screamed, and a man she had never seen before, his face covered with dirt, emerged through the smoke and ran towards them.

'Are you all right, love?' he shouted. 'You need to get away from here. We have to make the gas mains secure first before anyone can go down the street. Does she live here?' he asked the fireman who was holding Emily's arm.

Emily wasn't listening. She was looking at the face of her mother, who was lying on the roof of the house opposite where their own had once stood. Her arm dangling, she was looking directly into the street, her eyes open, free of pain at last.

'You all right, love? Seriously, I'm going to have to move you away from the gas.' The man was in front of her now, but she could not turn her head to look at him.

'Mam,' she whispered.

His eyes followed her own. 'Jesus! Fecking hell,' he muttered, putting his arm across her shoulder and trying to lead her away.

'We have to get my mam. I'm coming, Mam,' she shouted at the top of her voice. 'Richard! Henry! Richard!' she screamed into the heap of dust and rubble. 'Rita!'

She tried to move forward, but now more hands were pulling her back.

'Get her to the end of the street. Her da's there, he's still alive,' she heard a voice say. 'They won't let him down here because of the gas.'

'But Rita has the kids. She has to go with Mam to the hospital today. I'm coming, Mam. We'll get you down now.'

'Come on, love,' said a man she recognized from the Home Guard. He put his arm around her, holding her tight, so she couldn't move. 'No one can do anything. You don't need to go to any hospital now. No doctor can help. They're all gone, love. Everyone in that row of houses. We've been searching through the rubble all night. There's no one left except your da. He was on his way to fetch you when the bomb came down. Let's get you back to your da.'

She heard the conversations of firemen nearby, oblivious of her presence. The voices came from somewhere within the dust and flames, from the men searching the rubble.

'It was a bad one. A big bastard. Reckon there's a woman in here and maybe four or five kids, could be more, all dead.' For a moment the smoke cleared, and Emily saw that the speaker was standing in what had only the previous evening been Rita's kitchen.

'I have her coupons,' Emily whispered through her tears, knowing that, of the children he referred to, two were her own little brothers. 'I have her coupons,' she sobbed again.

CHAPTER 1

St Angelus Hospital, Liverpool, December 1951

St Angelus had begun life as a workhouse, proudly facing out towards the Mersey and across the Atlantic. It was built of a dark sandstone brick which had long since succumbed to smog and smoke and the dribbling black soot that ran down the exterior walls like icing on a cake. The many tall chimneys spewed out their lung-clogging smoulder from the basement furnaces which heated the Florence Nightingale wards.

Through the centre of the hospital ran a long, polished corridor that began at the main entrance and ended at the back door. The theatre block, the school of nursing, the medical school, the mortuary and the kitchens were housed in separate buildings dotted around the grounds and had been built at varying times over the past two hundred years. Some were constructed of brick, some more recent post-war additions, such as the prosthetics clinic erected to meet the upsurge in demand for false limbs, had been hurriedly thrown together from prefabricated units and covered with tin roofs.

Each area of the hospital, except those where patients slept, was scrubbed by an army of night cleaners, who shuffled along on housemaid's knees with metal buckets and brushes. They worked from dusk until dawn for five shillings a shift. St Angelus gleamed brightly and smelt strongly of Lysol, a smell so distinctive it struck fear into the hearts of the weak and anxious.

Martha O'Brien was the maid in the consultants' day sitting room at St Angelus and therefore, to anyone of any significance, was entirely invisible.

Martha knew it was her own fault.

That's what they would say, anyway. She had broken the rules. What did she expect? A person of no consequence. Laying the fire, clearing away the newspapers, plumping up the cushions and preparing the consultants' lunches for one o'clock on the dot. That was her job. She was meant to serve tea, not sympathy, they would tell her. But she had done it because she had felt sorry for him, not because she knew what the effect would be. If she had known, she would have run a mile in the opposite direction as fast as her legs would carry her, or better still, just kept her mouth shut. She had watched him, day after day, sitting in the chair, troubled and worried, and had wondered what it was that ailed him. It wasn't until Mr Mabbutt popped in for a cuppa and goaded him that the mystery was revealed.

'So, there are to be two consultants on gynae. Well, that's something. Yours will be the only department in the hospital with two firms.'

Mr Mabbutt, the orthopaedic surgeon, was addressing Mr Scriven, the obstetrician and gynaecologist. Mr Scriven shuffled in his chair and turned the page of the newspaper he was reading so sharply that it almost ripped. Martha knew all their names and what they specialized in, and given that she was a bright girl and they talked a lot when they met in the sitting room she knew far more about their personal lives than they might have imagined. Apart from Dr Gaskell, who had been at St Angelus for so long no one could remember a time when he was not there, Mr Mabbutt and Mr Scriven were the two longest-serving consultants. The reverence in which they were held by every nurse and doctor in the hospital conferred a godlike status upon both men.

They played golf together on Thursday afternoons, when they had finished their rounds on the private wing, otherwise known as ward five. Once a month, they also took turns to host a dinner, for other hand-picked surgeons, aspiring doctors and their ambitious wives. Due to the length of his tenure and his position on the hospital board, Mr Scriven was regarded as the senior consultant, second only to Dr Gaskell, who was chair of the board. Dr Gaskell sat on the regional TB committee and was respected and revered by all, and his word with regard to St Angelus was law. Mr Scriven had reach, undoubtedly, but not long enough to ensure that the board consulted him before deciding he must share the base of his power and source of unceasing adoration, otherwise known as ward two.

Neither man batted an eyelid while Martha wheeled over the tea trolley, or even appeared to notice her as they waited for a cup and saucer to be placed in their outstretched hands. There were nine consultants at St Angelus and Martha had only ever needed to be told once how many sugars they took, or how they liked their tea. Martha took her job very seriously. She dressed with care, her apron and frilled cap always spotlessly clean. Her long dark hair was coiled carefully and tightly into a bun, with every strand tucked neatly under her cap.

'Anyone would think you were the one operating yourself, you're that fussy,' her mother Elsie often shouted as she left the house to catch the ten past six bus every morning. It was true: Martha was as proud of the sitting room as her ma was of the parlour back at home.

Mr Mabbutt had collapsed into the comfortable brown leather armchair in front of the fire, opposite Mr Scriven, who, much to Martha's dismay, still wore his wraparound operating robe, instead of the day suit he wore for clinics and ward rounds. There were two theatres on the top floor of St

Angelus, and the two men had been operating simultaneously before finishing for the afternoon, leaving the registrars and housemen to deal with the post-operative checks on the wards.

Mr Scriven's gown remained gruesomely spattered with blood. None of the other doctors arrived to take their tea in blood-spattered gowns and Martha lived in hope that one day, maybe, one of the consultants would find the habit as offensive as she did and mention that he might like to be a little more respectful towards the room she spent her life polishing and cleaning and making comfortable. Not that she had ever said anything; that was not her place.

If only she had remembered just where her place was. How different things would be. She sometimes wondered if he was showing off when he strutted through the door wearing his theatre gown, when the other consultants took such care to remove their own. She was only a maid, but it seemed to Martha as though Mr Scriven liked to impress, or rather needed to impress, and even someone as humble as she was a worthy audience of one.

Educated by the nuns at St Chad's, she had learnt well and was a clever girl. Following the war, there were only the two of them at home and so the need to secure work with regular hours and pay was uppermost in her mind when the job vacancy arose. Both her da and her brother had been lost in action and Martha felt a strong responsibility to start earning for her mam and their home as soon as she could, even though it meant abandoning her dream of attending the new secretarial college in town and becoming a secretary in one of the shipping offices.

There were moments when she stopped scrubbing and cleaning and knelt with a cloth in her hand, letting the mixture of gloopy pink Aunt Sally and dark green Lysol drip on to the floor. With a sigh, she imagined herself setting off to work in the morning carrying a handbag, smartly dressed wearing kitten heels and a swing coat, on her way to run a smart office down on the waterfront. She felt no resentment. She and Mam were happy and Jake Berry, her childhood sweetheart, also worked at St Angelus, as a junior porter. Not that they were a couple officially. No, Martha would not allow Jake to assume that. Besides, they had only been on two dates since leaving St Chad's and they had been nothing more than to take a turn around the lake in Sefton Park on a Sunday afternoon after the roast dinner. On the last occasion, Jake had taken Martha's hand and slipped it through his arm.

'You will be my girl soon, won't you?' he had said. 'You're seventeen now. We could walk like this every day.'

Martha's blushes were saved by the musicians on the bandstand striking up a tune. Instead of replying, she gave Jake a shy smile and his arm a little squeeze. It was enough for Jake, who felt as though he would burst with pride, having by his side the girl he had adored since they were both children playing out on the street in rags and tags and shoes with holes.

Martha poured the consultants' tea and listened closely. She knew Mr Mabbutt's tone well. He hadn't finished with Mr Scriven, she was sure.

Mr Scriven fixed a rigid smile on to his face. 'Yes, Matron told me last week, after the board meeting.' Martha could tell that he was trying his best to sound casual. 'I can barely manage the numbers being referred to my clinic as it is. Emergencies are arriving via the receiving ward in their droves. The women in Liverpool are producing more babies than St Angelus can deliver, along with all the associated problems that can present later, as you know.'

Martha had read as much herself in the *Echo*, so she knew that wasn't a lie. Babies were booming in Liverpool. However, after a year of observing Mr Scriven at her leisure, she could also tell this was not a conversation he was enjoying.

She placed the cup and saucer on his upturned palm, but he neither acknowledged her nor said thank you as he picked up the spoon from the saucer and began to stir.

Mr Mabbutt appeared to have spotted a weakness and was openly enjoying himself. He was not about to let the wriggling Mr Scriven off the hook.

'Hmm, that's as maybe. Still, not sure I would like it much. My ward is my ward. Sister and the nursing staff know my ways and how I like things done. No, it wouldn't do for me, I'm afraid. Besides, we have all these new mad keen doctors now. The chaps who interrupted their training to fight in the war. The board favour them, of course, and they're flying up the ladder. Dr Gaskell's own son is one of them. He has an impressive war record, so I hear. God, no. I wouldn't want one of those hungry types working alongside me, trying to jump on my back and take my ward out from under me.'

Mr Mabbutt gave a fake shudder and then grinned. Mr Scriven struggled and failed to smile back. Mr Mabbutt had beaten Mr Scriven at golf four weeks on the run. This latest piece of information was yet another move on the chessboard in the battle for superiority and the unspoken acknowledgement of the position of senior consultant under Dr Gaskell. Mr Scriven took a long and carefully controlled breath. He knew perfectly well that his colleague had not yet finished taunting him.

'We are busy too, you know. They have allocated me an extra registrar and a houseman. It seems even the working classes are buying motors now. Just operated on a young lad with bilateral femoral shaft fractures from a scooter accident. Reckon there's going to be a lot more of that in the future. I wonder why they didn't just increase the size of your firm? Why bring in a new consultant? Regardless of how busy you are, it makes it look as though they don't trust your opinion, or the quality of your work.'

Bang. It was a direct shot and had hit its mark. Mr Scriven flinched.

He drank his tea to delay answering, because he had no idea what to say. He had asked himself the same question. He almost gave a sigh of relief as the call bell rang. Mr Mabbutt looked up at the consultants' alert board on the wall and saw it was his light flashing just as the telephone rang. He leapt up from the chair, splashing his tea all over his knee as he did so.

'Yes, on my way back up,' he barked down the receiver before slamming it down. 'Right, that was a short break. My last one is throwing an extended rigor in the recovery room and the anaesthetist can't raise his blood pressure out of his boots. Neither houseman nor theatre sister is happy. Poor lad, he's only sixteen. I feared he might not survive the shock. I didn't even touch the fractures. I was saving them until he was stable. All I did was sew up what cuts I could manage. l must have cleared half the dock road out of his wounds.'

He picked up his cup and swallowed what remained of his tea. As he walked towards the door he couldn't resist a parting shot. 'Anyway, do you know if you will be sharing a team, or will the new chap have his own housemen and registrar?'

Even in the midst of an emergency, he was not going to allow his advantage to slip away. He stood holding the door open, waiting for a reply.

'His own, of course. I told Matron I can't spare any of my team. We're working flat out as it is.'

'Ah, that's even worse, if you ask me. Competing teams on one ward, who needs it?'

His words hung in the air as the door swung shut.

Martha may have worked at the hospital since she was fourteen, but she was far from stupid. Mr Scriven had attempted to present a brave face to Mr Mabbutt, but Martha could tell he was both seething and miserable. She noticed that his hair, which a year ago had been grey only at the temples, was now grey all over. He had taken to wearing glasses, and she had thought it strange that, if anything, the dark glasses and greying hair had added to his attractiveness.

'Bastard,' she heard him mutter under his breath.

Without being asked, she refilled his cup and put two arrowroot biscuits on a plate for him. 'Nothing like a cup of tea and an arrowroot biscuit to cheer you up,' her mother had said every time an air raid was over and they slipped back into the house after a night in the shelter. It had seemed to work for her mam.

Mr Scriven was deep in thought. Leaning forward now in his chair, elbows on knees, fingers inter-linked before him, he tapped his straightened index fingers repeatedly against his pursed lips.

'A penny for your thoughts,' she said, as he automatically reached up to relieve her of the tea.

And that was when it happened. The moment

when she crossed the line, broke the rules, set in train the events which would destroy her world and everything she knew in life to be good and true. Those words, that impulsive moment of caring and compassion, would be responsible for pain and deceit, secrets and lies, and, the very worst of all, a death.

CHAPTER 2

A village on the outskirts of Belmullet, County Mayo,
Ireland, earlier, in the summer of 1951

'Dana, would ye wake up, sleepy head, and come downstairs and see Daddy. Your letter has arrived, look. He will be late for work if he doesn't leave soon.'

Dana blinked furiously. Her mother had pulled back her bedroom curtains and bright sunlight streamed into her room, replacing the damp rainy gloom of yesterday, and so many days on the windy west Atlantic coast of Mayo.

'What time is it?' she asked, as she put her feet out of bed on to the small bedside mat, avoiding the cold linoleum. A slithering notion of fear combined with excitement slipped into her belly.

It was here. The letter that would confirm whether or not she had been accepted for nursing training at St Angelus in Liverpool. If she had, her dreams had come true and her prayers been answered. If not, she would have to accept the offer of a place at a hospital in Dublin, and this she definitely did not want to do. Daddy had made it clear that if she trained as a nurse in Dublin, she would be expected to travel back to Mayo on her days off and holidays to help her mammy on the farm. Dana loved her parents, but being the only child had severe drawbacks.

'It's half past seven and would ye look at this letter, two weeks it's taken to get here. 'Tis a disgrace.' Dana's mother waved the brown envelope up and down as though she were furiously fanning her face. 'The war is long gone, and they are still blaming the Germans for post our donkey could deliver faster with his legs tied together. Come on now, quickly, I want to make the eight o'clock mass and Daddy's going into town in the van.' With that, her mother bustled out of the room and down the stairs, shouting, 'Noel, listen to me, don't be moving now. You've to wait until Dana comes down and opens her letter. Stand around the table now, both of ye.'

Dana pulled on her dressing gown, looking out of her bedroom window across the never-ending miles of mist-soaked bog. 'I won't miss you one bit,' she said to the wet, rolling earth. 'I want to have a life of me own, I do, and I do not want to marry flaming Patrick O'Dowd.'

As if on cue, she heard the click of the yard gate and, pressing her face against the window to see who it was, saw Patrick striding across the yard. As though he sensed her at the window, he looked up and raised his hand in greeting. Dana feebly raised her own in return.

Patrick disappeared beneath her window to make his way in through the back door. 'Bloody nosy Mrs Brock.' Dana cursed the postmistress under her breath, as she slipped off the dressing gown and put on her slacks. She must have told him I have the letter, she thought, and he realized what it would be. How else would he know to be here?

Now fuming, but determined not to show it, she pulled a sweater on over her head and made her way down the stairs into the kitchen, where she knew the family committee would be waiting. Her grandmother would have known before she did that the letter had arrived. Mrs Brock had antennae that spread as far as Sligo.

Dana had to play out the next twenty minutes very carefully. She knew she was blessed, in as much as her mother would not miss mass for the world, and her father had to go to town to pick up the newly arrived fertilizer before it sold out. He had spoken of nothing else over supper the previous evening. Her entire plan had been to think one step ahead of her father at all times. To anticipate his arguments and to be ready with a reply that he could not challenge. It was all so easy. He was a simple man, driven and motivated by religion and morals and some very strict rules, inherited from Dana's grandmother, who was now sitting in her chair by the fire. As for Patrick, he was the son of her father's best friend on the neighbouring farm. He was so familiar to her he could have been her brother, and he spent so much time on their farm he might just as well have been.

As she opened the kitchen door, the entire family was standing around the kitchen table, waiting. Her mother smiling, her father frowning, her grandmother gurning and Patrick looking as though his world might be about to collapse.

'I need the bathroom,' she said with a smile as she stepped into the room. 'God in heaven, would you look at you all, 'tis like a firing squad. Just give me a minute.'

As she ran outside, she grinned. Five minutes down. Only fifteen more to play for, once she got back inside.

'I'm not sure letting her apply to Liverpool was a good idea,' said Patrick to Dana's father, scrunching his cap around in his hand.

'Don't ye be worrying about that, Patrick,' said Noel. 'She will never get in. What girl who ever went to school in Belmullet ever made it to St Angelus in Liverpool? 'Tis all a dream. They only occasionally take a girl from the Notre Dame convent in Galway, although God knows why. You know what they say about that school, "Notre Dame, push a pram", so many of them get pregnant once they reach Liverpool.'

Patrick gave a leering grin. This was man talk. He had known Mr Brogan all his life and accorded him the same respect he did his own father.

'Look, I had to agree,' Noel continued. 'I have to keep a steady ship here, as the only man in this house. Dana's mammy, she has the devil in her sometimes so she does, and if I didn't handle things in a very superior and clever way altogether, those two would run rings round me. I have to give in on occasion, for a peaceful life now. Calm yerself, 'twill all be fine. She will never get in in a hundred thousand years.'

He picked up his mug of tea from the table and drank deeply to avoid having to say more. Damn that Mrs Brock. She must have got word to Patrick that the letter had arrived before he himself had collected the post. He was not as confident as he had sounded. His Dana had always been a smart girl.

'There's no surprise in that,' he told his wife, when Dana won the maths prize at school. 'All the Brogans won prizes when I was at school.'

Mrs Brogan knew this was an outright lie but she never challenged the assertion. She had learnt early on that the way to maintain calm in the Brogan house when Daddy was around was for no one to cross a word he said.

Noel cast his eyes around the room as he drank his tea, wishing someone else would engage Patrick in conversation. If Dana did by some miracle happen to be accepted by St Angelus, dealing with Patrick was something he didn't want to do. His priority this morning was to collect the fertilizer and the feed. He didn't have one of the most productive farms in the west of Ireland because he sat on his laurels and he had no time for lovesick young men.

'I wish Patrick would just leave everything to me and his daddy,' he had said to Dana's mother the previous evening, after a skinful of Guinness. 'She will marry him because I will fecking tell her who she will fecking marry. Nurse or not, she will do what is best for the family and the farm.' At that point he collapsed, as was his way, over the kitchen table.

Without speaking, Patrick picked up his own mug of tea. Patrick had plans. His sights were set on the Brogan farm. He knew that with no sons and only a daughter to speak of, Noel Brogan needed Dana to make a good match. Patrick was the eldest son on the neighbouring farm and it made perfect sense to combine the two properties. He had wanted Dana to be his wife ever since he could remember and their fathers had agreed.

'And sure, why wouldn't it happen?' Mr O'Dowd had asked when Patrick had asked him a year ago if he was certain Dana would accept him, as she didn't seem awfully keen. Every time he had tried to kiss her, she had given him short shrift. He still smarted at some of her more hurtful rejections.

'Have you ever seen a toothbrush, Patrick? Ye have green teeth that grow fur and they revolt me,' she had said, as he tried to pin her against the barn wall during harvest.

That was just before she thumped him. That was when he had been a boy. He had now altered in both stature and attitude. No longer the adolescent, he had grown up in a household where violence was commonplace and had learnt his father's ways of dealing with women.

'If Dana is keen, she has a funny way of showing it,' he had told his da. 'I've yet to feel her titties. She just pushes me away.'

He was not expecting the blow that had caught him hard across his ear and the side of his face, or the mouthful of dirt he had swallowed as he hit the floor. Driven all his life by envy of Noel's fertile land, Mr O'Dowd had plotted for years to ensure it fell into the hands of his own family one day.

'Don't ye be touching her, unless ye can be sure ye can stop yerself,' he had bellowed at his son. 'Take yer pleasure elsewhere in the village, and don't be darkening our doorstep. Noel Brogan is my friend and you cannot do better than marry his daughter and take that farm. You can have his daughter on the night you marry her and not before. Do you understand that?'

From his back, lying on the ground with a loud noise ringing in his ear, Patrick could see the frayed laces of his father's boot dangerously close to his already swollen eye. He knew that if he uttered one wrong word that boot would land with full force, straight in his face.

'Yes, Daddy,' he had spluttered back through his bleeding nose.

'Try that woman Monica who sits at the bar at the back of Murphy's butchers. She will sort ye out while ye wait. Dana is the catch; don't feck it up. That farm is a gold mine. Ye won't get a better opportunity than that, or land that grows as well, anywhere in these parts.'

Patrick had done as he was told. He had honed his skills with Monica and now he was ready to make his move. To ease Dana's disappointment when she was rejected by St Angelus. That's what his mammy had told him he must do, when Mrs Brock had delivered her news and he left their milking shed to make his way across the yard and down the lane to the Brogan farm.

'Jesus, everyone knows she would never get in. God knows why ye are having to go through this performance. It's not right keeping you waiting, so it isn't,' his mammy had said as he went. Her whistled words rolled over her gums, her teeth long since removed by his father's handy and mostly drunken fists. 'Play clever now, Patrick. Be nice and considerate when she gets the news. 'Twill make your proposal easier for her to accept if she knows ye are a nice understanding lad, like ye are. Sure, 'tis no pretence. Isn't he just the greatest-looking lad around these parts?' to no one in particular, as she milked the cow with one hand and soothed the yellowing lump of a bruise on her thigh with the other.

When Dana returned to the kitchen, her mammy handed over the letter with a shaking hand and a smile. If she had heard the parting words of Patrick's mammy as he left, she would have slapped

43

the woman herself. As Dana took the letter from her hand, she extracted a rosary from her pocket and began to pray. The last thing she wanted for her daughter was a replay of her own life, and if there was one man she didn't want her daughter to marry, it was Patrick O'Dowd.

'I want ye to do the things I could only dream of,' she had told her daughter. 'I want ye to see the places like the pictures in the magazine they sometimes get in the post office. Go on, go and get out of Ireland. Don't be me with chapped hands, varicose veins and haemorrhoids to boot, with only a hysterectomy to look forward to. Jesus, there has to be more to life than that in this day and age.'

Dana noticed that her father made as if to say something, as her mother prayed over the rosary beads, but thought better of it. Noel did not have the same control in his own home as Patrick's father had in his. Dana's mother had threatened to leave him if he ever raised his fists to her long before they were married, and he was smart enough to know that she meant it. Dana knew her mother was openly praying for good news, while her father and Patrick secretly prayed for bad. Whose prayers would win out?

'Open the letter will ye, for heaven's sake,' her grandmother gurned as she stuffed boxty bread and milk in her mouth.

Playing to the moment, Dana picked a knife up from the blue checked gingham tablecloth. It was covered in butter and she slowly wiped it clean with a cloth.

'Mammy,' she said, 'is there any tea in the pot? I'm parched.'

'Oh my Lord,' yelled her mother, blessing herself for having committed the sin of blaspheming as soon as the words had left her mouth. Her hand trembled slightly as she poured the tea and Dana knew she must put her out of her misery. Using the knife to slice open the envelope, she pulled out the letter.

'I think, 'cause 'tis a thick letter, 'twill be good news will it not?' said her mother, almost in a whisper.

Dana had thought the same thing. Slowly, she extracted the thick wad of papers from the envelope. 'Shall I read it out loud?' Completely ignoring her father and Patrick, she looked directly at her mother, who had moved to stand next to her, slipping her arm around Dana's waist so that she could look over her shoulder as she read.

'Go on then,' said her mother, grinning. 'Read, for goodness' sake, before her next door knocks on for me to go to mass and I have to send her away.'

Dana began,

Dear Miss Brogan,

I have pleasure in informing you that you have been accepted for state registered nurse training at St Angelus, Liverpool, following receipt of the results of your entrance examination and recent interview. Upon successful completion of the preliminary training school examination at twelve weeks, you will undertake a three-year course.

Dana's eyes blurred and the page swam before her as she clasped a hand to her mouth. She had prayed to the Holy Mother and St Agatha every day since her interview, asking for just this result and now here it was, written before her on the sheet of paper now trembling violently in her hands. She could hardly believe it. As she looked up and scanned the kitchen through watery eyes, silence was the only response.

It was more than an old wives' tale – it was a fact that St Angelus only accepted girls from the better families and schools in Galway and Dublin. The girls who were not one bit concerned at the prospect of walking through the doors of the Sherbourne Hotel in Dublin to attend an interview, because walking through those doors was something they often did anyway. Sitting in the drawing room and being served tea while they waited for their name to be called, a waiter filling their cups from a silver pot on an ornate silver stand kept warm by fancy candles, as Dana had done. Scared out of her wits. Neither Dana nor her mammy knew of any girl from a family in rural Mayo who had been successful in securing a place at St Angelus, for the state registration training. Some had been accepted to become state enrolled, but none had made it to the status of staff nurse. Dublin was where the nursing dreams of the country girls began and ended.

'I can't read any more, Mammy.' The tears began to trip down her face and her mother gave her the handkerchief from her own apron pocket as they laughed and cried and hugged each other.

Noel Brogan had wanted Dana's letter to provide him with an easy life. To fit in with the plans he and his neighbour had made in the course of many a whiskey-fuelled conversation over the years. Plans to save what generations before them had struggled to preserve. A productive marriage between Patrick and Dana was the answer to the future. It would make sense of the past and right the wrong and the shame Noel Brogan had been forced to endure because he had fathered a lone daughter and not a single son.

'Daddy, I made it. I'm in. I'm in,' Dana almost shouted through her sobs as she extracted herself from her mother's arms and turned to face him. But she was talking to the back of the kitchen door, which had slammed on her happiness.

CHAPTER 3

Dana worked throughout the summer both at Mr Joyce's shop in the village and on the farm, which her father now took every opportunity of mentioning would one day have to be sold, since the chances of her making a good marriage were so much reduced. Joyce's sold everything from tin baths to tinned pears and she worked twelve hours a day in order to save enough money to buy the books she would need in order to pass her preliminary training exam. Joyce's did not sell any of the essentials she had been instructed to take with her to Liverpool. When she asked Mr Joyce whether it would be possible for him to obtain some white kirby grips, he just looked at her, bemused. She worked on the farm in the evenings, to ease her mother's burden, knowing that her leaving home was going to make Mrs Brogan's workload heavier at a time when it should be getting easier. Even so, she gave thanks each day that her mother didn't have the life of Mrs O'Dowd next door. She and her mother both knew the source of the yellow and purple bruises that appeared on Mrs O'Dowd's face and arms from time to time.

'Never let a man use his fists,' her mother had confided. 'If he does it once and you let him away with it, he will do it twice. If he does it twice and he's away with it, he will never stop. Ask Mrs O'Dowd if you don't believe me.'

Dana wondered how you would stop a man as big as Mr O'Dowd using his fists. She did know that her mammy had some hold or other over her father, although she could not imagine what it might be, because Mrs Brogan most definitely ruled the roost and Dana's father did just what he was told, often claiming it was for a quiet life. He had never once laid a finger on her mammy, and he never touched Dana. That was more than could be said for her mammy though. Dana had felt the bottom of her slipper or a wooden spoon many times. She had learnt to be quick. In the time it took Mrs Brogan to kick off her slipper and bend down to retrieve it, cursing as she did so, Dana was off.

Noel Brogan begrudgingly agreed to allow his wife and daughter to accompany him to Castlebar on market day. The list of required essentials on Dana's list was long and could have been written in a foreign language. She was totally at the mercy of shop assistants, and in the end she bought nothing, but returned to her mother empty-handed and almost in tears.

'Stop now,' Mrs Brogan said as they sat in the café opposite the market. 'Ask Mr Joyce will he take ye with him to Galway. I'm sure now he will if ye ask.'

Dana knew there was an unspoken understanding between her mother and Mr Joyce.

She hadn't asked for the job in the shop. It had been offered to her, and the first thing her employer said every morning when she arrived was, 'And how's yer mammy this morning?' Not how are ye, or your pa, or the cow the vet came out to see yesterday? It occurred to Dana now, as she sat in the café with her mother, that Mr Joyce had never once asked about her father. She had no idea what stopped her, but she felt it would be better not to ask why.

'Would you give me a seat to Galway?' she asked the following morning. Mr Joyce was the only person, as far as she could tell, apart from her own mammy, who was delighted with her achievement. Jealousy was rife in their small village.

'Sure, I'll do better than that,' he replied. 'How about we make a day of it and take yer mammy too?' Dana wasn't too sure how her daddy would feel, but as it turned out he wasn't allowed an opinion even on that.

As Dana and her mother walked in and out of the shops, Dana dutifully ticked off the must-haves from her list. Mr Joyce had some business to attend to and had arranged to meet them at three o'clock outside the entrance to the hotel. They still had time to spare when they emerged from the last shop, and Mrs Brogan gave a sigh of relief. 'Do we have everything now?' she asked.

Dana read the list out loud. '"Two nightdresses; one candlewick dressing gown in a suitable colour; one wash bag with contents including medicated shampoo, toothpaste and toothbrush and soap; talcum powder; four pairs of black Lisle stockings" – why do you suppose I need four pairs, Mammy? – "two sharkskin full-length underskirts; one navy blue cardigan for night duty; one fob watch with pin; one pair of Spencer Wells forceps; one pair of nurse's scissors; one pair of black leather lace-up shoes, heel size one and a half inches; one sewing kit; two pillow cases with draw strings, clearly marked to be used as laundry bags; hair nets," and, the last thing, "white kirby grips and tortoiseshell hair clips for those with longer thicker hair".'

'They're right about the stockings,' her mother said. 'You'll be washing them every five minutes. All we are missing is those forceps things. Where in the name of God would we find those? What are they, anyway?'

'Mr Joyce said there was a medical and nursing suppliers at the bottom of this street and that is where I will get the scissors and the forceps from. Let's have a quick cuppa in the café over there, and then you can wait here while I walk down.'

Dana's mother looked relieved. 'Aye, well, Mr Joyce would know. There isn't much he doesn't know and the success of his business has proved that all right.' She extracted a wad of notes from her purse. 'I want you to keep the money he pays you to see you on for your first few weeks, because I don't want to think of you being hungry. But it's important we get your rig-out sorted now, so we'll use this to buy a nice day dress for yerself, and a couple of twinsets and a skirt. I'll just about have that pink cardigan finished by the time ye leave.'

Dana had seen the bundle of knitting on the chair in the kitchen and each night she had gone to bed knowing her mother would be sitting up well into the small hours, surviving on far less sleep than was good for her as she worked like a mad woman to finish the clothes she wanted to send Dana away with. Clothes she could be proud of. She had already knitted the navy blue cardigan on the list and was worried sick that the two little pockets she had worked into the front would make it unacceptable for wearing on the wards.

'The food is very different over there in Liverpool. It's not what you would be fed at home,' she whispered under her breath as she looked around the café, not wanting to offend anyone who might be visiting from Liverpool. As she spoke, the waitress placed two plates of buttered seed cake on the table. 'And I doubt there'll be any of that. I hear they are still on the rationing, God help them.'

But it wasn't the seed cake her mother really wanted to discuss, or the shortage of butter. That wasn't the reason she had agreed to hitch a seat with Mr Joyce, and traipse around Galway. She wanted time with her daughter alone, out of the house. It was the men in Liverpool she wanted to talk about.

'Listen while I tell ye, Dana,' she said, pouring the steaming tea from a large brown earthenware pot through the strainer balanced on her cup, 'the men in Liverpool, they can be very forward so they can. Different from Irish boys altogether. I want you to promise me ye will keep away from all men until ye have finished the training, and that ye will come home and visit me as often as ye can, so I can see for meself now that ye aren't wasting away. And Dana, ye must attend mass at least twice a week. Never miss mass, Dana, promise me that now, make me that promise. I know it's going to be hard with your shifts, but you must pledge me those three things, will ye? That's all I ask. Jesus, I don't care if ye never get married, not at all I don't. There are better things can happen in this life and I'm all for the nursing.'

Dana knew her mother was lying. As the mother of an only girl, Mrs Brogan wanted a lot more for her daughter than green-toothed Patrick and the house next door. She did want her to marry, and to marry an Irish boy at that, but she was also scared of losing her.

'I don't want to become one of those women who only gets to hear about her children in a letter,' her mother was continuing. 'Sure, Mrs McGuffy, she hasn't seen her lad since he left home five years ago, not once. Mind, ye have to ask why would he want to come home with a father like that. I'd keep well away too, but I feel sorry for her so I do, on the days when she's not soaked in the drink, anyway. I dread people asking me so how long is it since you've seen your Dana now, knowing full fine well I will have to lie to save me the embarrassment. I'll never be off my knees, I can see it now.' Her voice was beginning to rise as she contemplated having to atone for the sin of lying.

'I will, Mammy. I promise I will come home every holidays. Ye won't be embarrassed by me. Sure, I will be the most dutiful daughter. I want ye to be proud of me.' Maybe it was because she was an only child, but Dana knew she carried all her mammy's hopes and dreams for the adventures she had never had herself.

On her last night in Ireland, her parents threw a goodbye party in the village hall and every resident, other than the very elderly and the infirm, attended. When a free drink was on offer the village united, and everyone who had given out about Dana's being above herself, or accused her in whispered conversations of being no better than she ought to be, arrived with a generous gift in hand. If there was a party to be had, all was forgiven. Dana laughed at the prospect of trying to lift a case so full of parting gifts. She knew her mammy would make her pack even the small net of potatoes Mrs Gallagher had brought, tied with a ribbon at the top.

''Tis the first thing they all miss when they leave

home,' Mrs Gallagher whistled through her toothless gums, 'so best to be taking some with her.'

'Mammy, I cannot carry potatoes all the way to Liverpool. Surely to God they have them over there,' Dana hissed when Mrs Gallagher left their side, which she did the second someone asked her was she wanting a Guinness.

'I'm not saying they don't.' Mrs Brogan was offended. 'No one in their right mind ever had a bad word to say about a potato, Dana. But they won't have come from Belmullet and that's what's important. And, sure, ye cannot leave a gift behind. That would be most rude.'

'But Mammy, 'tis a sack of potatoes!' Dana was becoming exasperated.

'Aye, but it's only a small one, Dana, and would ye look at that lovely ribbon she's tied around the sacking. The time she must have taken threading that.'

Dana moved to stand near the main doors to greet her friends. Those who worked in Dublin had travelled back on the train to Galway. Her father had taken a trailer on the back of the van to collect them. It took a party back home to tempt them to leave the bright lights and the night life of Dublin town. Everyone knew someone who was working in Liverpool, and numerous pieces of paper and envelopes were shoved into her hand bearing the names and addresses of former Belmullet and Atlantic coast residents who had sailed the well-worn route across the Irish Sea before her. Some were nuns working in schools and convents, some were priests, saving souls on the back streets of Liverpool. She recognized all the surnames and that was all she needed. 'I'm a Brogan from Mayo,' was all she would ever need to say by way of introduction.

'There's a Brogan in Watford, now,' her da had said. 'My cousin who was gone when he was just sixteen, he finished up there. You'll find him easy enough if ye need help. Just ask anyone for Danny Brogan. They'll all know him.'

It was the first helpful thing he had said since the day the letter had arrived at the start of the summer.

Once the fiddlers struck up and the Guinness flowed she danced with the best of them, until, exhausted and hot, she stopped to fetch herself a glass of water and pay a visit to the privy. Some of her friends were having fun dancing with their peers, while others, exhausted from the journey back on top of a week's work, sat on the chairs to gossip. A neighbour's baby lay on her mammy's knee, thumb in mouth, sucking away. Dana caught Mrs Brogan's eye as she left the hall and made a sign between the dancing and jigging heads, that she was off to find herself a drink. Her mother nodded and smiled in response, tapping her feet to the music. Another neighbour sat next to her, nursing her own babby and waved across as well.

For a moment, a shiver of fear ran down Dana's

spine. If she hadn't got into St Angelus, if she had been pressured into marrying green-gob Patrick, in a few years from now that could have been her. Dana could see the pleasure on her mammy's face as she kissed the neighbour's baby on the top of his head, and she struggled to understand how a life of nothing but selfless giving and hard work could ever make for happiness. Dana had to do something, make something of herself, before she settled down to that. All her mother needed to experience bliss was for those she loved to be having a grand time. Even her da, standing at the bar with his friends, looked relaxed. She heard the familiar roar of laughter and could see his shoulders shaking up and down as a friend shouted something in his ear.

Slipping out of the back door, she stood on the step for a moment and closed her eyes to let the cool air lower the temperature of her burning cheeks. It was hot in the hall and perspiration trickled from her neck down between her breasts. She undid the buttons on her cardigan and pulled her blouse out of her skirt, shaking the material to let the cold fresh air waft up and over her body. Feeling better she started along the cinder path to the outhouse, and caught herself in surprise as from nowhere Patrick stepped out into her path.

'So, you're off then,' he said, putting a cigarette into his mouth and pulling hard.

She steeled herself and straightened her back,

and for the first time in her life in her own home town she felt uncomfortable and scared.

'I am, Patrick. I'm away in the morning. Isn't that why you are here, to wish me well and say goodbye?'

She sounded stronger than she felt. She had noticed a change in Patrick over the past few months. He had not concealed his disappointment well.

Patrick flopped to the side and, smirking, leant against the wall of the turf shed. 'Is that so? Do ye think ye will be marrying some grand and fancy doctor and selling the farm, then?'

Dana ignored him and, taking a breath, lifted her head higher than usual. Hoping she looked a great deal bolder than she felt, she walked purpose-fully on. Aware of every step she took, she felt her heart beat faster, her mouth become dry and the hairs on her arms bristle and rise. She wasn't scared of Patrick. He may have been counting on the fact that their fathers had been planning their wedding day and the unification of the two farms for more years than she could remember, but as far as she was concerned that was their plan, not hers. He may have been affronted by her lack of response to his clumsy romantic advances, but nevertheless, they had known each other since birth and played together when they were children. They had walked to school together every day until they had parted ways, he heading to the boys' side of the school and she to the girls'. He was her old playmate, whose shoelaces she had tied until he was ten because he could never get the hang of it himself.

As she came alongside him, she could smell the alcohol. He looked agitated. His eyes were red and wild-looking; his lip snarled in a way she had never seen before. This was not the Patrick she knew, and she felt her skin tighten in response to a rush of adrenalin, as goose-pimples covered her body.

As she quickened her steps and hurried by, he pushed himself away from the wall and stretched up to his full height, fixing her with his gaze, but he said no more. Once more, she had outwitted him. God, I'll be glad to be gone, she thought, as she rinsed her hands under the tap in the privy and splashed the cold water on to her face. She hung around, hoping someone else would follow her in, so that she could engage in bright chatter and wait to walk back with them into the hall. Or maybe Patrick would finish smoking and join his da and the other lads in the pub they had known since they were kids. Surely he would be gone by now. As she looked outside, she saw that her prayers had been answered. The path was clear, and all that remained of Patrick was his cigarette smouldering on the cinder path. Breathing a deep sigh of relief, she left the outhouse and walked down the cinder path.

She didn't see his hand shoot out from the shadows and grab at her arm, or feel him pull her violently towards the turf shed. It was all so quick that before she could scream he had pushed her inside and slammed the door with a bang.

'What are you doing, you fecking eejit?' she snapped, feeling instantly guilty for being in a dark enclosed space with him. Her nostrils filled with the smell of the dark brown peat, and she felt the cut bricks digging into her back as he pushed his weight against her. She knew that if she were seen in the shed with Patrick she would be viewed as the guilty one. It would be she who was whispered about, not he. No two people in a dark enclosed place would be believed to be up to any good. They would laud him as a bold lad and condemn her as a harlot.

Patrick didn't reply. He had other plans. As he pulled up her blouse with one hand and her skirt with the other, he pressed his wet lips on hers and she fought the instinct to retch. Whatever he had learnt with Monica, it had not been finesse. She managed to get both her arms in front of her and shoved him with all her might, but it was useless. Patrick had spent his entire life working on a farm. Each of his arms was the width of a newborn baby and his muscles bulged hard against her own. She felt trapped. Weightless. Despite pushing him with every ounce of her might, until she was drained of breath and gasping for air, she had made absolutely no difference. He hadn't moved an inch. She was imprisoned.

'Think you're too fecking good for me, do you?'

Patrick pinned her legs to the wall with his knees

and pain shot up her thighs from the sheer weight of him. Drops of spittle landed on her face as he spoke. Her stomach heaved with the stench. How could her own father ever have thought this was the man she should spend her life with? Her instincts were to scream, and as she tried with what was left of her breath, a thin reedy wail escaped. This isn't happening, she thought. He will come to his senses in a second. This isn't happening. It cannot be. Letting go of one of her wrists, he again tugged at her blouse, frustrated at the full-length underslip which covered her bra. He pulled down at the top hard to expose her breasts.

'I know what to do with you.' He spoke into the side of her face and she could feel his hot breath against her skin. 'I'm no eejit. You think I was going to wait for you?'

He laughed out loud and slammed himself into her again, until she could feel his iron-hard erection pressing an indentation into the soft flesh of her thigh. 'Ye just need to be shown what you'll be missing while you're away, missus. Think yer fuckin' bold with ye're fuckin' gobshite clever words? Ye won't be so bold when I've fucking finished with ye.'

At that moment, Dana realized, Patrick was too far gone and consumed by his own need for revenge. She was done for. With what breath she had left, she began to sob and begged him to stop.

'Patrick, don't. Let me go. I will talk about it

outside, so I will. I promise I will think about it all again. I won't go if ye don't want me to. Please, just stop.'

He wasn't listening to a word she said, and she felt consumed with horror as he thrust one hand up her skirt between her thighs and hurt her, his jagged fingernails stabbing into her flesh. Tears of pain flooded her eyes and she wanted to give up fighting, to give in and die, for him to be gone and the pain to be over. She could hardly breathe because of the weight of him, pushing against her with the full length of his legs and thrusting the hard bone of his pelvis into her soft belly. He was taller than she was and twice her size. She started to gasp for air as he forced the last breath out of her. She felt light-headed, and her head began to swim.

Pinning her to the wall with his forearm across her chest, Patrick fumbled with his free hand at his belt and trousers. Dana heard the leather belt slip as the buckle opened and it slid undone. His trousers fell to his knees and he pulled his langer clear of his oversized shorts before wrenching her skirt up and ripping the front of her knickers away. She knew the consequences of what he was about to do. At that moment she doubted she would leave the turf shed alive, convinced that Patrick would kill her once he had satisfied himself. Even if he didn't, she was sure she would be pregnant at the very least, and bearing a child to a man like Patrick would be as good as being dead.

'Oh, God, no.' She began to cry. 'What are you doing? Get off me.'

She let out one long, screeching wail, delivered by an overwhelming need to emerge from the ordeal alive. The future she had always dreamed of was at her fingertips, only days away. She no longer cared if anyone saw her. She was already someone. She was a girl from the villages who was leading the way for others. She was breaking free of the pattern of existence that had been the lot of girls like her for generations. Patrick swore again as he slammed his hand over her mouth.

'Fucking shut it. Shut it,' he hissed as he thrust himself against her. His knees jabbed into her thighs and she felt him, shockingly exposed, hard, wet and naked, jabbing, pushing his way further up her thigh, searching, grabbing at the flesh of her leg until she felt his dirty fingernails cutting into her skin once more.

He failed to find her. 'You fucking witch,' he hissed, forcing her legs apart with his knee until she thought she would split in two with the pain.

She bit into his hand, hard, her teeth ripping at his flesh. He pulled his hand away and she let out another terrified scream but still it didn't stop him. She knew he was on the brink of violating the most private and precious part of her life. She had no defence, no way of protecting herself. She was trapped in the vice of his thighs, and as the fight left her she slipped down the wall. Her only thought was that Patrick was about to destroy her life and her dreams.

Suddenly, Patrick pulled away from her sharply, and for a moment she failed to understand what was happening. The shed filled with light and she became aware that the door was open and that Noel, her own daddy, stood in the centre of the room. In a split second, he had made complete sense of the entire scene.

Patrick didn't know what had hit him as Noel Brogan lifted him by the back of his collar and ejected him from the shed. Dana heard the unmistakable snap of a bone as Patrick hit the ground outside. There was a scream, then Patrick's sobs and her daddy's swearing. The sound of the band and the dancing was louder and Dana almost wept in relief for small mercies. She knew a hail of blows must be raining down on Patrick. It was the Irish way. Fists and boots first, words later. She rearranged her clothes, desperately wanting to be out of the gloom of the turf shed and into the now fading light outdoors. As she stood in the doorway, clinging to the frame to hold herself upright, she saw Patrick scuffling across the cinder path and scrambling away, dragging his dislocated foot behind him. His nose and mouth were pouring blood and he was crying like a babby.

Dana's father retrieved his cap from the ground and busied himself with knocking the cinder dust away with the back of his hand to give her privacy while she straightened the rest of her clothes and wiped her eyes with the handkerchief that had somehow remained inside her skirt pocket. 'Is this your fault?' he asked her at last.

'Oh, God, oh God,' she cried. 'Did ye not see what he nearly did to me, Daddy?'

Noel ignored the question. His voice was as cold as steel when he spoke. Dana did not have the pull or the ways of her mammy when it came to her father.

'Did you ask him to come in here with you?'

Noel was unlike Patrick's father. He was not a violent man when it came to women, but he could give any man a good kicking if needed. But, he had to know it was for good reason. Men in their village talked with their fists and ended up in the gaol, but not Noel. It was yet another hold his wife had over him. 'Use your fists and I will leave you.' He was afraid she would, because he knew she had somewhere to go and someone who was waiting. Someone who had never stopped waiting.

'No, Daddy, I did not. Do you think I'm mad? Do you think I would want to do anything with that disgusting creature?' She was screaming now and pointing at the hobbling, retreating Patrick as she spoke. 'He dragged me in. He said he was going to show me what I would be missing while I was in Liverpool. Daddy, he was going to . . .'

Dana could not speak out loud the words to describe what Patrick had been going to do. Sex was not spoken about at home. Dana saw the temper flare up in her father; she watched as

65

the redness rose from his neck and spread across his face. He was angrier than she had ever seen him before. He looked as though he were about to explode, and when he spoke it was in a voice shot through with steel.

'Why in God's name was I not given sons?'

The tone, and the coldness of his words, frightened Dana. She had never seen him like this before. He wiped his mouth and placed his cap back on his head. 'I will deal with Patrick, but if I find you are lying to me, if you encouraged him or egged him on, there will be trouble. 'Tis here you will be staying tomorrow, not Liverpool.'

For the first few seconds after he had spoken, Dana was filled with disbelief. She felt the anger surge through her at the deep, hurtful injustice of her father's comment and she could barely hold back the torrent of words that rose in her like stale vomit. She wanted to scream and rage at him, but she knew that with her father this got you nowhere. With the strongest will she could summon to keep the telltale anger from her voice, she said, 'Do you know what I have just been through, Da? This is my night, my party and your best friend's son has just tried to rape me. The boy you wanted me to marry has just pushed me in here and tried to . . . to . . .'

Her words tailed off and her bottom lip trembled as her voice deserted her. She was choked by the tears that threatened to claim her. But she stared at her father defiantly.

'Yes, well, I will be asking Patrick questions too. But as I say, if I find out ye are lying to me . . .'

'How do you intend to work that one out, Daddy? Will you take his word over mine? Here, look at this!' She pulled up her skirt to reveal the indentations of Patrick's dirty fingernails and the blood trickling down her thighs. 'Do ye think I asked for this?' Now she was crying hard.

Her father had moved away, disturbed, having intended his words to remain unchallenged. He glanced back at her, and Dana saw him flinch when he saw her thighs. For a moment, there was silence between them.

'No, I'll take your word, Dana. Cover yerself up now. I have to believe ye, because your mammy's heart would be broken if there were to be any scandal about you in the town. You are her golden girl, and I don't want her to be made unhappy. But let this be a lesson to ye. Ye can't lead someone on the way ye have Patrick for all these years and not expect there to be consequences when ye let him down. What has happened to ye tonight, 'tis yer own fault. Now, pull yourself together and then come back inside as though nothing has happened. I will make sure Patrick is taken home.'

Dana's breath came in short gasps. She wanted to run at her father and throw herself at his back and pummel him with her fists. To scream at the injustice of it. To make him suffer for what Patrick had just put her through. She watched as he retreated down the path, knowing he would take her word, not because she spoke the truth, or because he believed in her, or because there was blood trickling down her thighs or because he was moved by her tears, but for the sake of her mother. His first instinct was to protect her mammy, not herself, because Dana had not been the son he had wanted to carry on the farm. He had never forgiven her for that. For a moment, she felt too weak to step back inside the hall. She was shaking like a leaf and all she wanted was to be comforted by her mother, who had loved her twice as much to compensate for her father, and to be back in her own bed in her own room. Her evening had been ruined in a way she would never forget.

In her heart, Dana knew she would never forgive her father for doubting her. For thinking she had led Patrick on. For doubting her morals and her integrity. It would be a long day before Noel Brogan's daughter ever spoke to him again.

The day she left home was both the best and the worst of Dana's life.

'Make us proud,' her mammy said, as Mr Joyce waited at the gate with his van ticking over, ready to take her to the station. He ran the closest thing they had to a taxi and serviced the villages for miles around.

'I will, Mammy. I'll try my best,' she said, as her grandmother shuffled out of the door into the yard and pressed a ten-shilling note into her hand. Her father remained indoors with his back to the fire, smoking his pipe, ignored. Dana had not confided the events of the previous evening to her mother. She knew all hell would erupt, and she was anxious that nothing should delay her leaving. One day she would tell her, just not now.

Suddenly she heard her name being called, and when she looked up the road she saw some of her friends running to catch her, their mothers and siblings running behind. Dana beamed and waved. Mr Joyce took her case and her heart sang while her friends clamoured around her, chattering and hugging her as between them they loaded the last of her bags into the back of Mr Joyce's van, and her mother cried.

'Go on now, get in the van and be away,' one of them said, 'before yer mammy's a wreck.'

Two minutes later, she was peering through the back window at the people she had known all her life, standing in solidarity, waving her off as a group. She knew that within five minutes they would all be in the farm kitchen drinking tea, her daddy being told to go and find something stronger to slip into it, this being the day Dana left for Liverpool. As the van moved down the road and along their bottom field she could see the cows impatiently lowing at the field gate waiting to be milked just as they had, twice a day, every single day of her life, and it occurred to her then that her entire life had revolved around that very routine and that now, from this moment, that would no longer be the case. The steadfast boundaries which had controlled her life were fading into small specks in the distance and in their place was nothing by which to count the hours of the day. She had begun to miss the cows and the stability they represented before they were even out of the village.

There was no sign of Patrick or of his poor beaten mother and greedy father. She had thought that as the van pulled away they might have slipped into view, knowing a free drink would be in the offing in the Brogan kitchen. She knew they would not be able to stay away for long, and that within the hour one or other would be round at the house to check that she had actually left.

'Mighty grand of you to be off to St Angelus,' Mr Joyce commented as the farm faded into the distance. He had cleaned the van in her honour, and her mammy had looked pleased as he pulled up outside the house.

'You'll be leaving in style, Dana. I like that.' Admittedly, the floor of Mr Joyce's van was carpeted with potato sacking and cabbage leaves, but it still smelt better than her father's, which had been used for transporting the pigs to Castlebar market only the previous day and had yet to be washed out.

Mr Joyce had told her every day she had done well to be accepted by St Angelus, usually within five minutes of her arriving at the shop. Dana was grateful for his praise. She had received little from anywhere else. Until the past few days, she had been made to feel as though having done well and winning her place at St Angelus were being perceived as a crime.

The road was rough and bumpy, cut into the hills a century ago by starving men in return for a handful of grain and barely touched since. Her mother's old leather handbag, given to Dana for Liverpool and now perched on her knee, was a weight in itself. Stuffed with the food her mother had made for the journey, it pressed down on her woollen skirt, prickling and chafing the scratches still raw on her thighs.

A feeling of relief washed over her as Mr Joyce put his foot down on the accelerator and the farm shrank to a small dot in the distance. As it did so, tears stung the back of her eyes. The village she had known and felt safe in all her life suddenly felt far too small, and dangerous. It was tainted. An entire lifetime of safety and comfort within familiar boundaries had been destroyed within seconds by the actions of one man. She had promised her mother in the café in Galway that she would return home as often as possible. How could she do that now, with a monster living next door and a father she felt she no longer loved?

She would cross that bridge when she had to. Right now, she couldn't get to Liverpool fast enough. A city she had never before set foot in suddenly felt like a safer and more comfortable option than living next door to Patrick O'Dowd. Patrick, who had grown into a threatening and violent man, who had Dana in his sights and would not be satisfied until she was his.

CHAPTER 4

Biddy Kennedy lifted her freshly baked apple pie out of the oven and shuffled across the concrete floor towards the sink in her oversized slippers, worn down at the back and holed in the toes, to set the enamel plate down in front of the window for the pastry to cool. There was no need to open the window, because the draught that whistled through the cracks did the job well enough. It was the fourth day in January, and as Biddy took a deep breath she detected a change in the breeze that blew up from the Mersey. The rain was pouring steadily, as it had been for most of the day, and the moonless winter sky was black and forbidding.

'Snow is on its way,' she said to the cat, who had jumped on to the wooden draining board and now pushed himself up against her hand, purring. 'Get down, you thieving bugger.' She picked him up and set him down on the floor before she shuffled back across the kitchen and closed the oven door.

And then opened and closed it again. A smile of satisfaction crossed her face as the door clicked shut. Her range had been damaged during the war and a month ago she had finally given up the struggle and surrendered to the new world, just as her New World cooker arrived. It was a treat to bake an apple pie without having to wedge the door on the range shut with the mop handle. Biddy loved her new oven, although she would never let on to anyone who asked. Not a great fan of change, she had tolerated her broken range for almost ten years and if truth be told she missed the warmth that filled the house whenever it was lit. But she was the only woman in the neighbourhood to own one of the new cookers and her nostalgic musing for her once hot range had been replaced by a sense of pride as her neighbours dropped in one by one, all curious to inspect Biddy's New World.

Biddy had enjoyed the attention, until she opened the tea caddy and discovered that she had used her weekly quarter-pound packet of Lipton's in two days.

'Bring yer own tea,' she shouted to anyone who asked if they could come and take a look at her oven as she trudged up the hill on her way home from work at the end of each day. The pride and novelty of a new cooker took second place to the injustice of having to re-mash the tea leaves thrice.

Taking her ciggies out of her apron pocket, Biddy sat down, slid the half-full ashtray towards her, lit up and awaited the arrival of her best friends, Elsie and Dessie.

Biddy lived in a row of terrace houses off the

dock road and worked as housekeeper at the school of nursing at St Angelus. She loved her job, but she was tired and she knew it. Tired of the repetitive daily struggle. Of being alone and having no one to moan to about her lot. Biddy sometimes wondered whether life would ever again bring her a surprise. An event she hadn't planned, expected or paid for. She often felt as though the future pointed downhill. Her hair greying, her varicose veins aching and worst of all her bladder leaking.

'It's last, getting old,' she said to the cat as she pulled in a deep tug of her ciggie. 'Bloody last.'

Elsie O'Brien lived in the adjacent row of terrace houses and also worked at St Angelus. Elsie was housekeeper in Matron's private apartment on the first floor, and also looked after the rooms that had remained occupied in the accommodation block by the four oldest sisters, including Sister Antrobus from ward two. Some of the remaining rooms along the corridor had become offices as St Angelus expanded to cope with the post-war demands of Liverpool's residents.

Biddy and Elsie were both members of the domestic elite of St Angelus. The A team. Not for them the drudgery of mopping mile upon mile of ward corridors. Each of them had carved out a niche for herself at the hospital, bagging the top domestic jobs, and as a result Elsie had managed to get her Martha a job as maid in the consultants' day sitting room. St Angelus was cleaned by an army of war widows, and in the pecking order

Biddy and Elsie were at the top. Dessie, a widower who had been demobbed in '46 and arrived home dripping in medals, worked as the head porter at St Angelus and lived in the corner house at the bottom of the street. A house that had stood empty from the day his wife died until his return.

Every Sunday evening at seven o'clock, he and Elsie would arrive in Biddy's kitchen to gossip about the week, eat, drink, talk about the war and listen to the Stargazers singing on the radio. Biddy and Elsie mothered Dessie from kindness. It was a kindness that had benefited them both over the years.

'Not right that he should come home a war hero and his wife died while he was away,' Biddy often said. That was when she was feeling generous. On her off days, her comments to Elsie were more cutting. 'Shame Dessie's wife was down the docks when the ship was hit. You have to ask, don't you . . .' she paused for effect as she exhaled a long plume of blue smoke, 'what was she doing down there in the first place, eh?' The comment was always followed by a questioning raised eyebrow.

'Should we tell him?' Elsie once enquired over the rim of her teacup. Biddy's reply had been unequivocal and swift. 'If there is one thing Dessie will die without knowing, it's that his wife was carrying on while he was fighting the Nazis, and if anyone does fancy telling him, you make sure that everyone in the alehouse knows they'll have me to answer to.' Biddy never set foot in the pub, the place her husband had scarcely ever been out of. The only cause of tension between Biddy and Elsie was that Elsie spent every Friday and Saturday night in the bar.

'I have the Guinness,' said Elsie, as the back door flew open in the wind and almost catapulted her thin frame into the kitchen. 'Jesus, the wind is so bad, it almost blew me curlers out. I didn't have to go into the pub. They've opened the side door and put in a hatch for fill-ups and take aways. Very fancy it is too. Means the kids can buy for their mam and dad and not risk getting a clout in the bar.'

She took the six bottles of Guinness out of her wicker basket and set them down on the kitchen table. ''Tis raining cats and dogs out there,' she said as she shook out her coat, and patted her wire curlers to check they were still in place. 'But not your cat, mind. Did you know he was on the draining board helping himself to the pie?'

Biddy shrieked as she ran to retrieve the plate and seized the mop to chase the cat out of the back door. 'That fecking cat,' she muttered as she hugged the pie protectively to her and laid it down on the kitchen table next to the Guinness. 'Is your Martha coming up later?' she asked as she took three glasses down from the press.

'No she isn't, not tonight. I left her in with Josie Jackson tying each other's hair in rags. They are going to do each other's nails too. She thinks I don't know, but Jake Berry is beginning to make his mark, you know. They've been out on three Sunday afternoons on the run, those two. Came back all smiles and blushes today she did. Won't tell me a thing, mind. You get nothing out of our Martha. I've told her, she would have made a better spy than Mata Hari. I could hear the two of them giggling like mad as soon as I closed the back door. The problem with Josie is she's a gob on her, that one, and before I was down the path I heard her yell "Has he kissed you yet?" and then Martha told her to shush so loud, you could have heard her down on the docks.'

'Well, you can't deny her that, Elsie. She is nineteen now, and Jake himself, he's twenty – almost a man. He'll have the key to the door on his next birthday.'

The kitchen filled with the sound of hissing as Biddy took the bottle opener that was tied to a piece of string hanging from a nail in the wooden draining board over to the Guinness and flipped off the lids.

'Oh, I know that. Me and my Charlie, we were married when I was just sixteen meself, and our little Charlie was born nine months later, just a week before me seventeenth. Our honeymoon baby he was. But what am I telling you that for? You delivered him, didn't you. Do you remember how big he was, Biddy, and how he never cried, not a sound? Always good, wasn't he? That's the only time I ever saw my big Charlie cry, when you put our little Charlie in his arms. The babby just stared up at his da with his big eyes. You would have thought he had been here before; they knew everything, them eyes, Biddy, and I always think to meself that the reason why he didn't cry when he was born was because he knew what was up ahead.'

Biddy turned her head sharply to look at Elsie. She knew what was coming next. A long moment of silence, a loud sniff, and then Elsie would shed tears as she removed her hankie from up the sleeve of her cardigan. Her little Charlie had died in 1944, two days before his father, big Charlie. They served in the same regiment and the only thing that sustained Elsie was the knowledge that little Charlie went first and wasn't left without his da. Nine years had passed and yet just the mention of either of their names was enough to bring a bout of weeping from Elsie. Not that Biddy minded that. She had indeed delivered little Charlie and witnessed the happiest moment of Elsie's life. Biddy was good at delivering babies and had been called in the middle of the night to many a house around and about, and often arrived before the midwife. Now she laid her hand on Elsie's shoulder, just as she had been doing for the past nine years. Biddy knew the drill.

She waited the three minutes it took for Elsie's fresh outpouring of tears to calm before she said in a soft voice, 'Here, take your drink, Elsie. It always helps.' She had known big Charlie well and could more than understand what it was that Elsie was missing.

The Kennedys and the O'Briens had moved into the neighbourhood in 1924. The streets were the last ones off the dock road and the closest to the hospital. Most of the residents in the area worked in one capacity or another at St Angelus. Dessie had been big Charlie's best friend, and it was this friendship which had helped catapult Elsie and Biddy into the most comfortable and secure domestic roles at the hospital. Dessie was a respected war hero. He was liked by Matron, a miracle in itself, and most important, he had influence. Influence and a fund of gossip worth nurturing with a home-made apple pie once a week.

Biddy had lost her own husband, but given that she only ever described him as a fist-happy drunk the event had come as a secret relief. Not one she had ever voiced to another living soul. Unlike Elsie's boy, Biddy's three sons had returned from the war alive and well. They had just never bothered to come home, remaining in London where the first leg of their homeward journey had set them down. Biddy never spoke of the past. Of the children who had deserted and forgotten her. The babies who had died in infancy or the husband who had buggered off and left her. Last spotted on Lime Street station, drunk, telling anyone who would listen he was off to visit his son. She was alone: she had to survive and survival left no room for sentiment.

Elsie had Martha at home. A perfect if somewhat

timid daughter and a living reminder of who and what Elsie had lost. Biddy lived with a cat, and a nuisance of a cat at that.

'Come on, Dessie will be here in a moment. Dry your eyes and get that Guinness down you. We both prayed for your men at mass this morning, as we always do, and one day, Elsie, you will stop crying, sure, you will.'

'I'm so sorry, Biddy,' sobbed Elsie as she removed her glasses and wiped them on her now damp handkerchief. 'I shouldn't cry, I know. We all have to get on with it, don't we? You never moan and you with the incontinence problem you have to put up with too. You're a martyr to your bladder and you never complain.'

'God the father, I have no bladder problem,' Biddy lied as she banged their Guinness bottles on to the table before she flopped into her chair.

'Well, no of course you don't. It's just that you have a lot more to put up with than I do, that's all. I'm in full working order down there.' Elsie raised her eyebrows. 'I imagine it must be awful for you, Biddy.'

Biddy was about to protest when the back door opened and Dessie came in.

'Evening, ladies, I have the pies. Biddy, get that radio on, or we'll miss the Stargazers. I heard the clock strike seven when I was halfway up the street.' Dessie's job on a Sunday night was to call at the hot van on the dock road.

'Pies, Guinness and a slice of our Biddy's apple

pie. We live the life, don't we, ladies?' Dessie threw his coat on to the nail on the back of the door and, leaving his cap in situ, began to remove the newspaper wrapping from around the food. 'Do you want this for the fire, Biddy?'

'I do not. Did you not remember, I have me New World?' Biddy took the plates out of the bottom of the oven as she spoke.

Dessie smiled. 'Oh, aye. I'd forgotten about that.'

He winked at Elsie and noted the wet eyes and the handkerchief being pushed back up the sleeve of her cardie. He hadn't forgotten at all. Every Sunday for the past month, a part of their evening had been spent discussing the new oven.

'The new prefab and tin roof houses are up in Litherland,' he said. 'Just bumped into Sid's lads from next door, carrying a pile of tea chests up the dock steps. Moving into theirs tomorrow, they are.'

'Sure, we'll be the only people left in these houses soon,' said Biddy.

'Not at all. Don't be worrying about that,' said Dessie, pulling out a chair, eyes fixed on the steaming pie before him. 'Most people round here either work at the hospital or on the docks, so why would they want to be travelling? I bet you anything you like the dock board won't shut Sid's house up: houses are in too short supply. It'll be another ten years before there's enough built for everyone after the war damage.'

'In that case, Dessie, you'll have a new neighbour

before the week is out,' said Elsie. 'The Irish are pouring in at the docks to work on the roads.'

'Wouldn't it be grand if it was someone from Cork with a bit of news from home,' said Biddy, setting the knives and forks on the table.

'Well, I know this: if our Martha does get wed one day, she would like her own house and I would like her nearby. It would be smashing, Dessie, if she got one of the houses round here.'

Dessie couldn't reply as his mouth was already full.

'You have a word with Jake, Dessie. You're his boss. Tell him not to drag his feet. She's a pretty girl, our Martha, and someone will snap her up soon if he doesn't.'

Dessie wiped a dribble of gravy away with the back of his hand. 'Jake Berry needs no encouragement from me, Elsie. I'll tell you a secret, but as God is my judge, don't tell no one else.'

Biddy and Elsie shuffled their chairs closer to the table and bent their heads in. 'Go on,' said Biddy, 'what is it?'

'I have to have your word, and especially yours, Elsie, because you'll be the one who finds it hardest to keep mum.'

'God in heaven,' blurted Biddy, 'leave that to me. I'll make sure she keeps her mouth shut, I will. What is it?'

Dessie grinned and looked from one to the other. 'It's Jake who has Sid's house. Being a docker's son gave him the right to apply and he's got it.'

Elsie and Biddy were speechless. 'How can he afford it, Dessie?' asked Elsie, when she had regained her breath. 'Jesus, his mother put up a new set of nets in forty-five to celebrate VE day and they haven't been changed since. They don't have two halfpennies to rub together in that house.'

Biddy jumped in. 'How can he afford the rent and everything else? The place is falling apart. They have the river damp in that house, I know that. I've been in and their range was more damaged than mine in the war.'

'Ah, well, now, that's where the real secret comes in. Our young Jake, he won on the pools.'

'He won on the pools?' Elsie and Biddy shrieked together.

'Aye, he did that, almost a month ago. He won over three hundred pounds.'

'Over three hundred pounds!' the cry went up in unison.

Dessie began to laugh. 'You should see the faces on both of you. Oh, God, you're killing me. Pass me me ciggies, Bid.'

Biddy slid Dessie's Capstan full strength across the Formica tabletop towards him. Her mind was racing. She had never met anyone who had won on the pools.

Dessie took his time lighting up. It was usually Biddy or Elsie who imparted the gems of Sunday-night gossip.

'Look, he came to see me when he won. Said he had been desperate to ask Martha out, but knowing he could never afford to give her a home of her own he wasn't sure, like. Wanted to wait until he became an under-porter and got a better wage. I told him, don't wait too long, lad, or someone else will dive in there. She's a cracker is Martha.'

Elsie drew herself up to her full height and grinned. Biddy scowled. Not that Biddy begrudged Martha a little happiness. God knew, the girl had helped her out often enough. It was the cat that had got the cream smugness on Elsie's face that irritated her. Friend or not, Elsie had so much more than Biddy to look forward to. A wedding, grandchildren and a growing family living nearby, whereas Biddy had nothing and no one. She had heard that one of her sons had married and was living in a place called Wandsworth, but that was six years ago and she hadn't heard a peep since. Not even a Christmas card.

Biddy looked at her cooker. Her only advantage. Right now, it gave her cold comfort.

'He hasn't told no one. Not even your Martha yet, but that's going to change. He said he'll tell her before he starts to do the house up. Said he's going to go in there every night after work, and when it's ready he's going to pop the question to your Martha and keep fifty pound back for a big wedding and a knees up at the Irish centre. So bob's your uncle. Your Martha has a good lad there, Elsie.'

Biddy had known what was coming; Elsie

pretended she hadn't, and gasped. Everyone had always known that one day the two best-looking kids in the neighbourhood would marry. Jake had eyes as dark as his hair and Martha, petite and frail with her deep chestnut hair and bright blue eyes, had always been hanging off his hand when they played in the streets as kids.

'Isn't that wonderful? Biddy, did you hear that? Jake Berry is going to propose to our Martha and he'll have a house all done for her.'

Biddy collected the plates and stood to carry them to the sink and fetch a knife for the apple pie. Her evening wasn't turning out quite as she had hoped. Neither of the others had mentioned the fact that her new cooker had kept the plates nice and warm, or that the crust on the apple pie was the same colour all round and not black on one side and underbaked on the other, as it had been for years.

'I heard. And I hope it keeps fine for him. Jake is a good lad, everyone knows that. Sure, I've never heard anyone say a bad word about him. Your Martha will be a very lucky girl.'

The smile dropped from Elsie's face. 'Well, I think 'twill be Jake who is the lucky one,' she bristled.

'Anyway, ladies.' Dessie could sense a change in the atmosphere. He hated it when Biddy and Elsie argued and they frequently did, often over the most ridiculous things. He knew they were best friends and yet they were riddled with jealousy,

85

although they all had so little he had no idea what they found to envy. His wife had hit the nail on the head before he had left to fight in the war.

'The problem is, Des, neither of them have nowt and so every little thing becomes something big. Especially with that Biddy, and she has a big gob that one. I'd never trust her.'

In fact, Dessie's wife had never trusted Biddy because she refused to go to the pub with the other women on a Friday night. The subtlety of the one-upmanship was lost on Dessie. He had seen friends blown to bits and found it hard to appreciate the significance of owning a New World cooker or boasting about a pretty daughter. Especially when his best mate, Elsie's dead husband, no longer supped with him in the Red Admiral on a Saturday night. Now he wanted to change the subject, fast.

'Anyway, as I said, it is one very big secret, and our secrets stay here in this kitchen, don't they?' Biddy and Elsie detected the tone of censure in Dessie's voice and bowed their heads, Biddy with a frown, Elsie unable to wipe the smile from her face. Dessie seized another snippet of news to bring things back on track.

'You have the new nurses intake starting in the morning, don't you, Biddy? You'll be run off your feet, then?'

'That's right. I doubt they will be any different from the last lot.'

'Oh, I wouldn't be too sure about that,' said

Elsie, seizing her moment to be back on top. 'Matron was furious about some of the girls your Sister Haycock has put on this course.'

Biddy was suddenly all ears. Sister Haycock was the director of nursing and had only been in post for a year, but in that year she had won Biddy's fierce loyalty. Sister Haycock was like Biddy, alone in the world, and even though Biddy was only the housekeeper at the school of nursing she would not hear anyone say a bad word about the new director.

'Oh really, and why would that be, Elsie? And since when was Matron ever happy about anything?'

'Well, I heard her on the telephone when I was polishing the brass. I think she was talking to one of the trustees. She said some of the girls weren't up to standard. "Not the usual sort," she said, and she was going to be keeping an eye on this intake as she felt your Sister Haycock had overstepped the mark by taking in girls from Ireland for the registered nurse course. "Not the St Angelus standard," she said.'

Biddy was ready to fire back at Elsie, but she kept her own counsel. She had to watch Sister Haycock's back for her, and her best source of information was Elsie: her own personal plant in Matron's office. Biddy knew that Matron was Sister Haycock's biggest enemy, and a dangerous enemy at that.

'Did she now? Well, that's interesting. Let me know if she says anything else, would you, Elsie?'

Elsie was spooning a large chunk of apple pie

into her mouth and nodded. Elsie loved the gossip and didn't share Biddy's strong sense of loyalty towards her own boss. 'Oh, I will, Biddy. I will that.'

Harmony restored, Dessie turned to Biddy. 'Turn the radio up, Biddy.' As Biddy leaned over to twist the dial, Dessie added, 'It's a lovely crust on this pie tonight. Best I've ever tasted.'

Biddy smiled, rinsed with pleasure, and silence descended as the sound of the Stargazers drifted into the kitchen.

Matron stood at the window of the sitting room in her flat and looked out over the empty hospital car park. What visitors there had been that evening had long since gone. The theatres and Casualty were quiet, but the hospital never slept. The radio played quietly in the background as she picked up her beloved Scottie dog, Blackie, and stroked his head, staring down at the rain bouncing off the porch roof over the main hospital entrance below.

'I think it's going to snow soon, Blackie,' she whispered to the dog, who, hearing his name, tipped his head towards her.

There was a time when the upper corridor had been filled with sisters who lived in. She could still sometimes hear the sound of the piano, the shuffle of shoes along the polished concrete, the whispers of colleagues long gone, but she knew it was only the ghosts of memories. The days of live-in sisters had ended with the war. Most of the rooms along the corridor now stood empty, waiting for the occasional visitor, or were used as offices. At night they were filled with a deathly, lonely quiet.

Sitting down at her desk, she tucked Blackie on to her knee and wrote a note to Sister Antrobus on ward two, inviting her for supper. It wouldn't seem that unusual. They were both single women and she had a notion that Sister Antrobus was very much like herself. The woman had the most fearsome reputation in the entire hospital, and it was not something Matron discouraged. She was aware that Sister Antrobus had a very particular manner, was a little too forceful when expressing her opinions maybe, and it was possible that her standards were a little too exacting for the probationary nurses, given the drop-off rate, but, all things considered, the two of them got along very well. Matron hoped they had many more things in common than nursing.

'Nothing wrong with that, is there, Blackie?' she said as she licked the flap on the envelope before writing Sister Antrobus's name on the front. They were the first words she had spoken out loud all day. Yes, there was nothing wrong with an invitation to supper. She had to do something to end the yearning loneliness which sat in her heart. She hugged Blackie to her to quell the ache and turned up the radio as the first strains of the Stargazers filled her empty rooms.

CHAPTER 5

Victoria Baker was kneeling on the floor by the side of her bed, packing clothes in her suitcase while her aunt Minnie ticked each item off the list.

'I don't think I've ever even owned a watch with a second hand,' said Aunt Minnie, lifting the navy blue velvet lid of the box that contained the Ingersoll fob watch and peering in. 'Oh, yes I have. The Cartier I got from your grandparents for my twenty-first had one. You should have that. It's in my jewellery box in London.'

Victoria packed the last few items laid out on her bed and leapt to her feet. She was leaving to catch the train to Liverpool in less than two hours.

She wandered over to the window and, looking out, saw Roland Davenport's car winding its way up the long driveway towards Baker Hall.

'Roland is on his way up the drive,' she said over her shoulder to Aunt Minnie, who rose from the bed, crossed the floor and placed her arm around her niece's shoulders.

'It feels strange to me that we only met Roland

a few weeks ago, and yet here he is, transporting you to the station.'

'Well, it doesn't to me,' said Victoria. 'Anyway, it was you who asked him to sort everything out.' She moved to the dressing table in case Roland saw her watching and attempted to rewind the long tendrils of blonde hair that had escaped her chignon, fixing them in place with a pin she selected from a pretty glass dish.

'Does my hair look all right?' she asked.

'You look lovely, my dear,' said Aunt Minnie. 'I really just cannot believe you are doing this. For once, I agree with your father. I blame your mother.'

'Well, I've no idea what else I could possibly do that would be useful. I would only get under your feet in London and besides, I'm just not ready to leave the north. Mother hated London and I'm very like her, you know.'

Victoria Baker, daughter of the sixth Lord Baker, was about to leave the life she knew to begin her nurse training at St Angelus hospital in Liverpool. Her perception of nursing had been wholly informed by the days she had spent as a child accompanying her mother when Lady Baker had visited the war wounded on the estate. Eight-year-old Victoria would help her mother load up the baskets on the fronts of their bicycles with food and basic medical supplies, doing her best to follow Lady Baker's instructions: 'Pack so the weight is balanced, Victoria. We have enough injuries without your adding more by falling off.' Before they cycled away, her mother would study the sheet of paper upon which she had written her list and say, 'Righty oh, darling, let's check who we are to visit today, shall we, and plan out our route?'

Those days of collusion and caring spent with her mother had been the most joyful time of Victoria's childhood. They had cycled out with pies and biscuits, fruit from the orchard and eggs from the hens who roosted in the stables. Her mother, who had never in her life made her own bed, plumped up pillows, straightened sheets and mopped brows. In the evenings, they made bandages and over-dressings from old sheets in the linen room.

They visited villages Victoria had only ever ridden through on her pony, accompanied by a stable boy. On two days a week, they joined a knitting and sewing circle to make socks and pullovers for the injured. The lads of Lancashire who had returned from the war with injuries would not want for anything Victoria's mother could provide, and she did much of her work with her only daughter at her side, watching and learning in awe and wonder. When Victoria thought of her mother today, it was those days she recalled first. The bloom on her cheeks when they returned from a long Sunday visiting her war wounded. The happiness in her voice when Mrs Armitage from Bolton came to the door with detailed instructions for the week ahead. It was the first time in her life Lady

Baker had felt needed, and she relished the challenge to do something useful, the only thing she could do, to help.

One thing never discussed at Baker Hall was the fact that the money had run out. Victoria's father found it almost impossible to accept that they could no longer afford to employ staff or even to fix the roof, which was now leaking in a dozen different places. It seemed to Victoria as though the rot had set in once the war had ended, but in reality it had begun long before. The war had simply provided a distraction. If her mother was busy attending to the wounded, she had no time to face the problems waiting at her own front door.

Baker Hall sat at the foot of the moors, far enough from Bolton to make a regular visit to town difficult, and looked just like a stately home with its towering walls and porticos and formally laid out gardens. The buildings adjacent to the house dated from the fifteenth century and included the original hall where Elizabeth I and her retinue had lodged on their travels through the north-west. There had even been a moat, although that was grassed over now. The grandeur of days long gone was everywhere to be seen, but behind the façade the truth was very different. When Victoria turned eighteen and the war-broken government was banging on the door for the final instalment of her grandfather's death duties, it was difficult for Victoria's father to see beyond the financial calamity before him. The estate was crumbling. There was only so much one man could do to keep the show on the road. The old and incompetent estate manager had to be let go, and the bottle became Lord Baker's new friend.

And then her mother went and died. Without a sound or any fuss, which was always her way. She simply slipped away in the night as she slept.

'A weakened heart, left by the rheumatic fever she had as a child. We know it can often damage the aortic and mitral valves quite seriously, but there is nothing we can do, even if we pick it up, which is often difficult. It's just impossible to know,' the doctor had said. His words of explanation were no comfort to Victoria. It was time to send for Aunt Minnie.

Aunt Minnie had stormed through the doors of Baker Hall like a whirlwind to attend Lady Baker's funeral, and it took her less than a day to understand the true extent of the damage.

'Why is the fire in the hall not lit? And for goodness' sake, Gerald, what is that food on your jacket? Where are the staff?' She went in search of Victoria. 'I'm here now, sweetie,' she said when she found Victoria with wet eyes and a book, unread, on her lap. She kissed Victoria on the cheek. 'Fear not.' But Victoria did fear, very much. Even with the protected life she had led, she was aware of the real extent of her father's drinking and the chaos which gripped Baker Hall. Aunt Minnie was as unlike her mother as it was possible to be. She was forthright, opinionated and used to having her own way. She was very much a Baker and Victoria was very much her mother's daughter.

Aunt Minnie spent her first month trying to bring some order back into the neglected hall and coaxed the remaining staff, who were as good as packed and about to leave, to remain. She paid them herself. The majority were approaching retirement. During the war, the young men had left to fight and those who remained, or returned still able-bodied, had been lured by the post-depression, post-war air of industry and prosperity which flourished in the towns and cities. Service became a thing of the past and no one wanted to work the hours or endure the routine of a stately home.

'I have paid the staff for the past three months and guaranteed their future stipend, Gerald, but I cannot run two houses and my inheritance will not last five minutes in Baker Hall,' said Aunt Minnie. 'We must find a solution soon, but first, we have to get this place back into some sort of order.' Aunt Minnie's husband had been an officer in the war and had left her widowed and well provided for at forty years of age, but unlike her brother, Minnie had chosen not to wallow in despair or to sink into a whisky decanter.

She had tasked Victoria and her father with the job of reordering and organizing the dusty library and of moving some of the books from the first floor to his study, while she herself took over the study and tried to make sense of the letters and demands from merchants for payment. The situation was far worse than she had anticipated.

After dinner one evening, Victoria came downstairs to get herself a drink and she overheard her name being spoken.

'What are we to do with Victoria?' Aunt Minnie was asking her father.

Victoria knew eavesdroppers heard no good of themselves, but she crouched down outside the large oak door and pressed her eye to the keyhole. Aunt Minnie was sitting forward on the sofa, staring into the fire, looking troubled, nursing a glass.

'That woman, she ruined us.'

Her father was slumped on the sofa and spat the words out as he pointed at the portrait of her mother hanging over the fire, before he gazed into the bottom of his soon to be auctioned glass. They were familiar words to Victoria. He had repeatedly blamed her mother when she was alive for not providing him with a son and heir. He took a gulp of whisky and swilled the ice around. Victoria shuffled from crouching to kneeling; it was more comfortable and she wanted to hear everything. She knew Aunt Minnie well enough to realize that she did not engage in idle discussion. If she had raised this subject, she must have a plan and so far, her plans had filled Victoria with horror.

'If we sell off any more farms, Gerald, we'll diminish the earning capacity of the estate. No one wants a house this size with no earning potential. What would be the point of that? An estate without revenue.'

'What choice do we have?' her father looked up from his glass with alarm.

Victoria could see her Aunt Minnie lean over and gently pat her father's arm, a gesture designed to coax him back from the pit of self-loathing to which he often retreated when Minnie brought up the future of Baker Hall, the family, the overdue taxes and, last but not least, of Victoria, his only child.

'I have an idea,' said Minnie. Victoria shifted her position on the floor – this could be interesting.

'I'm going to call in your solicitor and see if he can help.'

'He's not my solicitor any more,' said Gerald. 'His war wounds caught up with him. He died last year.'

'I am aware of that,' said Minnie.

Victoria could tell that Aunt Minnie was now entering the zone of decreasing tolerance. Pity for her brother stretched only so far. No one blamed the war for ever. They had all paid a price for freedom and now had a responsibility to look forward.

'His son is also a solicitor, and has taken over the practice. He is supposed to be a chip off the old block. It's time you realized that the tax man has no interest in heritage, Gerald, and certainly no love of privilege. The party you've supported all your life might be back in power but it won't keep you out of a debtors' prison. You need to wake up, and when you have you can tell me what on earth we are going to do about your wonderful, gifted daughter. In the meantime, I shall phone your solicitor first thing tomorrow. You need help, and I will not let you drag that delightful young woman down with you.'

Victoria only just managed to get back to her feet before the library door burst open and Minnie strode out. Without any thought as to what she was doing or why, Victoria stepped into her path and blurted out, 'Aunt Minnie, I want to be a nurse, just like Mummy.'

Two meetings with the solicitor and two weeks later, auctioneers' agents arrived to catalogue the contents of the house. Gerald was nowhere to be seen. He moved like a ghost from room to room, avoiding everyone, unable to bear the thought of dismantling his precious library.

'Choose the books you want to take with you to the dower house,' Minnie suggested.

The dower house only had six bedrooms. To Victoria's father, the very thought was a profound humiliation. Victoria had hoped there would be enough money left over from the sale of Baker Hall and its contents to keep them in some degree of comfort, but Roland had disabused her of that notion as she escorted him to his car after his first visit. Victoria had warmed to Roland as soon as he had arrived at the Hall. His manner towards her had been gentle and caring and as she had shown him to her father's study he had said, 'The last time I saw you, you were cycling away from my house with your mother, your pigtails flying behind you.'

Victoria had blushed. 'I was dreadfully sorry to hear about your father,' she said. 'Mummy was very fond of him, and I loved coming with her to change his dressings. He always had a toffee apple for me. It was worth the journey just for that.' They had both laughed and their eyes had met and held until they heard Aunt Minnie.

'Come along. We have much business to discuss.'

'The personal debts on the estate are enormous,' he had told her. 'It's not just the final instalment of the death duties. Your father has been borrowing against assets for some time just for the upkeep of the estate. Although the paintings should clear most of the debts, it may come to the point where the cottages and the dower house also have to be sold.'

'What? My father will be left with nothing? Not even a house?' They were standing in front of the stately home where generations of Victoria's family had lived. The portraits of her ancestors, which had hung on the walls for four hundred years, were to be sold on to strangers. She felt as though the fabric of her world was crumbling.

'My father tried his best to persuade him to sell the house years ago. From the time when your grandfather died and the first demands for death duties arrived. Of course now, due to the delay and with all the compound interest . . .' Victoria's eyes filled with tears as Roland fell silent. He could see that she was barely able to understand the magnitude of what was happening. 'I will do my utmost to achieve the best for you both. Are you going to be all right?' His voice was filled with concern, which he knew had grown from a feeling of protectiveness born of the fond recollections he had of her as a child and the care she and her mother had shown to his father. A feeling that had nothing to do with his duties as the family solicitor.

Victoria looked up at him. The genuine warmth in his eyes and the kindness in his voice was almost more than she could bear, and now her tears broke free and ran down her cheeks, unchecked. Tears she had hidden from her formidable Aunt Minnie, fearing that she would be regarded as weak, like her father.

'Dearie me.' Roland awkwardly put an arm round her shoulder. 'Your parents kept you out of the loop for your own protection. I know it makes all of this an enormous shock, but they were only trying to do their best for you. You know the estate will come to you, but frankly the debts are so huge . . .' His voice tailed away again, leaving unspoken the fact that no man would want to marry Victoria and take on such a huge financial burden.

Victoria lifted her chin proudly. 'I have already decided I want to become a nurse, like my mother,' she said, and Roland smiled.

'I still remember you wearing a nurse's apron.'

'Oh, yes.' Victoria brightened. 'I used to love wearing that apron and helping Mummy. Mrs Armitage made it for me. She said I was her youngest nurse. And I just loved helping and driving into Bolton to your house. Such a bonus, I remember, when we had petrol and didn't have to cycle.'

'I couldn't think of doing anything more worthwhile.' Roland opened the back door of his car and threw his briefcase on to the seat. 'There was something in *The Times* this week about restructuring the state registered nurse syllabus. Nurses are to take on some of the work undertaken by doctors. The NHS has a bit of a crisis on its hands, with the shortage of young men. We lost some of Britain's best brains during the war.'

'Surely plenty of young women could train as doctors?' Victoria felt slightly miffed.

'Oh, indeed, and they are, lots of them now. Most become GPs, but even then it's the old story. They marry and leave to start families of their own. Have you considered becoming a doctor?'

Victoria looked up at the gathering clouds scudding across the sky. A shadow fell across the drive. 'No. I want to be like my mother.'

Roland smiled at her tenacity. 'Well, for what it's worth, I think it's a good idea. My father always spoke very highly of your mother. She left an impression – well, you both did, actually.' His voice had dropped as he kicked up some loose gravel with the toe of his shoe. He was gazing at Victoria's hair, and he was overcome by an urge to reach out and remove the pin sticking out from the back of her neatly coiffed roll and watch it tumble.

Their eyes met and Victoria smiled for the first time since Roland had emerged from the meeting with her father. He smiled back at her and the warmth in his eyes made her feel lighter. Less troubled. 'I know I want to become a nurse but I'm not sure how to go about it. Where would I go?'

Roland, as keen as mustard to be useful, seized his opportunity. 'Well, I think I may be able to help you there. My brother Edward is a doctor at St Angelus in Liverpool. I could make some enquiries, if you like? You'd be close enough to return home sometimes, but far enough away to put some space between you and Baker Hall and all that's going on here.'

'Would you mind awfully?' Victoria cherished her mother's spirit, and held her heart in her own. She knew now that she would not stop until she got what she wanted. Nursing would become her vocation. It would give purpose to her presently empty life.

Roland wished he hadn't been so impetuous. If he could have done it without being noticed, he would have kicked himself. In wanting to help her, help this girl he had come to like so much, he now risked losing her. With his own promise of speaking to his brother and making enquiries about a nursing course at St Angelus, he was sending her away. Edward's way.

As Roland rang the bell, the dogs barked frantically.

'You do know he's sweet on you?' Aunt Minnie peered at Victoria as she fastened the lid on her suitcase.

'I do.' Victoria picked up the case, testing the weight.

'Well then?' Aunt Minnie took her niece's gloves from the bed and held them out to her.

'Well then what?'

Victoria and Roland had met a dozen times since that first day. He had driven her to Liverpool for her interview, taken her for dinner with his brother Edward, and been there for her every step of the way. She had told no one. Aunt Minnie and her father thought she was visiting a school friend in Manchester.

'You know perfectly well what. Are you sweet on him? Because if you are, please be careful. Your father would never approve, and for that matter nor would I.'

'Why ever not? Because he doesn't have a title, or land, or money?' There was a chill to Victoria's voice that her aunt had never heard before. Victoria reached out and took the gloves and felt immediately guilty. 'If Father thinks Roland is good enough to handle our financial and legal affairs, why would he not be good enough for me? After all, he is proving to be far more competent at managing the affairs of Baker Hall than Father ever was.'

Minnie struggled to reply. Victoria was of course absolutely right, but Minnie did not want her brother's incompetence to blight the plans she had for her only niece.

Victoria continued, 'Look, very soon I may have nothing. Absolutely nothing and then I won't be a catch for any man. What's more, my training will take three years. I have every intention of completing it and becoming a qualified nurse. If Roland is sweet on me, he has a long time to wait.'

Minnie stood on the steps and waved until Roland had driven through the gates. She was not unhopeful. She knew many eligible young men in London. Rich eligible men. They wouldn't have been classed as top drawer as short a time as ten years ago, but as everyone kept telling her, today it was a new world.

As she closed the large oak doors, her brother came up behind her. 'Has she gone?' he barked. He smelt strongly of whisky and despair.

'Yes, she has. She thinks she is going to stick it out for the full three years. I give her three months at the most before I persuade her to return. You may have lost the money, but she still has her lineage. I will make a good match for her, never fear. Right now, I want you to get on the phone and find yourself a new firm of solicitors. The sooner that young man has no business at Baker Hall the better.'

CHAPTER 6

Martha would have given anything to turn back the clock and as she lay under the covers, she wished with all her heart that she could. She used to love her work and the sense of responsibility it gave her. She had almost confided in her friend Josie, but when it came to it she didn't have the words to explain what was happening to her. When she tried, they sounded so disgusting, even to her, that she just couldn't say them out loud. He hadn't raped her, which made the rest of what he did hard to explain in a way that didn't make it sound as though she were at least half responsible. Besides, like everyone else who worked at the hospital, Josie thought Mr Scriven was the closest thing to a film star Liverpool had.

'Martha, what are you doing still in bed? It's almost half past six. Come on, up now. I'll make us some tea and pobs before we go for the bus. Is it thinking about that Jake Berry that keeps you in bed? Mark my words, when he's in there with you you'll be looking for reasons to get yerself up and down before he wakes.'

Elsie had put her head round the bedroom door to wake her daughter. There was usually no need; Martha was quite often the first one down the stairs and had the range lit and the kettle on before her mother woke. But recently Martha had been coming down later and later in the mornings, and there was an element of truth in Elsie's suspicions.

Martha loved the times when she woke with Jake filling her thoughts. She knew they were the luckiest and happiest couple in the world and her mother was wrong. The thought that they might one day be married and share the same bed sent a warm thrill shooting through her. She would never want to get up and go to work again. It was a thought so exquisite that she did not believe it would ever happen. Today, however, it wasn't thoughts of Jake that had made her wake. It was the nightmare that was Mr Scriven.

She racked her brains to think of a way to leave the hospital. Could she pretend she was ill, or find another job? That, she had decided, was what she would have to do. Look elsewhere for work. There was an easy way to deal with Mr Scriven and that was to make sure that he never saw her.

In the kitchen, Elsie was standing at the sink, peering into the pink plastic-bound mirror that was propped up against the kitchen window. She removed her curlers with the deftness of someone who went through exactly the same process every morning of her life.

'At last,' she said, turning round with what looked like a small pink plastic sword sticking out of her mouth. 'I thought you were never getting out of that bed. What's up with you? You don't want to be late, you know. We need to be setting an example to the others.'

Martha didn't answer but instead picked up the tea Elsie had already poured for her and began to stir in the milk, watching her mam remove the remainder of the pins. Elsie went through the same routine every day. The wire curlers came out one by one and were placed in a plant pot on the windowsill, and the first thing she did when she got back home at night, while the kettle boiled for a cup of tea, was to put them all back in again.

'There, done,' she said with a flourish, turning round with a smile. 'What's up with you this morning, Martha? 'Tis not like you to be so moody. Have you and Jake fallen out? Had your first row, have you?'

She took an earthenware bowl out of the oven. It was filled with stale bread that had been soaked with sterilized milk and sugar. 'Come on now, we have five minutes. I had to water the milk down this morning. I'll call in at the dairy and pay the bill and get the delivery going again after I've picked up me wages from Dessie.'

Martha had not heard a word her mother had said. She peered at the lukewarm bread and milk with distaste. 'Mam, do you think I could get moved from the consultants' sitting room to somewhere else?'

Elsie looked as though Martha had grown an extra head. 'Moved?' she shrieked. 'Are you mad? Ye have one of the best jobs in the hospital. Do ye realize there are women like Hattie Lloyd who would have ye murdered and yer body hidden if she didn't know I was watching her every move for a job like yours, and her with her new wallpaper all the way up the wall in the hall? All the way up it is. They haven't even painted the bottom half. That paper will be filthy in weeks with the kids running in and out and will look a damn sight worse than the paint, I can tell you. She won't be told, though. Always wanting to be on the up, that one is. God in heaven, no, you cannot move. She would have your place out from under you if she heard you saying that. 'Tis the only thing that keeps us holding our head up around here, having the jobs we do. Thanks to Dessie, between us we earn nearly five shillings more than everyone else. And we're saving it for a rainy day, not running down to St John's market every time there's a new roll of wallpaper in.

'She wants one of those electric steam iron things coming into the shops, she was saying. I told her, well, once it's spent it's spent, and you can't eat an iron, can you? Although I'm sure no one in her house would be able to tell the difference. Mrs Beeton herself would faint if she saw what Hattie Lloyd put on the table in the name of food. Move where? To what? Everyone would think ye had gone mad. No, you cannot move, you daft thing.'

Martha stared at her mother. It was no use arguing. She could not think of one valid reason why she would want to move from a job every other domestic in the hospital coveted. Except for the real reason, and she knew not a living soul would believe that. They would lock her up at the very least. Say she was as mad as a hatter. Accuse her of leading him on. And worst of all, Jake might believe them.

Mr Scriven had taken to visiting the sitting room more and more often, and each time he sought her out. He talked and talked until a kitchen orderly or another consultant entered the room. She far preferred being ignored. She had no idea how to respond or what to say or even why he wanted to speak to her. He had told her about his wife, who drank gin all day when he was at work and had to be put to bed when he got home. About his children, who attended boarding school and barely spoke to him during the holidays. He actually said, 'My wife doesn't understand me, Martha. But you do, don't you? You listen to me.'

'I make you tea and sandwiches,' Martha whispered, without expression or emotion in her voice.

His face was always etched with pain when he spoke, but the truth was that she didn't understand much of what he said and often felt as though the pained expression and long woeful looks were for effect. For her benefit alone. She knew he was a sad and lonely man, and she supposed that was why she hadn't screamed when he kissed her and placed his hands over her breasts. She had never been kissed before. She had thought about it and imagined what it would be like when Jake finally did it. But in reality her first kiss had been a crushing disappointment. She had hated it. It had made her feel sick and she had asked him to stop.

'I'm sorry,' he had said. 'I thought you would like it. Thought that maybe it was what you were looking for when you spoke to me that day.'

'Oh, no, Mr Scriven,' she had said, taking a step back. He was far too close; he had taken to coming into her little galley kitchen off the sitting room and trapping her at the end, so that she had no escape. 'It wasn't that. I just saw that you were troubled and I wanted to help if I could.'

'I see. Well, you did. I mean you have helped. It has been a relief telling you about my awful bloody wife and the way she has turned the children against me. All because I work long hours to pay for the school fees and the nice big house they want to live in.'

Martha almost smiled. 'Well I'm glad I did help, then. Would you like some bread and butter with your tea?'

Anything other than touch me again, please, she thought.

In answer to her prayers, the sitting-room door

opened and one of the other doctors walked in and shouted, 'A quick cup of tea, please, Martha.'

Martha let the breath she had been unaware she was holding escape without a sound.

Mr Scriven looked over his shoulder and beamed at the new arrival. 'Charles,' he said. 'Good to see you. Are you joining us for golf on Saturday?' But as he turned to walk away, to join his colleague in the sitting room, he bent slightly and whispered in Martha's ear, 'I'll be back, Martha. Later. With a treat.'

CHAPTER 7

Dana stood outside what she thought must be the Lovely Lane nurses' home with her overly heavy suitcase in one hand and a rain-dampened sheet of paper, extracted from her letter of acceptance, in the other. Home was just twenty-four hours away, but already felt like another lifetime. She had barely thought about Patrick, and the further she got from Ireland the more the memory had faded. When she realized how close she had come to being imprisoned in a life she had never wanted she felt herself begin to tremble, but she forced herself to stop. To put him and that night from her mind for ever, because the fact was, she was finally free.

Is it this door? she wondered for what felt like the tenth time. Before her stood an imposing building of large grey bricks on four floors. A towering black-painted door with a large polished brass handle stood at the top of a short flight of steps. The front garden lacked any flora or finery and comprised two finely manicured green lawns on either side of a short path. By the light of the street lamp she saw that the top of the low surrounding wall was pitted with holes which had once been home to a fine set of wrought-iron railings. The Lovely Lane home bore the scars of the war effort by shedding tears of rust every time it rained.

On the opposite side of the road was the Lovely Lane park, where branches once held back by railings grew out over the pavement and dripped rain from variegated leaves. There was no sign to announce that she was in the right place, and no number on the house. Her heart beat madly. She had never before approached such a building and she realized she would have to walk down the path and knock on that huge door. All she could think of was that it would be the wrong place and the owner would be angry at being disturbed. Her confidence was not what it was before Patrick had attacked her.

On arriving at the Pier Head, she had decided to walk to her destination. The letter she was holding said that Lovely Lane was only ten minutes from the docks, and she felt that the exercise might help to clear her thoughts a little. Her last moments in Ireland had been more eventful than she could ever have anticipated, and had done much to restore her deflated spirits. Mr Joyce had carried her case all the way to the ramp of the boat. He had spoken very little on the journey, as was his way, but when they approached the barrier he reached into his jacket and took out an envelope, which he held out to her.

'What's that?' she had asked in a voice loaded with curiosity. 'I already have me wages; ye gave them to me yesterday.'

'I know that now,' he replied. 'But I don't want yer mammy to be worried about ye. Here's something to keep ye going when ye are in Liverpool.'

Dana took the envelope and looked inside, and saw a brown ten-shilling note wrapped around a much larger bundle. Hesitantly, she extracted the money and counted it in the fading light. 'I can't take this,' she said, her eyes filling with tears as she stuffed the notes back in the envelope and thrust it back at him.

He had expected and prepared for this reaction. After all, she was Nancy's daughter.

'Well, it seems to me now that if ye give it back, and sure that is up to you, I'll have to put it in the post and hope that Mrs Brock in the post office doesn't find out and no postman on the way to Liverpool fancies it for himself.'

'But I haven't earned it,' Dana gasped.

'No, for sure, but when I tell yer mammy ye won't be going hungry or dependent on anyone for anything it will make her happy, and wouldn't that be a great thing indeed now. Your taking it would earn her that.'

Dana looked at the envelope in her hand and then back at Mr Joyce. She could not stop the tear that escaped from her eye and rolled down her cheek. Patrick, whom she had known since birth, had tried to rape her. Now another man from the village, with whom in all her life she had never held a conversation that was not about groceries or her mammy, was handing her two hundred pounds. She had seen her father return from market happy with a great deal less.

'Thank you,' she said, pushing the envelope deep down into her handbag. 'I don't know what to say.'

'Ye don't have to say anything, but do come home to visit now, won't ye? We will all be wanting to know how ye are getting along.'

It suddenly struck her that her mammy had said the same thing. She looked at Mr Joyce while she struggled to make sense of the coincidence, but there was no time.

'All aboard,' a voice rang out, and the next moment she was standing on the deck watching the lonely figure of Mr Joyce disappear into the crowd.

She had regretted her decision to walk the ten minutes to Lovely Lane in less than two and wished she had taken a taxi; the driver would have known exactly where to drop her off. The cabbies had shouted after her as she left the ferry and walked away up the rise, but she had placed her hand protectively over the envelope in her handbag and ignored their offers. She had money for the first time in her life and she wanted to keep it. She would not be wasting it on taxi fares.

'Can I help? You look lost.'

Dana almost jumped out of her skin. A young

man had approached her, also carrying a heavy suitcase, which he now set down next to hers. The first thought that crossed her mind was that she had never seen a man like this in Ireland. Even on Sundays, the boys at home never reached such a level of presentability. They were in a perpetual state of grubbiness from working every hour of daylight on the land. Those who could had done exactly what Dana was doing for herself and had left for Liverpool or New York. This man had not a speck of mud anywhere about him and his trousers were not ripped or tied up with twine. His teeth were white, his skin was clean and his hair was combed. A faint aroma hung about him, a light sweet and spicy smell infusing the cold damp air. This was not a man as Dana knew men to be and for a moment she stared, her mouth agape.

Recovering herself, she spluttered, 'Oh, thank you. I'm just looking for the Lovely Lane nurses' home. I'm not really sure if this is it?' There hadn't been a man in Dana's life till now that she hadn't known since she was a child. Being spoken to by a stranger was a new experience and she felt herself blush. His accent was crisp, with no hint of Irish, and his eyes, which were now crinkled up at the corners and smiling at her, were honest and kind. Dana knew in an instant that she had nothing to fear from this man. She marvelled at the sight of him, and realized that she was still staring. He grinned as he took a packet of cigarettes out of his pocket and offered her one.

'No thank you, I don't smoke,' she said rather primly. She was trying hard.

'Ha!' The man laughed. 'That will last for less than a week. I would bet there isn't a single nurse in St Angelus who doesn't smoke.'

Dana bristled. 'Well, there will be now. I made a promise to Mammy.' By now she was blushing furiously. She had made many promises to Mammy over the past few days. Mrs Brogan knew an emotional advantage when she saw one and had pushed it to the hilt, saving the best until last. Dana could still hear the whispered words in her ears.

'Never let a drink pass your lips, never smoke, and no sex outside marriage. I have only agreed to your moving to Liverpool because I know ye will swear to me, by all that is holy, to stick to those three promises, Dana.'

Dana had laughed in response. It was the first she had heard of it. 'Well, they are easy promises to stick to, Mammy,' she had replied. After Patrick, she had truly meant it. She had vowed never to speak to another man ever again.

'What else did you promise your mammy, then?' The young man exhaled a long plume of smoke and studied Dana carefully as he flicked his ash on to the pavement.

Dana prayed for the ground to open up and swallow her. How could she have been so naïve? Here was a man, a proper man, not one of the ignorant boys from the country. A man who smelt of cigarette smoke and something else she could not quite make out. A man who had the good manners to offer to help a girl who was obviously lost and not poke fun at her. This man, with his dark swept-back hair and deep brown eyes, with his polished brown leather suitcase, was a man of the world and Dana had been caught out. Her tongue was already in knots. Her mind was spinning and her mouth was dry with embarrassment. She knew if she spoke now, she would make even more of a fool of herself.

'Go on then, what other promises did you make?' She could sense he was on the verge of laughing again. 'Was one of them not to speak to strange men, by any chance? Because if it was, you have already broken it. But, I might add, you are perfectly safe with me. I work at the hospital. That's how I knew you must be a new nurse, looking so lost on Lovely Lane. So go on, I'm intrigued. What advice does an Irish mammy give to a daughter travelling to big bad Liverpool? Was it beware of strange men, and don't drink alcohol along with the smoking? I think that's what I would tell a daughter of mine if I ever had one.'

Dana found her voice. 'Well, as it happens, no, it wasn't. Not really. I am quite capable of holding a conversation with anyone, strange man or not, and ye don't look very strange at all. Mammy didn't need to warn me about that. I can look after myself very well.'

She was feeling more confident now. How dare

this man try to tie her up in knots? Gorgeous or not, she would hold her own. She felt her bashed and beaten confidence return with a surge.

'Well, I'm not going to give up until you tell me. I will regard it as my personal duty to find out, just in case it *was* don't speak to strange men. Then I'll know what my chances are of getting you to come out for a drink with me.' He held the cigarette packet out to her again. Dana felt her stomach somersault at the audacity of a man who was telling her that he wondered if he had any chance of being alone with her. That had certainly never happened before and her head was spinning.

'My name is Edward, by the way, and everyone calls me Teddy, but you will probably get to know me by a different name altogether.' He took two cigarettes out of the packet, lit one and held it towards Dana. 'What's your name then, Miss Lost in Liverpool? If you tell me, then neither of us will be guilty of talking to strangers.'

'I'm Dana. Dana Brogan. I've just got here off the boat,' she said and then fell silent, not knowing what else to say. This man was confusing her. She was determined not to sound like the country girl she was.

'Go on then, Dana, be a daredevil. We are practically best friends now by Scouse standards. Here, have a "welcome to Liverpool" ciggie.'

'Really, no thank you.' She smiled politely. She would have liked to try a cigarette but her mother's breath was still warm on her ear.

'Have you visited any of the wards in St Angelus yet?' Teddy asked. Dana felt on safer ground with this question and responded with enthusiasm.

'Oh, no. Not at all. I am dreading the wards. I'm near terrified.'

Teddy exhaled smoke before he replied. 'Well, I should think so. Some of the doctors are terribly fearsome.'

He grinned at her and the cold damp Liverpool air was banished by a warm feeling glowing inside. For a moment she allowed herself to compare this man with Patrick and shuddered.

'I've heard the ward sisters can be terrors,' she said. She felt a conspiratorial thrill at discussing hospital staff she had never set eyes on with a man she had met less than ten minutes ago.

'Yes, that is true, some can be. The best fun to be had is on nights. Not so many eyes around and lots of high jinks. Look, I have to go.' Teddy held out his hand, and, not really knowing what was expected of her, Dana tentatively placed her own leather-gloved one in his. 'I have to get to my own room,' he explained, looking down the street as though he were expecting to see someone. 'I look forward to meeting you again. Maybe next time I can work on getting you to break another of those promises you made to Mammy.'

Dana's eyes bulged as she remembered. No sex outside of marriage.

Teddy dropped her hand, grinned, and said, 'Go on, be brave. Go and knock on the door.' Then, with a wave, he was gone. Swallowed up by the smog. Dana watched him vanish, wondering if all of a sudden he might reappear. Return to say something he had forgotten. Rush up the road and say, 'Oh, by the way, Dana, if you ever need anything . . .' and she would make sure she would.

She felt as though she knew him already. His teasing words and laughing eyes were intoxicating. She had definitely wanted to talk to him for longer. She hadn't asked him what he did. Maybe he was a male nurse. She had heard that there had been quite a few working at St Angelus since the war. There was something about him that was both playful and worldly. She felt he was a man who had depths, and knew things that she couldn't possibly imagine. Gosh, what kind of man would just stop a woman in the street and tease her like that? Dana wondered what he had meant when he said she would get to know him by another name. She had been so flustered; she had had no time to organize her thoughts and ask him. At least that meant he was sure she would be seeing him again. He appeared to have been confident of that.

With a sigh, she looked up at the tall, dove-grey building. She had never before had to walk up a flight of stone stairs to knock on a door twice her height and felt nervous about doing so now. What if one of the fearsome sisters was on the other side? She straightened her hat, picked up her suit-case, and taking a deep breath, prepared herself to approach the door that would open on to her new life. She half hoped that someone nice inside would peep round the net curtains, see her loitering and open the door before she knocked to shout a welcome down the steps and say yes, this is your home for the next three years and it's lovely here, really it is.

Before she could move, she heard footsteps approaching, and a voice with a strong Liverpool accent called out to her.

'Are you all right, love? Are you a new nurse, like me?'

Dana turned and saw a girl with dark hair and a fringe, parted on the side and swept across. It was a look that Dana was sure absolutely no one in Ireland had seen on another human being – unless you counted Audrey Hepburn in the magazines which sometimes came to the post office. Dana's mouth almost fell open. Her shoulder-length red curly hair must look atrocious to someone so fashionable. She had heard her friends say that the women in Liverpool were the most elegant in the world, and had thought it must be an exaggeration, but now she wondered whether it could be true. Dana smiled. She felt as though she had smiled more in the last ten minutes than she had in the past week. She wondered, if she stood in the same spot on Lovely Lane for long enough, would everyone in Liverpool have stopped to speak to her?

'I thought I was lost,' she said, delighted to have

connected with another new girl just like herself, 'but a man who works at the hospital just stopped and told me I was in the right place.'

'Let's see that piece of paper in your hand.' The girl glanced at it briefly, then turned to the older woman next to her and said, 'Yeah, Mam, she's new too. We've got the same letter, her an' me.' She smiled at Dana. 'What a lovely name you have. I'm Pamela, but everyone, even the priest who christened me, calls me Pammy. Where are you from, love?'

'I'm from a village near Belmullet, in the west of Ireland,' said Dana.

Next to Pamela and her mother stood a man in a cap, lighting up a cigarette, and around them children of varying ages were excitedly jumping up and down. There appeared to be quite an age gap between Pammy and her siblings, a common consequence of the war, Dana had heard, with men fighting overseas for years at a time. Pammy seemed to have one younger sister and three much younger brothers.

'Are you all on your own, queen?' Pamela's mother asked. 'I'm Pammy's mam, Maisie, and this is our Stan here,' she said, pointing to the empty space next to her. Stan had disappeared. 'And this lot are our kids. Drive me mad they do. Lorraine, stop annoying little Stan.'

'I'm Dana – Dana Brogan. I'm new as well and I was looking for the nurses' home, but it seems I've found it.'

124

'Where's your family, love?' asked Maisie with a frown, looking beyond Dana, as though she expected to find a family of six crouching behind her.

'Oh, they aren't here. I came on my own. I know it says on the letter that your family can drop you off and see your room, just the once, but it's a bit far for everyone to travel from Belmullet. We're a long way from Dublin, and besides, there's the milking and everything. We live on a farm.'

'Oh yes, I know that, love,' said Maisie, nodding enthusiastically. Dana was taken aback for a moment, but then Maisie said, 'Everyone in Ireland lives on a farm. Anyway, love, my name is Mrs Tanner. We live just three roads away on Arthur Street, but our Pamela is moving into the nurses' home because in our house she'd get no peace to study or anything, would you, Pammy?'

Pammy, who hadn't been able to get a word in edgeways, smiled knowingly at Dana, who smiled back.

'Anyway. Stan, come here,' Maisie shouted to her husband, who was peacefully smoking his cigarette, leaning against a lamp-post and staring through the damp smog down the road towards the docks. Extinguishing his stub on the wet ground with the toe of his shoe, he headed back to the group, his steel heel- and toe-caps playing a tattoo on the pavement as he walked. He straightened his cap, sensing he was about to be given instructions, and he was right.

'This is Dana, Stan,' said Maisie.

'Hello, Mr Tanner. It's very nice to meet you. In fact, I'm relieved to meet you all, sure I am. I didn't know was I in the right place at all.'

Pamela's mother looked at Dana as though she were speaking in tongues.

'You know what, Pammy, I love that Irish accent, don't you?' Then, 'You see what it says on this letter, Stan? Your family's allowed to accompany you to your room on your first night for twenty minutes so that they can be . . .' she began to slow down as she reached the bigger words, '"reassured of the suitability of their daughter's accommodation". So here's what I'm thinkin', kids. Why don't we split up? Dana here hasn't got any family with her, because it's too far, so half of us will go in with her and half with our Pammy. And then if there's time, we'll swap over. There you go, love: you have a family now. A noisy one, but we're all yours.'

Dana felt the tears spring to her eyes in gratitude. She didn't say any more about her meeting with Teddy. She had no idea why not, but she knew it would be hard to explain. A handsome well-spoken man arrived from nowhere. He teased me, lit a torch in my heart, tried to give me my first cigarette, asked me out and then disappeared into the smog.

She decided not to mention Teddy to anyone else. Maybe after all he was just a ghost.

Pamela's siblings began to jump up and down

in excitement again, all of them shouting, 'I want to go with Dana. I want to be Dana's sister, not Pammy's.'

'Behave, you lot. Quieten down, or none of us will be allowed in. Stan, you and the boys go with Pammy. I'll go with our Dana here and help her hang her things up before I come to check that our Pammy's all right.'

A wave of relief and gratitude washed over Dana. She wiped the tears from her eyes with the new handkerchief one of her friends had given her as a leaving present, and sniffled loudly.

'I can't get over it, I can't,' Stan said suddenly. 'Our Pammy becoming a nurse and living in Lovely Lane and now she's already met a nice friend like you. Smashin' that, isn't it?'

Dana sniffed again, more loudly this time.

'Ah, c'mon, queen, don't worry. We're here now, love,' said Maisie. 'You've gorra Liverpool family now, hasn't she, Stan? Lorraine, 'ere, take Dana's hand.'

Dana was aware that the strain of the past twenty-four hours, the dance at the hall, the near rape by Patrick, the emotional goodbyes, the unexpected gift of a lifetime from the mysterious Mr Joyce and the meeting with Teddy had made her all of a fluster. If yesterday morning someone had told her this was how her arrival in Liverpool would be, she wouldn't have believed them. Her new experiences and the tiredness she felt after the long journey were beginning to have an effect.

'That's really kind of you, so it is,' she said, and she felt her hand being squeezed by Lorraine, who smiled up at her with large brown eyes. It occurred to Dana that those eyes were all knowing, and that they were telling her it was no use arguing. *You just do what Mam says.*

'Kind? Not really, love. It's what we do here in Liverpool, isn't it, gang?' said Maisie. 'You're gonna love Liverpool, you are, I can tell. Can't you, Pammy?' Pammy opened her mouth to speak, but before she could say a word Maisie shouted, 'Go on then, everyone, up the steps you go. Shurrup, you lot. Act all dignified now, not like the scallies from Arthur Street people will think we are.' Pamela and Dana strode up the steps together, with Lorraine still clinging to Dana's hand, and pressed the large doorbell. Everyone heard it echo out throughout the vast building.

A chain slipped on the other side of the door and a handle rattled and turned as the door was swung open to reveal a diminutive lady wearing a mid-calf dark grey woollen skirt and jumper. Grey hair of an almost identical shade was piled on top of her head in a tight bun, but the drab effect was broken by a large cameo brooch pinned to her thick pullover. Peering through her thick wire-framed spectacles the woman smiled in such a warm and friendly way at the girls that they both felt weak with relief, and the nervous giggles which had threatened to erupt just a moment ago disappeared entirely.

'Come away in out of the damp, all of you,' the

woman trilled, ushering them into the carpeted hallway. Pammy's siblings, raucous outdoors, had fallen as silent as church mice.

'I'm Mrs Duffy and I will help you settle in this evening,' she continued, once the introductions were over. 'You will see a lot of me. I come in each morning to prepare your breakfast and then an evening meal for when you get in from day duty, or before you leave for nights. I go back to my own house in the middle of the day and return in the evening to tidy the night nurses' rooms and to make a trolley of milky drinks with a plate of biscuits before the rest of you go to bed. I leave a good pot on the range every day for you to help yourselves when you get home from the wards. No one has ever complained about my dinners yet.' Mrs Duffy gave Maisie a knowing look over the top of her spectacles. It said, very clearly, *and no one is about to start now.*

'Well, that sounds lovely, doesn't it, girls?' said Maisie to Dana and Pammy.

'Mam, everyone talks funny around here,' chirped little Stan, pulling at Maisie's coat, and ignored by everyone as Mrs Duffy went on.

'At night, I sit in the lounge with the nurses for an hour while they have their drinks and chat about their day. Then I clear it all away at ten o'clock and I send the girls away to their beds before I leave for home.'

'Ooh, that's a long day, love,' said Maisie, concerned.

'Well, it is, but I enjoy looking after my nurses. I have no children of my own, after all. The morning maids come in from Monday to Friday to clean the nurses' rooms and make their beds, and for those who can't settle after nights, although that is a rare thing indeed, we serve coffee from ten o'clock in the morning. They are well looked after.'

Dana and Pamela looked at each other, amazed. This sounded like luxury.

'They make our beds and clean our rooms?' Dana said to Mrs Duffy, aghast.

'Yes, they do, but don't worry, love, you won't notice the benefit. You will be making thirty a day yourself once you have finished your preliminary training. That will all be explained to you in the morning by Sister Tutor when she arrives. But first, what would you all like? A cup of tea or hot chocolate, Horlicks maybe? We have twenty-five nurses living in Lovely Lane. All the new girls have already settled into their rooms, so you, young man' – Mrs Duffy took a plate of biscuits from the trolley behind her and handed it down to little Stan – 'can have your pick and be in charge of this plate. I spent the afternoon making them, just for you.'

Little Stan grinned from ear to ear. Mrs Duffy had just acquired an adoring fan.

Dana decided there and then that Mrs Duffy was lovely and not just because she made the most delicious hot chocolate she had ever tasted. The idea of arriving at the nurses' home had worried her sick every day since she had received her acceptance letter, and now she realized she needn't have worried. If her own mammy could have picked someone to look after her, Dana was quite sure Mrs Brogan would have chosen Mrs Duffy.

'You are the first girl to have been taken from Ireland for the registered nurse course,' Mrs Duffy said now. 'It's unusual, that is. We have had a few from Dublin in the past, for the enrolled nurse course, but not since the new exams began. It must have been difficult for you to study for the entrance exam. You should be very proud of that. They say that it is more difficult to train at St Angelus than it is at St Bart's in London.

'And, you know, Mrs Tanner, there has never been anyone here from the streets around the dock road before, either. This must all be down to the new director of nursing. They say she is making waves.' Mrs Duffy took Pammy's youngest brother by the hand. 'Come along, young man. We need to show them the way, don't we?'

'You've done me a favour, you know, Dana,' said Pamela, as they walked up the long wooden staircase to their rooms. Stan and the eldest boy carried the suitcases and Stan raised his eyebrows when he felt the weight of Dana's. 'Jesus, love, what have you got in here, a sack of spuds?' he said, and everyone laughed as Dana blushed furiously.

'How?' she whispered.

'By taking our Lorraine off me. She would have

tried to nick back half of me stuff. She has no idea I've got one of her best blouses in me bag. Me mam bought it for her on St John's market last week. It's lovely. She'd have gone mad.'

'Don't be soft, Pammy,' said Lorraine. She had heard every word. 'I took it back hours ago, before we left. I'm way cleverer than you.'

Dana looked at the name displayed on her door. It was typed on a small white card, within a polished brass frame. *Probationary Nurse Brogan.* 'Go on, queen, that's you,' said Maisie softly.

'Shall I turn the knob for you?' asked Lorraine, wanting to be helpful.

'Yes please, Lorraine,' said Dana, feeling as though she had known Pammy's family as long as her own. 'Go on then.'

Lorraine swung the heavy white-painted door open. Before them was a very large room with two sets of tall Georgian sash windows. The floor was covered in a rust-coloured carpet and the walls were painted deep cream. They stepped inside tentatively, Maisie pushing past Dana to take a closer inspection of the curtains.

Picking up the hem to feel the fabric, she said, 'Well, this is lovely, isn't it? You won't find anyone on Arthur Street with curtains of that quality. They never came from the market and that's for sure. Look, that's called interlining, that is. Our Pammy's going up in the world, Lorraine.' The room contained a small dark oak dressing table with a mirror and a stool, a large and shabby-looking velvet wing-backed chair next to an oak desk with a lamp, a wardrobe, and a small single bed. Mrs Duffy had shown them where the communal toilets and bathrooms were on the way along the corridor.

'This is better than what our Pammy has at home,' said Lorraine. 'Lovely pink curtains,' she added wistfully.

Dana agreed readily. 'Me too. I can't believe I have my own room. I have to share with my grandma at home.'

Maisie looked out of the window into the night. The street lights cast a marmalade glow beneath them. 'This house used to belong to one of the big shipping merchants,' she said. 'They say he employed twelve staff in here round the clock. Amazing when you think how some people live in Arthur Street, where we come from, just a few minutes away. Or even down on the dock road, where lots of the Irish live. That one man had all this to himself. They say he was a very good man to work for, mind. No one had any complaints and he was very generous at Christmas, or so the waitresses at the Grand say, anyway. He used to throw a Christmas party there every year apparently and one year he gave all the waitresses a present. A small blue box each, and when they opened it, they found a pair of real pearl earrings inside. Isn't that lovely?'

'It is, if they didn't all sell them the next day,' chirped up Lorraine.

Maisie carried on looking out of the window. 'Well, d'you know what, our Lorraine, I reckon he knew that might happen, or they'd pawn them more likely, but I reckon he also knew they would all have a bit of cash in their hand as a result and could have a nice Christmas.' Stepping back from the window, she pulled the curtains across. 'Come on, Dana love, let's get that bag unpacked. That Mrs Duffy is a nice woman, but she did say we were only allowed twenty minutes. I don't want to worry you, but she said you all need a good night's sleep because from tomorrow it all changes.'

'Have you seen the sign on your door? Look here.' Lorraine, who had been opening and closing drawers and generally examining the furniture, swung the door into the room wide open. 'Look at this. See your name here?' She pointed to the brass frame. 'Watch this.' She slid the name card upwards and out of the frame and showed Dana and Maisie the other side. It read *Probationary Nurse Brogan. NIGHT DUTY.*

'That's for when you're doing your night shifts. I bet it's so the others know to be quiet on your corridor during the day and the maids don't come into your room. That's why Mrs Duffy said she comes in and tidies up for you when you're at work at night. Isn't that incredible? Someone makes your bed for you, even when you've been lying in it all day.'

Dana was beginning to think that a probationary nurse could feel like royalty and very important indeed when she heard a unfamiliar voice from the corridor ask, 'Can I come in and say hello?'

Lorraine ran and opened the door to reveal a very nervous-looking young girl in the doorway.

'Of course you can, me lovely,' said Maisie. 'It's Dana's room; here she is. Give me that bag, Dana. I'll unpack for you while you girls become acquainted. I'm Maisie, love, Pammy's mam. She's just moved in too, down the corridor she is, on the bend at the top of the stairs.'

'I'm Beth,' said the girl. 'I'm in the room next door and I could hear you talking. I thought there was no point sitting on my bed looking at the walls and feeling scared.' Beth pushed her dark brown hair back behind her ears. She wore glasses that swept sharply up at the corners and she squinted slightly as she looked around the room. Dana thought she saw her nose crinkle as her scrutiny took in the clothes Lorraine was hanging up in the wardrobe.

Suddenly the door on the other side of Dana's opened and a timid but very cultured voice said, 'Oh, hello there, everyone. Would you mind terribly if I came in too? My name's Victoria. How do you do?'

Victoria could only be described as beautiful, Dana thought appreciatively. Her naturally ash-blonde hair, worn in a swept-up style, gave definition to her high cheekbones and large blue eyes.

She did not wait for anyone to respond, but went on, 'I don't know anyone either.' At which point her bottom lip trembled, and seconds later, she promptly burst into tears.

'Oh my giddy aunt. Come here, love,' Maisie said, putting an arm round Victoria's shoulder. 'Have you unpacked?'

Mrs Duffy appeared at the door with a tray of tea. 'I could see you were going to have your hands full,' she said to Maisie. 'First night is always the same, all woe and tears. I'm delighted you're here. Stay a little longer, would you, and have another cup of tea. You will be wanting to see Nurse Tanner settled in before you leave.'

It was nearly midnight and Dana was lying on her bed, talking to Pammy, Victoria and Beth. Pammy was sitting on the end of the bed, leaning against the wall; Beth was in the shabby wing-backed chair with her legs crossed and a list of instructions she had found in her own room on her knee. Beth left nothing to chance. She had already made a note of everything she needed for the following morning. Victoria sat on the desk chair, her legs primly crossed, while she removed her Cutex Shimmer Pink nail polish. They had discussed their backgrounds and shared their terror of what the next day might hold. Maisie had stayed with them as long as she could, mothering them all, and Mrs Duffy had chatted for a while when she slipped yet another tray of tea into the room, with her instructions for bed and a wink before she left.

Dana had produced a tin of seed cake and put

it on the desk, something that made the others gasp in astonishment. 'You carried that all the way here from Ireland!' Maisie had exclaimed, as she helped her unpack. That was before she unloaded the three brack breads, a boxty loaf, a bag of scones, the sack of potatoes, two onions, a deep yellow pat of butter wrapped in greaseproof paper, and a lump of cheese. All of which she handed over to Mrs Duffy.

Dana felt as though she was instant friends with Pammy. She liked Victoria too, but there was something about Beth she could not warm to, much as she tried.

'How did youse lot get on in your interviews?' asked Pammy, munching on the seed cake. 'I had a terrible time. It was the worst day of me life. When the big doctor on the panel, Mr Scriven, looked at the form and saw I lived in Arthur Street, I could tell he wasn't going to let me in. He asked me had I considered becoming an enrolled nurse instead. He said we've had them since the war, for girls like you. I said what do you mean, girls like me, but I knew very well what he meant. He thought I just wasn't good enough. But that nice sister sat next to him – Sister Haycock? The one with the lovely smile. She's in charge of the nursing school, I think. Did youse lot have her as well?' They all nodded. 'Well, when she took me to the door after the interview was over, she whispered to me, "Here's a little secret, Pammy. I was born in George Street." Well, I couldn't believe it. That's only just down from Arthur Street.' Pammy paused for effect. 'She said, "Don't you worry about Mr Scriven." George Street is really just bomb rubble now, though, so I don't know exactly where she lived. It's never been cleared yet – it's just where all the kids play, not really a street. Anyway, as soon as I got the letter, me mam, when she had stopped crying, read it and she recognized the name Emily Haycock and she said well I never, I knew a girl who was an Emily Haycock, she lived on George Street and I said Mam, it's the same one, she told me she was from George Street, and then me mam started crying again. I said to her what's the matter, Mam, and she said there wasn't anything the matter, but she gave me da one of her looks and he winked at her and said what comes around goes around, eh, love? Well that was all a complete mystery to me. I have no idea what they were on about, but they definitely knew who she was. I said to me mam, shall I say hello if I see her and she nearly bit me head off. "Don't be daft," she said. "No one's seen her round these parts for years. Don't mention anything, do you hear?"'

The others were amazed, as much by the velocity and volume of Pammy's chatter as by the story itself. Dana had no trouble in keeping up. She was from Ireland and there wasn't a woman in Liverpool who could hold a candle to an Irishwoman for gossip or chat. Beth was almost asleep. She had volunteered to copy her list for everyone, to make sure that nothing was forgotten, but no one was terribly interested and Beth had seemed slightly put out.

'I swear, if I hadn't had that cake to sustain me, I would have fainted from sheer exhaustion halfway through that story, Pammy. Just trying to keep up was an effort,' said Victoria. 'But your mother makes jolly good cake, Dana.'

Dana grinned with pleasure. Never in her life had she met or held a conversation with anyone who was as well dressed or as well spoken as Victoria.

Beth rubbed her eyes. The daughter of a former army sergeant, she had also been travelling since early that morning. 'My interview was a doddle,' she said. She appeared not to notice the astonished expressions of the others. 'I worked hard for my exams and I know I got top marks, so I would have been very disappointed if I hadn't got in. It was all fair and square with me, no help from a fairy godmother. My father is a stickler for doing things the right way. The army way.'

Victoria, Dana and Pammy fell silent. Beth's words were threaded with barbed wire. She had shattered the warm and giddy atmosphere of companionship and the excitement of new friendships formed.

'I suggest we all get some sleep,' she went on. 'I've left a list on your mirror of what to remember for the morning, Dana. Here are yours.' Beth held out two pieces of paper to Victoria and Pammy.

'I have no intention of setting a bad example on the first day. Night, all.'

The door had closed behind her before anyone had a chance to respond. 'Night,' the three girls chimed in half-hearted harmony.

'Gosh, well, she is a funny one,' whispered Pammy. 'I thought she liked us, sitting in here and eating your cake, Dana.'

'Imagine,' said Dana. 'What's got into her?'

'She's probably just nervous and tired like the rest of us,' said Victoria, putting the lid back on the cake tin and brushing the crumbs from the bed into her hand. 'Better not leave any evidence of our midnight feast, eh? It's like being back in boarding school.'

Pammy wasn't listening, and looked thoughtfully at the closed door. She had already decided Beth was one to be watched.

As Dana tried to sleep for her first night in a new room, she ran through the events of the past twenty-four hours. Nothing that had happened puzzled her as much as the tear in Mr Joyce's eye when she had said goodbye and boarded the ferry. Her thoughts then wandered to Teddy, the man with the impish smile, and she finally slept, smiling.

Less than a mile away, Teddy ran up the steps of the doctors' residence and almost bumped straight into someone who was leaving. 'Gosh, sorry. In a bit of a rush there,' Teddy gasped, dropping his case on to the top step with a bump.

140

'Not at all,' the other man replied, 'my fault entirely.' Teddy stared. The man was familiar, yet he was not. Teddy thought he knew him, but he didn't.

'Sorry to gape. I thought you were someone else,' he said, holding out his hand.

'Everyone does. You probably thought I was my father. Mr Gaskell.'

'Blimey, yes, I did. You do look like him. I heard his son was the new consultant on gynae. God help you, have you met Sister Antrobus?'

The young doctor Gaskell smiled. 'No, that pleasure awaits me. Do you live in, too? My parents want me to move back home with them, but I'm not sure I could manage that.'

Mr Gaskell senior was proud of his son and there wasn't anyone in the hospital who hadn't heard about his boy's work on the front line during the war. How he had suspended his training, been injured, returned to active duty, survived, and came home a hero. Teddy thrust out his hand. The man he had thought a mere junior doctor five minutes ago was in fact a consultant. An important man.

'It is an honour to meet you. Welcome to St Angelus.'

Dr Gaskell smiled back and shook the offered hand. 'Please, just call me Oliver when we're outside the hospital. I'm off to find a quick pint before bed. Care to join me?'

'Not half,' Teddy said. 'Let me just throw this case indoors.'

Two minutes later, the men walked in through the door of the Grapes. The parrot on the bar squawked 'Pint of Guinness, pint of Guinness', and as they laughed it occurred to Teddy that he was possibly the first junior doctor in the history of St Angelus to nip down to the pub for a pint with a consultant. He fleetingly thought of the Irish nurse he had tried to chat up. The country girl who, it turned out, had a smile to die for and dazzling blue eyes. Teddy felt good.

'When do you start in your new post?' asked Teddy, who dreamt of the day when he would become a consultant. Oliver Gaskell seemed so young.

'Not for months yet, believe it or not. I will be spending a little time lecturing at the medical school, until the new G&O lecturer arrives and I've promised to do the odd lecture at the nursing school here.'

'Gosh,' said Teddy. 'Don't you think it's weird? We spend years waiting to change from Mr to Dr and here you are, at the peak of your career and back to Mr'

Both men laughed. 'Not sure my father would agree with you there,' Oliver said.

'How long has he been at St Angelus?' asked Teddy.

'Do you know, I think it must be over forty years.'

'Make the most of your time in the med school old chap, because compared to ward two and Sister Antrobus, it will be a doddle.

'To the new world,' said Teddy, as they raised their glasses.

'To the new world,' Oliver Gaskell replied. 'Now, please, tell me all about Sister Antrobus.'

CHAPTER 8

The girls had agreed to meet in Dana's room at eight thirty the following morning, dressed in their uniform, ready to face the day. Mrs Duffy had instructed them not to be late. 'Cereal and toast with bacon rashers for breakfast. You will need a head start. You have Sister Ryan to meet and you'll need a strong stomach for that.'

No nurse ever skipped breakfast. It came before the mile-and-a-half walk to the hospital and three hours of hard physical work before they collapsed in rotation into the greasy spoon hospital canteen for mid-morning coffee and two thick slices of hot buttered toast.

Dana had been asked to send a great deal of information to the hospital in advance of her arrival, including her vital statistics. Hanging in the wardrobe she had discovered five starched palest pink uniforms with her name written on a linen tag, and five starched aprons. A pink petersham belt and a probationary nurse's polished buckle lay on the dressing table, along with five white starched and frilled caps and a handful of small brass studs. Dana picked up the cap. There were five holes at various places in the fabric. She picked up a brass stud and threaded it through one, then frowned deeply as she wondered what the other holes were for. On the back of the door hung a heavy, black, scarlet-lined cape with her name inside the collar.

Mrs Duffy had told the girls that after breakfast they were to gather in the sitting room, in their uniform, where they would be met by Sister Ryan for cap-folding instruction and a quick talk about dress and conduct. Then Sister Ryan would walk with them to the school of nursing within the hospital grounds.

Dana struggled with the uniform. The tiny linen-covered buttons were small and fiddly for a farm girl and almost impossible to fasten. There were more pockets in the dress and the apron than she could count. She was sure each one must have a purpose, but the meaning of the various shapes and depths was lost on her this morning. Her lace collar was so starched it wouldn't lie down flat at first, and when it did it scratched the back of her neck so much that her skin flared up bright red to match her hair. The fastenings of the apron were so incredibly complicated, with their long straps and the linen loops to thread them through, that she wasn't sure she had secured it correctly. Her red hair wouldn't stay behind her ears but curled and bushed out at the sides, thanks to the smog and damp air of the previous evening, and she had no idea what to do with the cape. She decided that she would wear it, and then almost staggered under the weight. At least it was obvious that the two heavy red ties crossed over the front and fastened with the buttons at the back. That was the easiest part of the entire uniform.

Thank goodness for the cape, she said to herself, studying her profile in the mirror, thinking that the heavy material at least covered up her now obviously incorrect fastening of the apron. She had seen a picture of a nurse wearing a cape on the notice board at the bottom of the stairs and felt quite accomplished. The cape was as heavy as she was and she felt instantly warmed, whereas in the cotton short-sleeved dress she had almost shivered. She wondered whether she should carry her purse or take her handbag, and hoped the suspender belt she had bought, which felt quite big and loose, would hold her lisle stockings up. Ah, there you go. What else could such big pockets be for, she said to herself, slipping her bulky purse, full of the change her mother had put in for the collections at mass and the small fortune from Mr Joyce, into her front apron pocket.

'Never take yer eyes off yer purse in Liverpool,' her mammy had said. 'Keep it with you at all times and separate from your bag. That way, when your bag is stolen as surely to God it will be, in such an awful place, ye will still have the purse and will be saved.'

Dana was doing as she had been told by her mammy. She knew no other way. She had yet to meet Sister Ryan.

She left her room and was greeted by the three girls at the top of the stairs outside Pammy's room. Her handbag was over her arm, her purse was bulging from her apron pocket, her hair was escaping from her cap and her face was glowing like a beetroot, and it was only eight twenty-five in the morning.

'Oh my granny's ghost. What are you doing with the cape on?' exclaimed Pammy, as soon as she laid eyes on her.

The stairwell was filled with the clatter of shoes, as new probationers like themselves and those further on with their training hurried down the stairs for breakfast. Dana was the only one wearing her cape and carrying her handbag. She heard some of them begin to giggle when they spotted her, and then one of them said, 'She's the Irish girl, isn't she? A peasant, I expect. Won't have a clue. What is St Angelus coming to, accepting bog jumpers as registered nurses?'

Dana felt the heat of shame burning up and spreading out across her face. Tears prickled behind her eyes, and she felt suddenly overwhelmed. She had spent her entire life on a small farm on the periphery of a remote country village, but no one had ever called her a peasant. The shame she felt was not just for herself, but for the hurt her mammy would feel if she had heard.

Pammy bristled and looked as though she were about to follow the two offensive girls down the staircase and give them a piece of her mind when another group swept past them and an older girl, who they assumed must be a third year, said kindly, 'Hello, girls. I'm Lizzie. Mrs Duffy wants me to keep an eye on you and help out if you have any problems. I'll catch up with you all in the sitting room tonight, but come on, don't be late on your first day. Sister Ryan eats girls who are late for breakfast.' She looked at Dana, barely suppressing a smile.

'Oh dear, what have we here? Help her out, girls. Leave the cape behind, lovey.' She nodded towards Dana and smiled at Pammy. 'I'm on the floor above. Don't take any notice of that little madam I just heard. She'll get her comeuppance fast enough. Her name is Celia Forsyth and she's already got people's backs up pushing leaflets under doors and asking who would like to make up a knitting circle. She's only been here for five minutes herself.'

'Lizzie,' a voice hissed from below them in the stairwell, 'get a move on.'

'See you later, loveys.' Lizzie tripped on down the stairs.

'Oh, no, am I doing this all wrong? Am I? I must be. Why is no one else wearing their cape?' Thanks to Lizzie's intervention Dana had recovered from the hurt she had felt and was now horrified at having got it so wrong.

'Because we're in the house and there's a big fire lit in the hall and the kitchen, soft girl. Here, let me help you get it off. You've tied it as tight as a nun's knickers,' said Pammy.

'What's that bulging in your pocket, Dana?' asked Victoria politely.

'It's my purse. Mammy said I wasn't to let it out of me sight when I was in Liverpool.'

Victoria gently extracted the purse from Dana's pocket. 'Well, that's as may be, but while we are here, I am sure you won't be allowed to take it on to the wards. Why don't you do what I've done? I have a ten-shilling note in my pocket, just in case I need it.'

'Oh, God, right, I will,' said Dana.

'Well, never mind about that for now,' Pammy interrupted, 'just put the purse back in your room and let's get a wiggle on. We don't want to be in trouble on our first day.'

'I have English money if you're stuck,' said Victoria.

Dana nodded. She was feeling as stupid as she was grateful. Victoria smiled sweetly and Dana was reassured. Victoria had a voice that naturally carried tones of kindly authority, and from what Dana had seen of the second- and third-year nurses there were lots of well-spoken Victorias and Beths and very few Danas and Pammys. If she hadn't already known that Beth had spent all her life in military camps, she might have guessed. If she hadn't been told that Victoria was the daughter of a lord, she would have known anyway that she was from a background much better prepared than her own to deal with life's challenges. Dana accepted that Victoria must be right.

'You poor darling, you look so out of sorts.' Victoria's voice was so sultry and refined that Dana immediately felt calmer. 'Come here, let me sort out your hair.' She took a couple of kirby grips from her pocket and clipped Dana's hair back behind her ears.

'I didn't think we were allowed to use them in our hair. I thought they were only for the caps,' whispered Dana.

Victoria smiled. 'Well, darling, if that's the case, we'll both be in trouble. But as the instructions clearly say hair must be worn up off the face and under our caps, I'm quite sure we will be safe.'

Dana looked at Victoria, amazed. She would have given anything to have her confidence. To have made a decision like that, all by herself.

By the time they had finished talking Pammy had undone the ties at the back of Dana's cape and slipped it from her shoulders. 'Where did Beth get to?' she asked, looking down the stairwell.

'I think she joined that nasty girl Celia Forsyth,' said Victoria.

'Well, that's nice, isn't it,' said Pammy. 'I'll be keeping an eye on that one, I will.'

Minutes later, without handbag, purse, cape and with her hair in some sort of order, Dana ate the last of the toast and bacon scraps in the kitchen and guzzled down her tea, before they all marched into the sitting room and sat in the armchairs, waiting for Sister Tutor to arrive.

'Stand up when she walks in, nurses,' Mrs Duffy had told them. 'As a sign of respect.'

Almost before Mrs Duffy had finished speaking, the door opened and the girls rose as one as the tallest, most forbidding-looking woman Dana had ever set her eyes upon marched into the room. It was as though the atmosphere in the sitting room crackled with the starch of her dress and exuded a sense of importance. She was a large stout woman, and beneath her tall, overly frilled and rigidly starched cap her hair was short, thick and jet black, with the occasional streak of silver daring to break through. Her lipstick was bright red, and the contrast with the blackness of her hair mesmerized Dana.

Her navy blue petersham belt had a silver buckle which was so highly polished that it glinted in the weak morning sunlight streaming through the window. Her starched collar was so stiff it looked as though it could support the weight of a bridge, and her shoes gleamed bright. Dana looked down at her own shoes and felt embarrassed.

'Welcome, ladies.' Sister Tutor had spoken. The new nurses sat frozen in fear. Unperturbed, she continued. 'Welcome to St Angelus Hospital. I am Sister Ryan and I will be known to you as Sister Tutor for the next three years. Over the next twelve weeks, you will attend your preliminary training, which is known as PTS. We shall be seeing a lot of each other.' She paused for breath and looked around the room, seeing the familiar spectacle of white, terrified young faces.

'You will attend the nursing school each day and spend your weekends studying either here or in the nurses' home, or wherever you like. The weekends are your own. I do not treat my probationers like children, because when you are on the wards I expect you to behave like adults. However, if any one of you fails to study at weekends and does not pass the preliminary exam at the end of the twelve weeks, you will not be given a second chance. Mrs Duffy will know your result before you do and will have your bag packed so fast that it will be waiting for you on the other side of the front door by the time you get back here. Do you all understand that?'

She paused again.

'I don't think I heard anyone say "Yes, Sister Tutor"?'

The room remained silent until one voice chirped up with a very confident 'Yes, Sister Tutor.' It was Beth. Pammy, Victoria and Dana gave each other a look.

'Thank you, nurse.' Sister Ryan smiled down at Beth. 'Don't think for one moment that I don't mean what I say. It happened twice last year with two nurses in the Easter intake. Let's try and break the cycle, shall we?'

Dana felt herself begin to shiver and wished that Sister Ryan would move away from the fire. She was blocking the heat with her huge frame.

'This morning I am here to ensure you understand a few very basic rules and show you the route from Lovely Lane to the St Angelus school of nursing. I'm also going to introduce you to the nursing director, Sister Haycock, and the tutorial staff. You, girl, what is your name?' Sister Ryan pointed at Pammy.

'I'm Pamela, miss,' Pammy replied with a smile. 'But everyone calls me Pammy. There's no one in Arthur Street ever called me anything else.'

'Really. Is that a fact? How amusing.' Dana suspected that there was something not quite right about Sister Ryan's tone of voice and she and Victoria shot each other a worried frown.

'And who would I be?' Sister Ryan was addressing Pammy once again.

'You are, er, miss,' said Pammy, nervously.

'OH NO I AM NOT!'

Sister Tutor shouted so loudly that all the new probationers shot upright in their seats. 'You are Nurse Tanner and I am Sister Ryan and you will never speak to me again without addressing me as either Sister Ryan or Sister Tutor. Do you understand that?'

'Yes, miss,' replied Pammy, quickly and nervously.

'WHAT DID YOU SAY?' Sister Ryan's voice bellowed out across the room. Dana felt her mouth dry and she was sure she was going to be sick.

'Sorry. I'm sorry, Sister Ryan.' Pammy looked as though she had shrunk into her seat and Dana thought that she might be about to cry.

'You are not Pammy, not to anyone at St Angelus anyway. You are Nurse Tanner and that is the only name anyone here will ever, ever address you by regardless of where you are. Whether it is here in the sitting room, in the kitchen, passing by in the corridor and very definitely at all times within the confines of the hospital grounds, you are Nurse Tanner.' Sister Ryan's look swept the semi-circle of terrified faces before her. 'Now, what is your name, girl?' she asked Pammy again.

Pammy's voice broke and trembled. 'I'm Nurse Tanner,' she whispered.

'Nurse WHO?'

'Nurse Tanner,' Pamela responded, slightly louder.

'That's better. And who am I?'

'Sister Ryan,' whispered Pammy.

'WHO?' the voice boomed again.

'Sister Ryan,' said Pammy. Dana and Victoria could see the tears welling in her eyes.

'Every one of you, understand this. You no longer have a Christian name when you are in the environs of St Angelus. Your Christian name has been amended to Nurse and you will only ever refer to each other by your surname. Do you all understand?'

A row of heads frantically bobbed in response.

'You only ever refer to patients by their surname and you accord every patient, no matter how lowly, the respect he or she deserves. Each time you address a patient, you will begin with Mr or Mrs or Miss and then you will follow with a surname only. Do you all understand? Christian names are overly familiar. They are for family and social use only and they shall not be spoken, regardless of whom they belong to, in St Angelus. Is that all clear?'

Dana felt her knees begin to tremble. Sister Ryan's strident tone was in such contrast to that of the gentle Mrs Duffy, that it was making her feel very uncomfortable, and she was beginning to wish she hadn't shovelled up the buttered toast crusts which the other girls had discarded before she had left the kitchen. Back on the farm, waste was a sin. No one ever left a crumb, never mind a whole crust. She could hear her nervous stomach rumbling and was sure that everyone else must be able to as well.

'Now, let us begin with our first lesson. Folding your cap.'

Dana broke out in a cold sweat. In all the confusion over her cape and her purse, she had left her cap in her room. She remembered placing it on the bed while she hung up the cape and put her purse into her dressing-table drawer. Everyone else was picking up the caps they had laid out on their knees.

God in heaven, why didn't I notice I'd forgotten the cap instead of worrying about the toast, she thought to herself frantically, her skin prickling in fear.

Pammy noticed at the same time. Shielding her face from Sister Ryan, she mouthed 'Put your hand up' and made a small upward stabbing gesture with her own raised hand.

Dana wanted to be anywhere but in that room. Helping with the milking on a cold, wet, muddy morning on the farm was suddenly a vision of comfort and bliss. Right now, she would regard feeding the chickens as the cold rain soaked through her hair and wet her scalp as a treat. She imagined that she could smell the raw aroma of cows in the shed, freshly in from the field, and it was where she wanted to be more than anywhere else in the world.

'Go on,' Pammy mouthed. 'Quick!'

Dana tentatively raised her hand. It barely reached above her head and trembled like a leaf in a stiff breeze.

'Yes,' said Sister Ryan, as she gave a deep sigh. 'I was waiting for the inevitability of this. It happens in every single intake. I had even wondered who it would be. Funny, I thought it might be Nurse Tanner here.'

'I've left my cap in my room, Sister Ryan,' Dana said.

Her voice was so faint that Sister Ryan left the fire and strode across the room to stand in front of her seat. She leant forward and placed one of her hands on each arm of the chair. Then she bent down, her face only inches from Dana's own, and spoke in a voice so cold and intimidating that Dana began to tremble visibly.

'You. Have. Done. What?'

'I have l-l-left my c-cap in m-my room,' Dana managed to squeak once again.

156

There was an audible intake of breath from around the room, with the faintest sound of a stifled giggle from the direction of Celia Forsyth, who was sitting next to her new best friend, Beth. Dana thought it was quite possible that she might faint, as she was feeling very light-headed. She could smell Sister Ryan's breath and it wasn't helping. Then, suddenly, Sister Ryan spoke in an altogether softer voice.

'Run along and fetch it then, there's a good girl, and I'll get Mrs Duffy to bring us all a nice cup of tea and some biscuits before we walk up to the hospital. On second thoughts, you run along and fetch it for her, nurse.' Sister Ryan had turned to address Celia Forsyth, who stared back open-mouthed. 'Chop chop. We haven't got all day. You'll miss out on the bourbons if you aren't quick.'

Celia rose slowly from her seat and took a nervous step forward. 'Yes, Sister Ryan,' she said, taking another tentative step, half expecting Sister Ryan to tell her to sit down. That she was only kidding, that Dana had to collect her own cap, but she didn't. She simply looked at Celia and smiled.

As the sitting-room door closed behind her, Sister Ryan straightened and walked back to the fireplace. 'That'll teach her to laugh when I am speaking. Never did like bullies.'

Dana had to clutch the now vacant arms of her chair to prevent herself from falling backwards.

CHAPTER 9

Dessie stood in the yard with his clipboard in his hand, marking each of the twenty-one wicker laundry baskets off his list one by one. It was the first thing he did each day as the porter lads drank their tea in the lodge, waiting to be allocated their wagon for delivery. Each basket travelled on eight wheels and was propelled along the corridor by two lads, one at either end. The January wind whistled through the yard and Dessie tucked his scarf down inside his buttoned-up brown porter's coat.

'Dessie.' The voice rang out from the opposite side of the yard.

Dessie looked up, pushing his cap back from his brow with the end of his pencil, and saw young Jake running across the cobbles towards him. He was almost out of breath by the time he came to a halt.

'Dessie,' he gasped, grabbing the handle of a laundry basket to steady himself. Putting one hand on his hip, he bent over to breathe and laughed as his cap tumbled off on to the cobbles.

'Blimey O'Reilly, what's up with you, lad? I don't

have to ask why you can't take that grin off your face. I would be the same if I'd had a windfall from the pools. Have you told your mam yet? She must be wondering where that new-fangled washing machine came from. Where's she put it? Surely to God it didn't fit in the house?'

'It did,' Jake replied. 'She's put it in the middle of the kitchen with a cloth over it and she's using the top like a table. You can't get in our kitchen on wash day now: it's full of women watching the rotor turn and the electric mangle go round. My underpants have never been so keenly inspected. I haven't told anyone about the win, Dessie, only you. That's not why I'm grinning. I've just heard you are going to make two of us into under-porters. Is that right, Des? The lads are talking about it over the tea.'

Dessie slipped his pencil behind his ear and tucked the clipboard under his arm. The wind was cutting and so he pulled his coat tighter across him to keep it out. 'Aye, lad, I may be. Tell you what, I'm gagging for a brew. Was there any left in the pot in the lodge when you came flying out like a bat out of hell?'

'Stop changing the subject. Do I have a chance, Dessie? Do I? You know why I'm asking. Even with my windfall, I can't ask Martha to marry me on a porter lad's wage, unless we live with my mam or hers and I know Martha wouldn't want that. She could have anyone, Dessie, you know that. I need to catch her and make her mine while I can.

Will one of the jobs be for me? You know I could do it.'

Dessie wasn't going to keep Jake hanging on any longer than he had to. 'Aye, lad, you're top of my list, one of my best workers. Anyway, I wouldn't hear the last of it from your mam if I didn't, would I now? But, listen here. Eight of those lads in there are going to be disappointed. They are all good workers and want to get on, so for now, keep it to yourself. Your first week's under-porter's pay should be at the end of the month, but not until I've made the announcement. I have to clear it with Matron first.'

Jake groaned at the mention of Matron's name.

'Aw, come on now, she's not that bad,' said Dessie. 'Just a lost soul who's never been lucky in love, that's all.'

'Is it any wonder?' said Jake. 'Any man would be terrified of waking up to find his balls chopped off if he was sleeping next to that battleaxe. Her bark is worse than her own dog's bite.'

Dessie picked up the clipboard and his eyes scanned the list. 'While ye're here, you may as well get a wagon out and get some linen delivered.'

'Can I do the theatre block first? Go on, Dessie, let me.' pleaded Jake.

Dessie tapped him playfully on the top of his cap with the clipboard. 'Now, that wouldn't be anything to do with the fact that the theatre is next door to the consultants' sitting room where a certain young Martha works, would it?'

Jake grinned from ear to ear.

'Aye, go on with you, but don't dally and don't tell anyone else what I just told you or you'll get me into trouble with Matron. It's not definite until she signs it off, but she never really disagrees with me.'

Jake swung a basket around by the handle. 'Just keep your hand on your tackle while you're talking to her,' he laughed. Then, bent almost double and pushing his shoulder and his full weight against the cart, he began to push the trolley past Dessie and across the cobbled yard towards the theatre block, negotiating the dips in the yard with the skill of a man twice his age.

Dessie watched him go. Without removing his fingerless gloves, he took his tobacco tin out of his pocket, lifted the lid and removed a roll-up he had made when he was eating his breakfast earlier that morning. A small flame illuminated his face as the loose Rizla paper caught alight. Slowly exhaling the smoke, he smiled with satisfaction as Jake successfully manoeuvred the trolley in through the heavy theatre block doors.

'Has Jake taken a trolley on his own?' asked a porter lad, approaching Dessie with a mug of tea in his hand. 'Here, Tom sent this out to you. He said you would be freezing your knackers off out here.'

Dessie laughed. 'Blimey O'Reilly, everyone is suddenly very interested in the welfare of my wedding tackle.'

The lad looked confused. 'Why, what did Jake say? He shouldn't be pushing that trolley on his own, Mr Horton, he'll make the rest of us look bad. If Matron thinks one lad can manage a full basket, she'll ask you to sack half of us.'

'Never mind about that, lad. Let's get inside where it's warm. Then I can tell you lads who is working where today.' As Dessie threw his cigarette stub into a puddle, the lad pressed him further.

'What did Jake say about your wedding tackle, Mr Horton?'

'I have to go and see Matron and he was worried that she might chop it off, if I'm not careful. With Matron being a bit sharp like. It's not my tackle Matron is after, though. She would have no interest in me or any man, even if he was Laurence Olivier himself, I am absolutely sure of that.'

'What do you mean, Mr Horton?'

The lad was fourteen and straight out of school, the son of a soldier Dessie had served with during the war. It was the Merseyside way. On the docks, in the hospital and in the factories. Workers looked after their own. The lad waited for a response.

'Nothing, lad,' said Dessie. 'Nothing at all.'

Jake almost threw the linen into the theatre linen store and then whizzed down the corridor towards the sitting room with the empty basket. He could have leapt for joy when he saw that the theatres were busy and there were no consultants in the

162

room. He knocked on the kitchenette service door and Martha opened it, with a tea towel in her hands.

'What are you doing here? You'll get me shot, you will.' Despite her stern tone, her smile lit up her eyes, telling Jake she was delighted to see him.

'Got a cuppa?' he asked. 'I have news, Martha, and I'm bursting to tell you.'

'Go on then, what?' said Martha, pouring boiling water from the urn into the teapot.

'I think Dessie is going to give me a job as an under-porter.'

Martha's face lit up. She threw the tea towel on to the table and clapped her hands together.

'Dessie said that? Jake, that's the gear. Can I tell me mam when I get home?'

'Well, it has to go through Matron first, she has to approve it, but it's what Dessie wants to happen. You know what this means, don't you, Martha?'

Martha looked at Jake with a blank expression on her face and dropped her hands into her apron pocket. 'No, what? Well, I suppose it means you'll have more money, doesn't it?'

'Yes, but it's not just that. It means that I will be able to plan for my future.' He didn't dare say *our future*. He didn't want to push Martha too quickly or scare her away.

'Well, fancy that,' said Martha, putting the heavy earthenware teapot on to the table. 'A man of means, you'll be.' Her heart was beating faster but it had taken a dip of disappointment when Jake had said *my* and not *our*.

'I don't know about that, but won't it be great? You won't be walking out with a porter's lad any more, I'll be a proper under-porter. They are making new jobs now, you know. There's going to be a porter just for the theatres, they're getting so busy.'

Martha crossed her arms and smiled at Jake's enthusiasm. 'There's no stopping you, is there? You've only just found out you're going to be made an under-porter and already you're casting your eye elsewhere.'

She turned to pick up a cup and saucer from the tea trolley and as she did so Jake caught the ties on the back of her apron. Feeling braver than he ever had in his life before, he spun Martha round and without even thinking about what he was going to do, he kissed her.

As he pulled away, he looked down into Martha's flushed face.

'Don't tell anyone,' he said half shyly, 'but that was me first kiss. I don't think there will ever be another like it, even if you let me kiss you every day, Martha O'Brien. Was it your first too?'

He looked intently into her face. Jake was in love with Martha and he wanted her to know it. He wanted to marry her and he had to fight every instinct he had not to ask her there and then. Martha's eyes filled with tears.

'Eh, what's up? Didn't you like me giving you a kiss, then?' He put his arms round her and buried her face in his chest, holding her tight. Martha could feel the coarse cotton of his porter lad's coat against the side of her cheek and she was glad that her face was hidden, so that Jake could not witness her shame. She breathed in deeply. He smelt of fresh linen and Wright's coal tar soap. How could she tell him that it had not been her first kiss? Mr Scriven had robbed him of that.

Jake pushed her gently away from him, his face creased in concern.

'Of course it was my first kiss,' she said as she wiped her eyes with the backs of her hands.

Embarrassed by her tears, she could feel her face burning with the shame of the memory. She had dreamt of this moment and now, here it was, it had happened. Jake Berry, the best-looking boy in Liverpool, had just kissed Martha O'Brien. She would never tell him that it had been Mr Scriven who had pawed her with his impertinent hands and slobbered with his wet mouth all over her face. She would banish that memory from her mind and never think of it again. It would not affect her. It would always be Jake who kissed her first, as far as she was concerned. She would banish both the memory and the moment to the wilderness. It never happened, Martha thought to herself. It never happened, it was all in my mind. All I have to think is that it never happened, and it didn't.

Jake grinned at Martha, and she grinned back.

'Where's me second?' she said cheekily.

Jake beamed from ear to ear and pulled her

towards him again. Martha smiled. Mr Scriven could not rob her of this. Of this tenderness. Of Jake's eagerness or this, her second kiss.

Nursing Director Emily Haycock lived in a bedsit. It was an upstairs room in a terrace house just off Lark Lane. The room was dull and depressing and the only thing of any beauty to speak of was the view out of the window and across the park overlooking the lake. This morning, the inner window was coated in a thin layer of ice, which obliterated the view and made the room feel smaller and more dismal than it already was. A grey gloom hung in the air and Emily shivered as she struggled to wash herself all over from a bowl of water she had fetched from the grey and chipped stone sink in the bathroom. The lodger in the next room had an unpleasant habit of impatiently banging on the door and pressing his face up against the opaque glass to see who was inside, and Emily had now taken to scuttling across the brown and cracked linoleum on the landing to bring a bowl back to her bedroom.

There was no electricity this morning and so she couldn't even make a hot drink on her Baby Belling. As she dried herself down, she swore that the time had come to find new lodgings. Things were becoming progressively worse and the landlady refused to do anything about the damp patch that had appeared underneath the windowsill. On at least two evenings this week Emily had had to light the candles because the electricity had suddenly gone off, plunging her into darkness. When that happened, it reminded her of the war, and that was the last thing she wanted. Emily had her own demons to live with.

As director of nursing, she wore her own clothes for work, with a white coat for protection when she visited the wards. However, she missed her sister's uniform. Life was so easy when she didn't have to give a second thought to what she wore. Fastening the buttons on the cardigan of her caramel-coloured twinset, she peered closely at herself in the cracked mirror hanging over the blocked-up fireplace. The silver had long since degenerated and peeled from the back. It was so grey and mottled she could barely see her face in the glass, but she could see her blonde curls as they bobbed and bounced on her shoulders.

'Thank you, God, for my natural curls. See, Mam, I did eat all my crusts,' she whispered to her reflection. Her shoulder-length hair took minimum effort to pin up at the back, before she was ready to place her hat on top and brave the air outside, which felt warmer than it had in her bedsit.

She bought the *Daily Post* on the way to work and on the bus searched the 'room to let' adverts from top to bottom. The trouble was, most of the people advertising rooms requested a 'professional gentleman'. There was no way Emily Haycock could get round that one, unless she knocked on the door anyway and was given enough time to persuade the owner she was a safe bet and a professional to boot. She had tried it twice and had been enraged by the attitude she had encountered.

'We prefer not to take ladies,' the last one had said, and then she had whispered, as though anyone else could possibly have heard on the busy road, 'We don't want any gentleman callers traipsing in and out, do we?'

Emily wasn't sure if she was expected to answer the question and stared in dismay at the woman who had black stumps for teeth, and was wearing a greasy wraparound apron. She could think of no response, other than to turn on her heel and walk away. She didn't trust herself to enter into conversation with someone who questioned her morals. She had given up so much to become a ward sister at St Angelus and then to work her way up to sister tutor and director in charge of the school of nursing. The unfairness in the implication that she would behave in any way improperly almost made her cry with the pain of it.

Emily closed the paper with a sigh. In the recent past, ward sisters had lived within the hospital grounds, but the war had changed all that. Today, in any case, she had other things to think about, and the fact was her funds were limited. She had obligations to meet and one particular obligation, her uppermost priority, always came first and left her little in the way of choice when it came to her own living conditions. She had a duty to honour. A commitment and a promise to keep, and for as long as was necessary that was exactly what she would do. If it meant that she had very little to live on at the end of each month, so be it.

Making a circle on the steamy window of the bus with her leather-gloved hand, she peered out into the cold grey morning. As they turned the corner of Church Street, she noticed that the Christmas display was still lit up in the shop windows. The man next to her and the woman on the seat in front were both smoking, and Emily held her newspaper over her mouth to stifle a cough. Thoughts of the new intake, and of what the day ahead would hold, filled her mind. The first week was always the hardest. Once that was out of the way, she decided, she would put every effort into finding somewhere respectable to live, closer to the hospital to save on the bus fare. She stood and pulled on the plaited brown cord above her head to ring the bell to let the driver know she wanted to alight.

Dessie stood and watched as the last laundry baskets disappeared through the back door of the ward block. The whoops of the porter lads as they raced each other to be the first across the yard had made him smile, just as they did every morning. Looking over towards the school of nursing, he saw that someone else had been watching.

'Morning, Sister Haycock.' Dessie removed his cap and replaced it quickly as the cold air stung his scalp. He felt the familiar sensation of his heart constricting at the sight of Sister Haycock. There was something about her that made him want to remove his porter's coat and wrap it around her. If ever there was a woman who confused him, it was Sister Haycock. She had flown up through the nursing ranks and been the talk of the hospital a year ago when she took up her new post, and yet whenever she spoke to him and he looked into her eyes he saw pain. He felt that she was vulnerable, lonely, and sad. Just like him.

'Morning, Dessie,' Emily shouted in response, and to Dessie's delight, she began to cross the yard towards him. 'It's such a cold morning.' Dessie felt his heart quicken as she approached.

'How are you, Sister? You have a new intake of probationer nurses today. Are they here yet?'

'No. I'm sure you'll see them arrive through the back gate.' They both looked towards the hole in the wall, where a beautiful pair of wrought-iron gates had stood until they were removed for the war effort. 'The porter lads will let you know, I'm sure. It is always such a source of amusement for them on the first day.'

'I'm sorry, Sister. I'll give them all a good warning when they return from the laundry delivery. They should behave. I always tell them to be respectful to the nurses.'

'Not at all, Dessie. I think it helps the new girls

to have a bit of fun as they arrive. They always give as good as they get.'

Dessie rolled his eyes, remembering the probationer nurses from the previous intake, who had locked two of the porter lads in the furnace wood store for 'a bit of fun'.

'They do that. Some of them break the hearts of the lads the moment they arrive.'

Emily and Dessie smiled at each other, and for a moment her sparkling blue eyes, watering in the biting January wind, seemed to peer into his heart. Save me, Dessie almost whispered to himself.

'Dessie, I wanted to ask you a favour.'

Dessie almost didn't hear what she was saying. He was made speechless by her closeness, and this morning she looked so beautiful, his heart ached.

'I have a friend who is in lodgings that she isn't very happy with. She is close to Sefton Park and she, er, she works in one of the offices on Water Street. She needs to move closer to town and asked me did I know of anywhere. I don't, but when I saw you I thought you might know of something that was available. She just needs a room; lodgings in a house, maybe? She's a very professional and respectable woman.' If Dessie did know of any suitable lodgings, she could make an excuse to take it for herself.

A frown crossed Dessie's face. 'There is still such a desperate shortage of housing. I feel for your friend, I really do. If I hear of anything I'll let you know.' For a split second, he saw fleeting

171

disappointment in her eyes and felt confused, but then, as quickly as it arrived, it was gone.

'Thank you, Dessie,' she said in a voice not nearly as bright as it had been just seconds earlier.

As she walked away, Dessie thought of Jake and how lucky he had been in securing his house. It was difficult for people on the outside. The dock-side community was almost locked to outsiders. Jobs, houses, lodgings, were all passed along to their own.

As Emily reached the door of the school of nursing she turned back to wave to Dessie, who struggled to tear his eyes away. She raised her hand before she stepped inside and he raised his own in response, then remonstrated with himself. Pull yourself together, lad. There's a rich and clever doctor waiting somewhere for a woman as beautiful as Sister Haycock. It was true she was no longer a girl, but as far as Dessie was concerned, that was her attraction. She will never look twice at the likes of you, he told himself, then slipping his clipboard under his arm and straightening his cap, he marched across the yard to the porter's lodge.

Once in her sitting room, which was attached to her office in the school of nursing, Emily could have wept with gratitude to discover that her maid, Biddy, had already laid the fire and the flames were licking up the chimney. She removed her hat and coat and hung them on the coat stand before turning to the fire and rubbing her hands together. She looked through the door at her tidy office. Even she knew how incredibly well she had done to have been awarded the position of director of nursing. She had been in the post for almost a year, and it had not been the easiest year as she struggled to make her mark and assert her authority with Matron and the board. It was a relief that Dr Gaskell, chairman of the board and the oldest member, was her biggest supporter. Without him, life would have been so much more difficult. Of course, Matron was still the boss, but the new reforms in Liverpool meant that Emily was responsible for the delivery of all nurse training. Warmed through now, she took the rubber bag from inside her own, extracted the wet pair of men's pyjamas and laid them over the wide single radiator in her office. Satisfied, she folded the bag away and sat down at her desk. Biddy had never asked and Emily had never explained. She was prepared, though, because one day Biddy would say something and she knew, when that day came, she would not be able to lie. Her secret would be out. She sometimes wondered if that wouldn't be for the best. Then she dismissed the thought as quickly as it arrived. No one would ever be able to say that Emily Haycock had been helped to reach the position she held. She had done it on her own and that was the way it would stay.

She shuffled her papers for the first lesson together, carefully counted them out into twenty-one piles, and then checked again that each pile contained the correct number of sheets before securing it with two paper clips and adding it to the stack in her leather wallet. She herself had personally typed out the information sheets for each of the new probationers, detailing the basics of the anatomy and physiology they would be required to learn, absorb and regurgitate over the following twelve weeks, until they sat their first exam at the end of the preliminary training school, known to all as PTS.

'Thank the Lord for carbon paper,' she muttered to herself, as she zipped up the wallet.

She wrote the words *The Epidermis* on the front page of her notes for this morning and checked off her tick list to ensure that she had covered every point she wanted to teach the probationers that day.

'Time for a cuppa before you head into the classroom?' Biddy popped her head around the door and then glanced over to the radiator. There was a moment's silence. Biddy left this moment free every time it happened, just in case Emily wanted to explain. Biddy would never ask. She would not push Sister Haycock to tell her what was going on, not until she was ready. Until she was, she would give her those few seconds and if she didn't fill the gap, well so be it. One day, maybe she would.

It was a long time since anyone had addressed Bridget Kennedy by the name she was christened with. She was Biddy to everyone at the St Angelus school of nursing, even to her boss, Sister Emily Haycock.

'I'd love one, thank you, Biddy. The new intake aren't due here until ten. Sister Ryan is walking them up from Lovely Lane to the school.'

'Ah well, they will all be in a good mood by the time they get here then. Bet you anything you like, she will pull that old trick of hers again. Scare them all half to death and then ask Mrs Duffy to bring in a tray of tea and bourbons before they walk up the way. She's wasted that one. She should have been on the stage.'

Emily chuckled. 'Tell you what, Biddy, I wouldn't like to get on the wrong side of Sister Ryan and that's a fact. She's a good help to me in running the clinical side of the school. I couldn't manage without her and there is no sister in this hospital who could teach the practical skills of nursing better, but still, I wouldn't like to cross her.'

'Oh, I agree with you there, me neither, Sister Haycock, because sure, I know she would come off worse and I wouldn't want to hurt her feelings now, or spoil the fearsome reputation she has built up around here.' Fearsome my fat backside, Biddy muttered to herself as she placed a sheet of paper on Sister Haycock's desk. 'Here you go, Mrs Duffy dropped this through my letter box on her way home last night. 'Tis the list of the new ducklings who will be waddling on their way up here right now I've no doubt. They all arrived, safe and sound.

175

No last minute dropouts. There's a Brogan on there, I noticed. That's a good name, Brogan. My daddy's cousin's brother-in-law's niece married one. We all went west for the wedding. Lasted days it did. Farmers they were, you know.'

Emily smiled while Biddy reminisced. If there was one thing Emily had learnt as a ward sister in a Liverpool teaching hospital, it was that the Irish never stopped yearning for home and talking of events that took place in a country they might not have visited for years.

Reminiscing was like cool salve on a burning wound of homesickness.

'I wonder who will be the first to faint on mortuary day on Friday?' said Biddy, moving on. 'We'll run a sweepstake in the kitchen, once we've had a good look at them. Let me know if you want to put a threepenny bit on, but you have to do it today, mind. Can't have you, with the inside information, making a bet at the last minute, can we? Mind you, if you don't want to be doing the sweepstake and you fancy tipping me off, that's allowed. You can always do that.'

Biddy lifted the scuttle to throw a few coals on to the grate. The school was mainly heated by a noisy stove, located in the basement and fed by a porter's lad. Emily turned her head away sharply. When Biddy bent down, the smell, if you were unfortunate enough to be behind her, was often none too pleasant. Emily was very sure that Biddy had an incontinence problem. Soon, she would tackle it with her in a sensitive way, but not today. She looked around her immaculate office.

The cleaning of the school was Biddy's responsibility as housekeeper, and the maids worked under her ruthless daily inspection. The dark wooden floorboards shone, and reflected the daylight from the gleaming windows. Emily thought that it must be a source of great sadness to a woman with such high standards of cleanliness not to be in control of her most personal hygiene. It was hardly surprising, though.

Biddy had confided in her that she had 'lain in' seven times and delivered big strapping babies, but despite their healthy appearance only five had lived past infanthood. Emily knew that was not an uncommon scenario in 1930s Liverpool among the Irish immigrant population. Emily would get today out of the way and then think how she could approach the subject and help Biddy. The first priority would be to let Biddy know she wasn't the only one to suffer and that it was a common problem among women who had delivered a number of babies, especially infants with a big birth weight. It was a silent cross many women had to carry and few thought to seek help for.

Putting the folder of notes to one side of her desk, Emily picked up the paper Biddy had laid in front of her and scanned down the list of probationers. With a start, she came upon the name Pamela Tanner.

'How could I have forgotten?' she whispered.

She traced the letters with her finger. 'She looks so like her mother.' She sat back in her chair, and as Biddy poked and rearranged the embers on the fire the memories of the worst day of her life came flooding back.

'I'm off for the tea,' Biddy said as she shuffled out of the office, but Emily didn't reply. The familiar feeling of loneliness swamped her as she stared at Pammy's name.

She had been just a young woman when she had last laid eyes on Pammy's mother, Maisie Tanner. Maisie with the cherry red lipstick and the wobbly lines drawn down the back of her white calves that looked nothing like a pair of stockings. Maisie from Arthur Street. They were like two peas from the same pod, Pammy and her mother. When Pammy had arrived for her initial interview, it had given Emily such a start that she had allowed Mr Scriven to lead with the interview. For a stupid moment, she had felt that maybe, knowing what she did, it was not her place to comment, or to question Pammy.

Mr Scriven was a man deeply steeped in prejudice and Emily had decided, almost as soon as she had been appointed to her new job, that replacing him on the panel which appointed the potential new probationers would be close to the top of her list. Everyone on the board knew that if a nurse applying for a job at the hospital was black or Irish Mr Scriven would reject the application on that basis alone. The only Irish girls he did let through the process were the daughters of Dublin doctors, and even then they were denied state registration and remained at the hospital as enrolled nurses. Many fulfilled exactly the same role as a staff nurse. They were just less expensive to the hospital.

Mr Scriven had been true to form on the morning of Pammy's interview, attempting to exert his authority over Emily by constantly trying to undermine her. His disapproval of the composition of the list of candidates she had put through for interview came second only to the fact that she had been appointed as director of nursing in the first place, when despite his best efforts to block her appointment the board had overridden his recommendation.

Within minutes Emily knew she had made a big mistake not to have led Pammy's interview herself. She felt conflicted. Should she say, 'When I was just a girl I knew her mother. We were together on the worst night of my life'? Mr Scriven had taken one look at Pammy's letter and decided that a girl from Arthur Street had no place as a professional nurse. How little he knew, Emily thought, silently fuming at his whispered words to the other trustees on the panel, while Pammy sat before them, earnest and red-faced, sweating hands clasped in her lap.

What had angered Emily more than what he had said was that almost the entire board of trustees, which met twice a year to interview potential probationer nurses, had nodded enthusiastically at his words of pious discrimination. All except elderly Dr Gaskell, who was also the chair of the Liverpool hospitals tuberculosis committee. It was obvious from his own look of dismay that he didn't like Mr Scriven and his narrow-minded prejudices any more than Emily did.

'She's from the bombed-out houses down by the docks,' Mr Scriven had blurted out. 'Not our sort. Can't let standards drop.'

Anger had flashed through Emily. She had no issue with the quality of nurses at St Angelus. It was one of the finest and proudest hospitals in the country. She was both delighted and honoured that St Angelus had been selected by the minister of health to trial the new entry criteria for state registered nurses in the north of England. She would not have wanted to train anywhere else herself and felt a fierce loyalty to the hospital. However, it was a fact that the body of nursing staff was largely made up from one stratum of society. There were almost no nurses in the hospital who spoke with a Liverpool accent. She knew that if things had been different and it had been up to Mr Scriven, who had no idea where she was born, she might never have made it into St Angelus herself, and the thought made her smile.

'Oh, I don't know. On the contrary, I think we very much need many more of her sort.' Dr Gaskell had spoken. No one dared to challenge him. And he had supported Sister Haycock, just as he always did.

She had voiced her concerns about the fact that hardly any of the nurses in St Angelus spoke with a local accent not long after she had taken up her post as the director of nurse training.

'What in God's name does it matter where you were born or how ye talk?' asked Biddy, who thought that the best way to get along was to never cross authority.

'Well, it shouldn't matter, because we have a new national training structure and examination process. Because we are to be a flagship hospital in the new structure. We need the best. Not those who speak with the nicest accent. The war is long over now and any woman who wants to nurse should be given a chance. We have a new national health service and the demand for our services is soaring, which means we have to increase the number of nurses we train. That is why I am here, in this post. I would like to get to a point, Biddy, where nurses don't have to leave their jobs, just because they want to marry. The training should be open to everyone. To all girls of all backgrounds and ages, and not just those seeking a doctor husband or a worthwhile occupation to wile away the time until they marry.'

'Well, I see no harm in it meself. There are worse ways to meet a husband if you ask me.'

Emily sighed in despair. 'The top positions should not be held only by men and spinsters, just

181

because they work to earn their own living. Oh, I know, I'm a spinster too. You don't have to remind me.'

'Look.' Biddy was concerned. 'Settle down a little first. Don't ruffle any feathers. And about Mr Scriven, I can tell you this and as God is my judge I maybe shouldn't, but I think you have a right to know. There was a man who wanted your job. Demobbed after the war he was and never settled since. Mr Scriven, he pushed like mad for him to get it. God, you have never seen anything like it. A golfing friend of his, he was. They had served together in North Africa in the medical corps, so Mr Scriven told Matron, and don't ask me how I know that. I have to have some secrets.' Emily was intrigued and didn't interrupt Biddy's flow.

'Mr Scriven near exploded when the board chose you for the clinical director's job. He couldn't believe they would give a woman such an important role, and it being one of the first in the country. They had made him look a right eejit, after he'd promised the job to one of his friends. Probably felt ashamed. Put himself about as the big I am, I reckon, and fell flat on his face by promising something he didn't have the power to give. God knows, he tried hard enough. Bought Matron a bottle of sherry. I felt like asking could I have a vote as well, thought I might get a bottle too.'

Biddy roared with laughter at the sight of Emily's expression. 'Look, I probably shouldn't tell you this.' She put her hands on Emily's desk and leaned forward. 'You do know, don't you, 'tis really me who runs this place. Everything is going to be fine, so stop yer worrying.'

The two women grinned at each other. Emily had known only too well that Biddy was the first person she needed to get on side when she took up her post. As housekeeper, Biddy did indeed run the school of nursing. Control over the tea urn and the daily delivery from the hospital kitchens, as well as authority over the kitchen porters, was power indeed, as the new director of nursing Sister Emily Haycock discovered. Being appointed to such a prestigious position did not give her access to the kitchen, and, as Biddy knew, that was where the real power lay when you were dealing with hungry staff and probationer nurses.

'I know that, Biddy. It was obvious from the day I arrived, but we have to put up some form of pretence here. Just don't tell anyone, eh?'

'Well, sure, I could do your job all right. There isn't anything I don't know.' Biddy dropped her voice a little. 'Look, I know this,' she said. 'You won by one vote. The twelve trustees were equally divided, but Dr Gaskell, he had your back. Now I'm no mathematician, but it seems to me you need to tread very gently for a little while longer, just till your feet are well and truly under the table.'

Emily had been dying to ask her, but had so far been unable to drum up the confidence, who had had the casting vote. Now she knew. Dr Gaskell.

This morning, Emily remembered that conversation. She had taken Biddy's advice. She had bided her time. A year had passed and she had won her first major battle, ensuring that Pamela Tanner from Arthur Street and the jolly Irish girl Dana Brogan had been included in this intake, and what a battle it had been. She had sorely ruffled feathers but she was also very confident. Mr Scriven and the trustees now knew for sure that she was very definitely no pushover.

Emily left her desk and crossed the room to sit in one of the two brown and battered leather chairs in front of the fire. As she watched the flames, her mind wandered back to the last time she had seen Maisie Tanner. When Pammy had walked through the door of the interview room and smiled, it was as if she had stepped back in time, all those years ago. She promised herself there and then, she would do whatever she could to ensure that Nurse Tanner succeeded. At the very least, she owed that to Maisie. As she watched the flames lick up the chimney, Emily had no idea that before the year was out she would risk everything, including her own job, to keep that promise.

CHAPTER 10

'**A** penny for your thoughts.'

Emily jumped at the sound of the unfamiliar male voice and turned to see the new gynaecologist and obstetrician, Mr Gaskell junior, standing in her doorway.

She herself had been a member of his appointment committee. Dr Gaskell senior was her biggest ally. He was her best friend on the board and she was in his debt for the care he had once shown to her mother. She was quite sure that he did not remember her as the young girl he had patiently explained her mother's condition to, but that suited Emily. Those days lived in a room in her heart. A room she visited when she was alone. She never wanted to talk about them to anyone, ever.

She felt no guilt about how she had cast her vote on that long day of interviews. She had quickly cottoned on to the fact that the other candidates were from the past – 1920s-trained and steeped in the old-school ways and traditions. Mr Gaskell junior had served his time in the war, interrupted his own career progression by working in field hospitals, and was now well and truly ready to specialize. His father had helped her in defeating Mr Scriven, time after time, and she knew he would be on her side when the battle was fought to allow married nurses to remain in work at St Angelus. Now his own son, standing at least six feet and four inches tall, with thick auburn hair and hazel eyes just like his father's, had arrived in her doorway.

'Oh, they aren't worth a penny,' she laughed, and for the first time in many years she blushed under the interested gaze of a good-looking man.

After the interview, she had tried to convince herself that only competence had influenced her decision. It had absolutely not been his tousled boyish locks or his charming manner. It hadn't even been the sense of sadness, which his father had explained was a legacy from the war. When Emily looked at him, she detected something she could not put into words. It was a feeling that was familiar, but which she could no longer identify.

'How have you settled in?' she asked. 'Is the room in the doctors' residence adequate?'

'Yes, well, thank you, and the room is fine. Although Mother would much rather I went home with Father every chance I got. But I don't expect I shall be spending much time in the residence – I want to be in the hospital and working. I am ready for the challenge.'

Emily laughed at his boyish enthusiasm, and raised her hand self-consciously to smooth her hair and tuck an errant curl behind her ear. 'Goodness me, you are going to have an impact on Sister Antrobus, I can tell. Have you met her yet?'

'No, not yet. I'm going through the motions of the paperwork at the moment. You did ask me during my interview if I would do some teaching, so I thought I would pop up to see when was it convenient to have a chat. I'm not familiar with the new nurses' syllabus and I thought now would be a good time, before I get cracking on the wards, to find out exactly what it is you want me to teach.'

'Were you familiar with the old syllabus?' Emily half raised a quizzical eyebrow.

It was now his turn to blush as he thrust his hands deep into his pockets. 'Well, as you ask, no, not at all. Are you sure you want me to lecture?'

They both laughed. 'I'm very sure. I want my nurses to learn about the new methods. We aren't in the nineteen thirties now, although if you spent a few minutes on ward two you could be forgiven for thinking you were. I know you are an advocate of some of the new thinking and we need that. You do know that on ward two, under Mr Scriven, ladies remain on bed rest for ten days following a simple D and C?'

Oliver Gaskell hit his forehead in mock exasperation. 'Well, it was the same all the way through my training. It was to do with hygiene and getting those poor women off their feet, although I'm not sure what happened to their children in the meantime. But you are right; we know so much more about the complications of prolonged bed rest now. The challenge is to convince others.'

Every word he spoke was music to Emily's ears. Dragging her eyes away from his face, she said, 'I agree, but effecting change in St Angelus isn't easy and needs to be set in motion from the top. I'm afraid Mr Scriven has just gone on as though everything is just as it was. It's as if the war never happened.'

Oliver weighed up his words as he spoke. 'It barely did happen for him, did it?' No one mentioned the fact that Mr Scriven had been sent abroad with the medical corps and returned after just months away, with an abdominal complaint. 'It's not just Mr Scriven, or indeed St Angelus. The war dominated everything for a long time. While we were on the front line, medical progress seems to have stalled back at home. Everything stood still. There were other priorities, such as tending to the injured. Some amazing work has been done in skin grafting and burns treatment, but now everyone is in a hurry to move faster and to change, change, change. It's almost as though if everything alters, the past can be caught up with, erased even. To be honest, after my own hellish five years, I'm all for that.'

Emily thought to herself that the past could never be erased. That for people like her, it could only be lived with as best they could.

Biddy swung the office door open and came in backwards, carrying her tea tray. 'They have all just filed into the classroom. Sister Ryan is settling them down. God, they made me laugh. The one called Pammy Tanner thought the dummies in the ward room were real. Can you imagine that? I've already placed my bet. Nurse Tanner will be the one who faints on mortuary day. If she can't tell a dead body from a real one, what chance does she have?' Biddy straightened up and started as she saw Oliver Gaskell. 'Well, I never did. How in God's name did you get in, through the window? I never heard anyone come up these stairs, I did not.'

Oliver took the tray from Biddy. Emily noticed Biddy flush and bluster as he did so. His charm had no boundaries when it came to age, she thought.

'Oh, well, it's an easy mistake, Biddy. The dummies do look very lifelike.' Emily hated them herself and couldn't bear to touch them. The staring eyes, the wax-like faces, the heavy, flopping limbs all made her shudder. It was a relief that she had Sister Ryan to teach the elements of practical nursing.

'Will I fetch another cup? Will I?' Biddy looked from Emily to Oliver.

'Well, I would love one, if you have time.'

Emily didn't have time. Biddy had just told her that the new nurses had filed into the classroom. They would all be on edge, nervous and anxious. Wondering what Sister Haycock would be like and what their morning would hold. She surprised herself, never mind Biddy, when she answered, 'Yes, I have ten minutes. Biddy, could you fetch a cup and saucer, please?'

Oliver watched Biddy go and then turned to Emily. 'Well, it sounds as if you are going to have your hands full with your Nurse Tanner.'

'Oh, I wouldn't write off Nurse Tanner just yet, Mr Gaskell. You never know, she may have her own guardian angel at St Angelus and surprise us all.'

The Epidermis.

The girls wrote the words Sister Haycock had written on the board very slowly and carefully on to the first page of the large notebook they had each been given. They sat in rows at the long wooden desks, the sound of pens scratching on paper almost drowned by the noise which came from the huge stove in the basement, which warmed the centre of the building and heated the noisy radiators in the large classroom. The large white clock on the wall ticked away the seconds as the probationers concentrated hard, trying to understand what it was they were writing down. The school of nursing had once been the laundry building attached to the workhouse and had retained an atmosphere of unease, which the girls had commented on as soon as they had arrived.

'What did this place use to be?' Dana had asked, as they walked down the corridor towards the classrooms. 'Why are the windows so high that you can't see out of them? Whoever fitted those had no notion of a view.'

They peered into a mock examination cubicle with white enamel trolleys lined up along the wall, and popped their heads into a mock practical room. Along a bench stood various open drums, and metal tins holding instruments laid on a white cloth, like newly polished silver cutlery.

'Oh, my,' gasped Victoria as she scanned the equipment, horrified at the sight of everything, from a scalpel to a pair of forceps. 'They look terrifying. Are we going to be using them on patients?' Her stomach felt weak.

'Well, of course we will,' said Beth, who, having lost Celia Forsyth, had tagged along with the three girls. She spoke with a far from pleasant assurance in her voice. 'Someone hasn't laid them all out for their own benefit. Those drums are where we will have to pack equipment to be sent away to be sterilized. If I'm not mistaken, some of them are for theatre equipment and some for ward equipment. I think that room is for the second- and third-year nurses to use.'

Pammy frowned. 'Bit of a know-it-all you are, eh, Beth?'

'Not really.' No hint of irritation in Pammy's voice was going to throw Beth off her stride. 'They have the same equipment in the military hospital in Germany. I saw the nurses packing them up once. They were just the same.'

'When did you see that?' Pammy was never afraid

to speak, or ask a question, and frequently said what the others were thinking. All three girls felt in awe of Beth and the knowledge she already appeared to have acquired. But before she could answer Sister Ryan's voice rang out down the corridor.

'Into the classroom, everyone, and after the first lesson you are to form a queue outside my office to collect your Evelyn Pearce anatomy and physiology books and sign your deduction slips.' Each nurse had to pay for her own textbooks and the cost would be taken from the first month's pay. Sister Ryan had spoken and they all hurried along, passing a long room with internal windows that appeared to be laid out like a ward.

'Look at those poor patients,' said Pammy, as they walked past the window. 'They must be cold. They have nothing on their arms.'

The girls began to giggle, but in a moment of clarity Dana became aware that Pammy wasn't joking.

'Oh for goodness' sake, they aren't real,' Beth said impatiently. 'They're just dummies. You really are ridiculous.'

'Oi, you. Don't call me ridiculous. How was I to know? I've never even set foot inside a hospital before today. I'm only here because of our Lorraine and me mam. Are you sure they are only dummies?' They all pressed their faces against the glass to take a closer look and Pammy shrieked with fright at the sight of the skeleton hanging in the corner of the room. Beth sighed.

As they walked in through the classroom door, Pammy pulled an exaggerated face at Beth behind her back and was spotted by Celia Forsyth.

'You won't be pulling that face, Nurse Tanner, when you fail your PTS exam.'

'Who says I'm going to fail?' Pammy hissed.

This was not a possibility that had ever crossed Pammy's mind and she looked both shocked and frightened at the prospect. Beth did seem to be terribly clever, and come to that, so did Celia Forsyth. Pammy glared at them both as she took her place along the bench. Beth sat next to Celia and they both smiled at Pammy. They could see self-doubt all over her face and Celia took pleasure from the fact that she had been the cause of it.

After a few minutes Sister Ryan walked into the room accompanied by Sister Haycock, who was wearing a white coat. The girls stood up like children in a classroom. Pammy recognized Sister Haycock from the interview and smiled at her, remembering that the nursing director had told her she was originally from George Street. It must have been a long time ago, at least before the war, Pammy thought; today, George Street was a make-shift football pitch and a playground for all the children who lived off the dock road. She was saddened by the fact that Sister Haycock didn't seem to recognize her, or smile back. But why would she recognize me, Pammy reasoned with herself. She must have interviewed dozens of girls. Maisie and Stan had been secretive, but it was clear that they knew who she was, just by the name on the letter. Pammy felt a sudden sharp sense of disappointment and knew it for what it was. She was sure she had felt a bond with Sister Haycock on the day of her interview. She had obviously been wrong.

'Sit yourselves down, ladies,' said Sister Ryan. 'This is Sister Haycock, the director of nursing. Some of you may have met her at your interview. She is in charge around here and will be taking you for all your anatomy and physiology lessons, and will prepare you for your final examinations in three years' time. Your ward-based tasks will be assessed by the ward sisters, who will mark and sign your work cards, which will be distributed shortly. Various assessments are undertaken by Sister Haycock and myself, and we will visit you on the wards ourselves in order to carry these out. Your initial twelve weeks will be in the classroom, at the end of which you will take your first exam, and then we let you out on to the wards before we bring you back in here for another week of lessons. If you pass,' she paused for effect, 'and let me tell you, I do mean if, because not all do. You will then begin your first full ward placements. Do you have any questions, nurses?'

Without hesitation, Pammy raised her hand. 'Sister Ryan, who does that skeleton belong to that's hanging up in the corner of the ward room? It gave me the creeps, that did. I mean, is it real? Was that a real person once?'

'I told you she was going to be difficult,' said Sister Ryan to Emily as she walked past her and out of the room.

As soon as they finished writing up the notes from the blackboard, Sister Haycock asked for a volunteer to hand out the papers in the classroom. Beth and Celia had their hands up first. Dana felt herself bristle as Celia dropped the notes on to her desk. She hadn't forgotten her sneering on the stairs earlier that morning.

She looked around the classroom at the other probationers. She felt a chill and wondered how they would cope, wearing what was in effect a summer dress in the dead of winter. She hated to have her arms bare at the best of times. Years of milking and reaping, cutting the turf and working outdoors had given her the hardest, freckliest arms, more like those of a farmhand than a nurse. Dana looked at the delicate, pale pink limbs of the girls around her and then down at her own, and wished she had anyone else's. Rubbing her forearms with her hands, both to warm herself and in a subconscious attempt to conceal them, she whispered to Beth, who was sitting next to her, 'I'm sure the dummies are fine, but why aren't we allowed to wear cardigans? Will we not be allowed to wear them on the wards?'

'Standards, dear girl,' Beth replied. 'That's what my pa would say, anyway. Mrs Duffy told me last night you can wear a navy woolly on nights, after lights out. When no patients or visitors can see you.'

Every time Beth spoke, she made Dana feel stupid. She made a mental note to write home and ask her mother to knit a second navy blue woolly as soon as possible. 'Do you have one, Beth?' she whispered, about to offer her mother's services. She knew her mammy wouldn't mind; in fact, she would be thrilled, and Dana was desperate to impress Beth in some way. But Beth just looked at her over the rim of her glasses.

'Of course I have a woolly. I have two of everything.'

Dana felt stung by her response. She had the strong impression that Beth would rather she didn't speak to her.

Pammy looked down at the notes on her desk and could barely understand a single word on the sheet in front of her. The diagram on the board, which they had to copy into their note-books, had been difficult and made her wrist ache. The passage headed *Squamous Epithelium* on the sheet in front of her was incomprehensible. Her head ached as much as her wrist, if not more. She had highlighted the different layers of skin, follicles, muscles and cells in various shades from the tin of coloured pencils which had been on the list of essential items to bring to the classroom.

'God, you need to be a Philadelphia lawyer to understand all of this,' she said out loud, quoting a well-used Liverpool expression with no clue of what a Philadelphia lawyer was.

Sister Haycock, sitting at her desk, bent her head and placed her hands over her eyes. She couldn't help herself: Pammy made her smile and that was not something she did very often. Recovering herself quickly, she stood to address the class.

'Care of a patient's skin will be one of your most pressing daily concerns,' she said. 'Many of your patients will be bedbound for varying periods of time. Even a dilatation and curettage on the gynae ward requires ten days' post-operative bed rest.'

Pammy turned to Victoria and whispered, 'A dittyation and what?'

Sister Haycock continued, 'If a patient is in poor health to begin with, or is suffering from the trauma of surgery, a deprivation of fresh oxygen-ated blood to the areas of greatest pressure will result in the skin quickly breaking down. Your job is to prevent this happening. There is only one reason for the existence of a pressure sore and that is poor nursing care.' She wrote the words *PRESSURE SORES* in big letters on the blackboard.

'If any of you ever make it to the giddy heights of being a ward sister, you will be judged by your management of pressure sores, sometimes called bedsores, although that is, in my book, lazy termin-ology and puts the blame on the bed, not on the nurse. If pressure sores occur as a matter of course on your ward, your reputation will suffer, badly.

197

It will be a mark of shame. Do you all understand that?'

A classroom of speechless young women, unused to their starched and precariously balanced caps, nodded carefully in unison.

'Sister Ryan will teach you the practicalities of looking after your patients well, but please never forget that the prevention of pressure sores will always dominate your nursing career wherever you may go. I am here to teach you the anatomy and physiology of the skin. By the time I have finished, you will understand how the skin works. But now you all look as though you are in complete shock. I reckon it's time for the break, and if my sense of smell is on form, Mrs Kennedy and the maids have lunch ready in the refectory on the ground floor.'

Dana could have leapt for joy. Her stomach had been rumbling for the past hour and she was sure others in the classroom could hear it.

'Leave quietly please, nurses,' Sister Haycock said, as the thumping and clattering of desk lids filled the room. 'Silence is a virtue and one you will all become familiar with when you are working on the wards.'

Dana looked around at the others and felt a sense of relief. Yes, they all looked as bemused and browbeaten as she must. Pammy exclaimed, far too loudly, 'God, me head is banging now. I don't know about them dummies, it's me what needs a lie down.'

Dana shot an anxious look towards Sister Haycock. She expected Pammy to be reprimanded for being noisy. Instead she was sure that she saw a faint smile twitch at Sister Haycock's lips, but it disappeared just as quickly and she couldn't be sure.

'Darling, me too,' whispered Victoria. 'What about you, Beth?'

'Oh, we'll all get there, I'm sure. It won't take long. Preparation and study is the key,' said Beth, and the others groaned.

When Dana wrote her first letter home that week, she wrote more about the food than she did about the hospital, but she knew her mammy would be interested in two things above anything else. Where she was attending mass, and what she was eating.

There is a room we all eat in on the ground floor of the school, but today we were shown the hospital canteen. That is where we will eat when we are out of the school and on the wards. We will have three breaks each day, called refs, which means refreshments, in case you don't know. One mid-morning and another mid-afternoon with lunch in between. The canteen was bursting at the seams with groups of nurses and staff walking in and out to take their morning refs.

At the bottom of the canteen, opposite the doors where you enter, are three big tables and on each table is a huge big urn of milky coffee, with a burner underneath to keep it warm. Mammy, I have never in me life tasted anything so delicious as the coffee. Why do we not have coffee at home? I never even knew what it was and Victoria must have thought I was a right eejit. In the afternoon, the urns are full of tea. The kitchen staff walk around the tables with a big wooden trolley piled high with slices of toast dripping in butter and they hand it out on plates and we don't have to pay for any of it.

Sister Tutor said nurses are very bad at eating in the mornings and too many faint too often because of it, so they make sure everyone has something on their stomach. We pay for the lunch, which we take it in turns to eat when the patients have finished theirs. There is a lady in the kitchen here in the school, her name is Biddy Kennedy and she is Irish. She was from Cork and she knows the Brogans in Belmullet. She says she has a sister whose mother-in-law knew Granny Brogan's cousin. I think I am her favourite, because she keeps slipping biscuits into my apron pocket and today she said when ye write home to yer mammy, tell her Biddy is looking after ye. She is very nice, Mammy.

I had sausages today with onion gravy and mashed potatoes and then a jam roly-poly with custard afterwards. Sister Tutor says we are all too skinny and need fattening up before she lets us loose on the wards. She's talking to the others when she says that, not me. I am twice the width of most of them and I've said they need to come back home and be fed by you.

She says that some of the patients we will have to lift will snap our backs in two if we don't put some muscle on. Mammy, I almost laughed out loud. Will there be a patient as heavy as the dead heifer the kids and I carried down from the field last year? I don't want to be put on the wards. I am scared stiff so I am. I am even scared in the practical room in the school. I've never had to touch another human body before. I'm happier with the pigs, but I will just have to get on with it, I suppose. Tomorrow is mortuary day. Jesus, I am out of my mind about that one. We have to go and see where the patients are taken to when they die and we have to see how they are labelled and placed in the fridges. Imagine that? If I don't faint, it will be a miracle.

Dana wrote about the new friends she had made, and that she had attended mass. She failed to mention that it was only the once. She knew her mammy would write back and want to know where and when. Who was the priest and where was he from? She knew her well enough to know that if she told her the priest was Irish, which he was, she would have tracked his family down and spoken to someone who knew him within the week. The priest had made an attempt to speak

201

to Dana as she left but she had rushed out, skirting around the ladies hogging his attention. She would escape his questioning for as long as possible.

Dana didn't tell her mother everything. She failed to mention the stranger who had churned up her mind or the impact the new medical students had on the girls.

'Oh my God, they are gorgeous,' Pammy had said as they stood upstairs in the school of nursing's main corridor on the first day, looking out of the window on to the car park below at a group of white-coated medical students parading across to the wards from the medical school. 'Holy Mary, mother of God, would ye look at him,' she went on, not specifying which particular doctor she was referring to.

'They are men,' said Beth, to a chorus of squeals and giggles. 'If you had ever lived on an army camp, it is a sight you would be used to. Men in uniform do nothing for me, I'm afraid, not even when they are wearing white coats and carrying stethoscopes.'

'Well, they do it for me,' said Pammy, who was beginning to sense that she might enjoy her freedom from Arthur Street more than she had anticipated.

Just as Pammy finished speaking, one of the medical students looked up at the window. Dana felt her heart beat faster. It was Teddy. He raised an arm into the air and laughed, walking backwards. She noticed that Victoria raised her arm in return and felt confused. Dark horse, she thought. The other medical students now looked up at the window and broke out into a rapture of wolf whistles.

'Oh my God, let me down those stairs now. Hiya, lads!' shouted Pammy, cupping her mouth with her hands to the glass, apparently having completely forgotten where she was. 'Look at the one in the front. Isn't he gorgeous? Do you think he's waving at me?' Pammy was now jumping up and down on the spot and waving back out of the window.

Dana was sure Teddy was waving to her. 'Well, would you look at you,' she said. 'We haven't even had the first lesson and you're after a doctor.'

'Yeah, but no doctor will look at me twice, I don't suppose, coming from Arthur Street. I would be ashamed to take a fella like one of them back to ours. I bet they all live in nice houses and went to a proper school. Mine closed down when I was there, twice. I have that effect on teachers. Me mam says it was probably my fault that the headmistress had a nervous breakdown, but it wasn't. It was nothing to do with me, I swear to God.' Pammy roared with laughter just as Biddy walked past.

'You need to keep that down, Nurse Tanner,' said Biddy, without slowing. 'You'll come a cropper if you don't lower the volume.'

Pammy pulled a face.

'Ah, don't,' said Dana, nudging her. 'She's nice.'

Dana had kept the story of her encounter with Teddy to herself, being reluctant to share it with anyone. He was her secret. She had thought about him often. She felt as though she had already known him for an age. She remembered the way he had tried to hand her the lit cigarette. The knowing, self-confident look in his eyes. He had made her stomach turn to jelly and every time she thought of him the same thing happened. It made her breathless and giddy and all from just a single five-minute conversation and that one smile from a stranger.

Mortuary Friday arrived far too quickly. The girls were unusually quiet as they made their way up to the school of nursing from Lovely Lane. Exhausted from the sheer amount of information their brains had been forced to absorb, they looked like four very different girls from the ones who had walked up to the hospital on Monday. The bounce in the step, the wobble of the cap, the bright smiles and cheery hellos to everyone they passed had been replaced with a slower march and bent shoulders as they held the fronts of their capes together against the stiff January chill.

'Lizzie says to eat a mint before you go in,' said Pammy. 'She knocked on me door as she passed this mornin' and left us these.' She thrust her hand into her apron pocket and produced a crumpled white paper bag. Inside were four damp and sticky mint humbugs. 'She says the sugar in the mint, as well as the smell, will help.'

'What a sweetie she is. She really looks out for us,' said Victoria. 'I think because your room is almost on the staircase you will have a lot of people knocking on your door, Pammy.'

Pammy had also seen the location of her room as an advantage. 'Do you reckon I will be able to sneak people in and out, with me being so close to the front door too?'

'My God, are you serious?' asked Dana, shocked. 'Like who would ye be thinking of? Who would you want to sneak in?'

'Well, I wouldn't mind one of those medical students for a start.'

And that was the last word anyone spoke until they arrived at the school of nursing. Thoughts preoccupied with surviving mortuary Friday.

'They all look a bit squeamish and they have yet to set foot inside the door,' Biddy said as she brought Emily's morning tea. 'Not one of them has taken her cape off. One of the poor things is even shivering. Getting themselves all worked up, they are in there. You look after that Irish girl, now. She's a dote, that one, though some of the others need a lesson in manners. I heard that Celia Forsyth, the one from Cheshire, giving out to the others about her. I'll tell ye what, if I hear her again, she'll be getting the sharp edge of my tongue. She has no nature, that one. Full of herself she is.'

Emily folded the morning paper and put it down on her desk. 'Trouble is, Biddy, this first week brings out the best and the worst in our new nurses. I think that Celia Forsyth has been rather spoilt at home, and now she's here she is out of her depth and it makes her behave in a way she may not ordinarily do. Dana, the Irish girl, has a good group around her. She'll survive. Don't worry, I've marked Nurse Forsyth's card. I will only tolerate arrogance and churlishness for so long, but for now, it's her first week. Let's give her the benefit of the doubt.'

'That's your trouble, you know,' said Biddy, with a frown. 'You see the good in everyone, and I would say that was a curse. You want to try and shake that off. I don't think it's a good quality for a woman in your position.'

Emily smiled at Biddy. She had taken to monitoring the odour on a daily basis and noted that this morning it wasn't so bad. That conversation needed to be had, but it would involve convincing Biddy to agree to an appointment with Dr Jackson and Emily knew that wouldn't be easy.

'Right, now, tea down and I'm off into the classroom for the pre-mortuary pep talk. I'll let the porter know we are off, in case I need a stretcher back.'

'It won't be the first time, if you do,' said Biddy, clearing the tea things back on to the tray. 'I just hope I win on the bet.'

Emily tried her best to look as though she disapproved. 'I hope you haven't told the mortuary attendants to walk like zombies again, Biddy. If someone faints and hurts herself, I would be responsible.'

'Don't be daft. When have I ever done that?' Biddy now had her back to Emily, as she began to carry the tray out of the room. Emily couldn't see the smile on her face, but she knew it was there.

The mortuary block stood some distance away from the hospital, at the opposite end of the car park. The building had been hurriedly erected as a temporary measure during the war, with grand plans for a replacement as soon as the hostilities were over. The grand plans had never materialized and the asbestos-lined square building had simply been added to over the past eight years to create a more imposing, larger, greyer square building.

'They say the men who work in the mortuary are really weird,' Pammy whispered to the others. 'Some say they are into black magic and suck the blood from the corpses when they arrive at the mortuary. Our Lorraine, she said that you can tell if a corpse has had the blood sucked out because they will be white, like zombies.'

'Don't be silly, Pammy. There's no such thing as zombies,' said Victoria. Celia Forsyth was walking directly behind, chatting to Beth, and Pammy overheard heard her say, 'Not zombies, eh? Then they must be Irish. Easy mistake.'

Pammy looked at Dana, but she was deep in conversation with Victoria and hadn't heard. Pammy turned round and fell into step between Beth and Celia. 'Oi you, I know who that comment was aimed at. Make one more like that and you will be very, very sorry. Did you hear me?'

If Dana or Victoria had heard her, they would have thought that she had gone quite mad. Her voice was cold and intimidating as well as loaded with meaning. She had grown up on the streets and was a fighter. She was also loyal to her friends.

Beth gave an uncomfortable cough. 'Steady on, Nurse Tanner,' she said.

Pammy swung round. 'Don't you go telling me to steady on. You had better decide which camp you are in, miss, because you can't be in both.'

'May I ask why I will be sorry?' Celia Forsyth raised her eyebrows. 'And who says so? On what authority will I be made to feel sorry? You and whose army? Your little bog jumper over there?' Celia Forsyth spoke the last few words louder and aimed them at Dana.

Pammy began to boil, but she could tell Celia was not quite as confident as she had been only a moment before and Beth was looking decidedly uncomfortable.

She took a deep breath before she waded back in. 'Listen here, I don't need any authority, or any army, girl. I've seen you and the way you look down your nose at Dana. Do it one more time, just once, and you will have me to answer to. Bog jumper, eh? Don't be so free with your name-calling, or some of us might have to use a few ourselves. You're not perfect, miss. From Cheshire are you? We have names for you Cheshire lot here in Liverpool, you thick woollyback. Kissed any sheep lately?'

Celia Forsyth blushed red with anger as some of the nurses walking around them began to snigger and the word 'woollyback' was repeated down the line. Celia had been trying very hard to make an impression on her peers. She was irritated to not have been born in the more stylish suburbs of London as many of the nurses had been, which she felt automatically carried a badge of sophistication, or in a country pile like Victoria. Celia's family were post-war northern industrialists and had done very well, but Celia was only too aware that new money was frowned upon in true society. Her parents were as far removed from farming as it was possible to be and only lived in Cheshire to put distance between their home and the smog of Liverpool. Celia smarted at the word 'woollyback'. Nothing Pammy said could have insulted her more.

'Say that again,' she hissed, threateningly, but there was no time for Pammy to respond as a hush rippled through the chattering nurses. An eerie calm descended as they came to a halt in front of the door to the mortuary.

Hearts missed beats. Throats seized as a man, stooped and bearded, with glasses as thick as the bottom of a milk bottle, slowly opened the creaking door. Each nurse instinctively pulled her cape tighter across her body and tucked her arms inside as he said in a low, menacing tone, loaded with a promise of impending doom, 'Good morning, nurses.'

'God,' Pammy whispered. 'It's worse than I thought.' Dana instinctively reached out for Victoria's hand. Victoria squeezed Dana's back and the two girls shuffled closer to each other. Beth was the only one among them who looked calm, but then Beth hadn't told any of them this wouldn't be the first time she had seen a dead body. Beth had played her cards close to her chest. She had often helped out as a volunteer at the army base hospital and had absorbed everything she had seen and heard, like a sponge.

'I've got a plan,' Dana whispered to Victoria. 'Let's close our eyes. That way, we see nothing at all.'

'That's a jolly good plan,' whispered Victoria back. 'No one will be looking at us. I'll hold on to the back of Pammy's cape and she can lead us in.'

'Would you look at that man.' Dana nodded at the mortuary attendant, slowly dragging his leg behind him as he walked ahead of them. Suddenly he stopped and turned to face the group of nurses. A few of the girls at the front let out a shocked squeal followed by a nervous laugh. For a moment, they thought he had forgotten what to say, but then he spoke in a voice that was slow and heavy.

'Will the last nurse in through the door close it behind you and bolt it. We don't want any of the corpses escaping, or one of you young ladies making a run for it.' Another nervous laugh rippled through the anteroom.

Sister Haycock frowned. 'Move forward please, nurses,' she shouted from the back, in a louder and brighter voice than usual.

'Come along, get a move on,' said Sister Ryan with an impatient efficiency, pushing the reluctant nurses forward.

The nurses unwillingly shuffled after the attendant into a large and very cold room. Many were now openly holding on to each other's capes and huddling together for the sake of touching someone alive who felt exactly the same as they did. The chilly temperature in the room quickly penetrated their bones.

'Sister Ryan will explain the mortuary service along with Mr Nightlinger here,' Emily's voice rang out. 'Mr Nightlinger works in the mortuary and has done so for the past forty years, haven't you, Mr Nightlinger?'

Mr Nightlinger didn't speak. He nodded, slowly looking at all of the nurses in turn and terrifying each one as he did so.

'Today we have brought you here as an introduction to the premises and the process of transfer from the wards. To show you what happens after you have completed last offices on a patient. You need to know, so that you can pass the information on to relatives and friends who may have reason to attend the mortuary. There will be some occasions when you will be required to accompany a porter yourself. This happens more often when you are on night duty and there are fewer porters around. I have no idea why, but the porters refuse to enter the mortuary alone.'

A sharp intake of breath swept the room. Sister Ryan, unperturbed, continued. 'It may be late at night and we don't want you losing your nerve then. This is why we find it so useful to familiarize you with the building now. Take a look around you. Remember what you see. This is your first time here, and the next time you visit I want you to feel confident and knowledgeable. You may well be looking after patients on the final stages of their journey before they are transferred to the chapel of rest. Performing last offices is a great honour, as I am sure you understand.'

Sister Ryan gazed pointedly at the rows of metal doors. She might have been studying the smile of the Mona Lisa in the Louvre. 'Right, those are the fridges in which the bodies are stored until the undertaker takes them away. Mr Nightlinger will show you a cadaver in a moment.'

Another audible group intake of breath. This time tighter, sharper and more fearful.

Any minute now, thought Emily, as she threw Sister Ryan a 'here we go' glance. The trouble was that nurse training began at the age of eighteen. An age when most girls appeared to possess a heightened sense of drama. It was inherent in almost every probationer.

'In your tenth week we study the heart and then

we shall return to attend and observe a post mortem. The coroner is very obliging and, along with Sister Haycock, will take you through that procedure. You will see the various chambers of the heart and the detail of the thoracic cavity, first hand and close up. This will be incredibly beneficial to your understanding of the body and how it works, and prepare you for your time in the operating theatre. The sounds and the smells, in addition to dealing with the end of life for the first time, will all be slightly new and difficult to cope with, but today we are just going to have a look round and open a few fridges so that you can pass the test of seeing a dead body for the first time.'

Sister Ryan stopped talking to make sure everyone was still standing, then:

'Mr Nightlinger, open a fridge, would you, and let the girls see their first cadaver.'

Mr Nightlinger had been perched on a wooden stool while Sister Ryan spoke. He slipped from the stool with no great hurry and walked towards a small square metal door. With a flourish, and with a movement so rapid that he took the girls by surprise, he pulled the fridge handle down. A body shot out among them on well-oiled runners. The screams of twenty-one nurses filled the air. Mr Nightlinger always presented the grimmest body he had in store. This one was an elderly tramp. Despite the best efforts of the mortuary staff and the frosty paleness of his skin, he did not look contented or serene.

A grin slowly spread across Mr Nightlinger's face just as a loud thud announced that one of the girls had passed out cold.

'Oh, what a shame,' said Pammy to Dana, as they turned round to see who it was. 'What comes around goes around, eh?'

Behind them, Nurse Celia Forsyth lay flat on her back on the cold grey tiled floor.

CHAPTER 11

Jake and Martha left the cinema hand in hand. Jake had sat with his arm around Martha's shoulder throughout the film. He felt more like a man than he had ever done before.

'That Diana Dors, did you see her hair?' Martha's voice was full of excitement. 'Everything about her was so sophisticated. I'll never be like that, Jake. My hair will never shine like that. It was so beautiful.'

It hadn't exactly been Diana Dors's hair or her sophistication that had impressed Jake. There were moments in the film when he had to remember to check that his mouth wasn't hanging open, but he was keeping quiet. He didn't want to do or say anything that would make his Martha feel less than the beautiful princess he thought she was.

'She was very pretty, but not as pretty as you, Martha. She has a long way to go there yet to catch you up.'

Martha squealed. 'Jake, you are full of the blarney sometimes. Honest to God, you are.'

Jake grinned and hugged Martha to him. 'I'm not. I just don't think there is any woman in

Liverpool as pretty as you, that's all. I've always thought so. Ever since you came off your three-wheeler when you were a toddler and hit the kerb with your mouth. Do you remember that?'

Martha groaned. 'Do you know, my gum still feels sore sometimes.'

'I'm not surprised. You knocked out every one of your front baby teeth and the ones that were left, they all turned black. Pretty as a picture you were. I led you with one hand and dragged the bike with the other, all the way to your front door. Yer mam, she almost had a fit when she saw you and all the blood pouring down the front of your dress.'

Martha giggled. 'She did, but that's the reason she likes you, Jake, because you looked after me. My mam never forgets a good turn.'

Jake felt his heart swell. Maybe it was because of that day, at age six when Martha had first made him feel like a man. The day she had turned her babyish face towards him and cried for help. Jake sometimes felt overcome by feelings of protectiveness when he was around Martha.

'I want to do that for ever, Martha. Protect you.'

Martha buried her face in his shoulder as they walked along in step. 'Don't let anyone hear you say that, Jake Berry,' she said. 'Someone might think you were proposing to me.'

Jake held Martha out at arm's length. That had certainly not been his intention when he collected Martha from her front door to take her to the picture house. In fact, it was something he thought would be at least another year down the line, when he had done the house up and had somewhere to take his new bride, but in a flash he was seized by the moment and before he could stop himself, the words were out.

'Martha, I am,' he said, surprising himself as much as Martha. 'I am proposing to you,' and in the middle of a busy moonlit street Jake dropped on to one knee. 'Martha O'Brien, will you marry me?' He almost laughed out loud at himself.

For a moment, Martha was so stunned, she could not respond.

'Go on, love, say yes.' A couple walking past them had stopped and were watching with amused grins on their faces, and now a small crowd of people leaving the Odeon began to gather around them. Jake began to feel very self-conscious as Martha, embarrassed and thrilled, began to giggle.

'Martha, will you answer me? Would you look at the cut of me, kneeling on the floor, me knees gone numb.'

Martha hesitated no longer. Without any idea she was saying yes to a man of some means, she put Jake out of his misery. 'I will, Jake Berry, yes, I will.'

Rising to his feet, Jake removed his cap and kissed his new fiancée. It took a moment for them to realize they were being applauded by a crowd of cinema-goers.

'That was better than the film, that, mate,' shouted one man, as he clapped.

'Make sure he always brings you tea in bed, love,' called his wife.

'May your first born be male,' shouted another. But Martha and Jake were lost in the bliss of the moment and the anticipation of a life ahead.

In Lovely Lane, Mrs Duffy had advised the girls to make the most of their weekends off, because once they were on the wards a free Sunday would be a rare treat. Off-duty preferences and requests were always granted to qualified staff first and then nurses who were further up the training ladder; new probationers were last on the list.

'The thing is, you have to bite your lip and get through the first year without complaining,' Mrs Duffy told Dana and Victoria, as they helped her clear away the hot chocolate mugs so that she could leave promptly.

The last thing Mrs Duffy liked to do each night was to ensure the catch was down on the front door before she left. During the day the door was left unlocked, for nurses coming to and from the hospital and for the cleaning maids. 'Let me hear the chain slide now,' she would shout through the letter box to whichever nurses on the other side had been persuaded to engage in the exaggerated performance of dropping the catch and slipping the bolt and chain across. 'Good girls,' they would hear her say once satisfied her charges were locked up as safely as chickens in a coop.

What Mrs Duffy didn't know was that as much

as she cared for her nurses, they cared for her back. They also had their own ritual, within the sitting room. 'Mrs Duffy is leaving,' the nurse on door and chain duty would yell down the corridor. This was the code for whoever was in the sitting room to put down her book or knitting and leave the warmth of the fire to stand discreetly behind the long dark velvet curtains in order to peep through the nets, which Mrs Duffy prided herself on keeping snow white, and watch her as she descended the steps to wait at the bus stop on the opposite side of the road, directly outside the park gates. The nurse on Mrs Duffy duty stood at the window until Mrs Duffy was seated on the bus and watched as it pulled away.

'It is not an exaggeration to say that as a new probationary nurse you are on the bottom of the pile, I'm afraid,' Mrs Duffy had told them, 'and you will spend most of your early days in the sluice room cleaning out bedpans. Bedpan rounds are every two hours, so just as you finish cleaning up after one another comes along. I've had some girls come back here at night in tears, unable to face food and complaining they can't shake the smell off. They don't last long. Usually gone before the year is out, so don't any of you fall into that trap. Just grit your teeth and remember nothing is ever as bad as it seems, and I've heard it all. There isn't one gruesome detail I haven't had described to me about bedpans, I can assure you.'

When Mrs Duffy said this, Victoria almost heaved.

'Come along, Nurse Baker. You are the daughter of a lord, aren't you? You should be made of stronger stuff than that. It will be your job to show a stiff upper lip to the others.'

Victoria racked her brains to make sense of why she, the eighteen-year-old daughter of a hereditary peer, should be made of stronger stuff than anyone else. If anything, she was the most terrified of them all.

Until recently, she had never cleaned her own toilet or washed her clothes and had not even contemplated the prospect of cleaning out a bedpan. In the circles Victoria had moved in at home, no one ever discussed such things. She had known that many patients spent a long time in bed recovering from illness and surgery, but it had never occurred to her that clearing away the products of a bowel evacuation would be her responsibility.

'You had another telephone call from home last night. Was it your aunt again?' Mrs Duffy was never nosy, but always chatty, which sometimes amounted to the same thing.

Victoria almost bent over with embarrassment. She did not want to lie to Mrs Duffy, but in recent weeks hardly an evening had gone by without a call from Roland via the pay phone that was situated on the wall in the laundry room. She had received a number of demanding letters from her Aunt Minnie, too, who seemed incapable of understanding that

Victoria could not come and go as she pleased. *Anyone would think you were in a nunnery*, she had written.

What Victoria didn't mention to anyone, not even Aunt Minnie, was the alarming letter she had received from Roland.

I have been dismissed from handling the affairs of Baker Hall, he had told her. *Your aunt has instructed a large firm from Manchester. It is a bit of a blow, I don't mind admitting. Doesn't bode well for me locally.* Victoria paced her room as she read this. 'Why? Why?' she said out loud. She didn't really need to ask; she knew the answer. It was Aunt Minnie's way. She had to be the one who was in charge. The decider and the controller. *Please don't tell them at home that I have written to you, but when it is time to visit, let me know and I shall collect you from the station and we can talk.*

Without a second's hesitation, Victoria had gone straight to the phone box on the corner of Lovely Lane and called Roland. Without even knowing it, Aunt Minnie had brought them closer together. Now, the most difficult part of telephone conversations with Aunt Minnie was not letting slip that she knew everything that was happening back at Baker Hall.

Victoria could not wait to see Roland again. With every day that passed and every telephone conversation they became closer and closer. She wanted to see Roland far more than she did her Aunt Minnie, who had telephoned Victoria the previous evening demanding that she return for a week. Victoria had explained to her that it was impossible. 'I have my PTS exam in a few weeks, Aunt Minnie. I can't just come and go as I please.'

'Well, that is just ridiculous. She says she can't come, Gerald. What? What shall I tell her? Your father says it's not a prison, Victoria, you must be able to get away sometimes. They aren't the bloody Japs. Life is not easy here, Victoria, I can tell you. Gerald, will you shut up. I cannot hear her. Victoria, your father wants to see you. He wants you to come home. He's not happy, what with everything as it is. Can't you come for a visit, dear?'

'I honestly can't, not until my PTS exam is over. Please understand that. It really is very important.'

'What I don't understand, Victoria, is why with so much happening here you have taken yourself off to bloody Liverpool, of all places, to prance around like this. Gerald, WILL YOU SHUT UP!'

Victoria heard the telephone receiver click back into place.

'It was Aunt Minnie, Mrs Duffy,' she said now. 'She would like me to visit home, but I told her I can't. Not until after my exams.'

'Well, you will be going straight on to the wards as soon as the exam results are known. It could be a while before you have time to visit home. Best wait until we know what your ward off-duty will be.'

Victoria could barely hide her disappointment, but it was Roland she wanted to see, not Aunt

Minnie. She was desperate to see Roland again. The man who had made her feel safe as her world fell apart. 'Of course, Mrs Duffy.'

'Oh, I nearly forgot. There's another letter for you.' Mrs Duffy took an envelope out of her apron pocket.

Victoria removed the clips from her hair and took off her cap before lying on her bed to savour the contents of the letter. She had recognized the handwriting immediately.

I hope you have managed to avoid my brother and keep your heart safe from him and ready for me, he wrote, only half in jest. *He tells me he has seen you about the hospital looking beautiful in your uniform and I don't mind admitting I am eaten up with jealousy.*

The truth was, being absent from Baker Hall had made her very sure that Roland had already won her heart. His brother Teddy could be the next Laurence Olivier, but he did nothing for her. Roland had lit a torch somewhere within her and nothing Teddy could say or do would alter that. She had told none of the girls anything about Roland. For now, he was her secret and she would keep it that way.

It was Sunday evening and the results of the PTS exam were due to be delivered to the nurses' home.

The girls waited nervously in the hallway for Mrs Duffy to return from Matron's office with the announcements and a list informing the new nurses which ward they had been allocated for their first placement.

'Oh my God, was there anything ever as bad as this,' groaned Pammy, who was sitting on the stairs.

'Will you move away from the window, Nurse Harper,' Dana snapped. 'Looking out won't make Mrs Duffy get here any quicker.' It was unusual for Dana to snap at anyone and the assembled girls fell silent, until Pammy, who could never keep quiet, chirped up once more.

'Oh, God, I can't wait to know which ward I'm on, never mind the results. I feel so nervous I want to be sick. Just think, tomorrow, if we have all passed, we will all be proper nurses.'

Lizzie burst in from a holiday at home, allowing a fierce wind to blow down the hall, and as she opened the front door, they all shrieked.

'Oh, it's you! We thought it was Mrs Duffy with the results list,' Pammy told her.

'Are your twelve weeks up already?' said Lizzie, amazed. 'Golly, that went quickly.'

'For you, maybe,' said Dana. 'Feels to me like the longest twelve weeks in my life, ever.' She meant it.

The routine of the classroom had become more difficult as they entered their last week of training and the prospect of being set free on the wards for a month, to learn the more practical skills and to nurse real patients, came tantalizingly close.

'I'm not sure whether I am nervous or excited,' said Victoria. 'I have a funny feeling in my tummy and I know I am not going to sleep tonight, no matter how much Horlicks Mrs Duffy forces down me.'

'You will all be fine,' said Lizzie, smiling. 'Just as long as you all pass and none of you are sent to ward two and Sister Antrobus, you'll survive.'

The girls had all heard the name Sister Antrobus. Her reputation was fearsome. It was legendary both in the school of nursing and on Lovely Lane. 'Pick your faces up off the floor, nurses,' Lizzie continued. 'I have heard that so many girls have dropped out after being allocated to that ward, they aren't going to place any more new nurses on ward two. They are going to save her for the hardened third years. I have a feeling it will be my placement before finals.'

She picked up her suitcase and began to hump it up the stairs. 'My mother has sent me back with the most ginormous fruit cake. I'll just unpack and then I'll put it on the night drinks trolley, if any of you fancy a slice.'

Just as Lizzie turned the bend on the stairs, the door opened once more and this time the girls fell silent. Mrs Duffy stood in front of them and to their surprise she was accompanied by Sister Haycock and Sister Ryan. 'Hello, Sister,' they all said at once.

'Evening, nurses,' said Sister Haycock brightly. 'I thought I would pop in to deliver the news. I remember what a dreadful time it is waiting for the results.'

No one spoke a word. Dana licked her lips. Victoria thought that if Sister Haycock didn't get a move on, there was a chance she might faint. Beth beamed with a self-assured confidence.

'Matron is responsible for the ward placements, and you have all done so well over the past twelve weeks that I thought I would like to break the news to you myself.' Still no one spoke as Sister Haycock unbuttoned her coat and hung it on the hat stand.

'Any chance of a cup of hot chocolate, Mrs Duffy? And maybe one of your biscuits,' asked Sister Ryan. Her stomach always came first.

'There is. Honestly, these nurses, a nervous wreck they all are. They've got me all of a dither, panicking all day they've been. 'Tis a mystery why Matron makes them wait until Sunday night for the results, is it not? Anyone would think they were awaiting a death sentence, not their first ward placements.'

'I'll put you all out of your misery in just a second,' said Sister Haycock. 'Nurse Harper, run and put the kettle on for Mrs Duffy. We shall all need a drink after this, if I'm not mistaken.'

Beth could not erase the smile from her face. She adored being given extra responsibility and had quickly become Mrs Duffy's little helper. 'I already have, Sister. It's simmering now,' she preened.

Undoing the knot of her green paisley headscarf and shaking the raindrops on to the floor, Sister

Haycock laid the scarf over the mahogany hat stand and moved towards the hall fire.

'Well, it looks as though no one is going to allow me to sit down until they know their fate, so here goes.' There were sharp gasps from the girls as they grabbed hold of each other's hands. Emily pulled the envelope out of her handbag while Beth scooped up a chair and slid it behind her and Celia, with a sickly grin, slipped one behind Sister Ryan. Beth had beaten her again and Celia was annoyed.

To make matters worse, Mrs Duffy gave Beth an approving smile from the doorway before turning her attention to Dana.

'Nurse Brogan, have you been to mass today?' she asked.

Dana blinked like a rabbit in the headlights. Sister Haycock opened the envelope and looked at Dana, waiting for her to reply before she began to read out the results. 'Only, I have to write back to your mother tonight.' Dana blushed with embarrassment until her face was the same colour as her hair. She wanted to scream. How could her mammy have interrupted this of all moments?

'Yes, Mrs Duffy,' she replied in an exasperated tone, and whispered to Pammy, 'I knew my mother would find a way into Lovely Lane.'

Sister Haycock began to speak.

'Nurses, I am absolutely delighted to inform you—'

Sister Ryan pushed a plate in front of the letter

and cut her off. 'Try one of these millionaire's shortbreads,' she said. 'Mrs Duffy made them this afternoon as a special treat. They're sublime. Go on, have one.' Sister Ryan winked at Emily, but no one saw her as all eyes were fixed on the letter in Emily's hand.

'Oh, thank you. I don't mind if I do.' Emily reached out and took a shortbread from the plate. 'Oh, yes. Mrs Duffy, they are delicious.' Crumbs fell from the shortbread on to the letter as she nibbled at the biscuit and made a slight rattling sound as they hit the paper. 'Can I have a hot chocolate too, please? It's always such a treat to come here, isn't it, Sister Ryan?'

'Are you for real?' This was from Pammy, who could contain herself no longer. Emily began to giggle.

'I am, Nurse Tanner, and so are you, a real nurse. Every one of you passed your PTS, and Nurse Harper, you have won the course prize for attainment. You got top marks in the exam.'

Mrs Duffy appeared carrying a tray filled with small glasses of dark brown liquid.

'I checked with Sister Haycock first and she said it was quite in order for a celebratory glass of sherry. It's not always the case that everyone gets through. Isn't that right, Sister? What a lovely night this is.'

Mrs Duffy placed the tray on the table.

'Go on, help yourselves, you are all proper nurses now, fancy that.'

For the following ten minutes, the Lovely Lane home was filled with the sound of excited chatter, congratulations for Beth, and the clink of glasses as everyone tucked into the celebratory millionaire's shortbread and the sweet sherry.

'Well, now we have to see who has been placed where,' said Emily at last, opening yet another envelope. 'Ward one, Nurse Baker, female medical, Sister Prior. Ward two, Nurse Tanner, gynaecological, Sister Antrobus.' There was a sharp intake of breath as the girls all turned to Pammy. None was paler than Sister Haycock herself, who looked as though she might faint.

'But, Sister Haycock, Nurse Lewis said no new nurses would be placed on ward two because so many had left before . . .' Pammy's voice tailed away in despair.

Sister Ryan came to the rescue and saved her from having to finish the sentence.

'Well, I'm quite sure I have no idea where Nurse Lewis got that idea from,' she said. 'These third years seem to think they know what colour bloomers I'm wearing these days. I will admit that there was some gossip about only third years being placed on ward two, but Matron has clearly rejected the idea.' Just at that moment, the kettle whistled deafeningly. 'Right, come on then, let's away to the kitchen to hear the rest. Let's not have the drinks late tonight. It'll be an early night for all of you if you know what's good for you.' As ever, Sister Ryan was keen to finish the biscuits. 'Next week will be one of the hardest of your life and we want you all to do well. Nursing is a vocation, not a job.'

Sister Haycock's brow was furrowed and she appeared troubled. 'That's a very good idea, Sister Ryan.'

Mrs Duffy led the way out of the hall, talking to Sister Ryan as she went. 'In my experience of looking after the probationers, Sister, there is always something that has brought each nurse through this door. An experience that makes them believe they are called to be a nurse in the first place.'

She looked across to Dana. 'Not everyone can do the job, you know, Nurse Brogan. It takes a special kind of person. If I can give you any advice, it would be to hold on to that. To whatever it is that brought you here. Whatever difficulty you encounter, remember the reason why you chose your vocation in the first place. Come on now, drinks.'

The nurses milled en masse into the kitchen, except for Pammy, who looked as though she would fall over her own trembling bottom lip if she moved.

'Come on now, Nurse Tanner,' said Sister Haycock. 'It's only Sister Antrobus, not a firing squad. She's not that bad.'

But Sister Haycock's reassurances did not quite ring true. Pammy stood, terrified, with tears flooding in her eyes, the joy of having passed her

PTS obliterated by the news that her placement was ward two with the dreaded Sister Antrobus. Emily wanted to put her arm round her shoulder and give her a hug, but she just could not. She was filled with anger at what Matron had done.

'I have to go into the kitchen now,' she said. 'I need to let the others know their fate.' She looked apologetically towards the kitchen door. Whichever ward the other girls were placed on, it would be a doddle compared to poor Nurse Tanner's.

As they huddled around the list, Dana grinned when she read that she was to be placed on ward eight, male surgical.

'Lucky you,' said Pammy. 'I would give anything to be on male surgical. They have charge nurses, not sisters, and Lizzie said they can be a right laugh.'

'Oh, I almost forgot,' said Sister Ryan. 'Nurse Harper, here is a little prize for coming first.' She handed an envelope to Beth, while Celia Forsyth bristled. She had expected the first place honour to be hers.

'Well done you,' she said to Beth, through gritted teeth.

'It's only a book token,' said Beth. 'You can have it if you want.'

'No, don't be silly. It's all yours, fair and square.' Celia thought Beth was being ridiculous, but as she was one of her few friends, she couldn't say so. It wasn't the book token Celia had wanted. It was the status, and the respect, that having come top in the PTS exam would have brought her. She turned to leave the kitchen, cocoa mug in hand, heading towards the stairs and her room.

'Don't worry about Sister Antrobus,' she said, as she brushed past Dana and Pammy. 'She only weeds out the students who aren't cut out to be nurses. I've heard that she gets them packed off pretty quickly.'

Dana saw the tears of fear in Pammy's eyes threaten to spill over. 'Well in that case, you wouldn't last five minutes on there, would you? So you'd better keep your opinion to yourself. Pammy will be just fine,' she snapped.

'Oh, shut up, Brogan,' Celia barked back.

'Steady on, Nurse Forsyth,' said Beth, who was following her out. Beth looked embarrassed.

'Nurse Harper isn't as bad as you think,' said Pammy. 'She's a bit of a stickler for the work and everything, but she's not mean like Celia Forsyth. I reckon she may be feeling a bit lonely, thinking that she's backed the wrong horse. I know I would, if I were her.' They heard Celia's voice boom down the stairwell.

'If I were you, Tanner, I'd be wishing I could do another twelve weeks in PTS' were Celia's parting words as her bedroom door slammed.

'Oh, blimey, Antrobus must be bad,' said Pammy. 'We will see each other every day, won't we, Dana?' she said, suddenly looking very young and scared. 'We can let off steam on the way home, can't we?'

Dana hugged her friend. 'We can. We just have

to make sure we don't do it on the ward, that's all. You'll be fine. You just show her what you're made of.'

'We might be on different shifts,' said Pammy. There was an air of despair about her and it caught in her voice. 'I may not ever see you. We may hardly ever see each other.'

'Don't be daft, Pammy. Remember, it all starts tomorrow. We become real nurses for the first time. Don't let anyone spoil that for you.'

Dana was not about to make the same mistake on her first day on the wards as she had made in the school, and so that night, before bed, she meticulously went through everything a dozen times. Yet, as she lay staring at her uniform hanging on the wardrobe door, her thoughts were not filled with what the following day would hold, but were full of Teddy. She had seen her doctor every day through the classroom window as he walked towards the main entrance of the hospital. He had no idea that she watched him. When she turned off her light at night he filled her thoughts, something she had confided to no one. Now, there was a chance, albeit a slim one, that one day soon she might bump into him on the wards, and she couldn't wait for that moment to arrive. If she had known that that meeting was but a few hours away, she would probably not have slept at all.

CHAPTER 12

The following morning the girls walked up to the hospital as usual, but when they reached the main entrance, they parted ways with shouts of good luck and plans to meet in the same place to walk back at the end of the day.

Dana's day began in the office, listening to the day's instructions and patient details, but her first report-taking was rudely interrupted by a phone call from Matron, just as the night staff nurse had finished handing over her report.

There was no ward sister on ward eight. It was run by two male charge nurses and neither of them was a favourite of Matron. She said, falsely, that their standards were lacking and that their manner towards both patients and nurses was overly familiar.

'She just doesn't like men!' the charge nurse exclaimed, after he had almost slammed the phone in the office down following a conversation about the number of old newspapers stacked up in the dayroom, the flower vases which hadn't been scrubbed properly and the general mess on his office desk. 'Did she come up here before the day shift began?' he asked the poor night staff nurse, who really couldn't have cared less about the papers. It had been a long and hard night. She just wanted to get home to her bed.

'She came in at seven. She has a bee in her bonnet about something today. Of course, it's the new probationers' first day on the wards, and she's been a bit crazy about that, ever since she lost control.'

Just as the night staff nurse stood to leave, her colleague, who had remained on the ward while the day shift were all in the office taking report, popped her head around the door.

'Charge Nurse, bed three, Mr Townsend, terminal prostate CA with metastases, he's just gone,' she said, an expression of sadness on her face. The charge nurse looked up and gave her a reassuring smile.

'That's OK, queen, you go now. You too, Staff; you have done enough for one night. Your twelve hours is well and truly up.'

'Thanks, Charge,' said the night staff nurse with a sigh of relief. If the patient had died on her shift, she would have been honour bound to perform the last offices and prepare the patient for the mortuary. 'Have a good day, all,' she said as she left the office. 'And you, love,' she added to Dana as she passed her. 'You'll be fine here. You're on a lovely ward and working with a nice lot.' She turned and winked at the charge nurse, who grinned back at her.

He turned to his day staff nurse. 'Staff Nurse Rowlands, will you do the honours and take our new Nurse Brogan here with you, and I'll carry on with the day report. The old fella's wife said she would be in first thing this morning to give him a shave and I said it would be all right. Sod Matron and her strict visiting hours. It's my ward. Nurse Brogan may as well dive in at the deep end.'

Dana had no idea what he meant or what anyone was on about. She hadn't understood a word the night nurse had said, but she knew her own name and that he was asking the staff nurse to take her somewhere. She followed the older girl obediently out on to the ward. Muted wolf whistles from the patients made the colour rise in her cheeks.

'Take no notice,' the staff nurse grinned as they walked. 'This is male surgical. You'll get a lot of that. Oi, you lot, pack it in,' she said to no one in particular. Then, 'Here we are, love,' making an opening in the drawn pale blue curtains which were fastened around bed three. 'You wait here, Nurse Brogan. I'll just nip back to the phone and tell the porter's lodge to be ready with the trolley for a transfer to Rose Cottage.'

Dana was so confused, her head hurt. *Wherever in God's name is Rose Cottage?* She saw the patient sitting upright against the pillows, and looked at the name above the bed. Mr Townsend.

'Hello, Mr Townsend,' she said. 'I'm Nurse

Brogan and I'm helping Staff Nurse to look after you this morning.'

Mr Townsend continued to stare straight ahead and didn't answer her. Dana looked around and wondered what she should say next.

'Did you have a good night?' she asked, trying her best to appear confident and professional and to remember what the night nurse had just said about him. She knew there had been something and that by the look on the nurse's face it wasn't good. 'Hello there,' she said again. Still no reply. 'Never mind. Are you not feeling very well? You definitely look a bit peaky to me. How long ago did you have your operation, then?'

At that moment the staff nurse opened the curtains and holding them together at the top, so that the other patients couldn't see inside, manoeuvred a trolley with a bowl of warm water on top and various towels and sheets on the bottom into place.

'What are you doing, nurse?' she asked.

'Well,' said Dana with a very serious face, 'Sister Ryan said that with every practical procedure we undertake, we must always chat to the patient. She said reassuring the patient was the most important part of a nurse's job.'

'And she's right, love, she taught me that too. But I'll tell you what, if I told her the patient was dead I bet she'd tell me not to bother.'

Dana gasped and put her hand to her mouth. Mr Townsend was dead. 'Come here,' said the staff nurse, lifting the covers from the foot of the bed and taking hold of one of Mr Townsend's feet. 'Get his other foot.'

Dana took hold of the other foot which was now cool to the touch. 'When I count to three, pull,' Staff Nurse whispered. 'One, two, three, pull.' They both pulled and Mr Townsend slipped down the bed and flopped back against the pillows. Dana didn't like the look on his face. His head had lolled strangely to the side and his bottom set of false teeth was falling out.

'Now we go to the top of the bed. See this clip? Push it to the side and the bedrest lifts back to a flat position against the headboard.'

The bedrest clanged against the frame. The pillows collapsed back, and with them Mr Townsend.

'Right, come on. Just copy me. He'll be as stiff as a board soon and it's not so easy to get the shroud on once they start to stiffen up.' Staff Nurse yanked the pillows out from under Mr Townsend, leaving just one under his head.

'There you go, love, I'll leave you one,' she whispered to him. 'You never liked lying flat, did you? He had Ménière's disease and used to feel a bit dizzy if he was laid flat on his back,' she explained to Dana. 'Always be careful with that. Patients with Ménière's can often pass out when you lie them down. And don't worry about talking to a corpse. I talk to them sometimes too, but I don't really expect an answer.'

Dana smiled sheepishly. She was desperate to prove she could be a good nurse.

'Right, let's get started. I'm going to fetch him a shroud, which I forgot, and his notes from the filing cabinet. They will need to accompany him to the mortuary. Never forget to send the notes with the porter on the trolley, if you ever do this on your own. I'll be about ten minutes. Don't try and lift him. Those pyjama bottoms are hospital issue and they've had it. Use your scissors to cut them down the front from the middle and then just lay them to the side. Remove the jacket and peel the dressings off his wound. There's a rubbish bag taped to the side of his locker. Put the dirty dressings in there and then use the tape to seal the bag. This is one time you don't have to worry about cross-contamination. We have to move quickly. The porters will be here in half an hour, rigor mortis is already setting in and I've still to collect our day list from the charge nurse. Our operating list begins at ten. Oh, and pop his top set of teeth in. Thanks.' Nurse Rowlands rushed out through the gap in the curtains and Dana was left alone, with a pair of scissors in her hand, about to cut the pyjama bottoms off a dead patient.

'Oh, God, no,' she whispered, freezing with fear. 'What did she say I had to do?' she said to Mr Townsend. 'Oh, God in heaven, what am I talking to you for, you poor man? You can't help me, so ye can't.' At that moment a loud noise escaped from Mr Townsend's mouth. It was too much for

Dana's nerves. She screamed and ran out between the curtains.

'Whoa. What's up, Nurse Brogan?' Clutching a set of case notes, Charge Nurse was walking down the ward towards her, with a doctor in a white coat, on his way to see a pre-operative patient.

'Mr Townsend,' she squeaked, 'he made a noise.'

'Hang on, doctor, just give me a minute.' The charge nurse handed the case notes to the doctor, put his arm round Dana's shoulders and led her back behind the curtains.

'Hello, mate,' he said to Mr Townsend. 'Lesson number one from me, Nurse Brogan.' As he spoke, he placed his fingers on Mr Townsend's pulse. 'Try not to run down the ward squealing. It doesn't exactly instil confidence in the patients. I like them to think that we might just know what we're doing. Yep, the night nurse, who is fifteen years qualified and has seen more dead bodies than you have hot dinners, was absolutely right. Mr Townsend is very definitely dead.'

'But he just made the loudest, most horrendous noise.' Dana was on the verge of sobbing. Everything had gone wrong in the space of five minutes. This was not how her first day was meant to be. She had wanted to shine. To be proud. When she had lain in bed the previous evening, she had imagined the charge nurse saying to her, 'It has been a delight to have you on my ward. You will make a fantastic nurse.' Instead, she had made herself look like a complete idiot.

'Aye, well, as you can see, you laid him down almost flat, and Mr Townsend often had a bit of wind. All the patients on this ward do, and I can tell you, they are not as shy about holding it in as they are on the ladies' wards. What you heard was air escaping from his body. Nothing to worry about.'

Dana felt rinsed with relief, and then overcome with embarrassment. Just then the doctor popped his head round the curtains. To her horror, it was Teddy, and she could tell he was only just holding in his laughter.

'Anything I can do to help?' he asked with a grin.

'Yes, as a matter of fact there is,' said the charge nurse. 'I need you to sign a death certificate before you leave the ward.'

'Sure, no problem,' Teddy replied. 'Let me do the check now.' He lifted his stethoscope from around his neck and placed the earpieces in before slipping the other end under Mr Townsend's pyjama jacket. Dana half expected him to shout, 'He's alive.'

Teddy winked at her. 'Yep, he's well and truly gone,' he said as he removed the stethoscope.

'Are you all right now, Nurse Brogan?' the charge nurse asked Dana kindly. 'Only we've got a busy day today.'

'Yes, of course,' said Dana. When the two men had left, she felt her cheeks burn as hot as coal. She felt useless, a hindrance, an idiot, and it was made all the worse by the fact that the doctor who had witnessed her humiliation was Teddy. The man she had spoken to on her first night who had barely left her thoughts since.

Without warning, the metal runners on the curtains swished back and Dana jumped out of her skin as Teddy popped his head round the curtain again.

'Bloody hell, Nurse Brogan,' he whispered. 'You want to do something about those nerves of yours.'

'How can I do something about my nerves when you spring on me like that?' Dana was mad, but she was finding it very difficult not to grin.

'Tell you what, why don't I give you a lesson about how not to scream while you're running down the middle of a ward and scaring the patients half to death, eh? We could discuss it over a drink in the Grapes on Saturday.'

'Get lost,' said Dana. 'I'm trying to make an impression here. It's my first day.'

'Thank goodness for that. Things can only improve. Are you coming to the doctors' social? It will be a laugh. If I know you are coming, I can work out how I am going to persuade you to dance with me. You see, I have two very clumsy left feet.'

'Did you not hear me?' Dana hissed at him. It was the second time that morning she felt as though someone was speaking Chinese to her. She knew nothing about a doctors' social. 'I have to cut this poor man's trousers off now, so will you go away.' She waved the scissors she was holding at him.

'OK, then, I'm off. I'm obviously going to have to turn up the charmometer for you, Nurse Brogan. I can see you are not easily impressed.'

Dana took a deep breath and forced herself to stop grinning. She was about to perform one of the most solemn and personal duties a nurse could undertake. Regardless of how loved someone was, or how popular, in the moments following death, when the soul fled the body, it was the nurse who had the privilege of being in attendance. To say a prayer, to open the window, to prepare the patient to meet his or her maker. Last offices were never rushed. Curtains were drawn, nurses spoke in whispers and full respect was accorded to the dead whether the deceased had been a lord or a road sweeper. In the final hour, they were equal. Washed with the same soap, dressed in the same shroud, and laid on the same mortuary slab.

This was no time to melt with shame and Dana recovered quickly, as she moved towards the bed with the scissors. She tentatively lifted the pyjama waistband and moved down to the crotch and began to cut. She was relieved she had managed to work the procedure out for herself. She worked from the crotch down one leg and then back up the other leaving a flap to cover his dignity in the middle. Replacing his top teeth took longer. Taking the denture out of the glass on his bedside locker, she put her fingers in his mouth, then pulled them out again. She tried once more. His jaw was becoming stiff and didn't yield very easily to her touch. She heaved. Her eyes were watering. She was successful on her third attempt, and managed not to heave again by turning her head to the side as with half-closed eyes she slipped the teeth into place, adjusting the bottom set as she did so. 'Oh, thank God. I'm sorry,' she whispered, very quietly. 'I'm so sorry, Mr Townsend. I've never done it before. It's my first day and you are my very first patient. Well, here goes,' she added as she tentatively removed each of the gauze and lint dressings from his abdomen, as gentle and careful with the patient in death as she would have been in life.

'Here we are,' said the staff nurse, arriving through the curtains with the shroud. 'Let's get cracking. I want to have him nice and clean as quickly as possible before his wife gets here.'

Dana couldn't help herself. She still kept talking to Mr Townsend, or rather apologizing to him, all the way through the procedure. 'Oops, sorry,' she said, when she had to bend his by now very heavy and stiff arm. 'Oh, sorry again. Silly me,' as she helped to roll him and failed to stop his arm flopping on to the bed when she leant over to tie the shroud. 'I hope this doesn't tickle,' tying his toes together with a gauze bandage threaded through a name tag.

'I'm sorry,' she said when the staff nurse giggled. 'You must think I'm mad.'

'Not at all,' said Staff Nurse. 'Look, if talking to

them helps you to get over any fear you have, you do it, love. Sometimes, when it's the early hours of the morning and you're doing this job all on your own on a dark ward, it does help. I know, because I've often done it meself. We all have.'

Dana breathed a sigh of relief. She knew she was holding her fear at bay. The only thing that had stopped her from running down the ward and out of the door was pretending that Mr Townsend was still alive. And, what was more, it had worked.

Just as they left the cubicle, Dana saw an elderly lady walking with a stooped back, carrying her shopping basket and greeting the patients on either side of the ward as she came.

'Morning,' she was saying. 'I'm just off to shave our Tom. He didn't manage very well himself yesterday, and it put him right out of sorts. I told him, don't worry, love, I'll come and do it in the morning. The charge nurse said he would let me. How have you all been? Had a good night?' She halted her to catch her breath and wait for a reply.

'OK, stick with me,' the staff nurse said quietly to Dana. 'If you thought last offices was tough, wait until you have to do this.'

For Mrs Townsend, it all happened in a flash. She wondered why the patient in bed two looked so embarrassed and threw a pleading look up the ward. She followed the direction of his glance and saw Staff Nurse Rowlands and Dana walking towards her, with looks of compassion on their faces just as she noticed the curtains were drawn around her Tom's bed. And then she heard Dessie shout in through the office door as he pushed a flat trolley on to the ward, 'Trolley for transfer to Rose Cottage.' Staff Nurse and Dana reached her side, and saw the fear fill her eyes as it dawned on her. The moment she and Tom had dreaded since the day he first became ill had arrived. And Dana thought it was a terrible thing to see.

For the remainder of the day, it felt to Dana as though her feet never touched the ground. For at least half of it, she scrubbed bedpans, washed out glass urine bottles and put into practice one of her first lessons from PTS, testing urine by using litmus paper. But as stomach-churning as all of that was, what preyed on her mind throughout the day were the tears shed by Mrs Townsend after losing her husband of forty-three years, who until his stay in hospital had never spent a night away from her since returning from fighting in the First World War.

'He saw the worst sights, you know,' she told Staff Nurse Rowlands and Dana. 'I've got all his medals at home. He has one from Mons. He said they all saw an angel rise over the brow of the field before they went into battle and he reckoned it was the angel what saved them. He thought you were all angels, and you are. He said to me, "Don't worry, Edna, whenever I'm in trouble there's always an angel around. I'm surrounded by them here." God knows, you were all so lovely to him.'

She put her cup back on its saucer. 'Well, I'll go and catch the bus, up to our Betty's now. I could ring the phone in the pub until someone answers and ask them to go and give her a knock, but I don't think I want to tell her that her dad has died over the phone. Best I go and get the bus.'

'Will you be all right on your own?' Dana felt brave enough to speak. Staff Nurse was holding Edna's hand. Dana knew that she must have been worrying about everything that still had to be done. It was already nine o'clock, and yet, you would think she had nothing other than all the time in the world for Edna.

'Thank you so much, nurses. I will be back with a present for you all.'

'Oh no you won't,' said Staff. 'You must only think about yourself now.' She gave Mrs Townsend a big hug.

'You're lovely and kind and I'm glad you were both with him when he died.'

Dana almost gave a guilty start.

'And you, little one,' Edna went on, returning Dana's hug. 'I've not ever seen you before. Tom said last night the new probationer would be on the ward today. They know everything, that lot, don't they, Staff? All I can say is, he would have been made up to have a nurse as pretty as you with him at the end.'

The nurses watched as Edna walked the lonely walk along the shiny polished wooden floor of the hospital corridor towards the main entrance. By the end of that walk, she would feel desolate, realizing that it was for the last time. She would never visit her Tom again, nor would he return home with her as he had so many times before, following his outpatient appointments.

'God, how sad was that?' said Dana. 'We weren't with him at the end, though, and she thinks we were. Is that all right? I felt terrible. I didn't know what to say.'

'Yes, thanks for not saying anything. That's the worst part of the job,' said Staff Nurse, 'but you'll get over it. It's just nicer for her to think it was us with him and not a night nurse she has never met. Sometimes a white lie in this game can be an act of kindness. There are some patients who never leave you and you just can't forget, and I'll tell you what, I'll never forget you chatting away to him thinking he was alive.'

'Neither will I,' said Dana, and with the feeling of sadness dispelled as rapidly as it often is, in a place where life and death frequently trade places, both nurses laughed as they walked back through the ward doors.

Dana was in the dirty utility room, putting the bed linen from Mr Townsend's bed into the basket which would be taken to the laundry by two porter's lads. Each time a dirty was taken away a clean one returned in its place, along with the twice per day fresh deliveries.

She was placing the used dressings in the drum

for the sterilizer and feeling very pleased with herself that everything was going smoothly when the door opened and someone clasped their hands over her eyes in a blindfold.

'Jesus, Holy Mother,' she yelled as she spun round.

Teddy was laughing out loud. 'Nurse Brogan, will you shush,' he said mockingly, wagging his finger.

''Tis you again,' she whispered. She tried to sound cross, but she could feel her heart banging and she knew without looking in a mirror that the colour was rising up her neck.

'What do you want?' she hissed in mock impatience.

'A date with you,' Teddy replied, 'and if I don't get one, I shall upend you into that dirty linen basket.'

'No you will not. That would be just disgusting.' Dana's eyes were wide with the horror of such a thing.

'OK, I won't, but will you tell me when you can come out for a drink, then?'

'I don't think I can.'

'Yes you can. You know you can. Come on, just give me a date and I'll leave you alone. I promise you, I am a man who is nothing if not persistent. I won't give up until you agree. I love those red curls, by the way. Do you know they have fallen out at the back and that they bob up and down on your shoulders when you are cross?'

Dana couldn't believe this was actually happening to her. Teddy was the best-looking man she had ever laid eyes on. His teeth were intact and they all seemed to be his own. A rarity among Irish boys in the country, by the time they had reached twenty-one. He spoke beautifully and he was a clever and educated man. 'Why the hell would you want to go out with me?' she asked, genuinely puzzled.

Teddy didn't waste a second. 'Well, you see, Nurse Brogan, it's because I like you and I truly would hate to see you being transported to the laundry in a dirty linen basket and never heard of again. It would be such a waste. It's happened to nurses more experienced than you, you know.' Teddy knew his strengths. He grinned at Dana and held her eyes.

'Do you make a habit of this, doctor?' Dana asked him tartly. 'Do you ask all probationers out on the threat of contamination with dirty linen germs? Would I be thinking now that that is the only way you can get a nurse to have a drink with you?'

Teddy looked affronted. 'I would have you know, I have never dated a nurse in my life. You would be the first, I swear.'

'You swear? Seriously, you swear? You see, I am not the sort of nurse who would go out for a drink with a doctor who made a habit of dating nurses. We Irish girls have a great deal of self-respect.' She wanted to roar with laughter at the change in expression on Teddy's face.

'Golly, you are a tough customer.' He had been leaning against the door, but now he stood up straight and ran his hand through his hair. 'Well, I did have a date with a nurse when I was just a medical student. But that was two years ago and anyway, she stood me up.'

Dana caught a hint of pain in his voice, but it was instantly replaced by his sudden infectious smile.

'Go on, give an overworked doctor something to look forward to. Say yes, would you? You know, your mammy would want you to make a homesick and lonely doctor very happy, and there is no other nurse in St Angelus who comes near you. Go on, please.'

Dana felt as though she were dreaming, or had been transported to another planet and was living someone else's life entirely. If Teddy hadn't been staring at her so intently, she would have pinched herself. She smiled back.

'Well, what can I say? You haven't met Celia Forsyth yet. I think you might find that she is far more interesting company than me.'

Teddy looked puzzled and scratched his head. 'But I don't want to meet this Forsyth, whoever she is. Come on, don't give a chap a hard time. You just have to say yes, or the dirty linen basket awaits.' He took a step closer to her.

'All right then, I might. Let me think about it.'

'Gosh, you are infuriating,' said Teddy. 'Well, you can't say I didn't warn you.' Dana didn't even see

him move. One moment she was stuffing the last
of the sheets into the basket, the next he had lifted
her up and she was sitting on top of the laundry.
As the sheets compressed under her weight, she
slowly began to slip down.

'Oh, my God, help me, you eejit, get me out,'
she yelled.

'Was that a yes, then?' said Teddy, grinning.

'No, it bloody was not. Get me out, now.'

Dana was saved by Staff Nurse entering the
room.

'And just what is going on here?' she said to
Teddy, hand on hip. Then to Dana, who was struggling to get herself out of a wicker basket which
was almost as tall as she, 'Nurse Brogan, are you
ready?' She seemed barely able to contain her
laughter. 'Honestly, Davenport, couldn't you think
of something more original? Is there a doctor's
manual for this?' She gave Dana her hand and
helped her out. 'Oh, and by the way, Mr Mabbutt
is marching up and down the ward waiting for
you and looking none too pleased. Nurse Brogan,
straighten your apron, quick.'

Dana was fixing her cap back into place as she
followed Staff Nurse out of the door and down
the ward, trying desperately to push the escaped
curls up and under.

'The first case is ready for theatre, so I thought
I would go through the checks with you first and
show you how we administer the pre-med.'

'Yes, Staff Nurse.' Dana looked down and noticed

that her apron had slipped round to the side. She felt more like killing Teddy Davenport than dating him.

'Look, Nurse Brogan, I'm not going to say a word, but if I were you, I would be very careful there. Half the nurses in this hospital are after Dr Davenport. He is a hot favourite. If you were to bag him you would make more enemies than friends, and I'm not sure that's something you want to do in your first year. Even as a medical student he caused chaos among the nurses.'

'Is he a bit of a flirt, then?' asked Dana, her heart sinking.

'He's that all right, but funnily enough he has never broken any hearts, as far as I know. He was famously stood up a couple of years ago by a second-year nurse. She married after she took her finals and so she left. Apparently he waited for her for over two hours in town, thinking she had got the wrong time. The medical students never stopped teasing him about it. They say she broke *his* heart.'

'Oh, I don't want to bag him,' Dana lied. 'I told him to get lost. That's why he dumped me in the basket, but honest to God, it was so fast I didn't even feel him do it.'

'No, I think they practise their technique over in the doctors' residence. I can assure you, it's been done a hundred times before. Right, theatre have rung for Mr Davis. We'll go through the motions and then take him down with the porters, and when we get back it's backs, beds and pans for you. You can give me a shout if there is anyone you need a lift with; don't struggle on your own. Lifting a fifteen-stone man on to a bedpan is something you should avoid doing by yourself, if you can.'

The two nurses came to a halt at the end of their patient's bed. 'Go on then,' said Staff. 'I'll let you go through the checks.'

Dana nervously picked up the notes which were ready on the bedside table.

'Er . . .' She racked her brain. This was her first test. 'Can you tell me your name please, Mr Davis?' For a moment, Dana had no idea why Staff Nurse and Mr Davis were laughing.

'Here we go, let me show you,' said Staff. 'Mr Davis. Inguinal hernia repair. Can you tell us your address, Mr Davis, and your date of birth?' She walked to the bedside locker and checked that his clean water jug and glass were ready inside for his return.

As they went through the pre-operative checks, Dana took and recorded Mr Davis's pulse just as Charge Nurse arrived at the end of the bed with a small glass gallipot.

'Here you are, Nurse Brogan, chlormethiazole for the pre-op.' He handed Dana the gallipot.

'I can't, nurse. Me throat's as dry as the bottom of a parrot's cage.'

'Really, Mr Davis, lovely.' Staff Nurse laughed. 'I'm afraid you are going to have to. It will make you woozy and relaxed. It's like having six pints of Guinness, all in one jug.'

Once Staff Nurse had left to call the porters' lodge to tell them they were ready, Mr Davis grabbed hold of Dana's hand.

'Eh, nurse, would you do me a favour? Only I'm a bit stuck like.'

'Of course, Mr Davis. What can I do?'

Mr Davis looked around the ward to see if anyone was listening.

'I have to tell you though,' Dana added, 'it's my first day. I'm afraid I don't know very much.'

Mr Davis looked slightly agitated and Dana thought it might be because he was nervous about going down to theatre.

'Apparently everyone is very nervous before being taken to theatre, so you mustn't worry.' Dana was quoting from her textbook word almost for word. *Reassure the patient at every stage of the pre-operative procedure*, Sister Ryan had taught her. 'I would offer you a cup of tea, but I would be kicked out within minutes. My first day would become my last.'

He squeezed her hand tightly. 'I'm a bit worried, like. I don't like hospitals. Had enough of them during the war, but it's not that. The thing is, you see, it's me wife. Charge Nurse has told her to come in at visiting, at six o'clock.' Dana nodded. She had been told at morning report that there was no afternoon visiting on operation day and visitors had to wait until six p.m.

'Yes, that is what they like to do on operation day. Charge Nurse likes to concentrate on the patients coming back from theatre and not deal with visitor enquiries.'

'I know that, love, he told me. The thing is, there is someone else who will want to see me, but she can't come in at the same time as the wife.'

'Oh, yes, she can,' said Dana, delighted that she could answer so many of Mr Davis's questions. 'You are allowed two visitors at the bed from six until seven. That's not a problem at all, Mr Davis.' A smile of sheer delight spread across her face. Her day had been a rollercoaster of new experiences and now here she was, truly putting into practice all she had been taught in PTS. 'You really mustn't be anxious. In half an hour, you will be fast asleep and—'

'No, you see, nurse, me wife, well, she doesn't know about me other visitor, if you know what I mean.' He gave Dana a nervous wink, as though imploring her to understand what he had failed to put into words.

Dana met his look with a puzzled frown. 'Well, that's not a problem. If you are under the anaesthetic still, I can tell her.'

Mr Davis became quite agitated. 'No, no, don't do that. If you do that, nurse, I'll have to go back down to theatre by the time the wife's finished with me. Look, love, if you could just tell me wife she has to go at about twenty past six. Tell her I'm not very well or something. That would be smashing. Would you do that for me, queen? Just in case I'm out of it. Ah, your name is embroidered on your apron. Brogan, is it?'

'That's right,' said Dana. 'My name is Dana Brogan, but don't call me that or you'll get me into trouble. It's Nurse Brogan.'

'My wife's sister's brother-in-law's cousin went out with a Brogan once. You might have known her, she came from Galway?'

'Well, I do know the Brogans from Galway, but never mind that. What am I to do about your wife? You are asking me to tell her a lie? That's a sin. I can't do that, and besides, I might get into trouble.'

'No, no, queen, you really won't, 'cause no one will know. Would you do that for me, please? Honest to God, you have no idea. I have a terrible life at home. If you knew what I went through. Please, queen.'

Dana sighed. 'Well, all right then, I will. But honestly, if you get me into trouble . . .'

Mr Davis had no time to reply because Staff Nurse arrived at the end of the bed, accompanied by Dessie. Minutes later, they were walking down the corridor towards theatre. Dessie pushed the head of the bed, Dana and Staff Nurse walked on each side at the foot, with a hand on the end, to guide it.

'I'm feeling a bit woozy here, nurse,' said Mr Davis with a hint of panic in his voice. 'I think I'm dying.' He tried and failed to grab the side of the bed to sit himself up.

'You're not dying, Mr Davis. It's just the effects of the chlormethiazole which Charge Nurse gave you as a pre-med. To keep you nice and calm.'

Within seconds, Mr Davis began to giggle and chatter like a man who had drunk six pints of Guinness, just as Staff Nurse had predicted.

'Valerie,' he shouted to every woman they passed on the way, 'Valerie, would you come and take me home, love? They've drugged me up here. I can't get up. *Valerie.*'

Staff Nurse looked puzzled, and opened his notes. 'I wonder who Valerie is,' she said. 'It says here his wife's name is Sybil.'

Mr Davis grabbed Dana's hand. 'We have a deal, Valerie, remember?' He was slurring his speech.

'I will be collecting you from theatre, Mr Davis,' Dana said. 'I'll see you when you wake up back on the ward. Just you relax now.'

They went through the basic checks once more in theatre, Staff Nurse making sure Nurse Brogan understood them all, and then their patient was handed over to the theatre sister.

'Are you coming for your tea? Charge Nurse has asked me to take you, before theatre start sending the patients back down. We need to be quick, so come on.'

Dana felt as though her legs wouldn't carry her as far as the greasy spoon. 'I could drink a bucket of tea and eat the place out of those crumpets,' she said. 'I thought it was hard work on the farm at home, but this is harder. 'Tis exhausting.'

Charge Nurse had overheard. 'The next few days will seem a doddle after today, Nurse Brogan, and besides, I'm a big fan of throwing people in at the deep end. You will learn more on one busy day like today than you will during the rest of the week.'

Dana thought he was probably right. Her head was swimming, but her confidence was also growing by the minute, as one new situation after another challenged her. Tomorrow she would work a split shift which meant she would walk back to the nurses' home at lunch time, and return to work at four o'clock, until the night staff came on duty at eight. She had planned to go into town, take a look at the shops, walk down to the Pier Head and watch the ferry come in. She now knew that all she would be capable of was sleep.

'Come along, Nurse Brogan,' said Staff Nurse as Dana scooped up her cape. 'We won't stop once the first post-op patient lands back on the ward, so we'd better get a wiggle on.'

Dana had never in her life tasted anything as delicious as those streaky bacon rashers, fried tomatoes and boiled potatoes smothered in butter. She washed them down with copious cups of tea and listened to the conversation of the nurses from other wards who joined them on their large circular table.

'Jam suet roly-poly and custard,' said the kitchen maid who now pulled a trolley alongside Dana and began to unload plates on to the table.

Dana scanned the cavernous canteen, looking for one of the other girls from Lovely Lane, but she appeared to be the only probationer in a hall full of far more experienced nurses. It seemed hard to believe that one day she would be exchanging hospital gossip and know exactly what everyone was talking about.

As they walked back in through the ward doors, Charge Nurse called out to them from behind his desk. 'Mr Davis is back from theatre, Staff. If you would like to go through the TPRs with Nurse Brogan and show her the post-op ropes for an inguinal hernia before she starts the backs and beds, please.'

Dana saw a woman sitting beside Mr Davis's bed and looked up at the large clock on the wall above the ward doors. It was almost twenty past six and her heart raced as she remembered her promise. 'Oh Holy Mother, I'm just in time,' she said, walking towards the bed.

'In time for what?' asked Staff, but did not wait for a reply. 'I'll get the sphyg for his blood pressure. You go and check his dressing, make sure it's not too wet and there's no blood on the sheets.'

Dana felt slightly panicked. How would she know how wet was too wet? What should she do if there was blood on the sheets? She had promised Mr Davis she would ask his wife to leave at twenty past six. She would have to do it right now, and checking Mr Davis's dressing provided a good excuse.

She was surprised at the sight of Mrs Davis. Mr Davis had made her out to be a harridan and Dana had an image in her mind of a stern-looking middle-aged person, not the peroxide blonde, red-lipped young woman in a fox fur stole sitting on the edge of his bed. Grabbing the curtain on the runner, she half pulled it around the patient, saying, 'Hello, Mrs Davis. Could I ask you to leave now, please? I need to check Mr Davis's dressing and we have to do his post-operative observations.'

The woman had hold of Mr Davis's hand. 'Oh, hello, nurse,' she said. 'I was just thinking his breath smells bad. Is that OK? He's out for the count, isn't he? Like a baby.'

Dana wasn't sure, but she had read that the anaesthetic could be smelt on a patient's breath post-operatively. 'Oh yes. I wouldn't get too close though if I were you. It's the anaesthetic; you may find you fall asleep.'

Mrs Davis laughed. 'Oh, God, imagine that. I'd have to stay in with him. No room in there for two of us, is there?' She leant over to speak to her husband. 'I have to go now, love,' she said. The only response from Mr Davis was a deep fume-laden snore. His wife rose. 'Thanks very much nurse,' she said.

'That's all right, Mrs Davis,' said Dana, glancing nervously at the clock.

'Oh no, love, I'm not Mrs Davis, not yet anyway. My name is Valerie. We're getting married at

261

Christmas, aren't we, love?' she said to the sleeping Mr Davis. 'We were sweethearts before the war, but I was a bit younger than Mr Davis and, well, me da wouldn't let us get engaged and then when he came home we had moved away to Chester where me da had been working. Took us to be evacuated, he did. We only met up again a year ago and, well, it's been romance all the way.' Valerie giggled as she took hold of Mr Davis's hand. Bending down, she kissed him gently on the brow.

'He never married, you know,' she said to Dana, who had lifted the sheets back and peeped underneath to see where the dressing was. 'Said he couldn't marry anyone after losing me, because he couldn't get me out of his mind. Isn't that lovely, nurse?'

'That's very romantic indeed, but we do have to see to his dressings now, so if you could . . .'

Neither of them noticed the stout woman, wearing a headscarf over her curlers, who had made her way down the ward and now positioned herself with folded arms at the end of the bed.

'Never married? Well, that's news to me, love. Who the bloody hell are you?'

Dana realized in a flash what had happened, but there was absolutely nothing she could do to alter the course of events.

Yet another woman appeared from nowhere, slightly larger than the first, who Dana had worked out must be the real Mrs Davis. The newcomer looked uncannily like her.

'What's up, our Sybil? Who's this?' the second woman said, nodding at Valerie.

'I don't know, but she had better get her skinny arse away from the side of my husband's bed, because if she doesn't it will be on the end of my stiletto any minute now.'

Dana felt her mouth dry and her heart beating rapidly. Frantically she looked down the ward and saw Charge Nurse heading towards her.

'Right, ladies,' he almost shouted as he reached the bed. 'Can we have this outside please?'

'Outside? I'm not leaving my fiancé,' said Valerie.

'Your fiancé.' Mrs Davis spat the words out. ''Ere, hold me handbag,' she said to her sister. 'Watch me ciggies don't fall out.'

She moved so fast, it took Dana a full thirty seconds to realize that Valerie was no longer standing by the side of the bed but was on the floor with Mrs Davis on top of her, and both women were screaming abuse at each other. Meanwhile, Mrs Davis's sister took the cigarette packet out of Sybil's bag, deftly transferred five cigarettes into her own pocket, and clicked the bag shut, all the while shouting encouragement to her sister. As if from nowhere, two of the porter's lads appeared in the ward while Dana, frozen to the spot, looked down at Mr Davis, who was snoring soundly, oblivious.

Victoria Baker had an altogether calmer day.

'Sister is a dote,' was the first thing Staff Nurse had said to her, 'and she won't make you do the bedpans every day. She thinks that's a waste of training. She is the only sister to let the ward orderlies help with the bedpan rounds, and that leaves you free to look after the patients.' Victoria could barely believe her luck and almost fainted with shock when Sister called her over.

'Nurse, the doctor here wants to examine Mrs Mulhearn. He needs an escort, so would you accompany him, please?' Victoria pulled the notes she had made out of her pocket, and to her relief Mrs Mulhearn was one of the first names she saw. She had been admitted the previous evening when the night staff were on duty, but no one was quite sure what was wrong with her.

Victoria pulled the screens around the bed, as she had been taught by Sister Ryan in PTS, and the first thing she noticed about Mrs Mulhearn was her pallor. It was very similar to that of her mother, when she had been alive. Her skin was translucent, like Dresden china. Lady Baker had worn lipstick every day and Victoria had sat next to her as she smeared her lips in cold cream revealing the thin blueish tinge beneath. Victoria blinked. This was not her mother. Mrs Mulhearn was an Irish mother, from the notorious Clare cottages, down by the docks.

'Now, Mrs Mulhearn, I just need to listen to your heart,' said the young doctor breezily. He placed his stethoscope against Mrs Mulhearn's chest, while Victoria held her nightdress open at the front.

'Oooh, that's cold. Could you not have warmed it up first, doctor? I got a slice of the chill there.'

The doctor wasn't listening to Mrs Mulhearn; he was trying his very best to listen to her heart. Then he made a signal to Victoria. She knew exactly what he wanted her to do. Assisting and escorting a doctor during an examination had been drilled in to the group during their last week by Sister Ryan. Victoria had done this before, on a dummy in the practice ward.

'Just lean forward a little please, Mrs Mulhearn,' she said. 'Doctor would like to listen to your heart from your back now.' She lifted up Mrs Mulhearn's nightgown and exposed her back. It was riddled with skin growths and blackheads the size of sixpenny pieces. Victoria felt as if she wanted to be sick and took rapid shallow breaths. Mrs Mulhearn had been bathed by the night staff as soon as she arrived on the ward, but the smell was still strong. The warm lingering aroma of stale faeces. The doctor's eyes met Victoria's.

'Thank you, nurse,' he said as he stood up. Victoria tucked the nightdress back into place and fluffed up a pillow, helping Mrs Mulhearn sit back so that she could be comfortable while the doctor chatted to her.

'Now, Mrs Mulhearn, you have breathlessness and fatigue and your pulse is a little fast, but are there any other symptoms you can give me?'

'Er, like what, doctor?'

'Well, are your waterworks all right? Do you have any pains in your heart?'

'Have I a pain in me heart? Well, that's for sure. My poor heart bleeds every day, as would yours if you had married a man like Padraig. He's never sober for long enough to recognize his own kids, and I swear to God he doesn't even know the last one was born. He went missing for two days and look at me belly.' Mrs Mulhearn wobbled the loose skin on her abdomen from side to side. 'He thinks I'm still carrying. Who wouldn't?'

'How many children do you have?' The doctor still looked puzzled.

'The last was the tenth.'

Mrs Mulhearn lost her colour when she spoke as a result of the fatigue. Yet again, Victoria noticed her pallor and the beads of perspiration which sprang up across her forehead. It was all sickeningly familiar.

'See that cyanosis on her lips?' said the doctor, as though Mrs Mulhearn couldn't hear him. 'Let me listen again.'

'Haven't ye just done that?' asked Mrs Mulhearn as Victoria sat her forward.

'He has, yes, but he wants to listen again. Try to stop talking if you can so that he can hear better.' Victoria smiled down at her. The blue tinge on the edge of her lips was beginning to disappear again.

'Thank you, nurse,' said the doctor. He looked exasperated and, thanking Mrs Mulhearn, rubbed his hair as he walked back to the office.

He forgot the case notes when he moved away from the bed, so Victoria retrieved them and hurried after him. 'Doctor, you left these,' she said, holding them out.

He was sitting in Sister's chair, looking as though the weight of the world was on his shoulders. Without acknowledging the notes, he looked up at Victoria. 'I'm going to have to call the consultant up. It's beyond me. She isn't having a heart attack, I'm sure of that, but I'm blowed if I know what is up with her. He'll be far from pleased with me. He's on the golf course today.'

Victoria took a deep breath. She had to share her thoughts with him. 'Doctor, do you think it could be heart damage caused by rheumatic fever?'

He shot up in his chair. 'The doctor who saw her last night and took the history hasn't mentioned rheumatic fever. I know, because I've read his notes twice. It is so common, it would have been the first thing he asked her.'

He picked up the notes and scanned the entry from the admission doctor to reassure himself that he hadn't missed anything.

'Mind you, the poor sod had been working five days and nights, straight through.'

'Maybe he didn't ask?' said Victoria.

The doctor looked at Victoria in surprise and then jumped up from his seat and strode down the ward. She caught up with him just as he reached the bed and heard him ask, 'Mrs Mulhearn, did you ever have rheumatic fever as a child?'

'Oh, yes, doctor. I was laid up with it for over two years. Couldn't move a muscle, I couldn't. The doctor in Ireland said it was the worst case he had ever seen. Ready for me to die, they was.'

Staff Nurse approached the end of the bed. 'Time for you to go with the first lot for coffee, Nurse Baker, and thank you. I will take over here now.'

Victoria almost floated down the ward. She had been a nurse for only hours and yet she was already in love with her job. She felt closer to her mother than she had since the day she died. Her heart cramped as she looked back at Mrs Mulhearn. If only someone had correctly diagnosed her mother. Would her tragic death have been avoided? And, if it had, would Victoria even be here today in Lovely Lane?

CHAPTER 13

As soon as Sister Haycock discovered that Pammy had been allocated to ward two, with Sister Antrobus, she demanded a meeting with Matron.

Known among the hospital staff as the Anteater, and military trained, Sister Antrobus had a reputation fiercer than that of any other ward sister in St Angelus. A trail of abandoned careers pointed to the fact that it was a reputation well earned and fully deserved. More nurses had given up partway through their training after a short spell on ward two than on any other ward. Her height, her width, her steel-grey hair and matching grey eyes perfectly complemented her stern personality. Sister Antrobus was both demanding and unforgiving.

Before the new training syllabus for professional nursing qualifications was introduced at St Angelus, nurse training had been Matron's responsibility, and it still was in many hospitals across the country, where the matron had been allowed to resist change. At St Angelus, Matron saw losing control of the new school of nursing as an affront to her own status. She was also of the opinion that Emily Haycock, always a pushy one, went too far with the board of trustees and got her own way a little too often. Although Emily, as director of nursing, was responsible for the training of the new probationers, the wards and every other aspect of running St Angelus remained firmly under the control of Matron.

A reply from Matron to Emily's demand arrived promptly, calling Sister Haycock for an early-morning meeting.

'Don't you let her eat you, now,' Biddy joked, just before Emily left. 'You know her bark is worse than her bite.'

'Don't joke about bites. You know she brings her flaming dog to work with her and he sits all day in a basket behind her desk.'

'I do,' Biddy almost shouted, impatient to disclose a piece of gossip that up until now she had forgotten. 'He bit Matron's housekeeper the other day and she hit him with the mop. Matron near went mad, so she did, and threatened to sack her. More worried about the dog she was than Elsie's leg, but Elsie's still here. That's what I mean. Matron's all bluster.'

'I heard about that,' said Emily. It was an understatement. Everyone had heard. The dog, Blackie, was a fierce and bad-tempered Scottie dog who put the fear of God into everyone when he was sent out on to the grass for his two-hourly comfort break. Office doors could be heard clicking shut and hurried footsteps scuttled across polished concrete floors. No one crossed Blackie's path. In the administration block, he was as powerful as Matron herself, and the confident way he strutted and held his head high told everyone that he knew it too.

'Here, take a biscuit, and if he gets a bit bolshy, throw it to him. Better that than your ankle,' said Biddy.

'Shall I do the same with Matron?' asked Emily. 'Shall I throw the biscuit at her if she gets a bit bolshy?'

As she walked into Matron's office, Emily saw Blackie sit up in his basket to inspect her. She felt the biscuit in her pocket and it gave her some comfort.

'Good morning, Sister Haycock. What can I do for you?' Matron didn't stand up. She remained behind her desk, looking down at a letter on her blotter. 'Lie down, Blackie,' she said, coolly. Emily waited politely for her to finish reading the letter and noticed that her dark, tightly styled hair was, as always, rigidly in place. A style which had never altered, not even by an errant wisp, in the years since Emily had first met her when she arrived at St Angelus. Now she was director of the school of nursing and responsible for all probationer training. This had provided her with an armoury of confidence and self-belief she had never before possessed. It was a change in attitude Matron had found disconcerting.

Emily knew that she had not been Matron's choice for the job, anything but. The huge changes imposed by the government had not been Matron's choice either. She had fought those tooth and nail and had even written a letter of protest to the Prime Minister. She would have preferred to continue in the old way, as a voluntary organization, as they had before the war and before the introduction of the NHS. Who would have thought the government would begin to exert such control over the running of hospitals? *As you have no experience of working in a hospital, Prime Minister, I feel that maybe you should leave the running of them to those of us who do,* she had written. *The methods prescribed by Florence Nightingale have served us all well until now. Regarding nursing as a professional qualification is a nonsense. It is a vocation.*

She had also remonstrated with the trustees, now under the control of the Liverpool Hospitals District Board. The government was interfering there too. *These girls marry and then that's the end of it. We don't allow nurses to be married. Nursing is for dedicated women. A job for life.* Matron had argued with members of the new board until she was blue in the face, but it was no use. The winds of post-war modernity were sweeping across the country and had arrived at the steps of St Angelus.

Emily had decided before she had walked into the office that, Blackie or no Blackie, she would stand her ground and take no nonsense from Matron. All the same, as she approached the administration block she felt a familiar weakness in the knees. Every nurse who had ever worked under Matron's authority knew that feeling.

'Shall I sit, Matron?' she asked, with an airiness she certainly didn't feel. Despite the biscuit in her pocket, her earlier confidence had stubbornly remained at the door.

Matron glanced up. Her olive complexion made her appear ageless although her hair, once jet black, was now shot through with grey. She looked Emily up and down with her dark and unforgiving brown eyes. It was her way with every nurse she met. Always looking for a crease or a stain on an apron, or a pair of shoes that required a polish. Now there was hurt in her eyes too as she examined Emily.

She had promoted Nurse Haycock to ward sister herself, only to have her stab her in the back and apply for the position of the director of nursing as soon as it became available. A position of which Matron did not approve, as everyone knew. It was almost as though Emily were waiting to apply for Matron's own job. Matron knew it, and she thought everyone must know that Emily Haycock was most definitely after her post. But although she might think Matron was heading for her dotage, she was wrong.

'We just have to be one step ahead of that little madam, don't we, Blackie?' she had confided, as they waited for Emily to arrive. 'We aren't stupid, are we? She is plotting to combine the roles of

273

director of nursing and matron. We just have to be a little bit smarter than she is, don't we, boy?' If she had to accept a director of the school of nursing, Matron would much rather the post had been filled by an outsider. Someone she could have taught her own methods from day one, but so much more than that, someone she could have made her friend. Matron so badly needed a friend.

'Please, do sit.' Matron raised her eyebrows as Blackie growled, but it was just a warning shot. His wicker basket creaked and crackled as he settled down. Emily craned her neck to check that he had in fact lain back and was not slipping out. Blackie saw her, lifted his head and bared his teeth before he closed his eyes. His ears remained pricked.

'How are the new intake progressing?' Matron asked with a chilly politeness, as soon as Emily was seated. 'It's their first day on the wards, is it not?'

'It is, Matron, and that is why I asked to speak to you. If you don't mind, I would like to ask for your advice about a very delicate situation.'

Matron visibly thawed and a smile almost reached her lips. This was more like it. Emily Haycock was seeking her guidance, rather than charging off with her own ideas.

She leant forward and put her elbows on the desk. 'I am happy to help, as you know. Of course I am. I looked after the probationers for forty years until the government thought it knew how to run my hospital better than I. What can I do to help? Would you like some tea? Shall I ring for Elsie? Blackie, no!' At the mention of Elsie's name, Blackie had growled.

Emily almost took the easy way out. Should she accept the tea? Ask imaginary questions, butter Matron up? Pander to her sense of superiority and self-importance? Would that serve any purpose? With a heavy heart, she decided it would not. The problem would still be there and it was one she had to fix. It was her responsibility. Her new probationer nurses must take priority. She would try as hard as she could to charm Matron, but her girls must come first. She took a deep breath and began.

'The problem is a little delicate. I . . . er, I . . . well . . .' Her voice wobbled and almost deserted her. 'I have grave concerns regarding the conduct of Sister Antrobus on ward two. You may not be aware of this, but she has been directly responsible for three resignations from the school of nursing in the past year.' Her confidence returned and she eased into full flow. 'Placing a probationer nurse on her ward is as good as saying goodbye to that nurse and I'm afraid I have to step in. I cannot allow this to continue. I have tried to speak to Sister Antrobus myself, but she simply will not . . .' She stopped mid-sentence as Matron raised her hand. The warmth that had been in the room just a few moments earlier had vanished in a flash.

'Indeed, I am aware that you've tried to speak

to her. She told me. I had wondered if you were aware that qualified staff are my responsibility, not yours?'

Emily swallowed. She was very aware that this was the case and wished it weren't. There was a difficult disconnect between the school of nursing and the general day-to-day operation of the hospital. If she had responsibility for the placement of the probationer nurses, she was sure, there would be far fewer problems. Blackie fixed her with a beady eye. The change of atmosphere in the room had made him positively bristle.

'I thought that you would already know, Matron. However, when it comes to the placement of probationer nurses, it would make my job impossible if I couldn't have any dialogue with the ward sisters. I assure you, I have a very good relationship with everyone on all of the wards, except for Sister Antrobus. She refuses to acknowledge the effect her manner has on probationers. Indeed, having been a nurse on her ward myself in my younger days, I can say that her style of nursing has a negative impact on patients too.'

Matron drew an audible intake of breath. It was one thing to criticize a ward sister for her failings and how they affected nursing staff, quite another to involve the patients. She placed the letter she had been reading back into its envelope with a calmness that concealed her inner flare of anger. Sister Antrobus was the nearest she had to a friend. Matron had appointed her, and they shared a dedication to the job as well as to the status of single women. Both vehemently opposed any notion of married women being allowed to nurse. Nursing and St Angelus were their life. They occasionally had lunch together. Matron was looking forward to cooking for Sister Antrobus this Friday evening. She thought a great deal of Sister Antrobus. In fact, she thought of her a great deal. It had worried her at first how much she thought about her, but she had decided that it was her own personal secret and no one else knew.

'Sister Haycock, I can assure you that I have received no complaints regarding Sister Antrobus, and having visited her ward only yesterday I can say with absolute confidence that I wholly approve of her *style*, as you call it. I had no idea that we were teaching our probationers *style* these days.' Her nose wrinkled in disdain.

Emily knew. Everyone knew, from nurse to porter, about the close relationship between Matron and Sister Antrobus. It was the basis of smutty jokes in the lodge among the porter's lads. Emily knew there wasn't a probationer who wouldn't have heard the hints within her first week. It was why Emily wanted to treat Matron gently. She would not tolerate a word of the gossip. In fact, any probationer nurse who did utter a word of jest at the expense of Sister Antrobus and Matron would find herself in Emily's office. Respect was the first thing Emily drilled into her probationers. For patients and for each other. For the doctors and senior nurses on the wards. For the teaching staff at the school. For Matron and Sister Antrobus, and especially for the people who kept the hospital running, Dessie, Biddy, Elsie and all the orderlies and domestics.

'Matron—' Emily never got the chance to ask her question. Matron cut her off yet again.

'Who is the probationer on ward two?' she asked abruptly. As though the name would make any difference at all to the overbearing behaviour of Sister Antrobus.

'Nurse Tanner.'

'Oh, yes, Nurse Tanner. She is resident at the Lovely Lane home, isn't she? The nurse whose corner you fought with Mr Scriven? He has asked me to keep an eye on that particular young lady.' Matron looked smug and Emily felt sick. 'As a member of the board, he has every right to do so.'

Emily wondered if she had just made things worse for Pammy. Matron, realizing she was on stronger ground, forged on.

'He would very much like to know how she performs once she is let loose on the patients. He is very concerned that we are allowing our standards to drop and I have to agree. She is the first nurse we have taken from the dock road. Mr Scriven thought you had gone quite mad.'

Emily felt her colour rise and took a deep breath before she spoke. Only the dog knew she was a hair's breadth away from losing her temper. Neither Matron nor any of the board members knew that the place of her birth and her true home had been only yards away from Pammy Tanner's. Emily swore to herself that one day she would let Matron and Mr Scriven know exactly where she originated from, but when she did, it would be at a moment of her choosing. Revenge was a dish best served cold.

'Are you telling me that you approve of the way Sister Antrobus intimidates probationer nurses with nothing more than her temper and an irrational bad mood? Do you think there is a place in modern nursing for such an overbearing and high-handed attitude?'

'I don't agree with your assessment of Sister Antrobus one little bit, Sister Haycock. If *style* is what you have come here to discuss with me, I am afraid you have wasted your time and mine. Given Mr Scriven's concern, I am delighted Nurse Tanner will begin her training on ward two. If she hasn't got what it takes, we will know sooner rather than later and she won't waste any more of our time.'

Emily had had enough. The ignorance and prejudice were beginning to suffocate her. She knew Matron was unmovable. Without another word, she stood and walked to the door. As she turned the handle, she plucked up an extra thread of courage and turned back.

'I'm afraid that if Sister Antrobus intimidates Nurse Tanner and I find myself with yet another nurse leaving before she has finished her probationary training, then I shall have to call an emergency meeting of the trustees to discuss Sister Antrobus's position. We invest a great deal in our probationer nurses. One loss alone costs the hospital a considerable amount of money, not to speak of the investment in time and effort that Sister Ryan and I dedicate to each course and each nurse. In the same way you will be watching Nurse Tanner, I shall be watching Sister Antrobus. She has frightened away her last probationer nurse. I cannot stand by and watch it happen again.'

With that, Emily opened the door and left the room to sudden barks from Blackie, who left his basket and flew across the floor towards the rapidly closing door. Emily almost leant against the other side. Her heart was beating hard, drops of perspiration had broken out on her top lip and there was only one place she wanted to be: with Biddy back in the school of nursing. Despite the trembling of her knees, she flew down the stairs and across the hospital grounds. No one ever stood up to Matron and she wasn't sure if she would be made to pay in some way for what she had just said.

'Well, I never. You gave her what for then,' said Biddy as she poured them both a cup of tea in the kitchen after hearing every detail of the encounter.

'I don't know about that, but I've done what I can for Nurse Tanner. Now we just have to pray.'

280

'Don't worry about that little girl,' said Biddy. 'I've already asked Branna to keep an eye on her. She's the cleaner on ward two, and she comes from Waterford. Her mammy's sister's son married a girl who was a Brogan. Isn't that just the thing, with us having a Nurse Brogan? I've told her, Nurse Tanner is the best of friends with Nurse Brogan, so Branna will keep a good watch out for her, and if things go wrong, she'll make sure I know about it pretty quickly.'

Emily laughed. 'You and your Irish Mafia. You're everywhere.'

'Ah, well, don't begrudge us that now, we have to be. We've been through a lot, so we have. We all have to look out for each other.'

Emily remembered the notices she had read when looking for lodgings. Time and again the adverts read *No Irish*. Emily knew exactly what Biddy meant.

As Biddy busied herself about the kitchen, Emily drank her tea and looked out of the window towards the main building and the wards. The sky had darkened and the rain had begun to fall heavily. She would leave herself before she would stand by and see another nurse driven from St Angelus in tears, abandoning a career she had been born to. If it came to that, she would take Sister Antrobus down with her. And whatever the outcome, Maisie Tanner's daughter would survive.

'Mr Gaskell came while you were out, the

younger one, that is. He left an envelope on your desk so he did.'

'Oh, yes. That will be the lecture notes he wants me to take a look at.'

'Really,' said Biddy, narrowing her eyes and fixing Emily with a meaningful stare. 'Are you sure about that? Because the thing is, he came twice before I could persuade him to agree to leave the envelope. Mighty keen he was to give it to you in person, if you ask me.'

Emily blushed. Biddy held her like a rabbit in the headlights as she tried to think of a suitable response. 'Well, I shall prove it to you,' she said at last, marching towards her desk. She masked her disappointment as she extracted four sheets of paper from the envelope. 'See, Biddy? Lecture notes, just as I said.'

Biddy was clearing away the tea things as she spoke. 'That's as maybe, but I'm no fool. He was keen to see you, and Dr Gaskell strikes me as a man in a dreadful hurry. I wouldn't keep him hanging around too long.'

Emily pretended to look offended as she placed the lecture notes in her desk drawer, ready to read later. She knew Biddy was right, but she had given so much of herself to her career that there had been no time for men, and besides, what man would take her once he knew her secret, what her life was really like? Would honour her obligation as his own? None, she was quite sure of that. She had made her decision, her bed and her promises, and now she had to keep them. She had little time left if she ever wanted a child. She knew that, and in her heart she also knew that she had sacrificed one love for another. She would never know the joy of holding her own baby in her arms.

Emily bit her lip. There was nothing she could do. She was trapped. She glanced at the ornate radiator and saw that they were gone, and looking at her shelf she spied the brown paper bag. Inside, would be the pyjamas, folded and ironed.

'I did them while you were gone,' said Biddy. 'You don't have to tell me, it's none of my business, but if there is anything I can do to help, you know where I am.'

Emily blushed and looked back down at her desk. 'Thank you, Biddy.' Her voice was the faintest whisper.

'Eh, did you know there's no limit on cocoa powder from this week? We can use the vouchers for something else. They've gone mad in the kitchens. I'll go and fetch us a couple of slices of the chocolate Victoria sandwich Cook has made. She's putting cocoa in everything. There'll be a dusting on the rashers at tea.'

Emily smiled. She knew exactly what Biddy was doing. She had skilfully changed the subject, respecting Emily's secret. 'Chocolate Victoria sandwich? I've never heard of such a thing.'

'Well, in ten minutes from now you won't be able to stop yourself from talking about it,' Biddy shouted back from the stairwell.

Dessie stood at the bottom of the stairs with a brown canvas toolbag in his hand. Biddy had told him that Sister Haycock's sitting-room door wouldn't close properly and he had arrived to fix it, the first free moment he had. He hadn't meant to eavesdrop, but he couldn't help himself. He had had no idea Oliver Gaskell was sweet on Sister Haycock. But of course he is. Why wouldn't he be? thought Dessie. What man wouldn't be? You are a fool, man, he told himself. Why would a woman like her be interested in a man like you? The truth was that Dessie had admired Emily Haycock since first setting eyes upon her, but each time he thought he might ask her to join him for tea at the Lyons Corner House in Church Street he was crippled by one thought. *Why would a woman like her want to be seen out with a man like me?*

'I'm here, Biddy,' he shouted out, as he placed his boot on the wooden stair Biddy had scrubbed only that morning. His steps were heavier and slower than they would have been only five minutes earlier, weighed down by the disappointment resting in his heart.

That afternoon, Biddy arrived home later than usual and found Elsie waiting on her doorstep.

'Jesus, aren't ye the lucky one, only needing to work this morning,' she said. 'I was lucky to be out the door by four today and I was on the overhead railway at half five on me way in this morning.

284

I thought the day would never end. Been waiting long, have ye?'

'I knew you were on your way, Biddy. Dessie came down the street half an hour since and he said you was on the same bus as he was, but that you were off to the shop.'

'Did he now?' said Biddy, as she put her key in the lock. 'Sure, I can't sneeze without you all knowing me business, can I?' She was only half joking and Elsie knew it.

'Oh, don't take on, Biddy. I was only after a natter. Tell me, when you went into the shop, were they all talking about our Martha and Jake and asking whether they're courting?'

'No, they were not. They were talking about the price of fish. It might surprise you to know there are some people in Liverpool who have no notion that your Martha is courting Jake and that he has an electric washer mangle machine on order from Blackler's for that house of his. Is that what you want to tell me, because I already heard it from Dessie this morning. Does this mean you won't be coming down to the Clare Street wash house with me on Saturdays any more?'

'Of course I will. There'll be no gossip to be had in our Martha's kitchen and besides, when would I get to see everyone?'

Since the day Martha and Jake had been courting, Elsie had spoken of nothing else except the possibility that they might one day wed and it was beginning to drive Biddy to distraction. The fact that Dessie had already imparted the riveting, all important electric washer mangle news had taken the wind clean out of her sails. Elsie had little in her life to look forward to. A wedding and an electric washer mangle for Martha would be enough to keep her bragging down at the Claire Street wash house for a year.

Biddy felt slightly guilty at the sight of her friend's crestfallen face. She knew that Elsie would have been waiting all day to tell her. An electric mangle was very big news. 'Fancy a cuppa then?' She knew full well that this was the best way to get around Elsie's disappointment.

'Aye, go one, if you're having one.'

'Ye know I am, and that the back door is always open. Ye could have had the kettle on by now, ye lazy mare.'

The front door creaked open, letting them both into the narrow, dark hallway. They were met by the wail of the fatter-than-was-good-for-him black cat, who darted from the shadows and pressed himself up against Biddy's legs.

'Ah, would ye come here, little fella,' she said, putting her heavy shopping bag down on the dark brown lino and bending down to stroke him. She had given the stray a home soon after she began having children. They had all long since left, but the old faithful cat sat on her lap at night and kept her company, and in return for his loyalty Biddy looked after him well and fed him half of every biscuit she ate.

'I have a bit of Spam for ye in my bag,' she murmured now as she picked up the string holdall and walked into the kitchen.

'Did you take that from the hospital?' asked Elsie in an accusatory tone.

'I did. It was being thrown in the pig bin. No harm in a bit of leftovers coming here for the cat.'

Elsie didn't like cats. She begrudged this one the large slice of Spam she saw Biddy take out of her bag. 'Would have done nicely for my tea, that, with a few taters,' she said as she watched Biddy purr over the animal. Elsie liked dogs even less than cats since Blackie had bitten her.

'We had your Sister Haycock in Matron's office today,' she said. 'I had my ear to the door. Gave Matron what for, she did. Sister Haycock did well to get out of the room before the dog went for her. Vicious, nasty little thing that it is.' As she spoke, Elsie reached down and stroked her leg where the bite had almost healed although the skin was still red and sore.

'Aye, well, she's not daft, that one, so she isn't and I'll tell you this, she holds her ground.'

'I've heard her mother was the same,' said Elsie, 'until she got sick, that was. Dessie tells me that bomb on George Street, it was more like a silver bullet, putting her mother out of her misery. But for the others, her little brothers God rest their souls, it was different altogether.' Elsie crossed herself as she spoke. 'Imagine, terrible. Those poor little 'uns.'

Dessie was the source and keeper of all gossip. The porter's lodge was the hub of hospital news and even Matron could occasionally be seen entering or leaving, in an attempt to gather her own intelligence.

'Sure, I've not mentioned the bomb to her meself,' said Biddy. 'She never has to me, either. I'd like to, mind. There are some days when that poor woman looks like she has the weight of the world on her shoulders and there's no man to speak of, ye know. I've not asked as much, but she would have mentioned someone, for sure. Told me she's in lodgings. She won't live in the Lovely Lane home, or in the accommodation in the hospital, where she could have her own room and a sitting room if she wanted. She said that if she did, it would be uncomfortable for the nurses.'

'No such luck for me,' Elsie snorted. 'No sign of Matron ever leaving her rooms at the hospital. I'll be cleaning those until I drop.' Matron's rooms were situated above the main entrance to the hospital, and from her windows she could see every person who entered and left St Angelus. 'And she's entertaining on Friday. I had to do the shopping this morning, as well as lay the table and polish the dining room for her. Our Martha has it much easier.'

'She's working on that house with Jake. That's a full-time job in itself.' Biddy poured the tea and flopped down on her wooden kitchen chair. 'Tea never tastes the same out of those green cups at the hospital.' She slurped loudly from her very chipped old china cup. Elsie tipped the spilt tea from her saucer into hers.

'Anyway, I have news,' she said. 'You need to keep an eye on your Sister Haycock's back. After she left today, Mr Scriven came into Matron's office not ten minutes later.' Biddy raised her eyebrows. 'See, I knew that would surprise you. He has it in for Sister Haycock. I heard him tell Matron that she had humiliated him in front of the board, and wasn't it bad enough that he had been overruled in the first place when she was appointed to be director of the school. He told Matron Dr Gaskell was making some very bad choices and his judgement was all out, choosing his own son and the wrong sort of nurses. It was his age, he said. Losing it he was, he said. You should have heard him going on, Biddy. He was mad. Ranting about the young Mr Gaskell, he was, said the shame of having two consultants on one ward looked bad on him. He didn't draw breath.'

'Well, that I can imagine,' said Biddy, taking out her cigarettes. She didn't like what Elsie was telling her. She could sense danger a mile away and her skin tightened with fear. Sister Haycock was her charge and Biddy would have her back if it was the last thing she did.

'Did he say anything else, about Sister Haycock, or any of the nurses?'

'Oh, aye, did he. Said he wanted an eye keeping

on the nurses he had said were not good enough for St Angelus and any slip-up from any one of those would be, er, what was the word?' There was silence as Elsie appeared to disappear inside her teacup. Biddy lit her cigarette and slid the ashtray across the kitchen table towards her friend.

'What, what was the bloody word?' she shouted.

'Hang on. It was a big word. I can't remember.'

'What? Remember, you eejit.' Biddy was growing impatient.

'Biddy, if you shout at me like that I will never remember.' Elsie looked flustered. 'Terminal, that was it, terminal.'

'Terminal,' Biddy repeated slowly.

'What does it mean, Biddy? I wish I knew, but I don't think that man is the saint everyone makes him out to be. He's trouble, that one. I think he bullies Matron a bit. Even the bloody dog is scared of him. We need to watch him.'

Both women raised their cups to their lips to finish the last drops of their tea.

'Hmm, terminal,' they both said, at the same time.

CHAPTER 14

'Well, unless I'm mistaken, there's not a lot of nursing can be done from there!' Pammy almost jumped out of her skin as a ward domestic in the customary mustard brown wraparound apron came up behind her with a bucket on a low wheelie trolley and a mop smelling strongly of Lysol.

Pammy had been hovering outside the door of ward two, wondering what to do and where she should go. She had been told by Mrs Duffy to report promptly to the door of the sister's office by eight forty-five, where she would be met by Sister Antrobus.

Branna had been given her instructions by Biddy. She was to watch Nurse Tanner like a hawk and report anything that appeared even slightly untoward. 'And if you so much as hear the word "terminal" mentioned, you get on the phone and tell me.'

'Terminus?' said Branna. 'And what would that mean?'

'I have no idea,' said Biddy, 'but it isn't good now so it isn't and you must let me know straight away.'

Pammy had stood on tiptoe and peeped through the two circular viewing windows in the doors. The previous week, the entire intake had been taken on a full tour of the wards and departments. Sister Ryan had taken one group, Sister Haycock the other. Now that she was standing here alone, Pammy's knees were almost knocking together in fear. She was about to face Sister Antrobus and all she wanted to do was run.

'Oh, God, I'm sorry. It's me first day,' Pammy squeaked.

'I know it is, love,' said Branna. 'I know who you are, too. I've been asked to keep an eye on ye. Now don't ye worry, just remember I'm here if ye need me, but don't go tellin' anyone else I said that now, do ye hear me? They don't like us and the nurses talking to each other, but we do it all the same. Mind, there's some nurses think they are too high and mighty altogether to talk to the domestics.' Branna whispered the last few words and winked at Pammy. Not trusting herself to speak, Pammy nodded. She had no idea what to say in response. How did Branna know who she was? Who had asked her to keep an eye out, and why?

'If ye have a problem, ask any of the orderlies or the domestics to find Branna. You got that?'

'I have, yes. Thanks, Branna, but what sort of problem might I have?'

'Oh, nothing at all. Sure, there will be nothing to worry about at all, not a thing, no, nothing.' It was as obvious to Pammy as the nose on Branna's face that she was lying. 'Now, when you go in through them doors, you see the first door on your left, that's the sister's office. They will all be in there, about to start report. Here, listen while I tell ye. See this door?' Branna pushed a dark wooden door behind Pammy. 'This is the ward cloakroom. Your uniforms will be delivered here and will be hanging on your peg each day. The laundry bag to put your dirty in is behind the door. It's a bit of a pain, but if you live in Lovely Lane best you change at night, before you leave, and go home in clean. That way, you leave all the dirty here in the bag, so.'

Pammy nodded. They had all been taught this in the classroom by Sister Ryan, but Pammy didn't want to upset Branna, who was being so helpful. Cross-contamination and barrier nursing had taken a whole day of lectures.

'Come here,' Branna said. 'Give me your cape. I'll hang it up for you. Here's another tip. I know your name is on the tape, but there's a little way to make it easier to know it's yours. You can usually tell – some are much older than others and there are nurses here who are wearing the same capes they had before the war – but if you're on wards with other new nurses you'll never know whose is whose. See this one here?' Branna stretched up and pulled back the skirt of a cape, and Pammy noticed a small lilac ribbon sewn on the inside hem.

'See that? That way, you only ever take home

your own cape. It can't be something obvious on the outside now, but just something to catch your eye when you pull the cape back, to save you having to take them all off the pegs to look at the name tapes.'

Branna put down her bucket and leant her mop against the wall. 'Now, you take one big breath, go through those double doors and knock on Sister's door. Remember, you are as good as anyone else in that office and don't let Sister Antrobus make you think any different.' With that, Branna slipped Pamela's cloak from her shoulders and almost pushed her through the swing double doors into the ward.

'Come in.' Sister Antrobus's voice was so loud that Pammy nearly jumped out of her skin. She tried to turn the round, dark brown Bakelite door-knob, but it wouldn't respond. She tried again. The knob rattled under the pressure and again the words 'Come in' rang out, but this time with more than a hint of impatience.

Suddenly, the door flew open. All Pammy had needed to do was push. She flushed red with embarrassment.

'Who are you?' Sister Antrobus looked Pammy up and down.

'I'm Nurse Tanner, Sister Antrobus,' Pammy responded.

'Are you really?' Sister Antrobus said sourly as she turned on her heel and walked back into the office. Pammy remained standing in the doorway.

Opposite Sister Antrobus sat a nurse wearing a woolly navy cardigan. She looked absolutely exhausted. Pammy assumed she had been on night duty and was handing over to the day staff. She turned her head and looked down the ward at the rows of beds lining the walls and saw another nurse. She was also wearing a navy cardigan. Pammy shivered. The first signs of spring had been in the air this morning as she had walked from Lovely Lane to the hospital. The sun had shone weakly, and for the first time she had heard a bird singing. It was a sound that stood out against the familiar daily call of the seagulls. A nurse in a light blue dress with a petersham belt secured with the St Angelus silver buckle also sat on another chair at the side of the large oak desk. The uniform indicated that she was a staff nurse. Behind her stood a row of girls, pencils and paper in hand, wearing the pale pink dresses and frilled caps of student nurses, who were clearly day staff. Sister Antrobus wore the dark navy sisters' uniform and looked every bit as severe as Pammy had been told she would. This was the moment when Pammy realized a truly dreadful fact. One which made her mouth dry and her legs turn to water. She was late.

'Stand there and listen.' Sister Antrobus didn't look at Pammy, but distractedly pointed to a group of nurses standing against the back wall. Pammy immediately did as she was instructed, thinking that maybe Sister's bark was worse than her bite and that the older nurses in Lovely Lane had exaggerated.

Sister Antrobus shifted her spectacles upwards with a twitch of her nose and peered through them at Pammy, as though she were a specimen to be examined and found wanting. 'The official start time for day staff may be eight forty-five, but on ward two, it is eight thirty. I like to begin early, in order to receive a more detailed report from the night staff.' Pammy thought she saw a look of weary despair flit across the face of the night nurse.

She watched with intense interest as the nurse lifted a card from a long wooden frame containing all the patients' details, concentrating so hard that she had almost stopped breathing. The nurse lifted the first flap and read out a patient's name. 'Mrs Toft, bed one.'

Pammy didn't want to miss a word and quickly looked at the nurses standing against the opposite wall for guidance. They had the advantage of standing behind Sister Antrobus. A second-year nurse had her pen poised, ready to write, and nodded towards Pammy's pocket, indicating that she should do the same. She smiled encouragingly at Pammy, who took her own pencil and small red Silverline notebook out of her apron pocket. Sister Ryan had told them they would need to have pen and paper with them at all times and be prepared to write down any instruction given by a doctor.

'Never try to remember it in your head,' Sister Ryan had said. 'That is how mistakes happen and mistakes cost lives.'

Pammy had no idea what she was supposed to write, but she reckoned that if she followed suit when the helpful nurse opposite began to scribble her notes she should be safe. She was too focused to notice that the other nurses weren't yet writing anything down.

'Mrs Marchmont, bed two, post-operative D and C and EUA. TPRs as normal. Pulse 80, BP 120 over 80 resps 22. PV loss now moderate to light. Visited by the houseman at ten p.m. when she complained of low abdominal pain. Analgesia given at ten thirty p.m. and now written up for dihydrocodeine PRN. Houseman says to remain on bed rest until PV bleeding is light for three full days. She slept well until three a.m. when we gave her a cup of tea and two more dihydrocodeine. She slept again once they had begun to work until six a.m. and ate a light early breakfast. She has passed urine this morning and had her bowels opened first thing, but of course, now she's on the dihydrocodeine, that won't happen again until the next Preston Guild. Mrs Sampson, bed three . . .'

Pammy looked down at her notes for Mrs Marchmont. The nurse had spoken faster than she could write and she couldn't remember all the abbreviations. Reading it back, she could barely understand what she had written and she was sure that she had taken much of it down wrong. She looked up anxiously and the sharp-looking, but obviously friendly nurse winked. Pammy breathed for what felt like the first time in minutes.

'What are you doing?' The question rang out through the office. Pammy felt her throat constrict and her mouth go dry. Sister Antrobus was looking directly at her. Pammy glanced around the room, hoping she was speaking to someone else.

'Nurse Tanner, I said what are you doing?'

'I was, er, writing down what the night nurse said, Sister Antrobus.'

'Really? It seems to me that you don't have a clue what you are doing. God alone knows what they teach over in that building. What a waste of money that was!'

Pammy thought she had to answer. That was her first big mistake. 'I, er, wasn't sure what I was supposed to do, Sister.' She looked towards the nurse who had guided her for reassurance and noticed that she had put her own paper and pencil in her pocket and would not meet Pammy's eye.

Pammy dried up and folded her hands, clutching her notebook in front of her.

'You don't write anything down until I issue the day report, and I do that when the night nurse has left. You write down the day report and instructions. You need only take note of what is to be done by you, not what the night nurses have already done. The night report is only for information. Do you understand?'

'I do now, Sister Antrobus,' Pammy replied with more confidence than she felt.

Sister Antrobus was unimpressed. 'In future, Nurse Tanner, simply reply yes Sister or no Sister. Again, I must ask you, do you understand?'

Pammy was not going to be caught out again. 'Yes, Sister,' she replied meekly.

She listened to the remainder of the night report in silence. Most of what the night nurse said sounded like a foreign language. Despite the past weeks in the school of nursing and the swotting up she had done on the gynae section of her book, she could barely pronounce, never mind spell, any of the words anyway.

The day report arrived soon enough and Pammy wrote down, for the first time ever, the names of patients, their conditions and what the day held in store for them. Then came the news she had been warned to expect.

'And you, Nurse Tanner, will be on the bedpan rounds, with responsibility for the sluice room. Staff Nurse Bates, will you keep Nurse Tanner with you today, please. If she leaves the sluice room or isn't scrubbing out bedpans.'

There were two staff nurses. Pammy could tell immediately which one was Staff Nurse Bates. She had lovely blonde hair, worn in the fashionable new urchin style. She winked discreetly at Pammy and gave her a warm smile. Pammy felt the breath she had been holding leave her body in relief.

'We have an entirely new clinical firm starting

on the ward today,' Sister Antrobus announced. 'The consultant is Mr Gaskell, the son of Dr Gaskell senior, our redoubtable senior medical physician. He has a registrar and of course his housemen and medical students. I already have his list of nursing requirements and I have to warn you, they are very different from those of our own Mr Scriven who has been consultant on this ward since nineteen thirty-two and knows exactly what he is doing. It would appear that we have some innovative methods coming out of the medical school, with the new wave of post-war doctors and their modern ideas. As if we haven't got enough to do. We are the first ward to have more than one consultant and clinical firm. We have Dr Gaskell to thank for that extra work.' Pammy glanced around at the other nurses in the office. Sister Antrobus seemed far from pleased about the arrival of the new consultant. The nurses appeared to be hanging on Sister Antrobus's every word. Too scared to even breathe, apart from the night nurse who was on her feet and ready to leave.

'There are many ward sisters in this hospital who will be envious of our status today, becoming a two-consultant ward. Think yourselves very lucky. Life may become more difficult, but that is a challenge we must be seen to relish. Brave face and all that. But remember this. It is Mr Scriven who is our first priority. He must and will always come first. This new Mr Gaskell has to earn his stripes.'

The night nurse, who had been trying to suppress a yawn, suddenly spoke.

'Sorry, Sister. There is a letter here for you. The porter brought it down last night.' She opened the desk drawer, took out an envelope and gave it to Sister Antrobus. Everyone thought that Sister Antrobus was about to explode. What if the night nurse hadn't heard what she said and had forgotten to give her the letter? A twelve-and-a-half-hour shift was no excuse. But Sister Antrobus was so intent on the letter that reprimanding the night nurse for shoddiness went clean out of her mind. She began to read the contents out loud as the night nurse slipped thankfully out of the room.

'Ah, it's from our new consultant, Mr Gaskell. I had thought it was from Mr Scriven.' A look of disappointment flitted across her face. 'He has written that he disapproves of long periods of bed rest.' Sister Antrobus looked over the top of her glasses at the assembled nurses, but if she had expected a shocked reaction she was disappointed. There was none. Shorter bed rest meant fewer bed baths. The day staff approved of Mr Gaskell already. She read a passage again, her lips moving rapidly, as if she couldn't quite believe what she had seen, before she continued, almost to herself: 'Well, I'm not sure I agree with that. As we know, Mr Scriven removes his post-hysterectomy abdominal sutures after fourteen days. Mr Gaskell is going to abandon the two-week rule and his are to be removed after eight days.' Sister Antrobus's voice had risen in disbelief. 'He also wants to introduce a new antiseptic wash called chlorhexidine instead of soap and water douches. He also writes that he *"will begin experimenting with metal clips for abdominal hysterectomies instead of catgut suturing"*. The chlorhexidine solution will be arriving on the ward today directly from pharmacy. He says we are to dilute one part chlorhexidine with twenty parts of warm water in a half-gallon jug. Don't anyone get any of that wrong.' She slammed the letter on the desk and looked round. Pammy felt her head lighten with the effort of absorbing all she had heard.

'Beds, now,' said Sister Antrobus. 'Every bed bath to be finished before coffee or there will be no coffee. I am off to Matron's office. Ward round is at ten. Theatre list starts at two. Don't anyone let Nurse Tanner give a nil by mouth a drink; we know how easily that can happen when a fool is on the ward.' With that, she flounced out of the room with the offending letter from Mr Gaskell in her hand and Pammy firmly on her radar.

As soon as Sister Antrobus had said 'Don't anyone get any of that wrong' Pammy had known her chances were slim. She had one stroke of luck, though: Staff Nurse Bates ('my name is Kate, but don't ever call me that on the ward') appeared to be nice and friendly, and Pammy thought she might at least survive the morning, if not the week.

'Come on then,' said Staff Nurse. 'Let's start

with the bedpans and then we can crack on with the beds.'

She walked very fast, and Pammy had to run to keep up.

'Gosh, stop. Don't ever run, will you? You'll be sent outside to stand in front of a firing squad if you do that. The head of the last nurse who ran on ward two is still on a spike on the banks of the Mersey.'

Pammy blanched, and Staff laughed. 'I'm only joking, you idiot. Right, this is the sluice room. And here is the bedpan trolley.' Staff took hold of the white enamel trolley at one end and swung it away from the wall. 'See how nice and clean the night nurses have left it? That is how Sister Antrobus expects it to be every minute of the day. It's not always possible, so just be aware, if she walks into the room while you are shovelling shit and thinking to yourself can life get any worse, it can. The Anteater can come in and show you by just how much.'

Pammy stood still, too afraid to speak or respond.

'Nurse Tanner, you will have to get used to something. Sister Antrobus will show you no mercy, ever. She will always find something wrong; she will never praise you for doing something right. Did you see the trick Nurse Jones pulled on you? Be careful there. She wants to be a staff nurse on this ward when she qualifies, and has a nasty turn about her. Sister Antrobus loves her. That won't be the only trick she will try to pull on you.'

'Oh, don't you worry,' said Pammy. 'I don't know how, but so help me God, I will get her back.'

'I bet you will.' Staff Nurse grinned. 'Of course, that post will be allocated by Matron, who will always be on the side of the Anteater. So don't say you haven't been warned. Right, now, listen.' She began pulling metal bedpans down from their resting place on top of a long warm pipe. Despite the pipe, the room was freezing, because the large sash windows were half open. 'Our bedpans on ward two contain more blood than anything else, and as you will see, a little goes a long, long way.' She laughed out loud as Pammy's own blood drained from her face once more.

'My best tip to you is to move as fast as you can and keep pulling the flush as soon as the tank fills. Just keep the water running. It helps with the smell, just a little.'

She had led Pammy to what looked like an over-sized toilet, with no seat and a huge tank attached to the wall behind it.

'Watch me.' She took an empty bedpan over to the long white shallow sink and filled it with water. 'See, you leave the sink taps running, don't turn them off ever. You take the dirty pan from the trolley, tip and flush at the same time – that way you get rid of the smell faster – then turn and shove it straight under the running tap, leave it and lean back for the next one. When you have two in the sink you begin the scrubbing with this.' Staff picked up a bristle brush and a container of detergent. 'Try not to get too much of this neat on to your skin; it bloody well burns. Then, with two pans clean, you pop them up on to the pipe and take the next dirty from the trolley and begin again.'

'Right, I've got that,' said Pammy. 'I've changed a few bad nappies in my time. I'll be fine.' Her voice sounded far more confident than she felt.

Staff Nurse smiled. 'Well, maybe you can tell me the difference after you have worked on one of the general surgical wards. Here's a couple of golden rules to help you survive. Don't ever be caught smoking in the bathroom when you are bathing a patient. Some of the new charge nurses are really fine about that on their wards and some will even slip you a ciggie to take in with you, but not on here. On some wards you can have a ciggie in the dayroom with the patients, and God love her, Sister on ward nine smokes when she's chatting to patients. She says it makes them feel better if she has one with them when she's giving them a bit of bad news. But on here, Sister Antrobus is very, very weird about it. She has a no smoking rule. When I'm desperate I sneak into the bathroom when it's empty and lean out of the window, and I actually saw her once, when I came back out, walking around the ward with her nose in the air, trying to trace the smell. She's never caught me, though, and by the way, the patients hate her. She never stops going on at them about smoking in their beds.

'Always be one step ahead of her. Never bring a whole packet on to the ward, just slip a couple into your apron pocket. You can always cadge a match from a patient. They all smoke, the patients. Every one of them has ciggies and matches in their handbags. The domestics clean the bedside ashtrays, not us, so you don't have to do that. We have enough to do.'

By the time ten o'clock arrived, Pammy had no idea how she hadn't yet thrown up. She had helped her mam and other women in her street change a baby's nappy often enough, and she had even cleaned up Lorraine's vomit when she was ill, but they weren't grown women and there had been no blood to deal with. There were times during the morning when, more than once, she had to hold on to the side of the huge white sink and let the water run clear as she swallowed deep, deep gulps of air. It was her first morning, her first bedpan round, and she wished it were her last. Four more rounds faced her before her shift was over. As soon as she had finished the bedpans, she headed straight back out on to the ward to find Staff Nurse Bates and help her with the round known as backs and beds. She was terrified she hadn't left the sluice room clean enough or had done something wrong, and worried that she had taken ages longer than she should have.

She found Staff Nurse behind a set of drawn pink curtains at the bedside of a patient. She was nervous, feeling as though she maybe needed to wait to be asked to enter, or knock on something.

'For goodness' sake, come in.' Staff leant over the bed and pulled the curtain back. 'This is Mrs Toft.' Staff smiled at the patient, who was lying flat on her back in the bed. 'Mrs Toft will be with us for a while, won't you, my lovely?'

Mrs Toft grinned back at her. 'I do wish you would call me Dottie, Staff Nurse,' she said.

'God, so do I,' Staff Nurse replied, 'but if I did, Sister would have my guts for garters. This is our new probationer, Nurse Tanner.'

Pammy smiled at the painfully thin woman in the bed. She recognized the name and knew from the day report she was a cancer patient healing from a radical vulvectomy, and she had to steel herself not to show a scrap of emotion on her face as she helped to remove the draw sheet from under her and replace it with a new one. Dottie weighed next to nothing and Staff said, 'While I hold her up, Nurse Tanner, you give her bum a good old rub for me.'

Pammy didn't need to have that explained to her. Sister Ryan had hammered home the care of pressure points and bedsores, and although she had only ever practised on a dummy she knew exactly what needed to be done. She tipped the surgical spirit from the bottle on the trolley into the palm of her hand and rubbed the bony coccyx of Mrs Toft as with almost no effort whatsoever Nurse Bates held her up off the clean draw sheet.

Staff Nurse set Mrs Toft back down for a moment while Pammy placed the top back on the brown ribbed bottle of surgical spirit.

'Now take the lid off the tin of zinc and castor oil cream and I'll lift her again. Are you ready, my lovely?' Staff Nurse smiled down at Mrs Toft and a look of trust and affection passed between them.

'OK then, one, two, three.' She lifted Mrs Toft but this time Pammy could see that the effort showed on her face. 'Cover her hips too.'

The antiseptic smell of the thick white cream filled the air as Pammy scooped out a generous amount and rubbed it in, working as fast as she could.

'Now, sprinkle some of that talcum powder on to her back. It stops the sheet pulling her skin one way while we move her another. Then slide the rubber ring into a clean pillow case and place it underneath her.'

Staff put Dottie Toft down for a moment and then lifted her again, and Pammy was touched by her tenderness as she whispered, 'Are you all right, my lovely? This isn't hurting you, is it?'

Dottie, a woman who had suffered a great deal, nodded. 'I'm fine.'

'Good, because that is all we want, isn't it? For you to be happy and to feel well again. Don't you worry about anything. We will have you right as rain as soon as we can.'

As they gently laid Dottie back down on the ring, Pammy saw Dottie's wound for the first time. She felt nauseous. *God, please no, don't let me faint.*

After they finished her bed bath, Staff picked up Dorothy's tin of Irresistible talcum powder and shook it under her breasts and arms. The air became filled with white powdery clouds as they all coughed and spluttered. 'And a bit for me too,' Staff laughed as she pulled open the top of her dress and pretended to tip the talcum powder down. Dottie giggled like a small child at her antics.

'Pass me a ciggie now you've finished, would you, love?' she said, smiling at Pammy. Pammy pushed the table across the bed, with her ashtray and cigarettes.

'There you go, Mrs Toft,' she said with a smile.

'For God's sake, don't set them curtains on fire again,' said Staff Nurse, wagging a playful finger. 'I've only just finished sewing the new pair to replace them.' She turned to Pammy. 'Matron made me sit up all night, she did, after our Dottie almost burnt the place down last week.' Dottie tried to protest at what were obviously Staff Nurse's mischievous white lies, but she was laughing far too hard and began to choke on her cigarette smoke.

'Right, enough of that.' Staff Nurse looked down the ward anxiously. 'Sister Antrobus will be back in a moment and if she sees you laughing she will be sending me to Matron on report.'

Once they had cleared everything back on to the bed bath trolley, placed the wire cage over Dottie's pelvis and covered it with a clean sheet that they folded down at the top to exactly eighteen inches, Pammy put the used bedding on the dirty linen trolley. As she turned back to say goodbye to Dottie and draw the curtains, Dottie reached up and gave her hand a little squeeze.

'Staff Nurse told me you were joining her and I would be your first bed bath. I hope I wasn't too difficult for you, and that thing down there, it wasn't too much of a shock?'

Pammy responded instantly. 'Oh no, not at all. I will never forget my first bed bath, and thank you so much for being so nice to a stupid probationer like me.'

Pammy knew she really would never forget her first patient. She had learnt more in those few minutes than she had in weeks in the classroom, the most valuable lesson being the way Staff had made Dottie laugh and feel better. As good as any painkiller or medicine. Nursing wasn't all about the tablets or the dressings or the bedpans. It wasn't about clean floors or an eighteen-inch turn-down; it was about really caring for your patient enough to brighten her day. She also knew she would never forget the overpowering scent of Irresistible talcum powder. It was something she would never smell for the rest of her life without thinking of Dottie Toft.

Jake and Martha sat on the low wall in front of the bins, while Jake rolled a cigarette and Martha held her cup of tea in one hand and his in the other. She watched as he carefully twirled his Rizla paper between finger and thumb.

'When are you going to tell your mam, then?' Jake asked. 'We can't keep the date a secret for ever. You will want to plan a nice wedding, won't you?' He slipped the tobacco tin into his overall pocket and lit up, then reached out to take his tea.

'We can tell her together on Sunday,' said Martha. 'Me mam has said I should take you to our house for yer tea when we come back from the park.' Jake grinned from ear to ear.

'Great, I can't wait. What do you bet everyone in the hospital will know, before we even get back into work on Monday morning?'

Martha laughed. 'Jake, everyone in Liverpool will know, never mind St Angelus.'

'Can I give yer a kiss here, Martha?' Jake asked, his eyes twinkling.

'No, you bloody well cannot,' said Martha. 'Get back to work now. I'm not marrying a man who hasn't got a wage.'

As Martha walked back to her kitchenette next to the consultants' sitting room, she grinned to herself. I want a hat, she thought. Not fancy, just a nice pillbox with a net veil and a pretty flower. She smiled to herself as for the hundredth time she tried to decide when and how she would ask her friend Josie if she would be a maid of honour.

He had been watching her through the window, his eyes never leaving her face. As he had left the house that morning, his wife had thrown a potted palm down the stairs and it had caught him between his shoulder blades just as he opened the front door. It had hurt, but not as much as it had dented his pride, or inflamed his anger. He had restricted her housekeeping allowance in order to limit her daily alcohol intake.

'Give me more money,' she had screamed at him. That was after she had thrown the plant and before she had slipped down the wall, like a rag doll, and slumped on to the floor. When he turned to look back up the stairs, he saw that her face was puce with anger.

'Give me some bloody money,' she screamed again.

Earlier in the morning she had been pleasant enough, claiming the money was for food and a few necessities. When he told her he would buy whatever she needed on his way home she lost her temper, and then she tried to kill him by aiming the potted palm down the stairs and at his head.

As he watched Martha and Jake, flirting and giggling, he felt a resentful anger bubble up within.

Martha washed up the dishes that had been left in the sink. She had put the last of them in the cupboard and was just drying her hands on her apron, ready to damp-polish the sitting room, when he took her by surprise. The doctors were all busy in outpatients and it would be another hour before any of them returned to the sitting room, half starved and looking for lunch.

'Hello, my sweet,' he said as he pushed his way in, forcing Martha backwards with him.

'Mr Scriven,' she said in an alarmed voice. But that was the last thing she was able to say for some time as his hand slammed over her mouth and she felt her knees buckle beneath her.

CHAPTER 15

As the four girls met by the back entrance of the hospital to walk home together, they fought for the gaps in the chatter to explain their day.

'I only nearly mixed up two blood samples,' said Victoria. 'A junior doctor just shoved them into my hand and asked me to shake them all the way to the pathology laboratory. I had absolutely no idea what he was on about, but a third year saved me and then when she took them out of my hand she said, "Which belongs to who?" Well, I had no idea and the doctor was on his way out of the door until she stopped him, and all the time she was shaking these glass tubes to stop the blood from clotting. It was enough to make one want to give up on the first day.'

'Well, I bet you didn't have a long conversation with a dead body, get flung into a dirty linen basket and start a fight on the ward,' Dana chirped, and in unison they all cried, 'Oh God, Dana, you are so Irish. Are you making all that up?'

'The bedpans,' squealed Pammy. 'Was there ever a job as foul?' But before anyone could answer her she had spotted a group of doctors and medical students in the distance, also leaving the back entrance of the hospital and heading towards them, down the lane. 'Don't move,' she said, putting up her hand to fix her hair. 'We need to get friendly with a few of these doctors. We all want a night out, don't we? I reckon it won't do us any harm to meet a few of these chaps. I recognize one from our ward today, really lovely he was. Stall, girls, stall. Dana, tie up your laces, go on, get down on the ground.'

'Not on your life,' said Dana, who dared not look to see if Teddy was among them, but could feel her heart beating wildly. She hadn't seen him, but she had sensed he was there; she just knew. 'Get down and tie up your own laces.'

'All right, don't then,' said Pammy, 'but don't move.'

The girls pretended to chat, Pammy laughing far too loudly as they surreptitiously turned round to face the doctors. As they approached, Dana recognized him and she was sure he had spotted her. She felt as though she had entered a world of her own. Her mouth had gone dry and all she could think about was the smile on his face and the feel of his strong hands on her waist as he had lifted her up and into the dirty linen basket.

Beth began to complain. 'For goodness' sake, do we have to hang around here? I would quite like to get back to Lovely Lane. We all have studying to do tonight, you know. We've got to fill in the worksheet Sister Haycock has given us for each night. It would be a disaster to miss the first one. Hello? Is anyone listening to me?'

No one was. Pammy was in a state of high excitement. She had complained lately how dull their evenings were. Twelve weeks of study and the confinement of the PTS had almost driven her crazy. They were all on days for the next month. Pammy badly wanted a night out.

'Here's our chance, girls,' she whispered. 'We'll ask this lot if they have any idea where a bunch of bored nurses can find some fun.'

'That's a bit forward, Pammy,' said Victoria. 'Maybe we should wait until they ask us.'

'Are you kiddin'? I'm not asking them to marry us. We haven't been out in months. I'm going to crack up if I have to spend another night in with a mug of Horlicks. I'll just drop it into the conversation all casual like. Watch me.'

'Listen to you, you mean,' said Beth. The doctors strode on and soon covered the ground between them.

'Nurses!' shouted one young man with dark-framed glasses and a short mop of equally dark and very curly hair. 'What a good job we bumped into you. We've all been wondering whether or not the new intake would be a good bunch.'

'We are,' said Pammy. Nothing was going to stop her from having her night out.

Dana had seen him at once. In a cloud of flapping white coats, he stood out from the rest. She wished her heart would slow down, that the colour she knew had risen in her face would subside, that she would remember how to speak when he reached her. He had broken away from the rest of the group. She clasped her hands to stop them shaking and swallowed hard.

He was grinning in that boyish way she remembered from the first night they met. Even when he had scooped her up and dropped her into the linen basket, her heart had beaten wildly. Now and again she had stolen a delicious free moment to relive it in her mind. She had almost torn herself apart wondering whether she had been too brusque. Played too hard to get. Had she let her Irish pride come before a lonely fall? His hair flopped over his eyes and bounced up and down as he walked. With each step, her heart beat faster. Was this an illness? He had filled her thoughts and the scenario of events from their first meeting had replayed in her mind like a film reel. She had laid her head on her pillow and imagined what it would be like if Teddy's head were on a pillow next to hers. If she could slip her hand across the sheets and touch his body, if he answered when she whispered his name. She had felt foolish today, trying to play hard to get. He had probably seen right through her. Thank goodness she had a second chance. Don't blow it this time, she thought.

She swallowed again as he approached. She forced herself to give him the biggest, most welcoming smile. Even her lips trembled.

He was almost upon her when she took a tenta-tive step forward to greet him. 'Hello,' she said. But he didn't hear, and her mind screamed in confusion as he strode straight past her to Victoria, threw his arms around her and kissed her on the cheek.

Dana's heart almost broke in two as she watched Victoria reach up and wrap her arms around his neck. Then Victoria kissed him back and whispered breathlessly, 'Teddy, I've found you at last.'

Emily Haycock decided that the moment had come. She had to have the conversation she had avoided for so long.

'Biddy, will you stay and have a cup of tea with me?' she asked when Biddy popped her head round the door to say goodnight.

'That tea on the tray? It's cold. Why would I want to drink that? Oh, I see. Is that just your way of getting me to make a fresh pot when I'm on me way out of the door? Would you get the cheek of you.' But Biddy had already placed her bag on the floor and taken off her coat.

Five minutes later she returned to Emily's office, bearing the tea tray and a smile. Biddy thought that Emily was dreading returning home alone. If only she knew, Biddy felt the same.

'They've all gone in the kitchen and I had to do it meself, so think yourself lucky,' she joked. 'I'll tell you what, this intake of nurses, they're a funny lot. They're a bit cheekier than the last bunch. Do you feel as though things are changing? People, I mean, not things. I've been here a long time and I've never known such a perky, happy group of girls.'

'I think they are, Biddy. I think the more probationers we try to recruit from the same background as the majority of our patients, the quicker the change will take place. I want some of the nurses in St Angelus to say bath, not barth.'

Biddy handed Emily her tea.

'Biddy, can we have that chat now? The one about your incontinence? Because I'd like to help.'

CHAPTER 16

Supper was over and the nurses of Lovely Lane were sitting around in the lounge, watching the new black-and-white television.

'Ssh,' said Lizzie to the room in general. 'It's news about the new Queen.' She leapt out of her chair and turned the dial of the fourteen-inch TV as far as it would go.

Mrs Duffy bustled into the room, pushing the drinks trolley in front of her. 'Draw the curtains while you are up please, Nurse,' she said.

As Lizzie looked for the cord down the side of the dark green velvet drapes, she stopped short. There he was again. Over the past two weeks, she had seen a young man lounging against the park bushes on the opposite side of the road on at least four or five occasions. At first she had thought he was waiting for the bus. Now, she was more suspicious.

'Mrs Duffy,' she said, without turning round, 'who do you think that young man is, opposite the house? He's been there every time I've closed the curtains for the past couple of weeks.'

Mrs Duffy came and stood next to her. 'Where, dear?'

Lizzie moved aside a little to give her room, and then exclaimed, 'Oh my, he was there just a moment ago. He's gone now.'

'Maybe he was just waiting for the bus?' said Mrs Duffy. 'Do you want me to mention it to Dessie? See what he thinks?'

'No, no, don't be daft,' said Lizzie. 'He looked harmless enough.' She drew the curtains together and took one last peep, just to be sure. Maybe he had just been waiting for the bus after all, she thought.

'Is it the news, girls?' Mrs Duffy said excitedly as she pushed the squeaky trolley against the wall.

'It is, Mrs Duffy. Don't worry about the drinks; we'll help ourselves. Come and sit down and watch it,' said Victoria, patting the seat of the empty chair next to her.

'I can't let you serve your own drinks after the way you nurses have worked all day,' said Mrs Duffy. 'I can do two things at once very well, Nurse Baker, and often do.' Victoria, anticipating the rejection of her offer, had already stopped listening and returned her gaze to the television.

From the far corner came the clatter of steel on steel. It was the knitters. This group had been organized by Celia Forsyth during the first week of PTS. Dana loved knitting, having been taught by her mother as soon as she could hold a pair of needles. She would have loved to join in, but felt inhibited by the fact that Celia Forsyth was the organizer. She had tentatively mentioned her interest to Beth.

'I love to knit,' she had said. 'I'm not as good as my mammy, though. She makes beautiful cardigans and jumpers. She knitted like crazy to kit me out before I left. Went mad she did because she only had a few months' notice.'

'Well, why don't you join us then? Take no notice of Celia. She may have organized the group, but she doesn't make the rules. There are no laws as to who sits in the knitting corner.'

'Are you joking?' Dana laughed. 'I'd be dropping my stitches every five minutes. Your one, she hates me, though I've no idea what I've ever done to deserve it. She put a note under everyone's door inviting them to join the circle. Under every door but mine, that is.'

Beth had already worked out that she had made a big mistake, being friends with Celia. The loudness of Pammy drove her to distraction and she had thought that forming an alliance with Celia was her best bet, but she had seen that whereas Pammy, Victoria and Dana had been genuinely delighted when she won the PTS prize, the smile had not quite reached Celia's eyes.

Tonight, Celia had herded her knitters, armed with their tapestry bags and needles, into the corner where she planned to deliver a lecture on blackberry stitch and to discuss the merits of a pattern she had seen in a magazine. Lizzie noticed some of the knitters straining over their yarn to see the screen in the corner of the room, and was sure they would much rather be sitting around the television with everyone else. All anyone could talk about was the new Queen Mother and her daughter, the Queen.

A nurse sat in front of Celia, holding a skein of wool in her hands while Celia wound it into a ball. As the nurse leant over to get a better look at the television, Celia dropped the ball of wool and snapped, 'Nurse Skeet. Sit up.'

'That one will make Matron one day,' Pammy whispered to Victoria.

'Let's hope we're far away when that happens then,' Victoria whispered back.

'My mother is posting me patterns so that we can knit some new clothes for the dolls on the children's ward,' said Celia in a deliberately loud voice, in order to do battle with the television and to irritate Lizzie. 'I will of course first check with Matron that it will be acceptable for us to do so.'

Almost everyone ignored her. Many had discovered that ignoring Celia truly got her goat. Pammy had turned her attention back to studying Evelyn Pearce's book on anatomy and physiology for nurses. Terrified of making a mistake on the ward and landing herself in Sister Antrobus's bad books, she had glanced at the theatre list for the following day and written down what operations were being performed, by whom and in what order. She didn't want to look like the first ward placement idiot she felt herself to be if someone asked her a question or spoke to her in acronyms.

Beth had moved slightly away from the rest of the knitting circle and was deep in a book, her needles lying idle. She was the most studious of the bunch, but could quite easily be jollied along into laying her work down. Some of the girls were dozing in their chairs, after a hard day on the wards. It was as much as some could do to keep their eyes open past supper but tonight, like Victoria, the majority were glued to the news.

Pammy lifted her head from her book and looked around the room for Dana. 'Have you seen Dana, Vic?' she whispered. They often used their Christian names between each other, as long as no one outside their group could hear them. If Pammy had spoken in tones of any volume, she would have addressed her friend as Nurse Baker. First names *sotto voce* and titles in regular tones had quickly become the accepted norm.

Victoria appeared not to have heard her question, so Pammy repeated, 'Do you know where Dana is? Is she sick, or what?'

'I haven't seen her since we walked home. In fact, one minute she was there, the next she was gone,' Victoria replied. Pammy looked thoughtful.

'Nurse Brogan isn't feeling very well,' said Mrs Duffy, interjecting. 'It's an exhausting ward, male surgical, having to lift those men up the bed all the time. She's gone to catch up on some sleep.'

'But she wasn't at supper,' said Pammy. 'If she

doesn't eat, she won't be able to haul anyone up the bed.'

'Don't you worry about Nurse Brogan,' Mrs Duffy replied. 'I'll take her a drink and a biscuit up when I've finished in here. Sister Haycock is coming down tonight to have a chat with you all, see how you are getting on on the wards.'

This was no longer a terrifying prospect to the girls. Sister Haycock was everyone's favourite sister by a country mile, and she often popped in during the evening to have a drink with them on her way home. They got to ask her as many questions as they liked. She always had time to listen and almost always made a point of asking Pammy how she was getting along.

Lizzie dived out of her seat and raised the volume on the television even louder. 'Shh,' she hissed as she collapsed back in her seat. The tinny and hissy voice of the announcer filled the room.

'If I told our kids we watched the telly every night, they'd all be around here, Mrs Duffy,' said Pammy.

Lizzie spotted an opportunity to save Mrs Duffy a job and walked over to the fire to poke it back into life, lifting the scuttle to pour on a few coals.

'Well now, that makes me very sad,' said Mrs Duffy. 'Maybe we should invite them around one morning when they are not at school?'

'Would you not need Matron's permission for that?' Celia Forsyth's voice cut across the room and silence fell. Victoria noticed that Mrs Duffy's face flushed with colour as she stammered out a reply.

'I hadn't actually thought of asking Matron, It was just an idea . . .'

'And a very kind one Mrs Duffy, said Victoria. I had never even seen a television until I came to live here.'

'We don't have one, and I don't know anyone in our street who does,' said Pammy. She was smarting at the kindness of Mrs Duffy's thought and the embarrassment she suffered as a result of Celia's comment.

'Well, my father says that everyone should have one, said Beth. 'I find it fascinating that we can actually see and hear Churchill. Such a great man. Daddy says everyone will own a television soon because people want to know what the government is up to. So many people love Churchill.'

'There's no argument there,' said Mrs Duffy. 'He was a great man during the war, was Churchill. We would never have got through without him.'

The television was now showing a picture of a smiling Queen Elizabeth standing next to Prince Philip.

'See? Everyone should be able to see those picture,' said Beth. 'Not just the lucky people like us.

'Well, wouldn't that be wonderful,' said Mrs Duffy, who loved the Queen almost as much as she loved her job and her nurses.'

'No, it wouldn't,' said Celia Forsyth. 'My father thinks that the masses owning televisions will bring about nothing but trouble. Could even bring the government down, he says. It will be the end of Churchill. The government will never let it happen.'

Victoria's mouth fell open as she saw Mrs Duffy walk towards Celia with her drink held out. She saw it happen in slow motion, but by the time she had registered the impending disaster it was too late to shout a warning. As Mrs Duffy reached over to pass Celia her drink, her eyes turned towards the television screen, the cup slipped from its saucer, sailed through the air and discharged its contents all on to Celia's lap, where they splattered all over her newly completed white matinee coat.

'Oh for heaven's sake,' Celia shouted, shooting up out of the chair and throwing the knitting on to the floor. 'You stupid, stupid old woman.'

There was an audible gasp from the assembled nurses, and, for a moment, time seemed to stand still before Pammy and the others jumped up to help, not Celia, but Mrs Duffy. Celia looked as though she were about to burst with rage.

Mrs Duffy began to apologize. 'I am so sorry. I will replace the wool and redo the knitting for you. All the time you have spent on that little coat, and it's so beautiful, too. I am so sorry.'

Celia Forsyth knocked Mrs Duffy's hand away and stormed out of the room, dripping cocoa. Not one person other than Mrs Duffy had looked at her.

'I wouldn't put up with being spoken to like that,

Mrs Duffy,' said Lizzie, as she helped the house-keeper to clean the chair. 'I think that Nurse Forsyth needs to be sent to Matron for her rudeness. It was an accident, for goodness' sake.'

Mrs Duffy's voice trembled. 'I can hardly send her to Matron, can I now, when it was me who spilled the drink and ruined her hours of hard work. No, it was my fault. Of course she's angry. I would be angry if someone threw a cup of hot cocoa all over me and ruined my knitting. No, it was all my fault.' Mrs Duffy held the matinee coat in her hand, looking distraught. 'I will try to wash it as soon as I've got the dishes done.'

Pammy thought she saw Mrs Duffy's eyes fill with tears as she collected the empty cups and moved the trolley out of the room. The girls looked at one another with expressions of disbelief. The only sounds were the fire hissing and the coals shifting in the grate.

'Well, that was a bit out of order.' Victoria broke the silence. 'That little madam needs to get her comeuppance.'

'She certainly does, Nurse Baker,' said Lizzie. 'I think some of us need to work on that. Her day will come, you mark my words.' Lizzie had known Mrs Duffy for over two years and they had become close. Just at that moment, Lizzie could have followed Celia to her room and thumped her. 'You lot, her so-called friends.' Beth and the others in the knitting corner looked up, their needles lying redundant in their laps. No one had the nerve to continue knitting. 'One of you had better run up those stairs and tell her not to come back down here tonight, because if she does she'll have me to deal with. And now I'm going to help Mrs Duffy, who looks after us all every day, to wash up the cups. Is anyone coming with me?'

Beth jumped to her feet. 'I will, Nurse.' For a moment, everyone was stunned. Beth had been Celia's closest companion.

'Thank you.' Lizzie shot a venomous look at the other nurses in the corner. They were looking mortified, and Pammy felt sorry for them. She knew they were as scared of Celia as most were of Matron.

'Best way to deal with a bully is ignore them, and if that fails, bring them down a peg or two,' her da, Stan, had often said. Pammy made a note that she and Lizzie needed to have a little chat about Celia Forsyth, soon.

Five minutes later, Pammy stood outside Dana's door and knocked gently. 'Dana? Are you feeling all right?' There was not a sound from within, only silence. Pammy stepped back and looked at the bottom of the door. No light was visible and all was quiet.

'Dana, are you asleep?' She whispered what she knew to be a stupid question. If she were asleep, Dana wouldn't be able to hear her or to answer. But Pammy was also aware that something was wrong. She had noticed a difference in the way Dana behaved as soon as they had begun to talk about their encounter with the doctors. Something must have upset her, Pammy thought. Dana wasn't ill. Someone had upset her and she wouldn't mind betting that yet again it was that bully, Celia Forsyth.

She made one more attempt to raise her friend. 'Dana, Sister Haycock is coming to talk to us, to find out how we are getting on. You don't want to miss her, do you?'

Receiving no reply and knowing that Dana would have loved to have seen Sister Haycock, she burned with anger as she walked back down the stairs to the kitchen to seek out Lizzie. It was time to make a plan. Ignoring Celia Forsyth had not worked.

Victoria only remembered the note in her pocket when she began to undress for bed. 'Darn,' she cursed as she slipped on her dressing gown and pattered along the corridor to Dana's room. She slipped the note under the door, and smiled to herself. After this, she would have to trust Dana with her own secret. It was something she was more than looking forward to. Having to keep quiet about Roland had been difficult. She had also been careful not to speak of Baker Hall. It was time for her to become more open with her friends. Victoria now knew, leave for her intake would not be until the end of the summer and her new friends would find the fact that she had kept news of Roland from them difficult to understand. It was time to share her own secret and she would start with Dana.

Dana had been awake all along, and lay still in bed while she waited for the footsteps to recede. She had heard the note being pushed under her door, and when she was sure that there was no one outside her room she slipped out of bed to retrieve it.

Not wanting to turn on the light, she tiptoed to the window and read the note by the light of the moon and the reflected glow from the sulphur orange street light. The notepaper glowed gold as Dana made out the neatly written words.

Dana, I haven't seen you since we got back to Lovely Lane so I'm writing this down to be sure I don't forget. Teddy has told me that he is on call every night for the next month, and he has asked me to ask you would you meet him for a chat at the bottom of the theatre steps tomorrow night? He thinks he may have been overly boisterous today and says he did actually throw you into the dirty linen basket! I will tell no one. I have my own little secret. Let's have a chat when you are feeling better.

Dana couldn't wait. She wanted to explode with excitement. She crept down the corridor to Victoria's room. 'I'm so sorry,' she said, when Victoria opened the door. 'It's just that I thought you must be sweet on him, when I saw you giving him a kiss.'

An hour later, Dana was still sitting on Victoria's

bed while her friend spilled out the story of the troubles at Baker Hall. 'And so, you see, Teddy's brother is my Roland and someone I *am* very sweet on.'

'Well, you must go home to see him.'

'I will, but never mind me, more important is, what are you going to wear tomorrow night, when you meet Teddy?'

Within minutes, almost the entire contents of Victoria's wardrobe had been emptied out on to her bed while Dana tried on one outfit after another.

'I feel so awful that I hardly have any nice clothes to speak of,' said Dana. 'To think, I thought I was arriving in Liverpool with a wardrobe to match Jean Simmonds. Now I wouldn't be seen dead in anything I own. God, I must be the only girl in Liverpool who owns a skirt hand-knitted by her mammy.'

Victoria laughed. 'Well, you look lovely in my silk blouse and skirt. Here, borrow my pearls, too.'

Dana objected and pushed Victoria's hand away. 'I can't have him thinking I'm someone I'm not, Victoria. I love you for offering, but I'm just a farm girl from Ireland. However much we object when Celia Forsyth says it, it is the truth. 'Tis who I am.'

Victoria was not about to challenge Dana's pride and quietly laid the pearls back in their box. 'You're quite right,' she said. 'Shame on me. Anyway, it would be ridiculous to wear pearls for a chat. They are really for dinner or a dance. And now you'll be awake all night with the excitement of it all. Get you, Dana Brogan, sneaking out for a date. What will your mammy say?'

Finally, Dana slipped back to her room with an outfit draped over her arm. She wondered whether she should knock on Pammy's door and explain. She heard the church clock strike midnight and decided against it. Her secret could keep a little longer.

Across the road, Patrick watched from the shadows of the bushes as the lamp in Dana's room flicked back on. He knew it was her room. He had seen her draw the curtains on half a dozen occasions. He would wait. His father had sent him. 'Don't return home until she has agreed to be your wife,' he had said as he dropped Patrick off at the station.

Patrick could not let his daddy down. He would wait until she left the home on her own, and then he would stop her and talk to her and put everything right.

Victoria dressed Dana while Pammy fixed her make-up.

'Stop, would you?' Dana squealed. 'I look as if I fell in the coal bucket, there's so much muck around me eyes.'

'You stop yer moaning,' said Pammy. 'That's the best, that, and it's only been in the shops for a few weeks. Elizabeth Taylor wears it and her eyes look incredible.'

'Stand up then, let's see you.' Victoria took Dana's hand and helped her out of the chair.

'Go on, spin round,' said Pammy.

'Spin round? I can hardly stand on these sling-backs of yours, Pammy.'

'Do you ever stop moaning?' Pammy pulled an exasperated face.

'Oh, I know, I'm sorry. I'm nervous, that's all. I'm just a country girl and this is me first big date, after all.'

'Well, all I can say is let's hope they improve. There has to be more to courting than a quick chat on the back steps to theatre.'

Victoria shot Pammy a stern look. 'Give him a break, Pammy. He's on call every night for a month. He must be keen if he can't wait that long to see her.'

Dana's face broke into a grin. If there was one thing she loved to hear, it was Victoria telling her how keen Teddy was on her.

Half an hour later, Dana was thankful that the spring rain had stopped. There was a full moon and the cobbled back road into the hospital glistened. Victoria and Pammy had sneaked down to the back door with her while Mrs Duffy was in the sitting room serving the drinks.

'I will slip along here when Mrs Duffy has gone and leave the snip up.' Victoria had told her. 'Make sure you drop it back down when you come in, or you'll get us all into trouble.'

'Don't worry, I will. I'll give you a knock when I return.' Then, with a hug and a blast of stiff wind through the back door, Dana was swallowed by the black of the night.

Victoria leant back on the door for just a second and whispered, 'Please, God, please, don't let there be an emergency and make him late.'

Dana took off her shoes as she ducked under the window of the sitting room and down the side path on to the road. As she walked briskly up to the hospital, she felt her mouth dry with a combination of fear and excitement. She thought she heard someone behind her and turned quickly, thinking she had forgotten something and it was Victoria or Pammy, but the road was clear. No one was following her. It's the heels, she thought. *What am I doing? Mammy would kill me.* But despite her anxiety her footsteps quickened as she hurried towards the back gate of the hospital.

As she neared the steps to the theatre block, she could see that the door was wide open and the lights were on, spilling out into the courtyard, filling the cobbled square with a bright white light. This was not what she had expected. There was no one standing outside having a cigarette, as there often was during the day. The theatre block was the only place in the hospital where smoking was strictly forbidden indoors, because of the oxygen tanks. Dana stood stock-still and wondered what to do.

She didn't want to be standing at the bottom of the steps in the pool of light. She felt this would be degrading and began to question herself again. If she was near the steps, waiting for him, when he came down, she would appear too keen. What had seemed the right thing to do when she read Victoria's note, suddenly felt wrong and inappropriate. He should be waiting by the nurses' home for you, she thought, even though she knew that, given his rota, this was impossible. Victoria had explained that he wasn't allowed to move any further from the hospital than the doctors' residence.

Spotting a row of cars, Dana dipped behind one and stood waiting where she had a clear view of the door, so that when he came down the steps she could hurry towards him as though she was late. That would be much more dignified. She almost stepped out twice, only to jump back in time when she could tell that the rapid footsteps did not belong to Teddy. The cold began to seep into her bones and she started to shiver. Through the opaque windows upstairs, she could see activity. The occasional shadow of a nurse or a doctor moved across the glass, blocking out the bright lights of the theatre. It was impossible to tell who it was or indeed if any of the shadows belonged to Teddy. The words of the staff nurse on her ward began to tap on her brain. *He was stood up by a second-year nurse. They say she broke his heart.* At first she dismissed them, but the longer she waited, the clearer and louder they became until they were banging on the inside of her head, blocking out all reason and deafening her. The church clock chimed twelve and she saw the lights in theatre go out, one by one. A rapid tattoo of feet descended the steps as the night technician and staff left the building and made their way over to the greasy spoon. Whoever it was they had been operating on, it was now over. Dana spotted Dessie, who had been working since six thirty a.m. and was yet to clock off. He was pushing a large oxygen bottle across the yard.

'All that young girl needs now is a prayer from us all as we hit the pillows,' she heard him say to a man who was taking a cigarette out of a tin.

'Aye, she'll be as right as rain in the morning. The doctors know their stuff.' The man lit up two ciggies and handed one to Dessie. 'At this rate, they're going to have to start opening the theatre at night on a permanent basis. We can't keep working these hours. You have to tell Matron we need more porters.'

'I'm on to it,' Dessie replied. 'I don't know what's happening out there. We've gone from being a nice quiet hospital to one that seems to be going mad, sometimes.'

'Aye, it's called progress, Dessie. Houses being built and babies being born everywhere. It's as though the war never happened.'

Dessie inhaled and Dana saw his face glow red in the light of the flaming cigarette tip. 'It's the opposite. It's because the war happened. Babies, houses, jobs, it's all about forgetting. It's moving on, more than progress.'

'Get you, Dessie. Always a deep one. See you in the morning, mate.'

The two men moved off in opposite directions, and suddenly the courtyard was plunged into darkness, as the final light was extinguished. The clock chimed once, for twelve fifteen. Despite the fact that she knew deep down he wasn't coming, Dana told herself she would wait for one more chime, at the half past, in case he was still inside. Writing up his notes maybe. Keeping hidden to give them some privacy, hoping they wouldn't be seen. When the lonely note of one a.m. rang out, Dana turned, and with tears of humiliation and disappointment running down her cheeks made her way back to Lonely Lane with the words, *He waited for her for over two hours. The medical students never stopped teasing him about it* playing over and over in her mind.

Celia Forsyth lay in her bed and heard the careful footsteps passing under the front windows and around to the back door. Minutes later, with her ear pressed to her door, she heard the shuffle as Victoria's door opened and gently closed. She also heard the stifled sob.

CHAPTER 17

The warm day had given way to a moonless dark, wet night. The rain fell steadily as Sister Haycock made her way up Princess Avenue, holding on to her umbrella with both hands as on tiptoe and with the lightest feet she sprinted across puddles to avoid drenching her shoes. By the light of the old gas lamps, she saw that her stockings were splashed and splattered with the wet debris of the street and she sighed inwardly. Yet again she would be worrying all the way back to the flat if there would be enough gas left in the meter to wash both the stockings and herself.

She turned down a small pathway and knocked gently on the door of the home for distressed and injured soldiers. It was late and they would be waiting for her. No need to wake everyone by ringing the bell. She was greeted by the night sister who, as always, looked delighted to see her.

'How is he?' she asked before the door had been fully opened. She felt guilty that she was late. She was always late and the guilt never diminished. She knew full well that the other soldiers in the home would probably have visitors during the day and believe that Alf, her stepfather, was unloved, when that couldn't be further from the truth.

'Oh, he's just fine, as always. Come in. He's been talking about you all day. We told him that you would definitely be here, as usual. I said to him, has she ever missed a day?'

The home housed thirty patients with varying degrees of problems but all shared the same criterion for entrance: each was entirely dependent on others to get through the day. The depth of Alf Haycock's tragedy had made him eligible and, indeed, almost a favourite with the staff. Emily had to provide part of the funding, which amounted to almost half of what she earned, but she had learnt to manage. She had become an expert at scouring jumble sales in the better areas of Liverpool. She ate at the hospital and went almost entirely without at weekends. The nurses at the home were all married, which prevented them from working at St Angelus, but in Emily's opinion they were the best. She had observed at first hand how caring they were, and had decided that marriage and motherhood were a bonus in nursing, bringing qualities of wisdom and compassion that even she could not train into her nurses. She had decided she would do her best to influence the board to drop that most stupid of rules.

'He's just had a cup of tea with a shortbread and he loved it. Asked for another, he did. I said to him, wait until Emily gets here and you can have one together.'

Emily's mouth watered. She had missed her tea at the hospital and her stomach rumbled at the prospect of her favourite biscuit.

'Have you come straight from work again?' The night sister asked the question with a hint of disapproval in her voice and Emily nodded, unable and unwilling to lie.

'Well then, it's just as well I saved you some supper in the kitchen, isn't it? You work too hard, you know. Mind you, in this new world, don't we all? You go straight in to him and I'll bring you both a nice tray.'

The night sister shuffled off down the corridor while Emily shook out her umbrella and leant it up against the front door, removed her headscarf and shook that too. Undoing her mackintosh and loosening the belt, she made her way towards Alf's room.

Alf had never recovered from the bomb that hit George Street. He had lost his wife, his sons and his mind, all on the same day. As she walked into the room, he looked up from the chair in which he spent most of his time.

'Hello, my Alfred the Great,' she whispered. 'I'm sorry I'm so late, but I'm here now. I can put you to bed.'

He smiled up at her. A smile full of remembrance and affection. She knew he still recognized his stepdaughter. Maybe not for all of the time she was there, but always in the first few seconds, she thought, although the doctors did not agree with her.

'You know your mother's watch?' Her father began talking before she had even sat down. 'I took it to the shop to be fixed. The little finger had stuck, and do you know, when I went to collect it today, they couldn't find it. Can you believe that? They asked me to go back tomorrow, so the owner can have a good look round for it. I told him, you had better find it, mate, it's made of gold that watch and it was me mother's before the wife 'ad it. Your mam said she keeps looking down at her wrist to see if it's there. Said she feels lost without it.'

Emily pulled her cardigan down to ensure it covered the watch, which she wore every day. The watch and her mother's wedding ring had been the only two items returned to her and she had worn both ever since. She felt the familiar warm metal of the ring on the chain beneath her dress.

'Well, that's terrible, Alf. I hope he finds it.'

'He will, queen, don't worry, he won't want the coppers knocking on his door and that's what I'll do if I don't get it back. I'll go to the Whitechapel station meself, if they don't find it.'

They had had the same conversation every night for the past thirteen years. Occasionally it varied as a different memory came back to him. One that had niggled at him during the day. The doctors often stared at her blankly, as though she were the

342

one who had lost her mind, when she tried to explain that she thought he saved things up for when she arrived, to share with her. There were moments during the day, she was sure from what the nursing staff told her, when he anticipated her arrival and looked forward to her coming, but the remainder of the time he spent with the ghost of her mother. In the first few years, she would show him the watch on her wrist, but it meant nothing to him. Nor did leaving the watch with him. He would look at it when she explained and say, 'Aye, that's right,' and then continue in just the same vein. Sometimes he would fret that he was late for a hospital appointment or that he had misplaced his blackout rota, or go on and on about the shoes he had to clean for her brothers for church, or worry that the kids hadn't come home from Rita's yet and must be driving Rita mad. She could never explain it to him, because even after all these years it was not a story she could tell without her eyes filling with tears and a catch in her throat. There was not a day when she too didn't think about Rita, the woman her brothers had died with. Or hear her last words and her brothers' whoops of joy when she said they could stay in Rita's house while she ran to the shop with the coupons for butter. 'You are such a love,' Rita had said.

Such a love. Such a love. Such a love. Sometimes, the words played over and over in a loop in her mind and she could hear Rita's voice, as clear as though she were in the next room.

343

There were half a dozen tableaux Alf could run through each night and every one of them reminded her of all that she had lost. Emily played her part as she washed and changed him and clipped his nails and brushed what was left of his hair. She asked the nurses to leave the evening routine for her. It made her feel less guilty, to be able to do something practical and worthwhile for him. To make him clean and comfortable, to feed him a drink and some toast, to chat away, to give him his medication and sleeping tablets and sit with him, holding his hand, until he fell asleep. His last words every night were 'Night night, my petal', his pet name for her mother.

When she left, she spotted the night nurse at her desk, writing by the light of the lamp. The home was filled with the sound of gentle wails and moans.

'Is that you, Gladys?' called out one patient. A former soldier, a lost soul, searching. There was no answer. Who knew who Gladys was, or even if Gladys was still alive? It mattered not; Gladys lived on in the home for distressed and injured soldiers.

'Are you off now?' asked the nurse, snapping the top back on to her pen. She got up and walked from the pool of light cast by the lamp towards Emily. In the dimness of the hallway her shadow loomed up the wall ahead of her.

'I am. He's asleep. I've got his dirty pyjamas in my bag and I'll bring some more clean ones back tomorrow. Did he eat his lunch today?'

'He did, love. Day Sister said he was great. They played bingo and he kept shouting "House". He thought he'd won every time. Loved it.'

The thought of Alf enjoying himself made Emily smile. 'Maybe we can do that on Saturday?'

'I'm sure you can, and you can be the caller. Sister was hoarse by the time she had finished.'

'Thanks for saving me the shepherd's pie,' said Emily.

'Not at all, love, it would just have ended up in the pig bin anyway. Someone who works as hard as you do deserves a little looking after. I'm baking tomorrow. I'll bring in a nice slice of cake for you.'

Emily smiled her thanks. In truth, she wanted to put her arms out and hug the night sister. Emily's job was a lonely one. She enjoyed the company of the nurses, but she was their sister tutor. She could not be their friend. All she had in the world was her da, Alf, and the thought of losing him one day was difficult to face. On the day he left her, she would be truly alone.

She had told no one at work about Alf. After the bombing, homeless and distraught, they had left almost immediately to stay with her mother's friend in North Wales. They could not accept the charity of their neighbours, those who had survived. They could not join the dispossessed, thronging into the town hall for help. They went by train from Liverpool to Betty's the same day.

They returned, just the once, to bury her mother and to visit Maisie Tanner. Maisie was hardly fit to receive visitors. Her tears fell as soon as she saw Emily; her new baby, lying on her chest, looked as though she wouldn't survive the day. The baby had been only seconds old when Emily had last set eyes on her. It was all just too much for everyone to absorb. The deaths. A new and delicate life. A broken community. The maelstrom of emotions had left the community reeling. Maisie's daughter, Pammy, made them tea, or tried her best, at least. Maisie's old mam fussed around, wearing widow's weeds. With wet eyes she repeated the names of the friends she had lost, winding her handkerchief into a knot, oblivious of the new life in her kitchen. The women who had shared in the birth of her own children had been blown apart by a bomb.

'Will you be calling on Rita?' she asked Emily and then realized her error, and wiped her mouth with her twisted hankie. 'God, I'm sorry. It was the Connors' house too, you know, and the O'Reillys'. Not a scrap of anyone or anything could they find, just dust and rubble.' She seemed to have forgotten that Emily's brothers had also been turned into dust and rubble. 'There's been a mass held in the street every day since.' The old lady's voice trailed away into an awkward silence.

What could anyone say? They had survived. They had lived. Emily and her father had lost everything. Life had changed so far beyond recognition that no one knew what to say any more. The familiar framework of conversation had been blown away with the entire street. What point discussing the weather, the washing or what was in the shop? Who cared?

As Emily said her goodbyes, little Pammy had held her hand at the door and asked, 'Will you come again?'

'Of course I will,' said Emily. But she knew she never, ever would.

Martha had been cleaning down the surfaces in her kitchen, counting down the minutes, waiting for the six p.m. klaxon to sound on the docks. She would make her way over to the porter's lodge and walk home with Jake.

The tap was running into the sink, and she was stacking the dishes on to the shelf and making such a clatter that she didn't even hear him come in, but she was ready. She had known he would be back. As he lurched towards her, she extracted the vegetable knife from her apron pocket in a flash. Her hand trembled so much she nearly dropped it.

'Do it again, and I will use this,' she hissed through quivering lips. She had thought her voice would betray her. That her words would stick or shake or, worse, not come out at all. Even she was stunned at his reaction as he reeled and fell back with such force, it was as though a dozen hands had heaved him off her and thrown him against the wall.

'Are you a lunatic?' Spittle flew from his mouth

and she felt it land on her cheek. 'What are you doing, you stupid bitch? Put that down.' She noticed he was hurriedly trying to button up his trousers, which he had half undone before he came to find her.

'I'm to be married,' she whispered. Her voice faltered, although she had intended to sound bold and strong. 'If you touch me again, I will tell me mam. She works for Matron and I will get her to tell Matron, I will.'

This obviously came as news to him because he visibly paled. 'All right, Martha, no need to tell anyone, now, is there? Put the knife down. I thought you liked it. I didn't know you were getting married, or I wouldn't have come anywhere near you. It will be just between us, all right? Don't tell anyone, will you? If you do, I can guarantee you will come off worse. I'm sure your boyfriend would like to hear about how you chatted me up. Who is he? Is it the porter's lad I've seen you flirting with outside? Shall I go and find him now and tell him?'

He was almost out of the door by this time and walking backwards, as though willing himself not to turn his back to her. She did not say a word in response. Staring him out with the hatred which shone from her eyes, she stood motionless until the door banged shut on his snarling face. Martha knew she had achieved her aim. He would not bother her again.

Moments later, she shook so violently that she

could not hold the knife any longer, and it clattered to the floor. Tears poured down her cheek as she retrieved it, terrified lest he should come back in through the door and snatch it to use against her. She slipped the knife back into her pocket, and that was where it would live, every single day from then on. On the day when Mr Scriven came into the sitting room, as he often did, acting as though nothing had happened, she would slip her fingers into her pocket and reassure herself that it was there and she was safe.

CHAPTER 18

Almost a week passed before Dana heard from Teddy, and when she did it came in the form of another note. This time she found it on her bed, on top of a letter from home, where the maids always left her post.

I hope you got my note on Tuesday saying I had been sent to the sanatorium in West Kirby. I will be back on Sunday. I couldn't say no when my consultant asked me to go – don't want to get into his bad books.

Dana tore the letter into a hundred tiny pieces and dropped them into her waste paper basket.

'You little liar,' she hissed at the basket, just as Victoria walked into the room.

'Talking to yourself is the first sign of madness, so they say.' Victoria went over to the basket and looked in. 'What's that? Couldn't you tear the pieces any smaller?'

'It's a letter from Teddy, that's what. Wheedling, whining, full of excuses. I hope you got my last note, he said. Well really now, what note, I would say. Said he was sent to West Kirby by his consultant. Do you know what I think? I think he's full of cow shite. That's what I think.'

'Well, it does seem a bit odd. This one arrived with no problem, even though it's torn into a million bits in the bin now and I can't read it.'

Dana's hand flew to her mouth. 'Oh, God, I'm so sorry. I was just so mad at the boldness of the man.'

'There's no need to apologize to me. Do you feel better now that you have ripped his letter up?'

'Do you know what? I actually do. I really do feel better. The little toad. I'll tell you what, he had better come nowhere near me, because if he does I'll set Pammy on him, so help me God I will.'

'Right, good,' said Victoria. 'I couldn't think of a better plan. There cannot be a man alive who wouldn't be scared of an angry Pammy. Now, it's ham, egg and chips for supper. Do you know, I had never in my life eaten such a meal until I got here. I'd heard of chips, but I'd never eaten them, and I bloody love them now. When Aunt Minnie finds out, she will have a fit.'

Both girls descended the stairs to the kitchen, Victoria chatting away to Dana, distracting her from the treatment she had suffered at the hands of her own boyfriend's brother, as she had been doing for the past week.

Never mind Pammy, she thought. The brute has me to deal with first.

Less than a week passed before Teddy tried to make contact with Dana again. He made the mistake of trying to do so through Victoria. Victoria gave him short shrift.

'Teddy, in no circumstances must you ever try to see Dana, ever again. Do you understand me?'

'But, Vic, I truly did give one of your nurses a note to pass to Dana. I couldn't help it – I was sent away to West Kirby because they were a doctor down. Truly, Vic. Give a bloke a break.'

Victoria almost believed him, but then the thought occurred to her that if what he said were true, the note would very quickly have been in Dana's hand.

'I'm sorry, Teddy, I'm afraid I just can't believe you. There was no note. Let's just leave it at that, shall we?'

Victoria's voice carried a trace of her aunt Minnie and she was very firm on Dana's behalf. Teddy knew there was no point in his continuing to try to persuade her. His only tactic could be to tell his brother that he had not let Dana down in such an awful way and see if he could persuade him to convince Victoria. Dr Edward Davenport was not a cad, and he was very sweet on Dana Brogan. She had ensnared him with her eyes and her red Irish curls and he was not a man who gave up on something he truly wanted.

Oliver Gaskell waited at the restaurant door while he smoked a cigarette. The autumn leaves were falling and blowing down the street and the wind was rising by the minute. He glanced at his watch nervously, then shot a glance down Bold Street towards where it joined Church Street. In the distance, he made out her figure striding purposefully up the road, head bent against the wind, one hand in her pocket, the other holding on to her hat. She hadn't yet seen him and he couldn't help himself: he grinned. The war had put his life on hold and he was done with waiting. Tonight would be the first step towards changing that. He wanted to be a married man and enjoy all that came with it.

'I'm so sorry. The bus was late and then two came along at once. You know what it's like.' She was flustered as she removed her hat. Emily didn't like to be late for anyone or anything. By her reckoning, being late was an inexcusable crime. This was not a good start.

'I saw you coming and so I knew I hadn't been stood up.' He watched, amused, as Emily, unused to wearing her hair down, tried to pat her shoulder-length tresses into some sort of order. His gaze travelled down her clothes. He was disappointed. He had seen them before. She was wearing what she wore for work. It crossed his mind that maybe she thought he wasn't worth dressing up for.

'Our table is ready,' he said. 'I ordered you some wine. Come on, let's have a drink and forget about the beastly buses. They're always late.'

Emily smiled up at him. Biddy was right, he did have a winning smile and he was very good-looking, but there was an enthusiasm, almost an impatience about his manner that made Emily nervous. He had asked her to have dinner with him almost two weeks ago and she had seen the look of disappointment flit across his face when she gave him the date of her next available free night. 'I, er, don't want to step on anyone's toes,' he had said, waiting for her to reassure him. To let him know that she was, as he suspected, a spinster of the parish just waiting for Dr Right to pop along.

'Is this your favourite restaurant?' she asked as they sat down.

'Yes. It was the first to reopen after the war. My parents used to bring me here when I was a young boy.'

For a second, Emily contrasted the difference in their backgrounds. She had never in her life visited a restaurant with her parents, and even now it was an all too rare treat. As the waiter handed her the menu, she looked at him gratefully and whispered a very sincere, 'Thank you.'

The waiter smiled.

'How are you?' she asked. 'Are you busy tonight?'

'Oh, no, miss. We are never really busy. I don't know how this place keeps going.'

As Emily scanned the menu, it occurred to her that at those prices they wouldn't need to be terribly busy to survive. Oysters from the Isle of Man, beef from Scotland and cheese from Wales. While she studied the menu, she stole a glance at Oliver from under her lashes. He hadn't so much as acknowledged the waiter, never mind thanked him. As she handed the menu back, she once again thanked the waiter and noticed that her companion barely concealed an irritated glance.

'Will you have the oysters and steak?' he asked.

For a second, Emily considered his words. He was suggesting what she should eat and had not trusted her with the wine list. He was, of course, quite right not to. Emily had no idea which wine to choose. She just would have preferred it if he could have involved her a little more in the decision. 'No thank you.'

Oliver raised his eyebrows in surprise.

'I would like the soup, please, followed by the chicken.'

Dessie had been helping to clean up the bombed-out church. His mother had been christened there and it had been attended by every member of her family. He had seen the notice in the *Echo* calling for volunteers to help clear the rubble and to sign the petition to rebuild the church and return it to its original glory.

He walked down Bold Street. At the bottom, he would turn left and carry on down Church Street to the hospital before he collected the pies and made his way to Biddy's. He wanted to check on the lads' rota first. Two were leaving to work for a firm of builders who were taking on in town. It had been years, but Liverpool Corporation had finally begun to distribute contracts for the new council houses to be built in Bootle. The Irish were once again flooding through the gates, ready to labour in gangs on the roads and houses. His lads were all Irish. He knew he was in danger of losing them to the rebuilding of Liverpool. More money to be made and excitement to be had that way than from stoking boilers or delivering clean linen.

He had no idea what it was that made him look through the restaurant door. It was a Sunday night. Town was quiet. Liverpool, famous for its party-goers and music lovers, radiated an atmosphere of calm, following the Saturday-night storm. He sidestepped a tankard of ale, standing upright on the pavement, half full, left and lost by some poor reveller the night before.

Music wafted out from an upstairs window above a tailor's shop and he reached the restaurant door just as a couple heading towards him on the other side of the road began to cross towards it. He turned his head to look into the golden light and away from the gloom of the street, and that was when he saw her. There was no mistaking her. Dessie stopped dead. She was no longer a young woman, but Dessie always thought, with each year that passed, that she had improved with age. Her cheeks were soft and pillowy and not like his wife's had been, gaunt and hollow. He watched as Mr Gaskell threw back his head and laughed, just before he reached out and placed his hand on top of hers.

The pain was so sharp that Dessie felt as though his heart had been pierced.

'Excuse me, sir,' said the stranger, who was now standing in front of Dessie on the pavement and blocking his immediate escape.

Dessie's heart beat faster, terrified that she might turn to the side and see him. What would she say? What could he say? Would she ask, 'Dessie, why do you look as though your heart has just broken in two?' Would he be able to say, 'The woman I have worshipped from afar all this time has just left the stage upon which my dreams were made'?

He stood in the pool of golden light and warmth which spilled out of the restaurant but he couldn't speak. He nodded to the man and tried to get out of his way, but his feet felt like weights of lead and refused to move. He couldn't tear his eyes away from her, or from Mr Gaskell. The woman with the stranger had dropped her fine leather gloves on the pavement and she was laughing. Dessie's good manners took over and he bent to pick them up.

'Oh, thank you so much. I am such a butter-fingers,' she trilled, in a high-pitched tone.

Mr Gaskell looked over. Sister Haycock was talking and yet he seemed to be distracted by the open door. He glanced Dessie's way. Please don't recognize me, Dessie thought. Please, don't.

He didn't. Dessie had spoken to him a dozen times since he began to work at the hospital, but Dessie recognized the distant look in his eyes when they talked. He was nothing like his father, a man liked by everyone who worked at St Angelus. The son displayed a lack of interest in anything other than his own goals and ambitions.

The door closed on the diners and he walked on, fighting an urge to stand at the window and stare. To become invisible so that he could observe her every expression, hear her laugh and wish with all his heart that it was he who was sitting opposite her and not Oliver Gaskell.

Biddy busied about her kitchen, waiting for Elsie to arrive. She was always a few minutes ahead of Dessie. As soon as Elsie reached the kitchen door, agitated and anxious, Biddy knew something was seriously wrong. Not least because Elsie's arms were not holding the six bottles of Guinness Biddy had been looking forward to.

'What in God's name is up with you?' Biddy laughed, more to ease her own rising anxiety at the state of Elsie than anything else.

Elsie grabbed Biddy's sleeve. 'Biddy, I'm at me wit's end with our Martha. She's acting so peculiar and she put me in a right position she did today. I've had to lie to Jake and tell him she was ill. They were supposed to be having their dinner with me and she told me she didn't want him around.'

Biddy stopped Elsie mid-flow. 'Elsie, I can hardly tell what you are saying, will ye slow down? Tell me from the beginning. What's going on?'

Elsie took her handkerchief out from the end of her cardigan sleeve and sobbed, 'Biddy, I cannot believe it. It's our Martha, she's been possessed. Altered beyond all recognition she has.'

Biddy knew Martha almost as well as her own mother did and she also knew that Elsie was more prone to exaggeration than most. Nevertheless, she realized that something was very wrong. 'Are ye sure? Why did you have to lie to Jake? That girl doesn't go to the outhouse without telling ye first. If something was up, you would be the first to know, surely.'

Biddy could see that Elsie was beyond worried. She was scared. Her face was pinched and white and her eyes were full of concern. Biddy felt unease rising in her belly as all her senses screamed that something was very, very far from well, and she almost didn't want to hear what Elsie had to say. With a sense of impending doom, she wanted time to slip back, to the moments when she had been looking forward to the arrival of Elsie and Dessie and her Guinness and pie.

Elsie jabbered on and quickly recounted the events of the day. How Martha had asked her to send Jake away when he had called round.

'Tell him I'm sick, Mam. I don't want to see him. I don't feel well.'

Elsie had done as Martha had asked, but she had felt ill at ease and annoyed with her daughter.

'"Have you gone off Jake Berry," I said, "the best-looking and hardest-working lad in Liverpool? Because if so, you need your head testing, young lady. I sent away a very disappointed lad, so I did."

"She's sick?" he said to me. "It's nothing serious is it, Mrs O'Brien?" Well, I had to lie through me teeth and all the time she was stood behind the door to the stairs, sat on the bottom step, in case he came into the kitchen.

'I could see how much that lad thinks of our Martha as plain as the nose on me face and I felt dreadful having to lie to him, what with the position Martha had put me in. "No, lad, she will be fine by tomorrow, a bad head she has," I said, "nothing an early night won't sort out. She's already in bed." God, I felt terrible, Biddy. He was so worried. "Will you tell her I love her?" he said. How many girls around here would die for a man like that, eh? "Aye, I will, lad, I will. As soon as she wakes," I said.'

'And is Martha sick?' asked Biddy.

'Sick?' Elsie looked thoughtful and Biddy knew that look. 'To tell you the truth, Biddy, I've been worried about our Martha for weeks. When she's at home she mopes around the house and she looks so miserable you wouldn't think she had a wonderful fella like Jake Berry. How could anyone whose fiancé buys an electric washer and mangle be miserable? I can tell that poor Jake is confused. She hasn't even been to the house this week, or mentioned the wedding once. They must be working her hard in the consultants' room because as soon as she gets home she's fast asleep on the settle and she's in bed before me at night. She spends half her morning in the outhouse. I thought maybe she

360

had eaten something. I'm worried she might be ailing with something bad like. She never complains, though.'

'Not like her mother then?' said Biddy. Elsie appeared not to notice the barb as she continued.

'She's been acting like she's older than me these past couple of months, she has so. Kids these days, they don't know they're born. How hard did we have to work when we were sixteen, eh?'

Biddy nodded, her expression inscrutable. She had known Martha since the minute she was born. It was Biddy who had boiled the kettles for the hot water when the midwife arrived and ran upstairs to tend to Elsie and the baby. Big Charlie was at work and little Charlie at school. When Martha had arrived, only Elsie and Biddy were in the house to welcome her.

Biddy had already put two and two together, but it appeared that she was way ahead of Elsie. She poured some steaming tea into two cups. When Biddy returned home from work, she could down a whole pot to herself. ''Tis the Irish way,' she often said to Dessie, who could only manage two cups in one sitting.

'When you get home, will you ask her to come and see me? Maybe there's something she can tell me, something private like. She could be worried or scared about the wedding, and sometimes it helps to have someone outside the family to talk to. Send her round. Tell her I need help with something.'

Elsie looked relieved. 'I will that. And do you need help with something, then?'

'I want to put a few old clothes up in the suitcase on top of the wardrobe. I need a clear out in my bedroom. That's a good excuse.'

Elsie's shoulders drooped with the relief of a burden shared with her oldest friend. 'Of course it is. Don't you go standing on that stool on yer own. We don't want nothing happening to you, Biddy. She's taken to her bed. As soon as she wakes up, I'll send her over. Whenever that will be.'

Biddy watched Elsie as she drained the last of her cup and poured herself another, and wondered what she would do if Martha didn't call round and she didn't get the chance to speak to her. If Biddy was right in her suspicions, Martha would avoid her like the plague. Truth will out, thought Biddy to herself. Truth will out.

'Anyway,' said Elsie, draining her second cup. 'How's your bladder been today?'

Biddy was almost speechless. 'Not as bad as yours will be, if you don't get down to the offie for the Guinness before Dessie gets here,' she replied tartly.

'Right you are, I'm off.' Before she reached the door, Elsie turned back to face Biddy. 'You are a good mate, Biddy. I don't know what I'd do without you.'

As the door closed, Biddy drained her cup. 'You'd manage,' she said to the door. 'You'd manage. No one would miss me.'

★   ★   ★

Emily let herself in through the front door and slowly climbed the stairs to her room. The last thing she wanted was for her landlady to wake and, in the nosy way she had, question Emily about her whereabouts that evening. As she let herself in through her bedroom door, she breathed a sigh of relief.

'Made it,' she whispered.

She left the light off as she brewed herself a cup of tea, and, standing at the window nursing her cup in her hand, she observed the Sunday-night activities around Sefton Park and thought of her mother. Sometimes she wished that she had a photograph. She had sifted through the rubble herself. There was nothing. She always felt a momentary flash of panic when she failed to recall her mother's face. The more she panicked, the less she could remember it. When that happened, she spoke to her mother aloud, willing her to appear, if only in her mind's eye.

'Is he for me, Mother?' she whispered into the dark now, pressing her forehead against the cold pane of glass. Nothing came back. No whispered words of maternal wisdom, just the darkness of the night and the dampness of the Mersey air.

Oliver Gaskell had made it clear that he had wanted to accompany Emily home. He had been a little too keen for that to happen, and she was far too embarrassed. Even if she had felt the same, she would rather die than let him see the neighbourhood she lived in.

'I shall wait with you at the bus stop then and no argument,' he had insisted. 'I won't have it any other way.'

She wished he would. There was only one direction her bus could be travelling in and the name Lark Lane on the front was a dead giveaway. She decided there and then, as she looked down upon a courting couple hurrying along the street hand in hand, that she would have to move into one of the spare rooms on the old accommodation corridor, along from Matron's office. She would have three retired old biddies and Sister Antrobus for roommates. The corridor was rumoured to be about to be emptied and converted to a new ward for critical admissions, but nothing was definite yet. It would give her time to find a better solution to her problems, and meanwhile the corridor had its own washing machine and bathrooms, with an unlimited supply of piping hot water.

Drinking the last of her tea, she battled with the question that often came late at night, when she was tired and emotional. She shivered as she slipped between her cold sheets. She had been happy to keep her promise for years without question. Now, dissatisfaction and loneliness were creeping into her life. It was Pammy Tanner. Seeing her at the interview and over the past few months at the hospital had resurrected the memories she had buried. The past she had successfully managed to forget. Or so she had thought.

And as often happened at the end of the day, in

the dark of the night, she heard the voices of her little brothers and her friend Rita. They were always followed by the sound of the exploding bomb, just as her tears escaped.

CHAPTER 19

Victoria Baker needed a holiday.

The long summer had passed, and as they had been warned would be the case, the first-year nurses came bottom of the list when it came to holiday requests.

'If Matron's flamin' dog wanted a break, he would come before us,' grumbled Pammy.

Victoria decided to take things into her own hands. Things were moving at Baker Hall, and Roland was growing impatient. 'Sweetie, I think you have to come home sooner rather than later,' he had told her on the telephone. 'I'm afraid the time has come where your Aunt Minnie and your father really need your help.'

Victoria had made an appointment to see Matron. She didn't know about Blackie. She had never seen the dog or even heard anyone mention him. She thought that Pammy was joking.

She knocked on the door at her allotted time, glad that Pammy had agreed to wait for her at the bottom of the wooden stairs, leading to the office. 'Don't be long,' Pammy had whispered as they passed through the large entrance doors. 'If she starts asking you about the latest hairstyles or does she suit the new Max Factor Coral Pink, tell her yes and run.' Victoria had looked down the stairwell at Pammy as she reached the top and only just suppressed a giggle. The thought of stern and austere Matron asking Victoria about hairstyles was beyond ridiculous.

'Come in,' boomed Matron. There was not a nurse in St Angelus who had not trembled upon entering that office. Not so Victoria, who strode across towards the desk with confidence. Half an hour later, she was tripping back down the steps to Pammy.

'How did you get on?' Pammy asked as soon as they were back out in the fresh air.

'Well enough,' Victoria replied. 'She said I can go tomorrow. I just have the one shift to do today.'

'That's smashing that, Victoria. Your dad and your aunt will be really pleased. It must be really hard, having to move house. They will want you to do your own room anyway.'

Victoria just smiled in response. Matron had been more than accommodating. 'Of course, Nurse Baker. Please give my regards to Lord Baker.'

'I'll tell you what, Pammy. I think Matron has a bit of a problem, you know.' They were almost at the ward block and about to go their separate ways.

'Why, what?'

'Well, it's really odd, but when I was talking, she

was growling at me. It's really disconcerting. I've never heard anyone growl like that before.'

If Victoria had not been granted her holiday that morning, by the time she had finished her day shift she would have needed it.

'We have a burns case being admitted from Casualty and we need someone to special her.' Sister had bustled down the ward where Victoria and another nurse were making beds on female medical. 'Nurse Baker, prepare the first cubicle please. She will be with us in ten minutes or so. Set up a trolley for an intravenous infusion, and oxygen too. I have no idea how bad she is, just that the burns are extensive.'

On every ward in St Angelus, the cubicle nearest to the ward office was kept free, reserved for the most serious of emergency admissions. Victoria dashed into the linen cupboard and loaded her arms with fresh linen. Staff Nurse met her when she came out. 'Here, I'll help you make the bed up. Although really and truly, I think all we will need is a bottom and a draw sheet, from what I hear.'

Victoria felt sick in the pit of her stomach. This was not going to be good.

When Dessie wheeled the trolley in to the ward, with Jake Berry helping to negotiate the corners, Victoria could tell by the shortness of his manner that he was concerned about the patient. A doctor trotted along behind the trolley with a set of case notes in his hand. It was all Victoria could do not to put her hand over her mouth in horror.

The patient lying on the trolley reminded her of one of the big logs that Hudson burned in the fireplace at Baker Hall.

The body was black from head to foot. There was no hair or ears or nose or lips. The woman's fingertips were burnt away, as were her toes, and she was covered in weeping blisters. Victoria was utterly shocked when the patient spoke to her.

'Hello. Do you know where our Eddie is?' she said. Her voice was strained, but as clear as a bell.

Victoria was quite unable to respond, but fortunately Dessie chose that moment to ask them all to move aside while he manoeuvred the trolley into the cubicle. 'Every bump hurts this young lady and I don't want to risk hitting the wall and jolting her to avoid you. Put your hands over the corners, Jake. That way, if the trolley hits a wall, it's your hand what gets it and she won't feel the bump.' The atmosphere in the ward had become tense within seconds.

'She's not going to survive the day, is she?' the staff nurse whispered to the doctor.

'I think she will,' said the doctor. 'Not so long ago, she wouldn't have stood a chance. Infection would already have been growing in the open tissue, but now . . . now,' the doctor spoke with a gleam in his eye and a hint of excitement in his voice, 'I can administer antibiotics via the drip and as long as she doesn't succumb to the shock she might make it. New skin will grow if we can keep the infection at bay. We can't replace her ears or her nose, but her husband will still have a wife and her children a mother.'

To Victoria's utter amazement, the patient spoke again.

'Am I all right, doctor?' she croaked. 'Will I be all right?'

They had all moved into the cubicle and positioned themselves around the bed, ready to help with the delicate transfer from the trolley to the mattress. Victoria had no idea how they were going to manage.

'You will be fine, Ivy. Just hold on in there, my dear. We're going to make a grand team, you and I, and I have new drugs to help. Now, you're a good Catholic, I'm sure. I have the means, and you must have the will, old girl. I'm counting on it. I just need you to listen to me and pray to the good Lord to help us both. Can you do that for me?'

'I can that, doctor.' For a moment, they were all silent. 'Is our Eddie here?'

Sister had gathered together a team of eight nurses to help transfer Ivy from the trolley to the bed. They stood around all four sides of the trolley with two at the foot and Sister at the head. 'Right, nurses, we will lift this patient using each end of the draw sheet from the trolley and your fingertips. We won't use the canvass and poles,' she said to Dessie. 'I will take your head, Ivy.' Each nurse looked to Sister, hanging on her every word. No one wanted to make a wrong move. Dessie and Jake took the bulk of the weight on the draw sheet. 'This will take less than ten seconds if we do it right.

'Ivy.' Sister leant over and spoke in an authoritative but reassuring tone. It felt odd to her to use the patient's Christian name, but the new doctor had yet to learn the ways of her ward and had not supplied a surname. 'We are lifting you on to the bed now. We are all here to help. You must try to relax, and not worry about a thing.'

It took only five seconds, and although they tried to be gentle, Ivy let out a chilling and ear-piercing scream as she was laid down on the bed.

'Right, I need a bottle of 9 per cent Saline,' said the doctor, swinging the trolley across the head of the bed. 'There was one vein I managed to get into. I need to get more morphine into her now, through the base of the tubing. I need some plaster to cover the puncture afterwards and we need to keep pushing the IV through, like this.' He opened the regulator on the tube situated close to the glass bottle. 'She has lost a huge amount of body fluid through the open burns. About half the surface area of her skin is damaged and she'll be as high as a kite soon on morphia. Those dressings on the burns are gauze soaked in liquid paraffin. The consultant is on the phone to a mate of his at the Queen Vic in East Grinstead. He was a doctor in the RAF during the war and specialized in burns.

We can't decide if the dressings should be changed frequently, or if we should just reapply more liquid paraffin over the gauze and see if the skin will heal and granulate underneath. These new IV antibiotics are a game-changer. You just keep an eye on her obs and let me know if there is any deterioration. I'm going to write up her pain relief and have a word with the pharmacist. We must keep on top of that. Find a way to keep the dosage constant.'

Sister tried her hardest not to, but she looked affronted. 'Doctor, I know you are new here, but if you don't mind, this is my ward and if you have instructions for my nurses, please do it through me in future.'

To Victoria's horror, the doctor was unmoved. 'I do apologize, Sister, but I'm afraid that at this moment the patient is my main concern, not the St Angelus protocol.'

There was a moment's cold silence before Sister said, 'You remain with the patient, Nurse Baker. Please do her observations while we sort out the pain relief.'

Victoria looked at Ivy and wondered how on earth she would take her blood pressure on her blackened and dressed arm. The drip was running through almost on full flow and this panicked her slightly too. It was the first time she had ever seen a patient being given so much fluid. A catheter had been inserted in Casualty, and yet still there was almost nothing in the bag. The fluids were going in, but not coming out.

'Hello, Ivy,' she whispered. 'Are you in any pain now? Does it hurt to breathe?'

'It was the chip pan, nurse. Our Eddie, he dragged me straight out, but when the pan fell on me he chucked some water on top of me and that made it worse. He's a soft lad, is our Eddie, but he always means well. The kids will be home from school for their dinner soon. They'll be wondering what's going on. I suppose Mavis next door will see to them for me.'

Victoria was amazed. The prompt rescue explained why there was no lung damage from the smoke so that Ivy could still speak, but it was hard to see how anyone could survive such extensive surface burns.

'Don't you worry about the kids or your Eddie,' she said. 'We need to look after you right now, Ivy. Just you. Remember the promise you made to the doctor? I'm just off to fetch a new drip bottle; I'll be back in two seconds. You say that first prayer Doctor asked for, to help him.'

Victoria was more like two minutes, but no longer. She risked a ticking off from Sister as she as good as ran across the corridor and flew into the clean utility room, grabbed a drip bottle of 9 per cent saline solution and shot straight back in through the cubicle door.

Before she had even reached the bedside, she could tell by Ivy's breathing that something was terribly wrong. By the time she had called the doctor back into the room, Ivy was almost gone.

'Get the head off the bed,' said the doctor. 'Quick.'

Victoria didn't know where she would find the strength. She placed both hands on the bottom of the metal headboard and tugged upwards. 'It's stuck,' she said.

'Here, let me help.' Staff Nurse had run into the cubicle. They lifted the headboard upwards and clear of the bed in one go, and looked at the doctor, but he shook his head.

'It's no good,' he said. 'She's gone. I can't even try to massage her heart; her chest burns are far too bad. Damn, damn, damn.' The doctor smashed his fist into the wall. 'I knew it, I knew it. I said that transferring her to the ward before she was properly stabilized would be risky. It was the shock. If we could just have kept her where she was for twenty-four hours. We need a unit near to Casualty for the more serious cases. I keep saying this and yet bloody Matron refuses to give up the space.'

Victoria just stared at him blankly. She hadn't heard the rumours, and had no idea that he was referring to Matron's own accommodation, which the trust had requested be turned into a casualty theatre and a serious admissions unit. A request Matron had steadfastly rejected. She knew that once she gave in, the four elderly sisters on the accommodation corridor, along with Sister Antrobus would be turfed out too. The four sisters had worked and lived at St Angelus for over sixty years. They had given their entire life to nursing the sick of Liverpool. She would protect them to her last breath.

As they covered Ivy with a sheet, a man with a blackened face and bandaged hands appeared in the doorway.

'Is that our Ivy, nurse?' he asked, his eyes filling with tears. 'They wouldn't let me leave Casualty till me hands were bandaged. What did she say? Was she in pain? Did she ask for me?'

To Victoria's relief, Sister appeared in the doorway. 'We shall go to the sitting room. Nurse Baker, perhaps you could bring a tray of tea. Mr Collins has had a very nasty shock.'

'Yes, Sister, right away.' But Victoria always regretted that she hadn't been able to tell him that Ivy had said he always meant well, and that her voice had been loaded with love and affection for her soft lad as she lay there with her life slipping away.

There had been much discussion in the group regarding who would take holiday leave and who would remain to cover. Victoria couldn't wait to return home to Baker Hall and yet she also dreaded it. For the past three months, every other weekend, Roland had driven over to Liverpool if Victoria had a day off and driven back on the same day. Over that time they had become even closer, and although he had never so much as kissed her they had held hands and never stopped talking. She knew it was Roland she wanted to see, more than the Hall. She had worked every weekend for the past month and so it had been five weeks since she had seen him. They had written to each other twice a week. She was tired of writing letters. She wanted to spend more than a day at a time with him and to know whether they had a future together, because difficult as not seeing him was, not being able to talk about him openly with her friends was equally hard. Dana knew, but Victoria had been too shy to say anything to the others until she was sure she had something to tell them. He had wanted to collect her, but it was a Monday and so she told him that she would take the train and arrive at Bolton at five thirty when he had finished work. She was glad of the day alone. Ivy and her distraught husband had disturbed her. She had wanted to do more. To visit Ivy's home, to help with the children. But Victoria knew her job was nursing at St Angelus, and she had to remember that. Not becoming involved with patients and their lives was going to prove to be her biggest challenge.

She saw him as soon as she stepped down on to the platform. He was difficult to miss, because he was running towards her, shouting her name. It was almost nine months since Victoria had taken the train from Bolton to Liverpool. She was aware a very different person was returning. At last, she had finally been allocated her holiday and she could barely wait to see Roland.

'Victoria, over here.'

She could see nothing now for the burst of steam from the engine, and then suddenly he burst through the white mist and she was in his arms.

'I thought they'd never let you leave that hospital,' he whispered into her ear. 'I was scared to look forward to your coming home in case it didn't happen.'

Victoria looked up at Roland and wondered how their friendship had become love. No words had been spoken. It had just happened. A seamless transition. He smiled down at her as though he had read her thoughts. 'Is it acceptable for me to do this?' he asked, and without waiting for a reply lightly kissed her on the lips.

'Well, I hope so,' Victoria replied, smiling back up at him, 'as you just did.'

'Well, that's a relief, then. I did worry I may have misread the runes. That maybe you had found a doctor who had stolen your affections, although I have to say Teddy came home last weekend and reassured me on that score.'

'Teddy?' Victoria almost shouted his name. 'Don't speak to me about your brother. I still haven't forgiven him.'

Roland slipped Victoria's hand into one of his and picked up her case with the other as they headed towards the car. He and Victoria had almost had a row about his brother and so he was happy to let the subject slip.

'Your letters sound as though you've been having a beastly time,' he said instead.

'Oh, no, I'm not. Not yet anyway. The beastly time begins when I return to my new placement, after the holiday. I am on ward two with Sister Antrobus. They call her the Anteater, because she almost looks like one. She near killed Pammy's nursing career stone dead. No one knows how she survived.'

'Has Pammy given you lots of tips?'

'Oh, yes. I've met a lot of women like the Anteater. Lancashire is full of strong women. She doesn't scare me one bit.'

Slipping into the passenger seat while Roland strapped her case on to the back, Victoria untied her headscarf, shook it out and folded it into a neat square on her lap as her hair fell down over her shoulders. She knew, deep down, that it was a lie to say she wasn't scared of the Anteater. She was terrified. She also knew that now, after Roland's kiss, they were officially courting, even if neither of them had said so. A life as a solicitor's wife in Bolton with Roland was very appealing, but she had resolved that she would continue with her nursing until she sat her finals in a little over two years' time. Since St Angelus didn't employ married nurses, one day she and the others would have to make a choice. For her it would be to be a nurse, or to be a wife and mother. To give up the job she was loving so much, the job that made her feel useful and vital and fulfilled on a daily basis, or not to marry the man she was sure she was now in love with.

They chatted as they drove about Roland's work, the estate, and the impending sale. About the fact that her father refused to take his calls and that Roland thought the new solicitor was probably dragging things out, helping himself to a large chunk of what was left of the estate.

'Gosh, Roland, I am so sorry. Aunt Minnie has gone quite mad. I can't even mention your name on the telephone without her changing the subject. That's why I haven't told them you are bringing me home. We will arrive together.'

Roland removed his hand from the wheel and slipped it into Victoria's. They exchanged a sheepish smile, shot through with the thrill of first love. Victoria found it difficult to stop grinning and, not wanting Roland to see that, she turned to look out of the side window. She breathed in deeply the scent of the heavy autumnal mist sweeping across the moors as they motored away from Bolton and out into the countryside. Despite everything, it was good to be home.

'What will you tell them?' he asked. 'Will you tell them we are together and we hope to be married?'

'Are we? Do we?' Victoria was still grinning.

'I jolly well hope so, unless you make a habit of letting men kiss you at railway stations.' He lifted Victoria's hand to his lips and kissed her fingers. 'I know I'm not supposed to mention him and I don't want to spoil the moment, but as you are looking so beautiful and serene and you are trapped in my car and cannot escape, I have to ask you again. Teddy's heart is broken, you know. He thought he had finally persuaded your friend to fall for his charms, but it's been months now and she won't even talk to him. He was home last weekend, full of woe.'

'I'm not surprised in the slightest. He's a cad. Asked Dana to meet him and then stood her up without a by your leave. At the very least, he could have made contact with one of us to let her know.'

Roland turned the corner into the driveway and Victoria could see Baker Hall standing proud against the skyline in the distance.

'But he says he did, that he gave a note to one of your nurses to pass on.'

Victoria gave a snort of derision. 'Roland, do you really believe that? That he would give a note to one of us and we wouldn't pass it on? No, I'm sorry, if Teddy doesn't know how to behave, then he can keep well clear of Dana. She has vowed that hell will freeze over before she'll ever speak to him again. And frankly, if he goes near her he will have me to deal with and then I shall hand him over to Pammy to finish off. No doctor plays around with or hurts the feelings of any one of us without having to face the consequences from us all.'

'Ouch,' said Roland, as he flinched. 'Remind me never to be late.'

'It wasn't that he was late, Roland. He stood her up entirely. The poor girl stood there waiting for

380

him for two and a half hours. She had to sneak out of the nurses' home. She could have got into serious trouble. Don't you understand?'

'All right, I do. I am no longer defending my brother. I well and truly rest my case; he can battle on alone.' Roland was laughing, but also thinking to himself how much more confident Victoria was since leaving Baker Hall and all the sadness that surrounded it. 'I hear on the grapevine that they are almost packed up at Baker Hall. Although the new solicitor won't speak to me, the agent is a good man and has been keeping me informed. I don't want you to be upset.'

Victoria saw the concern for her on his face. He was everything her father had never been to her mother. Protective, and caring, and she loved it.

'I won't be upset. I have had a long time to think and to realize that there are things in life far more important than an estate. Health for one. Roland, have you ever eaten chips?'

As Baker Hall came into view, Victoria was surprised to see removal lorries parked in front of the house.

'Have things gone already?' she asked.

'No, not quite.' Roland had avoided going into details on the journey, but now there was no getting away from it. Victoria would have to be told everything. 'I've seen some of the listings. The paintings are being sold at auction in London, but the rest is being sold here. Did you know that you

381

had almost forty horse rugs in the stables, or so the inventory said?'

'Yes. Some of them were there long before I was born. Mother looked after everything so well.' Victoria's eyes filled with tears and a sob caught in her throat. She had been desperate to come home, but suddenly, Roland or not, she wished she were miles away.

'Victoria!' Aunt Minnie ran down the steps. 'What are you doing here? I wasn't expecting you until this evening.'

Two men with folders in their arms came down the steps behind Aunt Minnie and Victoria guessed that they were the new solicitors. She felt Roland bristle next to her. Her aunt completely ignored Roland as she continued. 'I had hoped this would all have been finished weeks ago, but these men, they drink so much tea, it has taken them twice as long as expected. It's the war, you know; all the best workmen appear to have been killed off. I'm amazed this lot are tolerated by their employers.'

'I wanted to get here as quickly as I could. I've come to help, Aunt Minnie. You can't do this all alone. Where's Daddy?' she asked.

She felt anger bubbling up inside. She was no longer the shy and unsure Victoria who had left home nine months ago. This Victoria had made friends, passed exams, fallen in love and held patients' hands as they exited the world. She had worked long hours, been with people as they were told the best and the worst of news. In short, she had learnt about life outside Baker Hall. This Victoria knew her own mind. Roland had put the palm of his hand in the middle of her back and was exerting gentle yet reassuring pressure. If you fall, I will catch you, said his touch, as clearly as any words.

'Oh, your father. He's worse than the workmen. Sitting in his study. Hasn't lifted a finger. Shouted at them when they came in to take the pictures down. I told the auctioneer that he will have to sell your father as a job lot. He refuses to move.'

'Poor Daddy.' Victoria turned to Roland. She wanted someone who didn't really know her father and all his faults to agree with her.

'Poor Daddy my eye,' said Minnie. 'The dower house is lovely. You know, now that it is done, I cannot understand what has possessed us all to hold on to this crumbling pile for so long. I was dreading the auction only a few months ago, and now I can't wait for it to come. I'm afraid there is nowhere for you to sleep inside – all packed up. You'll have to go to the dower house and I will meet you over there.'

'I think I'll just take a look around the Hall, if you don't mind.' The pressure in the small of her back increased, just a fraction.

'But the dower house is so warm. There are no fires lit in the Hall. It's chilly in there. And I've had all your things moved over. Go and have some tea, darling. It will take a little adjustment.'

Minnie's voice had moved from assertive to pleading and Victoria instinctively felt she was hiding something. 'You don't want to traipse around the place now. I know you won't accept it overnight, no one knows that better than me, but honestly, in time you will feel just the same, glad to be rid of a freezing, oversized mausoleum.'

A sudden noise stopped all conversation.

A look of bewilderment crossed their faces as they stood united. Paralysed by disbelief. And then they heard a piercing scream from one of the maids and Roland moved ahead of Victoria, up the steps to the house. Still she could not move. She had heard that sound so many times before, but never inside the house. The sound of her father's gun.

Her father's dog put his head on Victoria's lap and stared up at her, his eyes dark pools of misery.

'That's the worst thing about dogs, you can't explain to them what has happened. They don't understand,' said Roland, as he sat next to Victoria on the big comfortable sofa in the library. The label attached to the string that hung from one arm said that it was lot number 147. They both nursed glasses containing the best brandy Baker Hall had left in the cellar. The funeral had been held that afternoon, allowing mourners time to travel from London.

Although her father had spent most of his time in recent years alone, brooding and blaming, now that he had gone the Hall felt to Victoria as though the life had been sucked out of it. Minnie walked into the room, still in her black funeral attire complete with her hat, and spoke in a voice that was pleading for forgiveness.

'May I join you?'

'Yes, of course,' said Victoria. 'Please, come and sit with Roland and me.' She slipped her hand into Roland's. Within an hour of the doctor having pronounced her father dead, she had taken charge.

'Baker Hall is now yours,' Roland had told her. 'You're in charge, not your father, God rest his soul, or your Aunt Minnie. It's you. I'm sorry, that's the solicitor in me, but I thought you should know. I documented your father's will. Everything goes to you. Many of your father's debts have died with him. Obviously, there are still death duties but things aren't quite as bad as they were. You can negotiate with the Inland Revenue as this is possibly an unusual situation. I'm sorry, Victoria, but I know you will want to know.'

Victoria knew that if Roland hadn't been at her side she would have been swamped by all that faced her.

'Right,' she said, looking at him through eyes blackened and smudged by tears. 'In that case, the first thing I am going to do is sack those solicitors. Is that all right with you?'

Roland smiled down at her. 'Darling, can I make that task a little easier for you? May I do it?'

'Did you see that woman, Lady Bella, at the funeral?' said Minnie now as she flopped down on the sofa next to Victoria. 'God, if only she knew the truth. She had been trying to catch your father's eye ever since your mother died. She would have loved to get her feet firmly under our table and bring her horrible children here.' Aunt Minnie shuddered at the thought. Victoria hadn't spoken to her much at all during the day and her aunt had felt it.

Roland had been wonderful and had seen each of the mourners out through the front door with a businesslike farewell. He had acted just as a husband would have done and that was not lost on Victoria or, unbeknown to her, Aunt Minnie.

He had helped to arrange the funeral, instructed the caterers, made small talk with the mourners. He had dealt with the police and the agents.

'I don't know how we would have managed without you this past week, Roland,' said Aunt Minnie. 'You went way beyond the call of duty and do you know, all the time, I couldn't stop thinking about my husband,' she tilted her head to remind Victoria, as though she could have forgotten, 'your Uncle Jamie.' There was a moment of silence while her remarks sank in.

'I appreciate that.' It was Roland who responded as he twirled his glass around in his fingers in a self-conscious manner. Victoria glanced at him under her eyelashes. This was his moment, not hers.

'All the men in this family have gone,' Minnie went on. 'I kept thinking, if it hadn't been for that hellish war, those young men would still be with us, at the head of our family today. I thought I saw their ghosts mixing with the mourners, and then I knew I was seeing them as they were, before the war, before they died. What in God's name did we all do to deserve this?'

'Don't cry, Aunt Minnie. Here you go, drink the rest of this brandy, and put your head on the cushion. You must be exhausted.' Victoria reached for a cushion at the small of her back and placed it behind her aunt's head.

'Thank you, sweetie,' said Aunt Minnie. She patted Victoria's hand.

'Do you think if I had come home earlier?' Victoria had been asking herself that question since the moment her father took his own life and now she had voiced it and steeled herself for the answer.

'Oh, no, darling. He was in his own world. I had told him you were coming a dozen times, he was lost to us all.'

'Baker Hall is really done for now, isn't it?' Victoria said to Roland later, as they took a stroll around the now overgrown formal garden.

'It is, my love, I'm afraid it is,' he replied gently.

Victoria began to cry again. 'I'm sorry, I just feel a bit sad. My father was a lazy old goat, but I was born here, you know, in my parents' bed. I feel as though we are doomed. Nothing my father or Aunt Minnie or the poor lost men in our family could have done, really. We are all powerless. If Hitler hadn't got us, the taxes would. How much are the death duties?' Victoria knew this particular sword had been hanging over her father's head since her grandfather had died.

'They want eighty per cent of the value of the estate.' Roland saw no point in holding anything back. She had to know. 'There has been no interest in the house itself.' He took a deep breath before he imparted the next news and reached out to take her hand. 'They are sending the bulldozers in. The house is to be demolished.'

'Demolished?' She stared at Roland in disbelief. 'Demolished?' she said again. 'Oh, don't misunderstand me, none of us should live here. It's over. Time to end the era. I think it's just sad that the house is to be demolished.' She shook her head. Roland could see that the news was proving difficult for his capable and competent Victoria to absorb.

'The contents, the cottages and the farms will raise enough money to appease the tax man – in fact there will now be some left over – but no one in this day and age wants to buy a house this large,' he said.

'Oh, I know that. That awful friend of Aunt Minnie's who came up from London for the funeral, do you know what she said to me?' Roland shook his head. 'She said, "Darling, you must not feel bad. I read in *Country Life* that they are demolishing a grand house a week." I just didn't think that Baker Hall would be one of them.'

★　★　★

Later that evening, when Aunt Minnie had returned to the dower house, Roland and Victoria sat on the sofa and drank the last of the brandy.

'If we drink it, it can't be sold,' she said, emptying the decanter into their glasses. She had cried all the tears she was going to. She wondered how many nights her father had spent on the same sofa, looking into the same glass, drinking the same brandy, asking himself what on earth he was going to do. How lonely must he have felt? How lost?

'Take a good look round,' she went on, slightly tipsy. 'Baker Hall won't even be standing soon, nothing but a pile of bricks and rubble.' She waved her glass in the air. 'Do you know what the really sad thing is? There's no one left, other than Hudson and ourselves, to care.'

Victoria was unused to brandy. She began to choke. 'Oh, Lord, I shouldn't really drink this,' she said.

Roland patted her between the shoulders and then, as it so often did, his hand rested in the small of her back, to comfort her. More used to brandy than Victoria, he was also feeling a little drunk. His inhibitions vanished. Filled with longing for the girl at his side, he slipped to the floor and balanced on one knee.

'Lady Victoria Baker, will you do me the honour of becoming my wife?'

Victoria sobered up in seconds. 'But, Roland, I'm a nurse now and I want to finish my training. They say that great advances are to be made as the NHS becomes more established. It's changed people's lives, you know, and with the advances in antibiotics and tuberculosis therapy, it's going to become even bigger.'

Victoria was quoting almost verbatim from the poster on the notice board in Lovely Lane. Roland could not quite believe what he was hearing. 'Victoria, have you read that somewhere?' he asked. 'And is that a yes or a no?'

'It's a yes, Roland, but you'll have to wait until I have sat my finals. I have to see this through, and then we can marry.'

Roland got back on to the sofa. 'Come here,' he said, and kissed her with a passion that took her by surprise. He wrapped his arms around her. 'Now that we are engaged, and I know you are mine, I can wait until you have sat your finals.'

'The time will fly by,' said Victoria.

'Do I have to wait for absolutely everything that marriage will bring?' he whispered into her hair. Victoria blushed furiously and buried her face in his chest.

'I was rather hoping not,' she whispered with an audacity she never knew she possessed.

It was all Roland needed. He scooped her up in his arms and carried her up the stairs to her room and to the carved four-poster bed with the brown label hanging off the post. What they were doing felt right and natural to Victoria. Generations of Baker women before her had done the very same. But she would be the last in Baker Hall.

CHAPTER 20

The Lovely Lane nurses were surprised to see Emily Haycock hurrying down the path for her second visit in less than an hour. It was immediately apparent by the expression on her face that all was not well.

'I won't beat about the bush, nurses,' she said as she entered the room. 'We have had some dreadful news, I'm afraid.' Mrs Duffy moved towards the television, ready to turn it off. 'Nurse Baker has had some very bad news. She will not be returning to Lovely Lane on Sunday as we expected. Her father has died, rather suddenly.' No sooner had she spoken than the news headline flashed up on the television screen behind her. *Lord Baker of historic Baker Hall in Lancashire has today taken his life using his own shotgun.*

Mrs Duffy stopped in her tracks as she stared at the television, waiting for the broadcaster to continue. Her hand hovered over the on-off dial as Emily said, 'Well, I suppose we will hear all the details now.'

A photograph of Victoria's parents taken on their

wedding day appeared on the screen, followed by a picture of Victoria in her coming-out gown. There was a sharp intake of breath from the girls. They had all known Victoria was the daughter of a lord and that she lived in a grand house – after all, there was a photograph of Baker Hall on the mirror in her room – but until this moment not one of them had realized quite how grand their Victoria of Lovely Lane was.

'Will she be coming back?' Pammy was the first to speak up when they had finished listening to the news.

'We hope so. She is a very good nurse and St Angelus will be the worse without her, but obviously, that was not mentioned in the telephone call. I imagine she'll call again in a week or so. Nurse Tanner, can I ask a very big favour of you?' Emily would never have imagined herself doing this, but Pammy had survived ward two and knew Sister Antrobus and all her ways and foibles. Tomorrow was the first day of the new placements and Emily was a dozen student nurses short. September was a favourite month for nursing holidays. Nurse Baker was one of a number to have taken two weeks' annual leave and one Emily hadn't known about until Matron had informed her. No matter what, Sister Antrobus would complain if she were a nurse down and Emily knew that somehow it would reflect on her. She needed someone to cover for Nurse Baker for a week or so. She couldn't use one of the third-year nurses; it would be too much to ask on top of their finals. Celia Forsyth had been her first choice, but she was about to go on two weeks' leave herself. Pammy was tough. She had survived once, she would survive again. She saw the look of dismay, quickly followed by pride, when she asked Pammy to cover.

'Of course I will,' Pammy replied. 'I'd do anything for Victoria, and I know she would do the same for me.'

'Bless you, Nurse Tanner. I know it is a lot to ask, but I immediately thought of you. I have every confidence you will be fine. I cannot begin to tell you how grateful I am.'

As Emily left the house, she noticed a young man darting across the road from the nurses' home towards the trees. Well, that's very funny, she thought. She remembered seeing the same young man months earlier, and the reason she had noticed him then was because of his suspicious behaviour. She went back inside to seek out Mrs Duffy.

'Have you noticed a young man hanging around outside?' she asked.

'Well, do you know, there was someone, but it was a while ago now. He disappeared. Is he back?'

'It looks like it. Don't say anything to the girls, but I think I will mention it to Dessie, see what he thinks.'

'Well, tell him to be sure he pops in to see me,' said Mrs Duffy. 'He loves my Scotch pancakes.'

'I'm sure he wouldn't miss them,' said Emily, grinning. As she walked down the steps, she noticed that the scruffy young man had disappeared, again.

CHAPTER 21

T he dining room was uncommonly quiet as the girls ate their breakfast. They were stunned by the news of the previous evening. Even Celia Forsyth had so far refrained from providing her usual waspish sarcasm.

Pammy dashed in with her cape on. 'Has anyone seen Dana this morning?' She studied her reflection in the mirror hanging over the fireplace, balancing precariously on tiptoes on the stone surround of the hearth so that she could stretch up to see herself. 'This mirror was definitely put up by a man,' she complained.

Mrs Duffy came in from the kitchen carrying a plate piled high with warm buttered toast, and Pammy turned from the mirror to sit down in one of the empty seats next to Beth. She had noticed a change in the other girl over recent weeks, ever since the night Celia had snapped at Mrs Duffy, and now she smiled at her as she helped herself to a slice of toast from the plate. 'Are you all right, Beth?' she asked. 'You are on paediatrics for your new placement, aren't you?'

Beth looked grateful that Pammy was speaking

to her. She knew that the girls had lost faith in her as a result of her friendship with Celia. The fact was, Beth had assumed that Celia was like her. She was wrong. Celia's manner was as efficient as hers, but her nature was unkind.

'I am. I have studied all I can before I start. I like children, when they behave, so that should help.'

Pammy grinned. 'Lovely,' she said. 'You should be all right then. Unlike me, having to face the Anteater again.'

Beth felt slightly disappointed that she hadn't been asked to cover for Victoria, but she also knew that no amount of study could prepare anyone to survive Sister Antrobus. She secretly admired Pammy for her forthright manner and immense gumption.

'Pass the cornflakes,' snapped Celia, who had been sitting at the table for the past five minutes and was ready for a second helping. 'My father has sent a car to collect me and I have to hurry.' Just at that moment, Lizzie arrived in the room. She reached over and grabbed the packet of corn-flakes from the table and out of Celia's reach.

'Say please,' she said, with as much menace as she could inject into her ordinarily gentle voice. 'Some of us haven't had our first bowl yet, so just wait.'

Celia helped herself to a piece of toast from the tower on the plate in the middle of the table and glared at Lizzie.

'I'll walk up with you, Pammy.' Dana stood in the doorway, with an envelope in her hand. 'I've written a letter to Victoria, everyone; I hope you don't mind. I said that it's from all of us. I told her we were all sorry for her troubles and that we were thinking of her, and wished we could all give her a hug. She's been a good friend to me has Victoria.'

'Well done you, Nurse Brogan,' said Lizzie. 'I had the same thought myself this morning. You've beaten me to it.'

Pammy stood and stretched to pin her cap in the mirror. 'I walked back down from the hospital last night with two of the doctors. They told me they're planning a dance in the new hospital social club. It has an official opening night six weeks from now. I'm all for that. I told them it would be a full house from Lovely Lane.'

Just then they all heard the front door shut and a car door slam, and looking out of the window saw Celia Forsyth being driven away.

'Would you look at that,' said Mrs Duffy. 'Not so much as a by your leave. I hadn't even noticed she had left the table.'

'Well, almost a full house,' Pammy muttered under her breath.

'You do know that if you are seen talking to men in the street, doctors or not, you will have Matron to answer to, don't you?' said Mrs Duffy.

'Oh, Mrs Duffy, what harm can it do? We were only planning a little dance.'

'I'm going into the kitchen now. I can't be hearing this. Poor Nurse Baker. She's all I can think about at the moment, not doctors and dances. She must be out of her mind with the shock.'

Dana stood next to Pammy at the fireplace as she ate her toast and fixed her own hair. As Mrs Duffy walked past, they exchanged a sympathetic glance in the mirror.

'Would you wait for me tonight?' Pammy whispered. 'I told the doctors I would walk down with them again. I'm dead keen for this dance to happen, aren't you?'

'Not on your life, thank you very much,' Dana replied. 'I've had my fill of doctors and that's a fact. They all think too much of themselves as far as I'm concerned.'

Pammy didn't know the full story. Victoria had been a good friend to Dana and kept the details of the broken date to herself, and Pammy knew better than to push the subject any further. She put Dana's antagonism down to the fact that she was a farm girl from Ireland and probably not very experienced at conversing with men, doctors or not. Neither was Pammy, come to that, but she wasn't quite as hostile to the idea as Dana appeared to be.

She checked once more that her cap was straight. 'God, I wish I could wear me lippy on the wards,' she said. 'I feel washed out without it. Let's hope our hats survive the breeze today.'

Pammy had no way of knowing that Dana's moodiness this morning wasn't anything to do with doctors, or even with Celia Forsyth. She had received a letter from home which she had read quickly. The contents made her blood run cold.

Patrick is working on the roads in Liverpool, her mammy had written. *He came home for the harvest, but has gone back again. Daddy says that men are earning a hundred pounds a day laying the new roads in England.*

Dana had shoved the letter back in the envelope and left it on the desk in her room to read again later. Her heart was pounding. Patrick in Liverpool? Why couldn't he have gone somewhere else? She talked herself down from the panic the letter had induced.

He doesn't know where you are. He doesn't know where you live. Liverpool is a big city. The new roads are being laid miles away. He will never find you. By the time she had reached the dining room, she was calmer.

'Shush now, nurses,' said Mrs Duffy, coming back from the kitchen to begin collecting up the plates. 'Let's have a bit of quiet. We are in the midst of death. You should all call into evening mass on your way home, if you can make it, and say a prayer for Nurse Baker.'

Beth, who was sitting quietly at the table reading her Evelyn Pearce, spoke up.

'Mrs Duffy, I didn't hear Celia go and she has my revision notes in her room. Could you let me in to collect them, please?' Celia was the only nurse in the home who kept her bedroom door locked. The rest of the rooms remained on the snip and nurses walked in and out of each other's rooms at will.

'Of course I will. Here, take my master key and run up now. Bring the key back down on your way out. Do you know where she will have put them?'

'Oh, yes, they'll be on her desk. I'll be right back.'

There was a clatter of chairs and dishes as the nurses helped clear away and a rumble of footsteps on the wooden floor as they dashed towards the stairs.

'Could you post this letter to Nurse Baker, please? I've put a stamp on it.' Dana held out her letter to Mrs Duffy.

'Come here, you,' said Mrs Duffy. Dana noticed that her eyes were watery. She threw her arms around Dana and gave her a bear hug. Dana took a deep breath. She wanted to stand there and melt into the hug. To sink into it and be repaired.

'You have a heart of gold, you, writing that letter to Nurse Baker,' said Mrs Duffy. Dana nodded her thanks, not daring herself to speak.

Her heart was heavy as they walked towards the hospital, her mind full of the letter from home. Concern for Victoria. Disappointment in Teddy. Fear of Patrick. There was an autumn chill in the air, and the girls had their caps tucked under their capes as though they were sheltering a newborn puppy. They had learnt, within their first days on the wards during a wet March, that wearing a cap on a damp day affected the starch and the cap, instead of standing firm, frill proud, wilted like a damp handkerchief. The Mersey mist had much to answer for.

'Have you decided what you are going to wear for the dance?' Pammy decided to chance her luck. 'The doctors are very keen and they have asked if some of us will help to organize it and be on the social club committee. There is always one nurse from each intake and I said it could be me. You don't mind, do you?'

'I'm not going,' said Dana unequivocally. 'Even if I wanted to, I don't have a dress for that kind of thing, and I don't care who is on the committee.'

She thought of the clothes hanging up in her wardrobe. The day dress she had bought on the market at Castlebar. The evening dress made by her mammy of black crepe, with six mother of pearl buttons placed in a neat row down the front, which at the time Dana had thought was gorgeous. Now, having seen the fashionable clothes Maisie Tanner had sewn for her daughter, Victoria's day dresses, bought in the best stores in London, and even those of studious Beth, Dana would rather die than be seen out in any of them. She had decided that her uniform was the best-quality dress she owned.

'But you must. You have to. We can't go without you,' squealed Pammy. 'Beth has agreed to go, sort of, and it will be just what Victoria needs when she gets back, to cheer her up like.'

They both turned as they heard the sound of Beth's footsteps running to catch them up. 'Did you find your revision notes?' asked Dana, who wanted to borrow them herself.

'I, er, I did, thanks.'

'You will definitely come to the dance, won't you, Beth?' said Pammy, who had now decided on a different tactic to persuade Dana to agree.

'Only under duress,' Beth replied. 'But, yes, I'll go to the ball and make a right spectacle of myself.'

'Oh, it's not a ball, Beth,' said Pammy with a look of astonishment. 'It's just a doctors' dance in the social club.'

Beth gave a rare smile. 'I do know the difference between the two, Pammy. It was just a figure of speech.'

Pammy laughed with embarrassment. 'Of course you do. I'm such a div. Anyway, Dana, we will speak to my mam. She'll sort you out with a frock. No one can resist Mam. She'll have you round her little finger and your measurements on her dressmaker's dummy in no time. You too will come to the ball, Cinderella, along with Beth here. You don't mind me being on the committee, do you, Beth?'

'Well, no, just as long as you run everything past me. These things have to be organized properly.

They don't just happen, you know. Maybe I should come to the meetings with you? Just to be sure.'

Even Dana, from the depths of her despair, could not resist a smile as they walked on up the lane. It only took five minutes in the company of her friends to calm her. It was obvious that the man she had thought of so much over the past few months was not who she had thought he was, but why would he be? She had experienced the full gamut of emotions, from upset and disappointment through to anger. Now she accepted that for girls like her there were only ever men like Patrick O'Dowd. Maybe if he bumped into her in Liverpool, she should just give in. Maybe that was how it was meant to be. She might be nursing in a big city, but she knew in her heart of hearts that she would only ever be a girl from an Atlantic-coast farming village, whose grandest sartorial concession had been to leave her dungarees and rubber boots back at home on the farm.

Men like Teddy were attracted to pretty, well-spoken, elegant girls like Victoria and not to tomboy daughters of an Irish farmer. She could not alter the ways of the world or even of Liverpool, and she most certainly could not change her destiny. She was Dana Brogan from the farm, and despite the pretty uniform and the cape and the frilled hat, notwithstanding attempting to discover a more exciting and brighter future, away from milking cows and planting potatoes, that was really who she was and always would be. Who was she trying to kid?

As she walked to the hospital with Pammy and Beth on a dank and dismal morning, Dana accepted that one day her future would be with Patrick O'Dowd and she had just better get used to it.

Beth hadn't been able to find her revision notes anywhere in Celia's room. Like all their rooms, it was tidy and well ordered. Mrs Duffy inspected them once a week to check that the maids were doing their job properly, and if anywhere was less than shipshape the offending maid and the nurse herself soon knew about it.

'Well, blow me,' said Beth out loud as she carefully looked through the papers on Celia's desk again. It occurred to her that maybe Celia had left for her holiday and taken Beth's handwritten notes with her. They had an exam in two weeks' time and Beth felt fury rising as it began to dawn on her that that was exactly what Celia had done, leaving her in the lurch.

'You are just the limit,' Beth whispered as she picked up Celia's book on trolley setting for nurses and then, intrigued, the sheet of paper which slipped out.

It had fluttered down on to the desk and Beth thought she could see the word *Dana* written on the front in a bold and confident script. Beth couldn't help herself. Slowly, she opened the letter.

'Why is this here?' Beth wondered out loud. Without knowing why, she slipped the note into her apron pocket then tiptoed out of the room, locked the door with the master key and went downstairs to Mrs Duffy.

CHAPTER 22

Matron fussed around the kitchen. She had invited Sister Antrobus for supper again and she was due in less than half an hour. She polished the sherry glasses and made sure the plates were warm.

'I hope she likes chicken, Blackie,' she said to the dog, who was almost leaning against the oven door, looking hopeful. 'Some people don't, you know. Oh, I know you do. Put that tongue back in, or you will burn it on the door. It's the first time I've ever made this sauce. Any sauce, really. Can you tell?' The dog looked up at her as she popped a lump of butter on to the potatoes, ears pricked, tongue at the ready to catch anything that might fall from the table. Butter was still difficult to acquire in the shops, but not so hard if you ran a hospital. She transferred the dish from the gas oven into the old warming oven at the side of the big chimney, feeling smug that she had insisted it remained when they removed the old range last year.

She wanted everything to be perfect when Sister Antrobus arrived. They had spent some of their off-duty time together. Matron had invited her to a concert at the Philharmonic Hall to hear the Messiah last Christmas. They had also attended a play together at the Royal Court Theatre. Matron had been thrilled on that particular occasion.

'Do you know, I haven't been here since before the big fire,' she had told Sister Antrobus.

'Well, we must jolly well come again,' Sister Antrobus had said and Matron's heart sang. However, no return invitation had been forthcoming. No indication that Sister Antrobus was keen to spend more time in her company was apparent and she was longing to spend another evening alone with her, just the two of them.

She remembered the first time she had invited Sister Antrobus to her private rooms in the hospital. She knew how people talked, especially the porters. But, realizing it would be odd to invite Sister Antrobus to another concert, she had become almost desperate. She felt covered in shame when she thought of the tactics she had deployed, and when the hour had actually arrived, her stomach had quivered, her mouth had felt dry and her hands had been shaking as she listened for the footsteps on the wooden stairs leading to the door of her flat. She remembered how it had taken her weeks to build up the courage to issue the invitation. At all costs, she must never reveal her true feelings.

Now, dashing into the bedroom, she ran a comb through her hair yet again and checked her fingernails. For the first time in her life, they were adorned with polish. Cutex Pink Shimmer from Woolworths. She looked at herself in the mirror. She very rarely wore her own clothes. Quite often she remained in her office until after the night staff had come on duty. She would have a word with Night Sister, walk Blackie around the perimeter of the hospital and return to her flat, take a bath and change into her night-clothes. Recently a television had been installed in the flat and she sometimes watched the news before she took herself off to bed. And that was her life. Work, dog walk, Horlicks, the news, bed. It was the same every single night. Night after night. Year after year, until now, at fifty, she was acutely aware that there would be no surprises left in life. She was who she was. Alone. Without family or friends, and she could see no way that would change. Unless she did something about it.

'How do I look, Blackie?' She turned from the mirror to face her affectionate companion. She had carried him into her room and sat him on the bed where he lay on her pillow, gazing up adoringly. 'Will I pass?' she asked, as she leant over to ruffle his fur. Smiling at the little dog, she looked into his doting eyes. She felt happy. It was not a feeling that was familiar to her, but tonight her favourite person was coming to supper and she was filled with delight. Yet it was not a happiness she would be able to share, because she had no idea how or where to begin. Her feelings would be her own. Never to be revealed to anyone, because she didn't know how.

'Well, I have to say, that was the most delicious sauce. I would never have considered putting a sauce on chicken. How very clever.' Sister Antrobus wiped her mouth with her napkin and, having devoured most of the chicken, leant back in the chair and raised her wine glass.

The wine was sweet. Matron was furious with herself. She knew nothing about wine and had sought advice from the woman in the wine store.

'I drink Guinness meself,' the woman had cackled, 'but we do sell an awful lot of it. Oh yeah, that's me bestseller on a Satdy night. You can't go wrong with that.'

Matron thought she must be right. How could she possibly go wrong with a bestseller? But now the wine, which was so yellow it looked more like a urine sample, had been poured into the glasses and she wanted to die with embarrassment. It was horribly sweet and sickly, but she noticed that this hadn't prevented Sister Antrobus from drinking it in rather large gulps. She thought that Sister Antrobus probably had to do that to disguise the taste.

Matron had already decided she would return to the wine shop tomorrow and give that woman what for. Bestseller my backside, she thought, and she had bought half a dozen bottles, too, as they were on special offer. She wondered whether or not the dust on the shoulders of the bottles should have been a giveaway. It had almost spoilt her evening, and if it hadn't been for the wonderful conversation and the fact that she and Sister Antrobus got on together so well it could easily have done so.

Laying down her knife and fork on her plate, she answered, 'It's called Sauce Diane. I saw the recipe in *Woman's Weekly* and thought I would give it a try. Like you, I thought it might be quite risky putting a sauce on a chicken, but as they say, one has to live dangerously every now and then.'

'Sauce Diane? Oh I say, that's terribly exotic.' Sister Antrobus laughed. The dreadful wine, on top of the sherry Matron had offered as an aperitif, had gone straight to her head. The sherry had also been bought from the woman in the wine shop.

'Try this one. Golden Knight. You can't go wrong with that,' she had said, failing to mention that the hardened local drinkers referred to it as golden shite.

'Now, to move to the reason I invited you tonight,' Matron lied. 'How has our chairman's son and new consultant Mr Gaskell settled down?'

Sister Antrobus took another sip of her wine, although being a woman of little finesse it was more like another gulp. 'Very well indeed. He has all his posts in place. However, I have no patience with some of their new methods. They discharged a post-op fibroidectomy today who was only operated on a week ago. Mr Scriven keeps his in for

410

a full three weeks. At this rate, we shall be run off our feet. For each patient Mr Gaskell discharges, another walks in through the doors.' Matron filled Sister Antrobus's glass with more wine. 'And do you think he will be good for St Angelus?'

Mr Gaskell had been trained in the army and as far as Sister Antrobus was concerned there was no better training. But her loyalties were divided. 'Well, I should say so. Ex-army, which in my opinion, as you know, Matron, is the best training a doctor can have, and I could tell as soon as I met him. But he's not really cut out for St Angelus, although what we can do about it I have no idea. With his own father having the casting vote on the board, it's not as though we can get rid of him.'

'No, but we can try,' said Matron. She was more desperate than she herself knew to say anything that would please Sister Antrobus. Anything.

'In my opinion, Matron, it would be hard to beat Mr Scriven. There's a consultant who knows how to run a firm. I don't mind admitting that I have told Mr Gaskell as much almost every day, in the hope that he will look to Mr Scriven as his mentor, but I'm sad to say they barely speak.'

Matron's heart melted a little as she listened to Sister Antrobus talk and chatter away. It was hard for her to concentrate on what she was saying. All she could see were moving lips and bobbing hair. She could have sat there all night, in that spot at the table and hung on her every word. As she leant over to fill Sister Antrobus's glass yet again, the thought *please don't let tonight end* flitted through her mind.

Sister Antrobus needed no encouragement. The wine had already loosened her tongue, and even though the notion that maybe she should slow down and stop drinking occasionally pierced the increasingly strange effects of the sickly wine, she continued to talk faster than she ever had before. The wine had made her feel warm and fuzzy and Matron was happy to let her continue. It gave her the opportunity to gaze on Sister Antrobus's steel grey hair, piled up into a bun, at the touch of daring rouge on her lips. She watched, fascinated, as Sister Antrobus waxed lyrical about the ward she ran as what she imagined was a benign dictator. Matron even loved the slight nicotine stain in a crack on one of her front teeth. She knew Sister Antrobus was a secret smoker and so she took out her own cigarettes and lit one up, sliding the packet across the tablecloth towards Sister Antrobus.

She studied Sister Antrobus's hands and thought to herself that they were indeed man-sized, but beautiful none the less. They could not be described as feminine by any stretch of the imagination.

As Matron looked at those hands, she wanted them to take her own and hold them.

Sister Antrobus had finished her wine.

'Cheese and crackers?' asked Matron.

'Oh, that would be something,' said Sister

Antrobus, lighting her cigarette. Matron refilled her glass.

'I suppose you have heard that your first year isn't starting on your ward tomorrow. Nurse Baker, Lord Baker's daughter. A terrible tragedy, poor man. All over the news it was. Thank goodness they didn't mention that she is here, training at St Angelus. Sister Haycock has replaced her with Nurse Tanner. You've had her before,' Matron called from the kitchen.

'I have, a scrawny little thing. I'm amazed she has lasted this long. Expected her to be gone in six months. Apart from anything else, she has an accent as bad as the patients', for goodness' sake. I don't mind telling you I was a little surprised she was ever taken on. Looks to me as though the standards in St Angelus will begin to slip if we start letting those kinds of girls in.'

'Well, please don't blame me, or Mr Scriven for that matter. As you know, she wasn't my choice at all. In fact, I saw Mr Scriven as I was leaving theatre today and told him about Nurse Baker. He had seen it on the news too. I asked him what we should do if they mention St Angelus, or if a reporter comes here wanting to speak to someone. Mr Scriven was wonderful. He told me to send any reporters to him and he would deal with it.'

'That's the measure of the man,' said Sister Antrobus. 'He wouldn't want you to know a moment's concern. A wonderful man, he is.'

'He told me you have a very busy day on

tomorrow and asked whether I had a replacement for Nurse Baker. I told him, Sister Haycock had allocated Nurse Tanner, and he asked me to request that you keep a very close eye indeed on that young lady. If you think there is anything we should know, make sure you repeat it to either Mr Scriven or myself.'

'I imagine he was not very happy when she was offered a place in this intake.' Sister Antrobus emptied her glass. 'He takes immense pride in ensuring that the kind of nurse we recruit is one that reflects our high standards, and I can tell you, Nurse Tanner falls a long way short.'

'Yes, I know. He usually decides which girls are accepted and which aren't, but in her case he was overruled by Dr Gaskell and Sister Haycock. He didn't like that at all and I am sure, having been a military person yourself, you can appreciate that. I know I can.'

'Oh, I am very aware of that, Matron,' said Sister Antrobus. 'Is Sister Haycock not aware of his rank in the medical corps or of the sacrifice he has made for our country? Maybe she should think on that.'

As she returned from the kitchen with the cheese and biscuits, Matron noticed that Sister Antrobus's eyes shone brightly and her speech had become slightly slurred. She laid the plate down on the table and picked up the wine bottle, then put one hand on the back of Sister Antrobus's chair as she leant over her shoulder to refill her glass. She could smell the lacquer on her hair, feel the warmth from the back of her neck. She smelt of woman, of perfume, of things that sent Matron's senses reeling in delight. As she stood there she allowed her hand to brush gently across Sister Antrobus's shoulders. She could feel the firmness and width of the bra strap beneath her fingers. The flimsy fabric of the blouse almost allowed her to feel naked skin and she caught her breath sharply. She swayed on her feet slightly and closed her eyes for a second.

Opening them again, she caught her breath and said, 'I am so pleased that you are enjoying the wine so much. I wasn't really sure if I was buying the right thing, but the lady in the shop assured me you would like it.'

She left her hand on Sister Antrobus's shoulder and was sure that the frisson which ran from her like an electric current would alert the other woman. Maybe this was all she had ever needed to do. To touch someone. It was surely not only she who could feel the chemistry between them; Sister Antrobus must feel that almost tangible current too. She felt that she wanted to die from ecstasy when Sister Antrobus placed her own hand over the top of hers and said, 'Matron, you're spoiling me, you know. I usually only partake on Christmas Day. I fear I may be becoming a little tiddly.' She giggled, and Matron felt as though her heart would melt right there and then.

Sister Antrobus dropped her hand to the table, with a slightly louder thud than was normal, and clumsily picked up her refilled glass. She appeared to have difficulty locating exactly where it was.

'I shall be delighted to report back to you on Nurse Tanner,' she said in an enthusiastic voice which was rising in volume. 'I will do it with pleasure. Sister Haycock has to realize authority comes with time served. How dare she go against yourself and the wonderful Mr Scriven? You must both find a way to re-establish your influence on the committee and I am very happy to be of assistance.'

She knew the wine had loosened her tongue. She was also aware that she was behaving out of turn, but now it all made sense. Matron had wined and dined her in her private apartment to ask a favour. But there was no need. She would have done Mr Scriven's bidding without any encouragement whatsoever.

'I'm sure Mr Scriven will be delighted to hear that. We can't have Sister Haycock getting all her own way. Those of us who preferred the old system must use every advantage we have to preserve standards and the good name of St Angelus.'

'Quite. I couldn't agree more.' Sister Antrobus banged her glass on the table. 'I don't know about you, Matron, but I am always happy to have a reason to visit Mr Scriven and this gives me a perfect excuse. I can tell you this, Matron, five minutes alone with me in a room and that fine specimen of a man would need to call on all his army training to resist what I have to offer. He's what I call a real man, and he still has some of his own hair, too. Any chance of putting a good word in for me? Seems to me he could do with the company of a no-nonsense woman who knows what's what and could bring the smile back to his face.'

Sister Antrobus tipped her head back and emptied her glass. She laughed and her eyes became disturbingly vacant, seconds before her head fell forward with a resounding crash into the middle of the cheese plate. Matron watched as a lump of best Cheshire flew across the table and landed at the grateful Blackie's feet.

Matron remained seated. She waited while her heart finished breaking and her disappointment settled to the point where she could begin clearing away the dishes without fear of dropping one or stumbling into something. It was difficult to see through the tears pouring down her face. She wiped her eyes with the backs of her hands and then fumbled for the handkerchief she had secured inside the sleeve of her cardigan. She picked up the wine bottle and filled up her hardly touched glass to the top.

'If you can't beat them, join them,' she said to Blackie, and downed the glass in one.

Dessie had been standing just inside the park entrance for almost an hour and had decided to give it one more cigarette before he called it a night. Not like Sister Haycock to be fanciful, he thought. But there is definitely no peeping Tom hanging around here.

Looking over to the Lovely Lane nurses' home, he recognized Dana as she switched on the light in her room and moved over to the window to draw the curtains.

He promised himself a bag of chips on the way home and a bottle of Guinness to go with them. Taking out his packet of matches, he was about to strike one when he heard the sound of a twig snapping on the pavement, on the other side of the bush from where he was standing. A match flared and Dessie saw the face of a man as he lit his cigarette, threw the match to the ground and placing both of his hands in his pockets, his ciggie lodged in his mouth, turned his eyes up to Dana's window.

Dessie moved cautiously to the edge of the grass where his bike lay on the path and pedalled his way to the police station, as fast as he could.

CHAPTER 23

Pammy bumped into Branna as she burst in through the doors of the cloakroom on ward two to hang up her cape. 'Am I late?' she called.

'You're back,' Branna said. 'Holy mother. As God is true, you must be a glutton for punishment, you.'

Pammy had forgotten she needed to be on ward two earlier than on other wards and, looking up at the clock, saw that she was late by three minutes. She had run as fast as the wind up the last five minutes of Lovely Lane, ahead of Dana and Beth.

'I didn't have a lot of choice, Branna,' she said, throwing her cape in the direction of the hook. 'Have you not seen the news about Nurse Baker's father?'

'Seen the news?' asked Branna in disbelief. 'The whole hospital is wild with the talk so it is, the poor girl. But listen now, you aren't late, but Sister Antrobus is and I can tell ye this, it's never happened before, not ever, not once since the day I started here. Nor has she ever had a day off sick.'

She bent down to pick up Pammy's cape, which

419

had landed on the floor. 'Now, listen while I tell ye. Dessie has told me to pop in as he has a bit of news for me now, he does, so I'm off out to the lodge. I wouldn't dash if I were you. Staff Nurse is about to take report, I heard them all say so, and my, won't she just be loving that.'

Pammy felt both relieved and concerned at the same time. 'I hope nothing awful has happened to Sister Antrobus.'

'Well, she may have gone under a bus for all we know,' said Branna as she carefully manoeuvred her mop and bucket into the corner of the cloakroom. 'We can but hope, I suppose.'

She blessed herself and, without another word headed up the corridor faster than she ever moved on the ward.

Pammy joined the assembled nurses in the office and took her old place at the window. There was a buzz in the room as the nurses began to realize there was no Sister Antrobus.

'She will go down as a DNA for today,' whispered one of the second years.

'Nurse,' barked the senior staff nurse, 'Sister has never failed to attend anything.'

'Well, pardon me,' said the nurse. 'I thought I was just stating the obvious.'

'Just pay attention, will you,' the staff nurse snapped. 'We will hear shortly, I'm sure. There'll be a perfectly good explanation as to why she is late.' She secretly hoped that they didn't hear, that Sister Antrobus didn't turn up. She was excited at the prospect of a day of stepping in. Of being in charge and testing her skills.

Pammy turned slightly and looked out of the window, where she had a view of the entrance to St Angelus. She watched as the other lucky nurses, who didn't have to begin fifteen minutes earlier than anyone else, poured in through the gates and milled around chatting. She spotted Beth and Dana, whom she had left only minutes before, walking in together. Beth seemed to be handing Dana a letter, or a sheet of paper, and whatever it was made Dana stop dead in her tracks.

'Hellooo, Nurse Tanner.' The voice cut through her daydreaming.

'Yes, Staff,' she said, realizing that everyone in the office was staring at her.

'Did you hear a word I just said?' Staff Nurse was hoping to be promoted to the rank of sister at the earliest opportunity and now practised her sternest voice.

Pammy looked around the room, confused. She had been deep in thought, watching the other nurses arrive for day shift and thinking how pretty they all looked. Capes loose and swinging, white caps bobbing, pink and white dresses and aprons crackling and her own good friends in their midst. She had completely failed to notice the night staff leave, or the fact that the staff nurse had slipped into Sister's chair. She was instantly annoyed with herself. Daydreaming had been a problem throughout school. She had been determined that she would not succumb to it when she became a nurse.

Before Pammy had time to answer, the office door swung open and Sister Antrobus stormed in. Pammy thought she heard the sound of chins hitting the floor. The words *You look dreadful* were on everyone's lips, but no one dared to utter them.

'Have you begun?' she demanded of Staff Nurse, with not so much as a good morning. Her intimidating tone was far from unusual, but a waxen-looking Sister Antrobus, with fixed, blood-shot eyes and a spittle-streaked chin, was very unusual indeed.

Staff Nurse, who had only seconds before made herself very comfortable and whom Sister's chair suited rather well, began to stammer.

'Er, I was just about to start, Sister. You weren't, er, here . . .'

Sister Antrobus didn't seem to be listening. She appeared to be breathing deeply while noisily swallowing saliva and staring at the sunken inkwell carved into the desk. Her colour faded from a waxy tallow to a deathly grey before their eyes. They waited for her to continue speaking, to renew her tirade, but nothing happened. The office was silent, tense with anticipation as nurses exchanged fearful glances and wondered what would happen next. It was as though she had lost the will or the ability to continue.

It was the staff nurse who found the courage to break the silence with a slightly sharp 'Sister, you don't look at all well. Would you like me to take over for you? Maybe if you had a little lie down in the treatment room for half an hour or so you might feel somewhat improved?'

Pammy was aware that as she spoke Staff Nurse rose a couple of inches in the chair. She may have been feeling brave, but for the remaining nurses it was as though the air had suddenly left the room. Pammy could not quite believe that Staff Nurse had just said what she had. Some of the nurses half closed their eyes, as though to protect them against the explosion which was surely about to follow. Sister Antrobus appeared to be on the verge of recovering as she fixed her eye on the staff nurse and opened her mouth to speak. She placed her hand on the desk to steady herself.

'Mr Scriven,' she said and then nothing, as she leant forward and pressed down. She lifted her head with what appeared to be a great effort and began again.

'Mr Scriven . . .' Again, nothing. Everyone waited with bated breath for her to continue. Clasping her hand to her mouth she ran from the office and headed towards the sluice room.

Staff Nurse, who dreamt of one day ousting Sister Antrobus from her post and bagging the prize position on ward two, seized her opportunity.

'Dearie me. Sister should obviously not have reported in this morning. I have no idea what is going on there, but continue we shall. We have poorly patients waiting.'

For a brief moment the air was filled with the shuffle and crackle of starched aprons as pens and notebooks were extracted from pockets, to a backdrop of violent retching from the sluice room. Then, suddenly, the telephone rang.

Staff Nurse listened carefully to the caller, asking the occasional question – 'Is she bleeding? How is her blood pressure?' – and then slowly replaced the receiver. 'Well, today is just going to get worse,' she said. 'There is a young girl in Casualty. A botched abortion. Problem is, she is very pregnant. Twenty-eight weeks' gestation, Casualty Sister said. Amazingly, she seems quite stable and is on her way down to us. Staff Nurse Bates, I would like you to take this case with the assistance of Nurse Tanner as I shall be busy running the ward. The patient will require special nursing until we know exactly where we are. The doctor on duty is coming down with her until they locate Mr Scriven. I'm sure we will all learn more when he arrives.

'We have a new domestic arriving on the ward today to work with Branna. I will ask her to help in the sluice and assist with bedpans. None of us like these cases, but if the mother's life is in danger we must do our best.

'Staff Nurse Bates, you've dealt with cases like this before. Nurse Tanner, you can assist with the bathing and bedpans, as normal, until the patient arrives, and when she does Staff Nurse Bates will let you know. Right, let's whip through the day report quickly; thankfully bed one will be the only unusual event of the day. Well, I suppose there are two, if we count Sister Antrobus.'

Pammy beamed with pride. She felt as though she had been singled out for special treatment and she loved working with Staff Nurse Bates. They had got on so well together the last time Pammy was on the ward. Sister Antrobus would have kept her on the bedpans all day long and never let her near assisting in a serious medical situation.

'I suppose as abortion is illegal, we shall have to report it to the police,' she said to Staff Nurse Bates as they hurried out of the office and into the linen room to grab the sheets for the cubicle bed.

'Oh, God in heaven, no, Staff Nurse won't, although if it were Sister Antrobus, she would and does. She can be such a bitch. No sympathy. Treats them like lepers, she does. The doctors usually send them to Maternity, to keep them out of Antrobus's way. This must be someone who doesn't realize that the poor girl will have been through enough already. It's a real dilemma, to be honest. If we protect the girl, or the woman, by not informing the police what has happened, we are also protecting the abortionist. We rarely get to know what the back story is.'

Pammy loaded sheets on to the metal trolley as Staff Nurse Bates spoke. Her initial excitement at being given a patient to special had evaporated, to be replaced by fear of nursing the unknown.

'We had one in last week,' Staff Nurse Bates continued. 'She was about ten weeks' gestation. Died only a couple of hours after arriving on the ward. She had spent too long at home, terrified of being prosecuted. Tried to make herself better. By the time she got here, there was a pocket of infection in her perineum the size of a tennis ball. Mr Gaskell took her as his case; made an incision and inserted a drain to draw out the infection and give the antibiotics a fighting chance. He threw everything we had at her, but it was no use. The infection was everywhere, already in her blood. She was a widow, had three little ones, and died in her own mother's arms. Mr Scriven ran a mile. Wouldn't touch her. Thank God Mr Gaskell had started, at least someone tried to save her. Tragic case.'

'That must have been awful. The poor kids.' Pammy's eyes filled with tears. 'Our Lorraine was born at twenty-eight weeks and runs circles round us all, and she lands the toughest punch.'

Lorraine's birth was the one big family drama that her mother never mentioned, despite the fact that Lorraine was now a teenager and as fit as a fiddle: her arrival in an air raid shelter on the night of the worst dockland bombing of the war, which had destroyed half of George Street in a direct hit and killed so many people.

Pammy knew it had been hard on her mam in the early days because she herself had helped a great deal. Lorraine required feeding every hour and for her first week she had serious trouble breathing. The army of women who lived in their street had rallied round. Early births and poorly babies were not an unusual occurrence in an area of high poverty.

The women had arrived at the house, uninvited but expected, as soon as the word was out, and were welcomed by Maisie and her elderly mother. The years between had dimmed that time in Pammy's memory, but she remembered the kettle boiling on the range all day long and all night too. She could recall neighbours arriving with a shovel of coke to keep the range going in one hand and a plate of food in the other. Doors and windows remained locked as the kitchen filled with steam. Lorraine had been almost too weak to suckle and so a midwife came out to the house and helped Maisie express her milk.

'Mother of God, come into St Angelus, will you?' the midwife had pleaded. 'We can look after the baby for you.' But Maisie wouldn't budge.

The arrival of Lorraine hadn't been the only calamity that had drawn on the resources of the women of Arthur Street. The strongest women Pammy had ever encountered. The bomb on George Street had pulled the community even closer together. Toddlers had been orphaned, adults widowed and children killed before they could even put on their shoes to run to the shelter. The birth of Lorraine on that dreadful night had seemed almost symbolic. She had arrived in the midst of chaos and reminded them all that there was hope. Pammy still shivered when she thought of those days. She remembered long, tearful faces, mounds of rubble and the clouds of dust that had hung over the streets for days. George Street remained almost unaltered from that day to this. It had been razed to the ground and still was nothing more than derelict land and piles of rubble.

She could also recall the nights of concern and anxiety. The times they scraped money together for the doctor. In the early days, her nana would knock on doors in the street to ask for help, and she never had to travel far. Everyone gave for the doctor to visit a poorly child. The coming of the NHS and free health care had been a blessing because often, while Lorraine grew, the doctor had to be called in the middle of the night. Lorraine got sicker than any other child on the street when she was younger. Often the doctor called in every day, a luxury they could never have afforded before the establishment of the NHS. However, Lorraine was a tough little fighter and she survived.

'Was she a war baby?' asked Staff Nurse Bates.

'Yes, she came just as our streets took the worst bombing of the war. Trust our Lorraine. Always likes to make a fuss. Too close to the docks, we were. Me mam had her in the shelter, where she was stuck all night. I was only a kid at the time, but it was an awful night, that. Awful.'

'Does she get her own way a lot, then?' asked

Staff Nurse Bates, smiling because she could see that Pammy obviously thought the world of Lorraine. 'Your mam probably feels she's very lucky to have her. Do you remember much about that night? Where were you?'

'I can remember some of it, but I wasn't with Mam, because I was at home with me nana when the siren went off. We ran down to the end of our street to the shelter that was nearest. Me mam was at the shop on the other end, nearer to the docks, so she was separated from us. I reckon that's why our kid's such a tough nut.'

'Wow, that's very dramatic,' said Staff Nurse Bates. 'Were there people with her?'

'D'you know what, I don't really know, but I s'pose there must have been.' Pammy leant on the trolley with her elbows on the sheets as Staff Nurse Bates reached up to the top shelf for fresh pillows. 'Me mam never talks about what actually happened and I don't suppose I've ever asked. Not the kind of thing you talk about, is it? To be honest, you'd think the war had never even happened on our street. No one ever talks about it, despite the fact that everyone walks past the rubble to the docks and back.'

'That's not just on your street, Pammy. I think with the King dying and the new Queen, new beginnings and all that, no one wants to talk about the past.'

As Staff Nurse Bates balanced on a step and passed linen down to Pammy, Pammy remembered that her mother had carried Lorraine against her chest for months. Tucked inside her jumper and held up with a scarf. 'It's the closest I can get to popping her back in,' her mother had explained, when a jealous Pammy had complained.

Pammy and Staff Nurse Bates parted ways, Pammy to head down the ward, Staff Nurse Bates into the cubicle to make it ready for their expected patient. Half an hour later, Pammy was at the ward door, holding a wheelchair and saying goodbye to Mrs Toft, who was in the process of being discharged.

'How lovely that you are here on my last day, nurse.' Mrs Toft beamed. 'Almost a year of my life I've spent on this ward and you are one of the angels I will remember the best. I won't forget your kindness. Or the other angels'.'

'I won't forget you either, Mrs Toft,' said Pammy. 'You were my very first bed bath and I think it's lovely that I get to say goodbye to you. It may have taken a year, but just look at how well you have done. Now, let me check. You have got all your medication in that brown paper bag, haven't you? Any worries, get your Tom to ring the ward office and we will explain everything to him.'

'I have, nurse, everything. Staff Nurse brought them to my bed this morning and explained them. It's only painkillers, you know. That and some vitamin drops. There's nothing more medical science can do for me. It's only thanks to all you lovely nurses and doctors and everyone that I am going home at all. It's no surprise people call you angels.'

'And you,' said Pammy. 'Half of it has been you, wanting to get better as much as you did. We couldn't have done it without you.'

Mrs Toft took Pammy's hand. 'You won't see me in here again, nurse,' she said. 'If the cancer comes back, I'm staying at home. I'm done with hospitals now. A year away from our Tom has been too much for me. We had enough of being apart during the war. Seven years he was away and he spent two of those in a hospital. Can you imagine that? Twice as long as I have been in here. Terrible that, all that time we've wasted. We want to be together now. Done with hospitals we are. To think, I used to never stop moaning about the old bugger. Life's short, you know; it's meant to be. You won't see me back here.'

Pammy smiled and, bending down, gave Mrs Toft a big hug. 'We don't want to see you back in here, either,' she said. 'And it's not coming back. It isn't. I know you, you won't let it. You've years ahead of you yet.'

She turned the wheelchair round and the ambulance driver took the handles from her. 'I've been told I have to watch this one, nurse, is that right?' he said to Pammy with a wink. 'Dessie down in the porters' lodge told me that she can get a bit fresh and eats ambulance drivers for breakfast, but not until she's felt the size of their muscles first. She's a bit fussy, I've heard.'

Mrs Toft laughed so hard, Pammy thought that if they weren't careful she would be back in her bed sooner than they had anticipated.

'Don't worry about me though, nurse,' he went on. 'I've put a jumper on this morning, so she can't get at the buttons on me shirt.' Tears of laughter almost leapt from Mrs Toft's eyes. Pammy thought they might need to give her oxygen if he carried on.

'You've got to be kidding,' she said. 'You wouldn't be saying that if you saw the size of her Tom.'

Now the ambulance driver laughed and swept Mrs Toft and the wheelchair around and away down the long wooden corridor to home.

'Bye then,' shouted Pammy to the retreating raised hand.

'Go on then, one last wave,' said the ambulance driver, swinging the wheelchair round to face Pammy before performing a perfect pirouette towards the exit and the waiting ambulance.

Just as she was about to go back into the ward, Pammy saw Dessie pushing a trolley from the opposite direction. A nurse from Casualty ran alongside him, holding a set of case notes and carrying a glass drip bottle. Pammy immediately noted the look of concern on their faces and in a fast heel-toe trot made her way to the cubicle and Staff Nurse Bates.

'She's on her way,' she said. 'I can see them coming down the corridor.'

No sooner had the words left her mouth than the ward doors burst open. 'Straight into cubicle one,' said Staff Nurse Bates, and the trolley immediately swung left into the cubicle. Seconds later, the nurse and the new Casualty doctor Anthony Mackintosh hurried in behind them. 'Close the door,' snapped Dr Mackintosh to Dessie. 'The fewer people who know about this sorry mess, the less chance there is of the police at the door. Who's in charge here?'

'I am,' said Staff Nurse Bates.

'We have no idea how she got to the hospital in this state. She just turned up on a chair in the waiting room. We have no name or age, nothing. She seems to be mute and it looks as though an amateur abortionist has inserted a catheter through the cervix and then tried to flush the foetus out with a mixture of carbolic and water. I have nothing to go on other than the burns and the smell. When will these witches realize, that if a lay person wants to kill a developed foetus they have to kill the mother first? If it was so easy, there would be no need for caesarean sections. We could deliver babies on demand.'

Pammy and Staff could tell he was angry.

Just as Dr Mackintosh finished speaking, the patient came round and began to scream. It was the most terrifying noise Pammy had ever heard. She felt her own internal organs crunch in response and her arms prickled with goosebumps. The girl screamed again, long, pitiful, horrifying. It chilled the air as the patients in the ward ceased to chatter and silence fell.

Pammy must have looked as scared as she felt.

'Her uterus has been distended,' whispered the nurse from Casualty, who was still holding the drip bottle. 'It's the most painful thing any human being can experience, to have a hollow organ distended. Though this one seems to have a seven-month-old baby inside. A curse of women, of course. Couldn't happen to a man.'

When the screaming subsided, the doctor took the patient's pulse. His brow furrowed as he concentrated.

'We have listened to the foetal heart in Casualty,' he said. 'Amazingly, it's still beating, but it's too fast. The foetus is distressed and so is the mother. She has stopped bleeding, but only just, and this baby is definitely coming, and why wouldn't it? It can't feel very safe in there with someone trying to force carbolic water down its mouth. Probably fancies its chances a little better on the outside. But we have seven births on Maternity today, so there's no room up there.'

'So, she's around twenty-eight weeks, then?' asked Staff Nurse Bates.

'Aye, she is, twenty-eight weeks and alive. It's a miracle. The procedure she has been through can induce primary obstetric shock and it's instant. Blood pressure falls into their boots and they end up in heart failure. She is so young, too, to have survived such an ordeal, but let's not count our chickens, eh? We've a long way to go till this young girl is out of the woods. Her bladder may have been perforated, her bowel even. It's too soon to tell. She is in the danger zone at present, and all we really know is that there's a premature baby on the way who is so distressed it will probably be dead before delivery, and that for some reason this young girl desperately wanted to be rid of it.'

'Are there any internal injuries we should know about?'

'Oh, aye, the carbolic solution the abortionist used to flush out the baby was far too concentrated. The girl is burnt and blistered to bits internally and probably the lining of the uterus is in the same state. The abortionist managed to break in through the amniotic sac, but the cervix is rock hard.'

'How do you know she didn't do it herself?'

'I don't, for sure, but can you imagine any woman being able to do this to herself? At the very least, the baby, if it lives, will be blistered and probably blind.' Pammy thought the doctor was about to cry.

The patient opened her eyes and focused on Pammy. Her pain appeared to have ebbed and a feeling of calm momentarily filled the room.

'Do we know how long?' Staff Nurse Bates asked the Casualty nurse.

'We don't, I'm afraid. It could be twenty minutes or twenty hours. Look, I'm taking a patient up to Maternity in a minute. I'll see if they have a spare midwife who can come down and help, but with deliveries on the way in it's not likely. I don't know what they've put in the water in Liverpool. The number of pregnant women coming into St Angelus is ridiculous and almost more than we can cope with. Who was it who decided that hospital was a safer place than home to give birth? They must have been mad.'

Half an hour later, the room was calmer as Pammy, left alone with the patient, checked her charts were in order.

'Hello there,' she said to the frightened young girl, who looked vulnerable and frail. Her skin was pale. Beads of perspiration stood proud on her top lip and across her eyebrows. Pammy slipped her hand into hers. It was cold and damp.

'Well, you are the mystery one. You just turned up out of nowhere and had no one with you, they said, and in the pain you were in too. Was there really no one with you? Come on then, love, what's your name at least?'

The girl looked at her through wide and frightened eyes but didn't speak a word.

'You don't have to tell me now if you don't want to. Don't worry. You just catch your breath and take your time. Tell you what, shall I fetch you a cuppa? A piece of toast? Something nice and warm?'

Pammy saw the girl's eyes fill with tears. 'Hey, come on,' she said, and although it was against Sister Antrobus's very strict rules she sat on the side of the bed and took both the girl's hands in her own.

'Don't cry, love. I know this is awful and I don't know all the details, but Mr Scriven is the consultant on this ward and he's the top man on call today. He's the best, so they say. He will come and see you soon, I'm sure.'

Pammy wasn't really sure she actually believed this. Mr Scriven had a reputation for being less than charming towards his patients, but she desperately wanted to say something to reassure this young girl, to wipe away the look of terror from her eyes. But her words had the opposite effect.

At the mention of Mr Scriven's name, the patient clasped Pammy's hand. 'No,' she hissed. She could say no more before she was seized by another contraction.

This girl was too young to go through this, thought Pammy. The pain was just too severe. Something was definitely wrong. 'There, there, my love,' she whispered. 'Breathe and blow through your mouth, and it will pass quickly. The doctors will be here soon.'

Pammy's kindness seemed only to make things worse. The girl let out a stifled sob.

Pammy peered inside her bag, to check for a nightdress or toiletries. Had she expected to be admitted? There were no overnight things and the ring on her wedding finger was almost falling off. If Pammy had to guess, she would say it was neither gold nor the girl's. It looked more like a curtain ring from Woolworths and Pammy wouldn't have minded betting that it was.

'Do you want to talk to me?' she asked in a tender voice. 'I won't say anything to anyone. Everything here is strictly confidential, if that's what you're worried about. Cross me heart.' She made a sign of the cross on her chest and smiled at the girl. 'You look to me like you need a shoulder to cry on.'

'I can't. I'm not allowed.' Again, the young girl emitted a stifled sob.

'Oh, God, come here, queen,' said Pammy as she scooped her up into her arms.

The gesture released a flood of tears and the girl sobbed violently in Pammy's arms. Pammy knew that if Sister Antrobus walked into the room, or even if Staff Nurse were to catch her hugging this young patient, they would disapprove of such a personal display of comfort. Her actions were unprofessional. She knew it and she didn't care.

'I'm frightened.' The words sounded tortured and pathetic and were whispered into Pammy's shoulder.

Once the first torrent of tears had subsided, Pammy held the girl a little away from her, while still holding her gently by the arms.

'Do you have a mam? Is there anyone I can contact to let them know you're here, in St Angelus? What's your name, queen? Are you going to tell me?'

The girl shook her head, with such conviction that Pammy realized there was no point in pressing her.

'OK. Well look, I'm going to leave you for one minute, to find out what you can eat and drink and get you a bedpan, but I will be back in a jiffy, so don't worry.'

She plumped up the pillows with one hand, supporting her patient with the other, and laid her back with tenderness.

As Pammy headed to the office in search of Staff Nurse Bates, the senior staff nurse marched past her with the drugs trolley.

'Have you seen Branna?' she asked in a voice loaded with new-found self-importance. 'That woman treats ward two as a social club. She never stops chatting to the patients and when she isn't wasting time doing that, she's harvesting gossip from the porters' lodge.'

'The ward is lovely and clean though,' said Pammy, looking down at the shining floor.

Staff Nurse sniffed and looked down her nose. 'I didn't ask for your opinion, Nurse Tanner. If you see Branna, please tell her I'm looking for her.'

Feeling deflated, Pammy walked into the office just as Staff Nurse Bates put down the phone. 'God, I can't believe it. She's almost as bad as the Anteater. She's just near bitten me nose off.'

'Yes, well, never mind Miss Bossy Knickers. She's only a year ahead of me and I get it too. I've just spoken to Sister on Casualty. Our mystery patient arrived on her own. They didn't notice her until someone saw her sitting crying on one of the seats. There was a puddle of blood under the seat, apparently. Mr Scriven is being very evasive on the telephone. His light has been up for ever and he only just called me. Said he'll be down presently.'

'What do we do then?' asked Pammy. 'She wouldn't tell me anything either, but she's just had a good cry.'

'I'm damned if I know. I've never had a nameless patient before. Let's start with the usual procedures. You set up the examination trolley for when the doctor arrives. Put a jug of chlorhexidine solution on it while we wait for our masters to let us know what's going on and who this poor terrified creature is. They're sending a delivery pack down from Maternity. Keep an eye on the drip, it's there to keep a vein open in case they need to give her any drugs.'

'A delivery pack?' asked Pammy with a hint of surprise in her voice.

'Yes, well, we are delivering a baby. She is at twenty-eight weeks' gestation, or thereabouts. No one can say if this baby will be born dead or alive. Your Lorraine survived. This one may do and could be your first delivery.'

Pammy rushed to set up her trolley in the clean utility room, as she had been taught. She mentally checked off each item and prayed there was nothing she had forgotten as she counted out her speculums.

'Sims', Cusco's, Ferguson's, a uterine sound,

rubber gloves, three enamel kidney dishes, sterilized rubber gloves and a towel. Yes, that's it,' she whispered and popped into the sluice room for a warm bedpan from the hot pipes. She slipped it into the paper cover and on to the bottom layer of the examination trolley and filled a large metal jug with the chlorhexidine solution.

As Pammy pushed her trolley back towards the cubicle, she bumped into Branna leaving the domestics' room. 'Branna. Where have you been? Staff Nurse is looking for you and she's in a right strop. On the war path for you she is.'

'Well now, you wouldn't believe it if I told you. Looking for me in a strop, is she now. I knew her when she first started here. Wouldn't say boo to a goose, she wouldn't, terrified of her own shadow she was and now she orders everyone about, those who let her get away with it. Where are you rushing to with that trolley? Sure, you will slip on me wet floor if you don't slow down.'

'We have a mystery patient in the cubicle. Just waiting for a doctor and some notes to arrive, so we know what to do next. Hasn't spoken a word she hasn't. Poor thing is terrified.'

'Aye, well, sure, 'tis a mystery to some maybe,' said Branna. 'I'm off to the school to see me mate Biddy. If Staff Nurse asks again, tell her I'm on me break.'

'But you've just had a break,' said Pammy.

'Yes, well, I'm having a second one now. I don't save lives like you lot so I don't, and while the

441

cat's away I'll make the most of it. Besides, I have important business to see Biddy about and it cannot wait. Mysteries and secrets everywhere they are.'

Pammy looked at Branna suspiciously. She was hiding something. But there was no time to wonder what.

Staff Nurse Bates walked out of the cubicle. 'Don't leave her. I think it will be best if we make sure that there's always one of us with her. I'm not happy about this case. I wouldn't trust this one not to run away. She looks like a scared cat.'

'I'll get her a cuppa and some toast from the kitchen,' said Pammy.

'Yes, well, it will give her some strength,' said Staff Nurse Bates. 'The poor thing is going to need it, in more ways than one.'

Pammy tried again to get the mystery girl to talk to her, after she had gratefully eaten the tea and toast. 'So, are you from around here then, love? Or have you travelled far?' She talked about everything other than why the young woman was actually lying in the bed in an attempt to encourage her to provide them with some information.

Some of the other nurses were bristling with disapproval. They could barely conceal their moral indignation. 'I would refuse to nurse a case like that,' one of them said to Pammy as she passed her on the ward. 'Tell them you are a Catholic and it's against your religion. You'll have to go to confession, you know.'

'I'm here as a nurse, not a nun,' Pammy snapped. 'We aren't here to judge, that's not our job. I don't know about you, but I'm here to look after people who are sick, whatever the reason.'

Staff Nurse Bates had overheard the exchange, and smiled so sympathetically at Pammy that Pammy's indignation boiled over.

'Never let me behave like some of those pious madams,' she said in a fierce whisper as they disposed of the towels they had used to wash their patient in the laundry trolley outside the cubicle. 'We are supposed to be nurses. I can hardly believe them. That poor girl, she's no more than a child herself. A waif and stray and she's in agony. I've never seen anything so sad. Do they not have hearts, that lot?'

'God, I know. They make me sick. There was a reason why Staff Nurse asked us two to nurse her, you know. She may be a bit big for her boots today, but she's not stupid, or unkind. There but for the grace of God go all of us,' Staff Nurse Bates replied.

Pammy thought that wasn't strictly true. She had never done more than hold a boy's hand. A situation she hoped to rectify at the doctor's dance. 'Do you think she's married? That wedding ring, it's not real, is it?'

'I have no idea, but look at her. How old do you think she is?'

Pammy peeped through the door at the girl who was now lying back against the pillow with her eyes closed. 'I don't know. The same age as me? Eighteen, nineteen maybe?'

Both nurses fell silent as Mr Scriven walked in through the ward doors. He recognized Pammy instantly, and frowned.

'I will examine the patient now, please, Staff Nurse Bates.'

'Yes, Mr Scriven, but you do know, sir, we have no information about her. All we have are the notes taken by Dr Mackintosh in Casualty. We don't even know her name, because she won't speak to us.'

'Hardly a priority given the circumstances, Staff Nurse Bates. I am more interested in what is happening from a gynaecological perspective.'

They both saw the expression on the girl's face when she heard Mr Scriven's voice before he had even entered the cubicle. She looked terrified.

'Her contractions are erratic,' Staff Nurse Bates continued after a short pause. 'No regularity whatsoever, but all the same, she's in a great deal of pain.'

Pammy had just taken her pulse and blood pressure. Both were high. Pammy wondered if she dared to say anything to the godlike Mr Scriven. First-year nurses never spoke to consultants, unless it was one who was friendly and encouraged it. Taking what felt like her life in her hands, she said, 'Mr Scriven, her pulse is now 120 and her blood pressure is 170 over 100. It has risen since she arrived with us thirty minutes ago.'

Mr Scriven ignored Pammy. It was as though

she hadn't spoken. He picked up the fluids chart to check the input.

'Is she still bleeding?' he barked at Staff Nurse Bates. 'What's her PV loss like?'

'Very little to speak of, sir.' She shot a quick glance at Pammy, and the two girls frowned at each other. Something wasn't quite right, but it was not their place to question the consultant. What Mr Scriven said was law.

'I will give her an injection to speed things along. The foetus will be delivered dead. Call the porters and have it sent down to the incinerator immediately, and I mean without delay. She will suffer some sickness and diarrhoea as a result of what I am about to administer, but that will help with the delivery. She may develop a temperature, but it won't be anything to worry about. My registrar will check the expulsion is complete and that there are no retained products from the pregnancy and then she can be discharged and sent home. Wherever that may be.'

Staff Nurse Bates was so stunned she could barely speak. It was unheard of to send someone home so quickly after such a traumatic procedure. Mr Scriven was known as a bed blocker. He kept his patients in far longer than Mr Gaskell.

Mr Scriven turned to the young girl, who had kept her eyes closed and her head turned away. She was terrified. Pammy saw that her fists were clenched tight. Mr Scriven looked as though he was about to say something directly to her and then decided not to bother. Instinct took over and Pammy moved to the side of the bed to take one of the girl's hands in her own.

Mr Scriven raised his eyebrows. It didn't take a clairvoyant to tell anyone that Mr Scriven didn't like the new nurse.

'I have seen her in clinic before today. Her name is Jane Smith,' he barked, in a tone which left Pammy and Staff Nurse Bates in no doubt he was in a foul temper. They were also amazed. Both nurses wanted to ask *How did you remember that?* Mr Scriven had needed to be reminded of Mrs Toft's name almost every time he came on to the ward and she had been an in-patient for over a year. He knew his patients by their condition, not their name.

'Well, at least we have a name to put on the charts,' said Staff Nurse Bates in a sceptical voice as she filled out the blue TPR forms. And to stop people from asking her what her real name is, thought Pammy. She felt a shiver run down her spine. Pammy was streetwise and sharp. Mr Scriven was lying about the girl's name, and the question now banging in her head was *Why?* Why was Mr Scriven lying?

'Please prepare a trolley for induction, nurse,' he said to Staff Nurse Bates. 'I will put some of the drug into the drip first and get it running. In the meantime, I will perform an examination.'

'Yes, Mr Scriven.'

Pammy positioned the examination trolley she

had laid up earlier against the side of the bed. Both she and Staff Nurse Bates were shocked by Mr Scriven's roughness. In less than a minute he had pulled the girl's legs up without any explanation and inserted a Sims speculum.

'She's burnt,' he announced, removing the speculum and pulling the covers over her knees. 'The solution they used was too caustic. Probably carbolic and water. I've seen worse, but we had better get her delivered. Let's set up and get on with the induction, nurse.'

Before she left the cubicle for the clean utility room, Staff Nurse Bates found the courage to ask one question. 'Mr Scriven, I hope you don't mind my asking, but as we have no notes and I shall be nursing this young lady, do you remember how old she is?'

'She's twenty.'

Staff Nurse Bates gasped. 'Twenty?' Her voice was incredulous. The girl kept her head turned away and her mouth shut tight.

Pammy was aware that an oppressive and slightly alarming atmosphere had slipped into the cubicle. Something was deeply untoward, but she had no idea what.

'Where is Sister Antrobus?' barked Mr Scriven. He was now clearly irritated. Neither nurse had spoken, but they hadn't needed to. He took a clean handkerchief from the pocket of his white coat and wiped his brow. 'It's hot in here. I hate these cubicles. Open the bloody window,' he snapped.

Pammy obliged. She had decided during her first spell on ward two that the dislike was mutual. She far preferred Mr Gaskell and wished he were here instead of Mr Scriven, but Mr Gaskell was not at the hospital today. They knew that much at least from Dr Mackintosh.

Staff Nurse Bates mumbled something about Sister Antrobus being ill and, aware she had over-stepped the mark, scuttled out to fetch the trolley so that she could set up for the induction. Pammy did not bother to offer to find the senior staff nurse. She had seen her heading off with the other nurses for their coffee break, Staff striding out ahead with the juniors trotting along in her wake like obedient pink little ducklings. If Staff Nurse had had any inkling whatsoever that Mr Scriven would be calling into the ward himself, she would never have left for coffee. Securing the position of sister on ward two would involve Mr Scriven's approval one day, and even Pammy, inexperienced as she was and unused to the ways and politics of St Angelus, knew Staff would never miss an opportunity to ingratiate herself. She would have hung around all day waiting for Mr Scriven, and would be blisteringly mad to have missed him when she returned.

Pammy had also noticed on her first spell on ward two that whenever Mr Scriven was present, Sister Antrobus became quite giggly. She flushed and preened when he was due on the ward for his round. She held him in higher regard, almost, than he held himself. She would often disappear to the cloakroom before his mid-morning round began and return smelling of hairspray, lipstick and eau de cologne.

Once the round was over, she would order Branna to leave a tray of tea in her office, to be drunk as they devoured a tin of Huntley and Palmers while she wrote his instructions in the case notes.

'She'll try any way she can to get into a man's trousers, that one,' Branna used to say, to the shock and horror of any prim and proper young nurses who happened to be around to hear her. 'Someone needs to tell her it takes more than a custard cream.'

Staff Nurse Bates returned to the cubicle, pushing a trolley with one hand and a heavy drip stand with a fresh glass bottle on with the other. She struggled as they rattled along, each intent on going its own way. Pammy rushed to the door to help her through, and taking the drip stand from her wheeled the heavy contraption to the head of the bed. Staff Nurse Bates smiled her thanks.

'Would you please hold, er, Miss Smith's hand, Nurse Tanner, while I assist Mr Scriven,' she said.

Pammy took the girl's hand and squatted down beside the bed. 'Mr Scriven is going to give you an injection, love, to help the baby on its way,' she whispered. 'But you can hold on to my hand and you just squeeze away as hard as you want.' Her face was only inches from the side of the bed. She could feel the patient's warm breath on her cheek. Mr Scriven had not explained what he was about to do.

She looked towards Mr Scriven, who had snapped off the top of half a dozen or so glass vials containing a clear solution with a faint straw-coloured tinge. The syringe was a large one and the needle about eight inches in length. Pammy felt her skin tighten as with little finesse and not even a glance at the patient's face, or a word of encouragement, he pulled back the sheets to reveal her swollen belly. Pammy saw the girl's abdomen jerk to the side and then ripple back again, as though the baby within objected to the sudden cold and exposure. She had seen Lorraine and her brothers move in much the same way when they had been in her own mother's belly. 'Doesn't like lying on me spine. Too bumpy,' Maisie had laughed as she had laid her own hands protectively on her abdomen. This baby was kicking away in protest. Just like Maisie, the girl placed her free hand protectively over the area where what appeared to be a tiny heel, or a fist, pushed outwards, distending the smooth and stretched skin.

Mr Scriven had not noticed. He was drawing up the solution into the syringe from the last remaining vial.

'Swab the area with iodine, nurse,' he snapped at Staff Nurse Bates, who, with an unreadable expression, responded to his instructions.

Both girls wanted to scream, *What are you doing?*

This girl isn't twenty, and surely she is too far gone? Just leave it a while and see if she settles, if the baby holds on. Doesn't it deserve that chance? But both of them were only too well aware that if either of them did so, they would be sacked on the spot. Their role as nurses was to support the consultant, not to challenge him.

Staff Nurse Bates opened a brown ribbed bottle of iodine and poured a small amount into a white enamel kidney dish. She then clamped two swabs of lint into her Sinus forceps and dipped them into the cold solution before laying the forceps on the dish and moving the trolley closer to the bed.

'This will feel a little bit chilly,' whispered Pammy, 'but I am afraid it is necessary to sterilize the skin.'

She was aware of the proximity of other patients in neighbouring beds on the other side of the thin plasterboard wall, and was by now well practised in keeping her voice low. There was not a flicker of acknowledgement. Pammy knew she would be in charge of the patient's TPRs for the day and had been counting her respirations. At the beginning of the process they had been a steady twenty-two per minute, but they were now greatly increased. The girl was extremely distressed. Pammy's heart was heavy as from her crouching position she watched Staff Nurse Bates swabbing away. Stark yellow rivulets of iodine ran down the side of the girl's swollen white abdomen, soaking the fresh draw sheet on which she lay.

The solution was cold and the response from the life within became stronger as the baby kicked even more furiously. It seemed to Pammy as though the girl's belly had a life of its own. The patient gave a tight sob as Pammy brushed the damp fringe away from her forehead. Her brow was now soaked in perspiration. Her eyes were squeezed tightly shut and her face was beaded with sweat that smelt of fear. The air in the cubicle was filled with the antiseptic smell of the iodine and Lysol from the newly washed floor.

Despite the fact that her eyes were tightly closed her tears would not be contained, and as the iodine solution ran down her belly, puddled in the valley of her groin and spilled over her exposed thighs, they flowed out from under her eyelids and ran down her face. Once again she moved her hand protectively, to cup her lower abdomen with her hand, and Mr Scriven barked roughly, 'Don't touch. That area has just been sterilized.'

Pammy reached up and took the patient's free hand and held them both together in her own. She felt as if she was holding the girl prisoner, and as she thought of Lorraine the tears prickled behind her own eyes. She knew that that gesture, the move to caress her baby, was instinctive: protective, loving, possessive. It was what all mothers did. The first touches, separated by a layer of muscle and skin, but each letting the other know hello, I am here. I am here.

'Good work, nurse.' For a moment, Pammy

didn't appreciate that Mr Scriven was talking to her, but far from being made to feel proud she felt ashamed to be praised for assisting in such an act. She was sure he had lied about the patient's name and age, and she intuitively knew that this was not an induction, but an abortion, and it was not happening because the mother's life was in danger. He was acting no better than a back-street abortionist. She felt utterly helpless. Everything that was occurring before her eyes screamed out to be challenged, but she was the lowest of the low in terms of medical rankings and felt unable to question or intervene.

Still holding both the girl's hands in hers, she leant in yet again and whispered, 'Don't you worry, love. You aren't alone. We are here with you and we won't be leaving you.' Her reward was an almost imperceptible squeeze of the fingers.

'Right, all systems go. I am about to inject, so do not move a muscle. It will feel like a sharp scratch to begin with, but I'm injecting into a sac of fluid and you won't feel anything after the first minute. It will be just like a bee sting.'

The mysterious Miss Smith still didn't look at Mr Scriven, but kept her head turned away and her eyes tightly shut.

He lowered his tone to almost a whisper. 'She needs to be kept calm.' Ignoring Pammy again, he spoke directly to Staff Nurse Bates. 'There will be some wriggling. The foetus always kicks up a fuss when the amniotic sac is penetrated, but she won't feel much at this stage. All she has to do is keep perfectly still. You need to keep absolutely still,' he said more loudly, as though the girl was deaf. He studied her, waited for a response. She gave a slight nod of her head to indicate that she understood. Now both Pammy and Staff Nurse Bates noticed that Mr Scriven was trembling. Staff Nurse Bates had never seen that before and it made her even more convinced that all was not as it should be. She had never seen any doctor carry out a procedure such as this before and even though she was yet to be placed on Maternity, she had also never heard of a pregnant woman being injected into the uterus through the abdominal wall.

'Right, hold her still, nurse,' he said to Pammy. 'Staff Nurse Bates, you had better move to the opposite side of the bed.' He winked knowingly at the staff nurse, as if to indicate that things could become difficult. That was when Pammy realized he was lying about the pain, the bee sting. That wasn't true either.

As the needle pierced the abdomen, the girl let out a small scream. It was her first audible display of emotion and it erupted from somewhere within her heart. Mr Scriven was right. The baby within thrashed and flailed about as the needle pierced the uterine cavity and Mr Scriven roughly palpated the abdomen. Pammy, feeling slightly sick, thought it looked as though he was trying to locate the foetus, to inject it. At last he appeared satisfied.

'There, we have it,' he said. Pammy saw him begin to depress the syringe, and the solution gradually moved down the markers on the glass, disappearing as slowly as the life that was ebbing away within.

Tears now threatened to stream from Pammy's own eyes. She saw that Staff Nurse Bates's face was white and set. They were assisting in the ending of a life. A life that Pammy knew could thrive if allowed to settle down, to repair and grow. To be born.

Dr Mackintosh had said that the girl's cervix was as hard as a rock on examination. Surely, if she was just allowed to rest, there might be a chance? A slim one, perhaps, but a chance at least? The atmosphere in the cubicle suddenly felt so thick and hot it was unbreathable. Pammy felt compelled to release the hands she was holding, open the curtains, throw back up one of the sash windows and gulp in some fresh air. And still the young mother had not spoken a single word. With each moment that passed, the atmosphere in the cubicle became more suffocating. At last Mr Scriven removed the cannula with a flourish and threw it into the kidney dish with a clatter.

'There, done,' he said. 'It won't be easy, but she should repel the foetus at around eleven o'clock this evening.' He pulled on the sterilized rubber gloves, pulled up her knees, and almost roughly performed a PV examination. The girl flinched and again squeezed Pammy's hand tight.

'As I would have expected, her cervix is still hard. There is no dilatation. The surface of the cervix is burnt and blistered. We have to get this baby out as a measure to save her life. We have no idea how bad she is internally. It will take at least the full twelve hours, but if it hasn't happened by this time tomorrow we'll take her to theatre.'

Pammy wanted to place her hands over the girl's ears. She had flinched as Mr Scriven spoke.

'The thrashing about,' he inclined his head towards the convulsing abdomen, 'will stop within a couple of minutes. I'll telephone in a few hours. If Sister Antrobus returns, tell her to ask the switchboard to put my light on and I'll pop down for a word.' Without so much as glancing at the patient again, he turned on his heel and left.

Staff Nurse Bates stood rooted to the spot. Pammy pushed the girl's hair back from her head and wiped her brow with a cloth she had soaked in cold water and placed on the trolley, ready. The young mother cried silently and the two nurses watched her abdomen settle as life slowly left the seven-month-old baby in the place which was meant to be the safest of all.

CHAPTER 24

Pammy marked the hours that passed by the clock on the wall and by her religious fifteen-minute observations that she never failed to complete on time. She continued to try to engage her patient in conversation.

'Would you like a cuppa now?' She had changed the draw sheet and nightdress, washed the girl's face and pulled up the bedclothes to tuck them around her. Once again she brushed the now wet and matted hair back from her face, almost overcome by an urge to bend down and kiss her. The patient shook her head. 'Come on now, there's a good girl. I'll go and fetch you one, and something to eat. Might be best to get something down you now.' The words *because very soon you may be in too much pain to feel like eating and need every ounce of energy you have* weren't spoken, but hung in the air.

Pammy slipped into the kitchen and began to lay a tray. 'What's going on in there?' asked Branna, nodding towards the ward.

'I wish I knew,' said Pammy. 'We have a young girl who won't speak a word or tell us anything.

Sister Antrobus has gone missing. Staff Nurse is barking so many orders she seems to be practising for national service. Mr Scriven is in a very bad mood and Staff Nurse Bates and I don't know if we are coming or going. Apart from that, everything is fine.'

'Jesus, this place might as well still be an asylum. 'Tis mad so it is. I can tell ye where Sister Antrobus is. That was this morning's mystery. She's on the sofa in Matron's sitting room. Throwing up something terrible, she is. Elsie says her and Matron downed a few bottles of some disgusting wine last night. Elsie knows how bad it was, she finished off the last one. She said she had never tasted anything so awful in all her life. Nothing like Guinness so it isn't. I tried a bit too. 'Twould peel the paint off the walls it would and God alone knows, it would be the day Elsie disappears off the face of the earth. Dessie can't find Jake either. You couldn't make it up, could you? Mad this place is, mad.'

Pammy tried to disentangle the thread of Branna's story to decide what was relevant enough to comment on.

'Sister Antrobus is on Matron's sofa?' she said. 'Well that's very good of Matron. Would she do the same for any of us, if we was sick?'

'Ah, well now, that's not the best of it. Dessie tells me Sister Antrobus rolled out of Matron's flat last night, as drunk as a coot, and it was gone midnight. What Dessie didn't know when he told

458

me that was how many bottles of wine they had drunk.' Branna winked at Pammy. 'I don't believe what the porters say about Matron and the Anteater. Sister Antrobus is too fond of the men by half, she is. Beats me why she wanted to work on a women's ward. She has not a drop of sympathy for the women's troubles.'

'My head won't take any more, Branna,' said Pammy, totally confused now. 'I need to concentrate on what's happening here.'

She and Staff Nurse Bates took it in turns to sit with their patient while she slept. 'Are you all right with this?' Staff Nurse Bates asked when they had slipped outside the cubicle for some fresher air. 'It's pretty full on. I was just wondering, after what you were telling me about your Lorraine being born at twenty-eight weeks, whether this was all a bit much for you. I can ask Staff if she could put someone else on to special, if it is.'

'God, no. Don't be daft,' said Pammy. 'It's not easy, I'll admit that, but I can't leave her now. I want to see this through and get this poor girl better. I don't believe she's twenty, do you?'

'Not in a million years. I don't believe her name is Jane Smith either. Look what I've got.' Staff Nurse Bates took one of the empty glass vials Mr Scriven had used earlier out of her apron pocket.

'What are you doing with that?' Pammy's eyes widened in surprise.

'I've just been into the office to look it up in the British National Formulary. What Mr Scriven did

459

to her, I have never seen done before.' Staff Nurse Bates lowered her voice. 'It's oxytocin, and it should have been given either as an intramuscular injection or IV. It doesn't say anywhere in the BNF about injecting it into the amniotic sac, or into the baby, as I'm sure he was trying to do. The contra-indication is a ruptured uterus. We need to watch her like hawks.'

'Why didn't he just take her to theatre?' asked Pammy.

Both nurses inclined their heads to check on their sleeping patient, and Staff Nurse Bates leant in closer to whisper, 'Because if he did, the baby might have been pulled out alive, that's why. Or that's what I think, anyway, and don't ask me why he wouldn't want that to happen, I have no idea. I just know this is all wrong. I've never seen a doctor try to inject a baby when it was in the uterus. Did you see the way he was palpating her abdomen?'

Pammy let out a long sigh.

'Flamin' heck,' she said. 'And here was me thinking the worst thing that could happen to me today would be working with the Anteater. I'm not leaving her, you know. I don't know what time this will all be over, but I'm not leaving this ward until it is. Matron will have to throw me out first.'

Staff Nurse Bates grinned. 'Some of us pray for that to happen, some days.'

Six hours later, towards the end of Pammy's official shift, the girl began to complain of bad pains.

'Are you going for tea?' Staff Nurse Bates popped her head around the curtain. 'Is she still sleeping?'

'No,' Pammy replied. 'She's just woken up.' As she spoke, the young girl let out an enormous groan, struggled to sit upright and vomited across the bed.

From that moment on, Pammy felt as though her heels were winged and her feet never touched the ground. The girl they could only call Miss Smith developed a high fever. She shook and shivered. She asked for a bedpan, which remained almost permanently underneath her as the diarrhoea poured, and she screamed and cried and begged for someone to take her pain away. Pammy knelt on the side of the bed and tried to adjust the back rest behind her and stuff pillows down to bring some relief. She felt the pain in the small of her own back as she attempted to hold the girl up on the bedpan. She knew that if she let go she would surely fall off.

Staff Nurse Bates whacked up the metal cot rail on one side of the bed, giving the girl something to hold on to for support.

'Is there nothing she can take to relieve the pain?' Pammy begged, while the girl screamed and clutched at her in agony.

'I don't think we have anything that will touch it. Let me see if we can get some Entonox from the maternity ward.'

'Why is it so bad if she is only seven months?' A rare moment of calm had descended upon the cubicle as the girl closed her eyes and laid her head against the snowy white pillow.

'I think it's because the womb doesn't really have a great deal to clamp down on, I suppose, so it's having to push down harder to eject the baby. I don't know, Nurse Tanner, that's just a guess. I haven't done my midwifery yet. I'm going to fetch Sister Antrobus, sick or not, because she is a trained midwife and she should be here.'

Pammy wished she wouldn't, but their first concern had to be for their patient, who with each moment that passed appeared to be more and more out of it. Pammy wrung out a flannel in the bowl of water she had fetched and wiped her brow.

'There you are, my love,' she whispered. 'Not long now and it will all be over.'

The girl opened her eyes, and the look she gave chilled Pammy to the bone. Her eyes were distant, her pupils like pinpricks. Pammy took her TRRs. Her pulse was fast, her temperature 103 and her blood pressure had fallen dramatically. It was now only 95 over 65.

'I'll be back in a minute, queen,' she said, squeezing the girl's hand. Whacking up both cot sides she dashed from the cubicle to the office. Staff Nurse Bates was talking to Sister Antrobus, who appeared to have her head in her hands, but this didn't deter Pammy as she charged in.

'Sister,' she said with a degree of alarm she knew a more experienced nurse would manage to contain,

462

'we need a doctor. Her pulse is very fast and her blood pressure has dropped to 95 over 65.'

Sister Antrobus didn't snap at her, which surprised her. 'Go back to her, both of you,' she said. 'I will call for Mr Scriven.' As the nurses hurried away Pammy heard her pick up the telephone. 'Put Mr Scriven's light on, please, and ring theatre in case he's there. We need him urgently on ward two.'

Back in the cubicle, Pammy took the girl's temperature again. 'God, it's 104 and rising. What's going on?'

'I don't think the temperature is anything to worry about,' Staff Nurse Bates replied. 'It's the blood pressure which is more alarming. She may be bleeding internally. That can often happen with a ruptured uterus.' They whispered, but there was no need. Their patient was entirely unaware of her surroundings as she screamed with the pain.

The room fell quiet. The young girl was now panting, rather than screaming. For a moment, Pammy felt a calm descend upon them all. The fresh bedpan wobbled as the patient sat far forward. The nurses dropped the cot sides and placed their arms round her back for support. Only minutes before, Pammy had swabbed her down with the chlorhexidine and changed her into yet another clean gown and fetched yet another clean pan.

The girl leant forward, almost as though she was looking down into the bedpan, and without warning she groaned deeply, her groan turning into a grunt. Pammy and Staff Nurse Bates looked at each other in alarm as they heard something plop into the metal pan.

'Jesus, lift her off quick,' said Staff Nurse Bates. They interlinked their arms under her legs and across her back and lifted her clear, Pammy expertly slipping out the bedpan from under her before they laid her back, with as much care as possible, on to the pillows. But not before their patient had grabbed the side of the bedpan and pulled it towards her. Staff Nurse Bates picked up the Spencer Wells forceps she had ready on the trolley and clamped and cut the pulsating cord.

'Get it to the sluice,' she said. 'I will see to the rest of the delivery. We will need another bedpan in here for the final grand contraction. You call into the office on the way and tell Sister what has happened.'

Just at that moment, the door swung open as Mr Scriven and Sister Antrobus stormed in.

Pammy snatched up the bedpan before Mr Scriven could reach it. She looked in at the contents and there lay a perfect little boy. He was breathing and helpless and he stared right back up at her.

'Oh my God,' gasped Pammy, stating the obvious. 'It's a baby.'

'No it is not. It is a foetus,' snapped Mr Scriven. 'Leave it in the sluice room and Sister will arrange for it to be transferred to the incinerator.'

'It's a baby boy and he's alive,' Pammy responded without thinking.

Mr Scriven ignored her, keeping his gaze fixed on the TPR chart in his hand. 'What is her blood pressure now?' he asked Staff Nurse Bates.

'Get it into the sluice room, now,' Sister Antrobus hissed.

Pammy looked frantically at the girl, at the doctor and back at Sister Antrobus. As she opened her mouth to speak again, she felt herself grabbed sharply by the top of her arm. Sister Antrobus marched her out of the cubicle and down to the sluice room. Pammy didn't feel the pain in her upper arm, she could only think of the baby boy, alive in the bedpan she was clutching. As the sluice-room door slammed behind them she squealed, 'Sister, it's a baby boy and he's breathing.'

She shook her arm free and, laying the bedpan down in the long stone sink, scooped out the baby. She grabbed a towel from a trolley that someone had left ready just inside the door for a bed bath, and wrapped it carefully around the tiny body.

'Oh my God, would you look, the little love, what can we do? Should I run down to Maternity with him? Should I? Or up the stairs to the children's ward. What shall I do?'

Pammy never forgot the moments that followed, or the words spoken while the struggling baby boy lay in her arms. His eyes wide open, deep blue eyes looking up at her imploringly. He was begging her to help him. He was gasping. His mouth making small shapes as he desperately tried to part his lips to breathe. There were blisters down his right arm, Pammy assumed where he had been touched by the carbolic solution, but his eyes were clear and knowing. They were pleading to live.

'It is NOT breathing. Give it to me and telephone the porter for transfer to the incinerator, now.'

Pammy let out a small scream and clutched the baby to her. 'No.' She pulled the bundle closer, but as she did so the little boy cradled in her arms lost his fight for life. She saw his eyes close and his chest become immobile as it ceased to rise and fall. He had lived for less than five minutes.

Memories of Lorraine flooded Pammy's mind as she clutched the little man to her. She lifted him up and began to cry pitiful tears on to the unknitted scalp that had never known a mother's kiss. She had been there at the moment of his birth. Hers were the only eyes to look into his own. She felt responsible, and if no one else stood up for him, she would. She was aware that the only person in the whole world who cared that he had lived was her. He was her responsibility.

'Give him to me now, if you know what is good for you,' hissed Sister Antrobus. Her tone was vicious.

'No, I won't. He lived. He needs to be buried, not put in an incinerator. He needs a priest and a birth certificate and everything. He is a little boy, not a severed limb. I want the priest now. I may be only a first year, but I know what a little life deserves. He lived. He did. I saw him.'

Pammy was by now on the verge of hysteria. She had lost all reason and was oblivious of the potential consequences of her actions. But she truly didn't care. She had held a living, breathing baby in her arms and they would have to put her in the incinerator before she allowed them to take the baby boy who had gone from feeling firm and alive to being a limp weight in her arms.

Half an hour later, Pammy sat on a chair in the ward office. Opposite her sat Sister Antrobus, her face like thunder. Matron sat behind the desk and there was a heavy and troubled silence while they waited for Mr Scriven to join them. Pammy had been assured that the baby would not be taken anywhere and would remain in the sluice. She was not budging on that one and Sister Antrobus knew it.

Mr Scriven looked like thunder as he walked into the office and closed the door tight behind him. Glancing through the window, Pammy could see Staff Nurse Bates in the cubicle with their Miss Smith.

'What have we here?' Mr Scriven asked in a cold voice.

'Nurse Tanner believes the foetus breathed and lived, Mr Scriven. I have told her it could not possibly have done so. Nurse Tanner is stepping well beyond her station and is requesting a priest. I thought we should inform you.'

'Come with me,' said Mr Scriven to Pammy. 'Now.'

Pammy jumped up out of her seat and followed him out of the room, with Sister Antrobus trailing behind. Pammy could hear the crackle of the starch in Sister's dress as she moved. She knew that she was in dreadful trouble. Her earlier bravery had almost deserted her and she felt herself weakening in the face of the opposition lined up against her. Now that Mr Scriven had joined them, she wasn't sure what she would do. Maybe they were right. Had she been over-emotional?

Mr Scriven stood under the central green glass lampshade in the sluice room and picked up one of Branna's buckets. He placed it under the sluice sink tap and began to fill it with water.

'You see this?' he snapped. 'If that baby breathed and lived, when I put it in this bucket of water it will float. If it didn't, it will sink.'

'It was a he, sir,' whispered Pammy.

'What?'

'It was a he. He was a little boy.' Pammy saw a vein in Mr Scriven's neck twitch and pulsate and she thought he was about to explode. Instead, he placed the bucket on the floor.

'Is this it?' he asked Sister, who nodded an affirmative.

Pammy was aware that someone else had joined them in the room, but her eyes remained fixed on the bundle of towelling.

Without looking at the child, he took the towel to the bucket and plopped the dead baby into the water, where it floated, face down. Pammy could hardly believe what she was seeing. She was incredulous.

Mr Scriven looked startled. For a split second, he hesitated before he snatched the baby back up and wrapped him in the towel. 'See?' he said. 'He sank.'

'But he didn't,' Pammy whispered. 'He didn't sink. That's not the truth, sir. He floated.'

'Take it to the incinerator,' said Sister Antrobus.

'But . . .' Pammy faltered. She was frozen to the spot. 'I can't, Sister,' she muttered. Her mind was reeling at what she had just witnessed.

'I did not ask for a reply. I gave you an order. Do as you are told.' Sister Antrobus was almost shouting again. She looked to Mr Scriven for confirmation that this was what he wanted and he nodded back, the expression on his face cold and unmoved.

'I shall take the waste product to the incinerator myself, Sister,' he said coldly.

Sister Antrobus looked humiliated, and she blushed red. She had been late on this fateful day, and now it would appear to Mr Scriven as though she were losing control of her ward and her staff. There was a moment's silence, broken shockingly by Matron, who, unbeknown to Pammy, had stood silently in the sluice room and witnessed the entire scene. 'You are a disgrace to nurses everywhere.' Her words sliced through the air. They were full of menace and sent a chill of fear running through Pammy. 'Get out of this hospital, pack your

469

belongings at Lovely Lane and be out before this evening. You will never set foot in St Angelus again.'

Pammy tried to move, but her legs had turned to jelly.

'Get out of this ward and this hospital. Do it now. I shall send you an official dismissal by post.'

'But Matron, it was a baby boy. Don't you understand?' Pammy's voice wobbled. Her words petered out and she realized that somewhere in Matron's eyes there was a gleam of human kindness, but not for Pammy. Not for the nameless little boy who had just died in her arms.

'If that baby goes anywhere, I'm calling the police.' As soon as she spoke those words, her knees began to shake.

She was already trying to work out what she would tell her parents, but she knew instinctively that they would understand. They would even praise her actions. At home in Arthur Street, a welcome would be waiting. That thought emboldened her.

'You are a liar,' she screamed at Mr Scriven. 'A liar, do you hear me?'

She had nothing to lose and was beyond containing her anger. With tears pouring down her cheeks, Pammy took her cape down from its peg in the cloakroom. Her eyes searched for Branna, but she was nowhere to be seen. Feeling very alone, she wrapped her cape around her and shivered. She would have liked to say goodbye to

Staff Nurse Bates, who was tending to their patient. They would never see each other again, and Pammy wanted to say thank you. But they would never let her, and anyway she felt a need to be out of this place and in the fresh air. The condemnation of Sister Antrobus and Matron and the coldness and anger of Mr Scriven were all too much for her. She had never been shouted at like that by anyone in her life before and the experience had been deeply upsetting. She had barely eaten since her snatched breakfast, and as a result she felt weak. Her emotions had been assailed by events and she still could not comprehend what she had witnessed, although she was sure she would never forget the image of the floating baby or the deep blue eyes staring up at her.

She was on the verge of storming back into the office and shouting that Mr Scriven was a brute. Her mind screamed out, rejecting the reality of what had occurred. Putting the baby in a bucket of water to test if he had lived had been the last straw. Pammy began to shake. Her arms were crossed defensively and she felt her fingernails digging deeply into the skin of her forearms. The speed of events had left her speechless and tearful. Could she have got this all wrong? In the world of hospitals and surgery, of medicine and nursing, the world she had chosen, how could a baby be born and breathe but be condemned and written off? But Pammy was her mother's daughter, and even as she doubted herself she thought of Maisie and asked herself what would her mam do. In a flash, the thought gave her strength. Pammy had seen her entire community, women with a dozen children each, fight to save the smallest scrap of a life and if her mam were here she would have done the same as Pammy. Her instincts had been right.

She felt weak with relief and the tears almost cascaded from her eyes. Pulling her cape around her for warmth and protection, she opened the cloakroom door to leave. Then she heard Branna's voice, and turning towards the ward she saw that the doors were wide open. Branna was standing outside the cubicle with her arms folded, and her words clear for all to hear. It looked as though she could be the second person to be dismissed that day on ward two.

'Is anyone here going to tell Elsie what her missing girl Martha is doing in that bed?'

In the school of nursing, Biddy picked up the telephone. Another minute and she would have been gone. Her bag was packed, her scarf was fastened and she had been heading for the door.

''Tis always someone wanting something,' she muttered as she picked up the handset. She recognized the voice right away. It was Dessie.

'Biddy, where the hell have you been? I've been trying to call you all day.'

'We haven't had no phone all day. You know that, for pity's sake. 'Twas you what organized to have the new phone put in. I haven't been anywhere but here.'

Dessie had spent his whole day running up and down to Maternity with gas bottles. The requests were never-ending, and Jake had disappeared. Dessie could hardly believe it. There had been no word, not a message from his mother or another of the lads, nothing. He banged his fist to his forehead. 'How could I have forgotten?' he said.

Dessie didn't bother to argue with Biddy. Not least because she was right. He had ordered the new telephone system to be installed in the school of nursing. It was a measure of how frantically busy he was that he hadn't remembered that fact.

All day long he had been trying to call Biddy each time he was anywhere near the lodge.

'I have news, Biddy, and it isn't good. Are you sitting down?'

CHAPTER 25

Biddy ran down the entry as fast as was physically possible with a wicker shopping basket in one hand and a seven-pound bag of King Edwards in the other. By the time she reached Elsie's house she was out of breath and had to set both down on the floor in front of her before she could push open the back door.

For a brief moment, she stopped and smiled as it dawned on her that she had completed the journey without embarrassment.

Biddy, you have to know that almost all women who give birth to a large number of babies in rapid succession suffer with your problem.

Emily had taken her to Dr Jackson's clinic. It had been an uncomfortable experience and she had thought that the ring he had placed inside her would surely fall out, but it hadn't. He told her that it didn't work for everyone, but maybe life wasn't always that bad, because for Biddy it had.

'Elsie,' she roared, almost falling in through the door. 'Elsie, I'm nearly dying from lack of breath here. Where are you?'

Elsie's neighbour Hattie had been bringing in

her washing. She was Welsh. Biddy didn't like the Welsh. She thought that every English person who claimed the Irish were dirty should visit the home of a Welsh woman first.

Hattie wore a blue floral housecoat and a red and green paisley scarf, worn like a turban, to cover her wire curlers.

'Get them feckin' curlers out,' Biddy had jibed at her during the war. 'Jerry's using them to get a signal for his bombers, so he is.' She only said it once. The following morning, after the worst bombing of Liverpool, Hattie whipped out her wire curlers with their holding spike antennae and put them in a box under the bed. She did not put them in again until VE day.

'What you yellin' like that for? There's no one home. She'll be down the bingo, either that or still looking for their Martha. Not settled, she hasn't, since Martha went missing. Told me she was calling on Josie's mam. What news have you got then?'

Hattie was peering over the wall between her back yard and Elsie's. She took the stub of a roll-up ciggie out of her apron pocket and lit up, expecting to be standing around for at least five minutes to chew over Biddy's news. She squinted as the blue smoke rose upwards and tears stung her eyes in protest.

Biddy was tempted to share. To tell Hattie that she knew where Martha was. It took every ounce of her willpower to keep her own counsel. 'Just tell her to come down to mine when she gets back, will ye? Tell her I have something for her now.'

Hattie wasn't going to let her away that easily. 'Why don't you tell me what it is and I'll pass a message on? I'm reliable, me.' Hattie crossed her arms and leant on the wall. 'You wouldn't be running like that if you didn't have something important to say. I haven't seen you run that fast since New Year's Eve in 'forty-six when you realized your Mick was in the pub with yer purse. Generous man your Mick.'

Biddy blessed herself, remembering the night. 'I shouldn't have bothered running and put my heart in danger like that. The bloody purse was empty by the time I got there. The bastard.' Hattie smiled. This was more like it. She knew mentioning their Mick would distract Biddy.

Due to its close proximity, almost everyone who lived in the community worked at the hospital in some capacity or another. Hattie was a night cleaner who nursed a deep resentment that after all these years she had never progressed.

'What is it? Go on then, tell me,' she said. 'You know me, I'm the very soul of discretion I am. I'll tell Elsie as soon as she gets back. I might even go up to Josie's to fetch her for you, if you like, seeing as how you're all out of breath. Course, I'd 'ave to know what it was I was going to fetch her for first though, obviously.'

Biddy looked down at her shopping bags. It was no good. Elsie wasn't here, she needed to get word

476

to her and what better way of doing it than telling a woman with a gob the size of the Mersey Tunnel. She took the path of least resistance.

'Tell Elsie to come down to mine as soon as she gets back. Tell her I know where Martha is.' With that, Biddy picked up the potatoes and her basket and trotted out of Elsie's gate, and back up to the entry to her own house.

'Biddy,' shouted Hattie, throwing her cigarette over the yard wall into the cobbled entry. 'Biddy!' But there was no reply. Hattie decided there was nothing for it. Placing her washing on the pulley in the kitchen and hoisting it up to the ceiling, she left via the front door and began knocking on doors to spread the word. Biddy knew where Martha was. Now all they had to do was find Elsie.

'What a day this has been,' Biddy said to her welcoming cat. 'If the Holy Mother told you herself what had gone on, you wouldn't believe her.'

Letting the cat out and placing the kettle on the range, she began to unpack her shopping. She watched the cat through the kitchen window as he leapt from the roof of the outhouse up on to the entry wall.

'Find Elsie, would ye?' she said to him. She often talked to the cat, believing she got more sense out of him than from most people.

As soon as Biddy had put the phone down on Dessie, she had made her way to the classroom where Emily Haycock was teaching a class of final-year students, and gestured frantically through the glass in the door. Emily had frowned but, realizing that it must be something serious for Biddy to disturb her, said, 'We will finish early today, nurses.' A murmur of appreciation had swept around the room.

Biddy didn't wait for the students to leave.

'Something bad is happening on ward two. I think your Nurse Tanner may need your help.'

Biddy had no need to say another word. Emily didn't even wait to collect her cape. She was off and down the stairs as fast as her feet would carry her.

CHAPTER 26

The hush which had descended on the Lovely Lane home was unnatural. Even the knitters were subdued. With Celia Forsyth away on holiday they were not obliged to discuss the latest pattern or argue the merits of stocking stitch or moss stitch, and their comments were confined to 'pass the wool' or, 'dash it, lost count again', over the clickety clack of their wooden needles.

Sister Haycock had arrived with Nurse Tanner and the two of them were presently closeted in a small downstairs study room. When the door had closed behind them Pammy had thought for a brief moment that Sister Haycock was going to hug her. She was certain the nursing director had reached out for her hand, but of course she hadn't. It was just her imagination. Emily asked her to go over and over again the events of the afternoon. She let Pammy cry as she gazed down on the girl's now unkempt and flowing hair, her red bloodshot eyes and swollen red nose and thought, I've got this, Maisie. I've got her back for you. My turn to help your family now. It also occurred to her that one day soon she would have to face the past and turn to the future. Doing that would mean having to knock on Maisie's door.

'I've let everyone down,' Pammy sobbed. 'Me mam, me dad, you, Mrs Duffy, everyone.'

Emily let Pammy cry it out, and handed over her own handkerchief. 'Look, Nurse Tanner, everything always appears worse at night, especially on a wet and miserable night like tonight. Listen to that wind. There's a storm brewing out there.' She was trying to divert Pammy's thoughts, to lift her out of the well of despair she had fallen into. 'I know Matron was harsh and Sister Antrobus was worse, but that was tonight. Matron has agreed that we can go back to her office tomorrow to talk about this. You haven't gone yet, Nurse Tanner. As far as I am concerned, you are still a part of St Angelus and I will do everything in my power to keep it that way. Let's pray for a miracle. Matron's word is law, but perhaps we can persuade her to change it.'

'I think it was all a bit of a shock, to be honest,' said Pammy, as she wiped her nose. 'I've never seen an abortion before. I don't suppose I would have, with them being illegal. He said he had to do it, because of the carbolic. Said she was blistered and burnt. But he did something very odd. He injected straight into her uterus through her abdominal wall. Staff Nurse Bates said the drug was only supposed to be given intramuscular by the drip. She said that a side effect of the oxytocin

– that was the drug he gave her – was that her uterus could have ruptured.'

Emily retained her composure. That was a piece of information to be filed away.

'What would you have done, Sister Haycock, if you had been me? Some of the nurses were turning up their noses at the girl, you know, and that's something else. We didn't even know her name. Mr Scriven said it was Jane Smith but we knew that was a lie.' Pammy's voice began to rise.

'There, there, don't get upset again. The other nurses should have known better. Whatever one's religion, it has to be left at the ward door in cases like this. The moral position would be to ensure that abortion is available free on the National Health Service for all women in the early stages, to prevent cases like the one you saw on ward two today. Women should not have to resort to visiting butchers in back streets.

'You hold tight, Nurse Tanner. I need to think. Things always seem better in the morning. And, remember, pray for that miracle.'

Dana and Beth had colonized the far corner of the sitting room, and when Pammy returned to join them they absorbed their tearful friend into their midst while she recounted events. 'Look after her,' Sister Haycock mouthed to Dana as she popped her head round the sitting-room door before she left.

'He refused to accept that the baby had lived

and said it hadn't and that I was imagining it, but I know it did. I saw it with my own eyes,' Pammy said.

Dana blessed herself and gasped, 'The poor little mite.'

'Why did she have an abortion in the first place?' asked Beth. 'Did you get to find out?'

'No, not a word. We didn't even have any name or address or anything.'

'Well, that's most odd. If you ask me, something is very untoward there,' said the stickler for standards, Beth.

Dana looked thoughtful. 'What did Sister Haycock say when she came to the ward?' she asked. 'What a stroke of luck that was altogether. Imagine. She just chose that moment to pop in to see Sister Antrobus. A few minutes later and it would probably have been too late. See, there is a God. You must pray to him tonight, Pammy, to say thank you for sending Sister Haycock to the ward for ye.'

Pammy dried her eyes for what seemed to be the twentieth time that day.

'You should have heard how Sister Antrobus shouted at me when I went back into the ward to find out what Branna meant. Sister Haycock heard her and told me to sit on the visitors' benches in the corridor outside while she went into the office to speak to Matron, and then when she came back out she said, "We have until tomorrow to make a case to keep you at St Angelus. I told them a decision made in the heat of the moment would not be wise and very unprofessional." While she was talking to me we could hear Mr Scriven in the office complaining to Matron and Sister Antrobus. He's a nasty piece of work, that man.'

The girls listened attentively. Pammy didn't mention the part about Sister Haycock telling her she needed a miracle to happen tonight. She couldn't truly acknowledge to herself what a precarious situation she had landed herself in. It had all happened so quickly. She had allowed her emotions to get the better of her, and Pammy knew that was a recipe for disaster. Her friends hadn't been there. They hadn't seen the look on Sister Antrobus's or Mr Scriven's face, or Matron's for that matter. They hadn't heard any of them shouting. The hopeful conclusion her friends had reached, that she would survive this, sounded empty and hollow to Pammy. If she had left her personal feelings to one side and acted in an entirely professional manner, she would not be facing the prospect of returning home, her dreams shattered.

It was the midwife who had visited the house every day to attend to premature Lorraine who had inspired the young Pammy to become a nurse. Pammy wanted to be just like Nurse Heather, who had sucked out Lorraine's airways with her little tube and massaged her back for over half an hour every morning, with the baby almost hanging upside down on her knee. She had weighed her, bathed her, and instructed family and friends how to manage until she returned the following morning. On the day she announced her visits would have to cease, when Lorraine was twice the size she had been at birth, she left Pammy a little card for when she arrived home from school. On the front was a sprig of pressed heather. The delicate paper-thin lilac and purple petals were almost transparent. Pammy thought it was the most beautiful thing she had ever seen. On the inside the midwife had written the words *To Nurse Pammy. Thank you for being my little helper. I shall miss you. You were the best nurse I have ever worked with. Look after your little sister for me. I discharge her into your care. Nurse Heather.*

What had happened in the sluice room that evening could not have been further from the image of nursing that Pammy had carried with her since that day. Now she wondered to herself whether she really wanted to be a nurse any longer. Did she honestly want to work with the likes of Sister Antrobus and Mr Scriven, people who had denied a birth and a life?

'If it had been a little girl and not a little boy, she may well have survived,' said Beth matter-of-factly.

'Why?' asked Pammy, taking a fresh, dry handkerchief from Beth's proffered hand. Pammy's own was by now a soaking wet rag, beyond use.

'No one really knows, it's just that baby girls are much stronger than boys at the same stage of gestation and tend to survive more often. It's a mystery, but that's how it is. You will hardly find any premature baby boys that survive. It's always the girls.'

Pammy thought it was equally mysterious that Beth was being so understanding and kind. She had moved seamlessly from being a very definite fan of the ambitious and unpleasant Celia to a supportive member of their group.

Mrs Duffy's progress towards the sitting room could be heard long before she appeared. The wheels on her trolley squeaked and groaned under the weight of steaming copper jugs of milky drinks and home-made biscuits as she made her way from the kitchen to the sitting room.

Emily had popped into the kitchen before she left to explain what had happened.

'I think we all need an early night tonight, nurses, don't you?' Mrs Duffy said to the room in general as she handed Pammy her drink. Pammy looked up at her and, not daring to speak, simply nodded. She felt as though she had let Mrs Duffy down along with everyone else.

'Things always look better in the morning, and goodness me, we all need that, don't we? So, let's be having you all up the stairs as soon as you've finished.' Mrs Duffy was afraid that if she didn't spur the nurses on they would sit there all night, chewing over a situation which not one of them could influence by anything she said or did. There was only one woman who could make a difference and she was already on the case. Sister Haycock was Pammy's only hope.

None of the girls would dream of arguing with Mrs Duffy, whose kindness and wisdom had inspired much respect from all of them except Celia, who fortunately was not around to inflame the situation. Half an hour later, everyone was tucked up in bed. Dana and Beth had run out of words of comfort, and had to agree with Mrs Duffy that waiting for the morning was now the only thing to be done.

Pammy lay in her bed and stared at the moon and stars through her window, wondering what tomorrow would bring. Sister Haycock's words rang in her ears. *Matron's word is law.* She knew it might be the last night she would ever spend at Lovely Lane. She heard the thunder seconds before the flash of lightning illuminated the cosy room she had come to love. As a lonely tear ran down her cheek, Pammy said aloud, 'This is it. You've done it now, soft girl.'

She didn't want to leave her friends, Lovely Lane, or her familiar room. She thought of Mrs Toft and of her appreciation and their laughter when she said goodbye. She remembered how Martha O'Brien's face had been filled with gratitude when she had helped her through her pain by holding her hand. Helping people, being a good nurse – and despite her earlier doubts she knew she had been a good nurse – was the only thing she could be proud of and the only thing in the world that she knew she truly wanted. The sound of her sobs was drowned by the thunder which rattled at the windows.

★　　★　　★

Dana sat on the side of her bed and for the first time since that morning, reread the letter Beth had given her as they had walked in through the hospital gates. She was missing Victoria. She had no idea what to do, but she knew Victoria would know.

'Heavens above, what a mess,' she whispered as she read Teddy's words yet again. He must have asked Celia to pass the note to me and she hid it in her room. Celia wasn't even there to take to task. Dana stood and walked to her window to watch the storm. 'You can't hide for long, Celia,' she said as she looked down at the rain bouncing off the cobbles on Lovely Lane. 'You will be back.'

CHAPTER 27

The curtains had not been fully drawn in the cubicle and Martha could see outside into the hospital garden. The night sounds of the patients, the crepe-muffled footsteps of tiptoeing nurses and the distant murmur of the occasional porter's voice provided her with distraction as sleep eluded her. The pains in her abdomen were sharp and stabbing and brought tears to her eyes, but it had been two hours since anyone had even popped a head round her door. The night sister didn't think much of her, she could tell.

'So you're the one who is causing all the trouble,' she had said, when she began her rounds earlier. 'Maybe you should have thought of the consequences before you dropped your knickers, miss. You young girls from the dock road, you're all the same.'

She picked up the charts at the end of Martha's bed and glanced down at them.

'Have you been in here before?' she snapped. 'You look familiar.' Martha was beyond being capable of a reply. There was no way she could speak, or even shake her head. She wanted her mother. She wanted Jake, but most of all she wanted the baby she knew had lived. She was on the edge of asking for Elsie, but she knew that if she did, Elsie might lose her job. This was all such a mess, and she had no idea how she had ended up here.

She thought of the woman who had 'helped' her. Helped to near kill her, more like. She closed her eyes and drifted into an exhausted and fitful sleep, back into her nightmare day.

'I have half an hour,' the woman said as she spread old newspapers out over her kitchen table. 'Get your knickers off and then get up on the table. Put your backside to the edge so I can put your knees up. How far gone are you?'

It had taken Martha two weeks to find the name of an abortionist. In the end, she saw an advert in the paper from a woman offering herbal potions for a list of ailments, one of which was ladies' stomach cramps.

'Come back with five guineas,' said the woman, 'and then I'll sort you out, dear. You won't feel a thing. All over in a jiffy.'

Martha had been saving for the wedding and had exactly five guineas in an envelope in her bottom drawer. She had saved the money by adding half a crown every week for months and topping it up with sixpence or a shilling whenever she could. She would have to find a way to lie to Jake. To say it had been stolen, or lost. She was hardly showing and had barely put on any weight, she had been so ill, but she knew exactly how far gone she was. He had only raped her the once. As the abortionist spoke to her, her fingers slipped to her protector. To the knife in her pocket.

'I can't do it 'ere,' the woman said. 'It's illegal. I have to do it at your own place.'

'I can't,' said Martha. 'My mam would find out.'

Begrudgingly, the abortionist agreed to perform the abortion in her own kitchen. 'I don't like doing that, mind, although there are a few on Upper Parliament Street who practically run bloody clinics, women in and out all day. The police don't bother us, not unless they want a bit of business.' The woman cackled and Martha had no idea what she was talking about.

She returned with the money the following day. The abortionist's house revolted her. It smelt of stale cabbage and cats. She still had the blackout curtains up from the war and the sink was piled high with dirty dishes.

'I'll have you out of here in no time,' the woman said, 'and don't you tell no one that you was 'ere, you got that?'

Martha nodded and watched as the woman opened a cupboard and took out a piece of rubber tubing and a jug.

'Take this first, girl,' she said, handing Martha a drink. 'Knock it back in one, go on. It makes me job easier.'

Martha did as she was told. She wanted to be

out of that kitchen even faster than the abortionist wanted her gone.

She began to feel light-headed and dizzy. So light-headed she could no longer stand without swaying. 'Whoops-a-daisy, there's me lady,' said the abortionist, grabbing her by the arm. 'Up you get, come on, love. Shuffle yer bum to the edge, there's a good girl. Feels lovely that, doesn't it?' She grinned toothlessly at Martha, who lay rigid with terror.

'I like a bit of that meself now and then, but I can't always get me hands on it you know.

'Now, hold your knees against your chest, put your arms around them and put your hands together. There you go. Don't let go now or you might knock me arm. You'll feel a little sharp prick down there, and then I'm going to mix some carbolic with water and flush your womb out. You're quite far gone. Too far for anything else. Just cross your fingers it works, queen, but I'm not promising anything 'ere.' It occurred to Martha that she hadn't said that before she took the five guineas.

The woman lied. It was not a small prick. The tube felt like a searing hot knife as it was inserted through her hard-clamped cervix.

'I've mixed more carbolic than usual with the water,' said the woman. 'You're so far gone, you need it. Most of the women who come to me are only a couple of months gone. Get here a bit quicker next time.'

Next time? Martha could not believe that this

woman would think she would ever want to visit her dirty kitchen again.

'Does the fella know?' Martha's mouth would not work. Whatever she had been given to swallow allowed her to hear, but not to speak. Her tongue felt thick and filled her mouth.

The pain that followed was like nothing Martha had ever experienced in her life before and hoped she never would again. She felt something cold and liquid slip down between her buttocks and soak the newspapers. She was holding her knees against her chest for dear life, but the wooziness made it hard and she felt herself sway. 'Keep bleedin' still, I told you,' the woman snapped, as Martha pulled her knees in tight.

What followed was a pain in her abdomen so sharp that she thought she was surely about to die, and all she could think about was Jake and her mam. It felt to her as though the people she loved most now belonged to a different world that was as far away from the nightmare she was living as it was possible to be.

Her first reaction was to convulse with the vomit that threatened to explode over the table.

'Don't worry, love,' said the abortionist as she lifted her up into a sitting position. 'It's just a bit of shock. It always happens when you use the flushing method. Don't know any woman it hasn't happened to. What d'you think I put the old *Echo*s on the table for? Don't want me kitchen messed up. It will go in a minute.'

It will, or I will, thought Martha, as she screamed with the pain. Her insides burnt with intense heat and, with a sense of horror, she watched as the blood ran down her legs. She tried to lift her head from vomiting, before everything around her turned black and she passed out.

Martha woke with a jolt. Her room was dark. Hours had passed. No nurse had checked on her. Her mouth was dry and thirsty, but when she reached for the jug on her bedside locker, it was empty. The sound of thunder and heavy rain filled the cubicle as she rested her head, too heavy to hold up, back on the pillow.

She saw the grass outside the cubicle light up a luminous bright green in a flash of lightning. It occurred to her that Matron had seen her many times before, when she was little, as she had sat for hours on end on the hard-backed chair near the main entrance to the hospital while she waited for her mother to finish working. She was very lucky Matron hadn't recognized her today. She had felt badly for the young Nurse Tanner when they had all turned on her in a fit of temper. Martha had heard them in the corridor, shouting.

She had heard Nurse Tanner say, 'He's alive', but when she asked Staff Nurse Bates only minutes later the staff nurse told her it wasn't true. 'No, I'm sorry, love, he was dead. But that was what you wanted, wasn't it? What we need to concentrate on now is getting you better. You have been through a tough ordeal, Miss Smith. I can't imagine what it was like for you before you got to St Angelus.'

Staff Nurse Bates had raised her eyebrows. Martha guessed she was hoping she would contradict the Miss Smith and confess her real name.

'So, it was a boy?' She was sure she had heard that too. 'It was a boy?' She had grabbed at Staff Nurse Bates's hand and squeezed it. 'Are you sure he's not alive?' she had asked, between sobs of grief. 'It was a boy?'

She had no idea why she had cried the way she had. She had tried to abort her baby. Taken great risks, used all her money, lied to Jake, made herself ill. She had had her insides burnt out, and yet through the pain she felt nothing but overwhelming sadness and grief.

'I had no choice,' she sobbed, as Staff Nurse Bates stroked her fringe back from her forehead. 'I had no choice. I didn't know what to do.'

Staff Nurse Bates gave her a look of such deep sympathy and care that it actually made her feel worse. She would have preferred to be hated. For Staff Nurse Bates to have been rude to her, as the night sister had just been. That would have been so much easier. The kindness dissolved her and she was scared.

'I had no choice,' she sobbed to herself quietly again, while the thunder boomed outside her room. Jake would never have spoken to her or looked at her again, and would have married someone else. Her mam. God, her mam. The shame and disgrace. She would have had to leave her job and what a mess that would have put them both in. But it was the thought that she would lose Jake, that she would lose the boy she loved so much, that had driven her to do something that had almost killed her.

At first, she thought the noise was the thunder. The lights in the ward flickered and then they went off. Seconds later they came back on, but as the lightning struck they flickered again and the ward was plunged into darkness.

'Don't worry, ladies,' she heard the night nurse say. 'The generator will be on within five minutes. Happened all the time during the war.'

But then she heard it again. It wasn't thunder but the sound of boots, running down the main corridor. Pounding and urgent, getting closer and closer, and the pounding and urgency sent a chill down her spine and a shiver across her body. It was night. It was dark. The generator had not kicked in. It was Mr Scriven. He was coming back to hurt her. Or had he sent someone else? Were they coming to kill her? To silence her and to keep Scriven safe. She heard a match strike, saw the glow of a paraffin lamp through her window and let out a sob. They were almost upon her. The merciless, pounding, urgent boots. She froze as the object of her new terror was almost upon her, and screwed her eyes tight shut. Her hands flew instinctively to her abdomen before she remembered there was no baby there. No little life to protect. The ward doors burst open and she heard the unmistakable voice of Jake as he roared 'MARTHA!' at the top of his lungs.

CHAPTER 28

Sister Haycock walked through the main doors of St Angelus and headed for the stairs that led to the old sisters' landing.

She had been so distracted. Before she had said goodnight to Mrs Duffy, her mind had been racing. Trying to find a solution to a problem for which there seemed to be no answer. Pammy was in desperate trouble, but she now had at least one bullet to fire. Mr Scriven had injected a drug into the girl's abdomen that the BNF said was for intramuscular and IV use only. She made a mental note to slip on to a ward and check a BNF for herself.

Why had he done that? It was only a small bullet, but it opened up a line of questioning that might lead somewhere. Pammy said Staff Nurse Bates had only managed to keep one of the vials. She thought another drug had been used. What had that been?

She was desperate for a bath. Sad that she had missed her visit to Alf. Daunted at the thought of what tomorrow would bring.

Only three sisters remained in residence on the

landing and she was now the fourth. The fact that she and Sister Antrobus were now neighbours depressed her. She had noticed that the night porter's lad was nowhere to be seen. He sat in a wooden cubicle at the bottom of the stairs, just in case the sisters needed anything.

It was Biddy who had finally urged her to move in. How right she had been. 'I think you might discover a thing or two on that corridor,' Biddy had said.

As was often the case, Emily had no idea what Biddy was talking about. Right now, all she wanted to do was have a bath and kick off the soaking wet shoes she had been wearing for the past eighteen hours. 'Bath, here I come,' she whispered as she removed her shoes and picked them up from the floor.

There was no end of hot water in the bathroom on the sisters' landing. Sheer luxury after what Emily had endured over the past two years.

She slipped behind the desk on the landing to remove the key to her room. The clean hospital towels were kept behind the desk and she removed two large fluffy ones. The best were kept for Matron and the sisters' landing. As she held them to her face, she felt foolish for having attempted independent living for so long. The fees for Alf had made it impossible for her to afford anywhere respectable to live alone. She should have just given up and moved in ages ago, she thought.

As she tiptoed along the carpeted landing in her

bare feet, not wanting to disturb the sisters, she thought she heard music coming from Sister Antrobus's room and the murmur of voices. She stopped and listened. Maybe she had friends round? How could she, after the way she had behaved towards Pammy and the case they had dealt with? The two very much older residents had told Emily that they were in bed by eight in the winter, and visions of frilly nightcaps and teeth sleeping in jam jars had flown into her mind.

All was quiet as she moved along towards her room. She had deliberately chosen the furthest one away from everyone else. The corridor suddenly flooded with light; someone had opened a door. Instinctively, she shrank back against the wall, into the shadows, and was glad of the cover as her eyes adjusted. She almost gasped aloud at the sight before her. Then a smile crept across her face.

Mr Scriven stood in the corridor outside Sister Antrobus's room. There was no mistake. The light from the room shone on his face and besides, Emily had met very few men who were as tall and imposing.

Stepping into the pool of light from the door and throwing her arms around his neck was Sister Antrobus. Emily could hear every word reverberating back to her from the high domed ceiling. She almost wished she couldn't as she cringed.

'Will you come back tomorrow, darling?' she asked.

'I can't. It's my golf day, you know that. Maybe

next Monday? I came tonight, my loveliness, because I wanted to thank you for today.'

Emily put a hand over her mouth. Loveliness? In Emily's wildest dreams she could never have imagined anyone calling Sister Antrobus 'my loveliness'. She stood stock-still, not wanting either of them to hear or see her. She knew that the next few moments could prove to be incredibly useful.

'That silly Martha girl. I was only doing my best, trying to help her. I know it was wrong of me, but I thought that as she worked at the hospital I would do all I could. You know how it is. We must look after our own at St Angelus.'

But Sister Antrobus plainly had other things on her mind. She wasn't paying attention to a word he said.

'I'll have died of longing by Monday. I can't wait a whole week. Please come back inside.'

Emily closed her eyes for a second, unable to bear to look as a gesture of intimacy passed between the two.

'I can't, my dear. You know how it is. If my wife suspects anything she will threaten to tell the hospital board. I've explained all this before. I've a terrible life at home, you know that.'

Emily was surprised at the whining edge to his voice. The pathetic nature of his pleading.

'You were top spot today, helping cover for me with that silly girl.' He had now taken hold of both Sister Antrobus's wrists. 'You know how important it is that you back me up in this, don't you? The girl is ashamed of what she has done. She may feel pressured to make outlandish and ridiculous claims to cover her own back. You understand that I may need your further support in this matter, don't you, my loveliness?'

'Yes, of course I do. If she tries to damage your reputation she'll have me to answer to. You've been too good to that girl.'

Emily saw a look of relief pass across Mr Scriven's face. 'Matron did the right thing, dismissing that common nurse. Good girl,' he said. 'You obviously have influence over her.'

Now he had her attention. 'Oh, yes. I do. She'll be retiring soon and I'm hoping I will be first in line for her job. Don't you worry about Matron. I can play her like a finely tuned fiddle. You will be safe with me.'

A thought occurred to Emily and then ran down her spine like a trickle of icy water. In order to leave the corridor, Mr Scriven would have to walk past her. She would be caught listening, eavesdropping. She almost fainted with a combination of repulsion and relief as she heard Mr Scriven say, 'Not sure if the old boy is up to it, but you know I can never resist you. Back inside, my loveliness.'

Sister Antrobus giggled as they turned back towards the door.

Emily knew she had to seize her moment and she had to do it there and then. It was no use letting them simply slip back into the room. What she had heard and what they were doing was her lucky break. Why did he want her support? Why value her influence with Matron? Why want Pammy dismissed? There was more to this, to what Mr Scriven was saying. Every scrap of intuition was screaming out that he was hiding something. Pammy had been suspended and it was Emily's job to save her. She didn't yet know what was what, but, by God, she would find out.

She coughed. They didn't hear a thing. She tried again, just as the door began to close. 'Mr Scriven,' she said loudly.

Mr Scriven froze, and then he and Sister Antrobus stepped back into the corridor looking confused. Neither of them could see her, concealed as she was in the shadows. 'Mr Scriven,' Emily said again. 'What a surprise to see you here.'

She moved away from the wall, holding the towels out in front of her, and stepped into the light. Tiredness and her desperate need for a bath were all but forgotten. She wanted to laugh out loud at the expression of guilt and horror on both of their faces.

Pammy, she thought, I think we have our miracle.

CHAPTER 29

'What on earth is going on?' Martha heard the night nurse say, her voice loaded with indignation. 'How dare you push past me? I shall report you to Matron, right now.'

Martha heard the ting of the telephone bell, just as the door to her cubicle burst open and Jake was standing in the doorway. A flash of lightning lit up his face. He looked terrified. His hands hung by his sides and for a moment it was as though he could not believe that it was his Martha in the bed. That he was checking. Scanning her face with his eyes, a face which was now so pale and wan, that it was not how he had ever seen his Martha look. He was soaked through from the torrent of rain that beat against the windows. The only sound in the cubicle was that of water dripping from the peak of his cap, on to the floor. Without another word, he ran across the room, almost knocking over the drip stand as he scooped Martha into his arms.

'God, Martha, Martha. I have been all over Liverpool looking for you and all the time you were here. There isn't an inch of the dock road I haven't covered.'

The stubble of his cheek pressed into the side of her face. His cap lay on the bed where he had thrown it. He was unshaven and rough, but she did not care. The feel of his arms, the smell of him, worked better than any of the painkillers she had been given. The damp of his jacket penetrated her hospital gown and it was like a balm. It was Jake.

Sought out by a frantic Elsie that morning, he had walked the streets all day long. He had scoured every inch, the Pier Head, the dock road. He had been out of his mind with worry.

He had known that Martha was out of sorts. Had put it down to wedding nerves. Excitement. Fear. He wondered whether the work on the house had become too much for her and wanted to kick himself.

'Shh, shh, shh,' he said as he rocked and rocked and rocked her, back and forth on the bed. She was upright, almost in his lap as he clung on to her.

'Shh, shh, shh,' he said again.

Martha, the grief for her lost baby raw, blurted out the whole story to Jake. As the ward lights flickered back on, she saw that his face was whiter than she had ever seen it before. As he pulled her back into his arms, the only words he uttered were 'I will kill him', and Martha was scared that he meant it.

And then Matron walked into the cubicle and Martha saw the recognition on her face.

'Martha. Branna told us it was you, and I've been trying to locate your mother. You have had us all in a bit of a tizzy, young lady.'

Sister Haycock stood behind her, looking exhausted. Soaked, tired, anxious. Martha wanted to ask a useless and practical question: what time was it? She had always lived her life by the clock, to the minute. Her thoughts were scampering, distracting her with useless meanderings. Not wanting to hear what Matron might be about to say.

The possibility that she, her mother and even Jake could be about to lose their jobs was unthinkable.

She was concerned that if Jake let go of her, he would leave the cubicle and do something to Mr Scriven. Something they would all live to regret. But her worries all faded to nothing as a new wave of pain claimed her whole attention.

She placed both her hands over her abdomen, as the pains became stronger. She could feel the perspiration breaking out all over. She was as wet as Jake. She was hot. Her sheets were cold. She hadn't been offered a bedpan by the night nurse, not since it was all over. Now she felt a warm dribble escape her and knew it was blood. The wave of pain came again and this time she cried out loud. It was too bad, almost unbearable.

'Mam,' she screamed. 'Oh, Mam.'

'I'm here, Martha.' Martha opened her eyes and saw that her mother stood next to Sister Haycock. Her friend Biddy hovered by the door. The cubicle was filling.

'How bad is the pain, Martha?' Matron asked. 'Show me where it is.' She pulled the sheet back.

'What's wrong, Matron?' asked Elsie, terrified.

'I'm quite sure this can be sorted out with some painkillers and a dose of the new antibiotics, followed by a quick examination to check that the uterus has been fully evacuated. But not until the painkillers are fully working.' She laid her hand on Martha's shoulder to reassure her and looked her directly in the eye as she spoke. 'The examination will be simply to check there are no retained products left behind. It will be as nothing after what you have been through, my dear.'

Matron looked round the room. She noted the empty water jug and glass. She walked to the end of the bed and picked up the TPR chart. The last person to complete an entry had been Nurse Tanner, and before that last entry, the log had been written up every fifteen minutes on the dot. The charts were meticulously filled in until the point where Nurse Tanner had left.

Martha grasped at her abdomen and groaned as the pains returned.

'Sister Haycock, you stay here with her while I find the night sister and fire up a rocket,' said Matron. 'I believe Dr Mackintosh is on call. Could you ask reception to put his light on? Let's ask him to take a look at her, the poor thing. I have known her since she was a child.'

As Matron stormed out on to the ward, Elsie grabbed hold of Martha's hand.

'I've been worried sick about you,' she said as soon she saw that the pain had subsided and Martha had opened her eyes. Jake was now standing next to Elsie, holding Martha's other hand. The presence of Matron had calmed him a little and now, like Martha, he was concerned for their jobs.

Elsie was still speaking. 'I don't know what's been going on, but Sister Haycock went and knocked on Matron's door. Luckily I was already on my way here, and we met in the corridor. Dessie got a message to Biddy and she tracked me down. Me and Jake, we've been looking high and low for you all day.'

Martha didn't speak. She knew what was coming next. The why and how. The disappointment and disbelief. But Elsie said, 'Don't you worry, queen. Matron will have you sorted soon, but, love, you're gonna have to tell me what's been going on.'

'Well, am I glad to see you out through the other side of this mess.'

They all turned at the sound of Dr Mackintosh's voice in the doorway.

'If you all wouldn't mind stepping outside while I see to the patient? Sister Haycock, could I have a nurse to assist, do you think?' Elsie and Jake left the cubicle, Jake scooping his cap back up off the bed as he went, and joined Biddy, who had waited in the corridor

Emily didn't move. 'Do you mind if I assist?' she asked.

'Not at all. The director of nursing herself. Now that is an honour, at the end of what has been a truly mad day.' He turned to Martha. 'Now, you have been through enough. We are going to be very gentle with you.'

Once Dr Mackintosh had given her a strong injection of painkillers, had examined her and reassured himself that her uterus was empty, he gave her an intramuscular injection of antibiotics and added an extra dose directly to the drip bottle.

'And now I'm going to have to return to the bedlam that is Casualty,' he said, 'but you won't be going anywhere, young lady. Preventing infection is going to be our main task here. So you need to settle back and relax. That's all you have to do now. There'll be no putting your feet on that floor for at least a week.'

Martha laid her head back on the pillow. A lone tear rolled down her cheek. Dr Mackintosh and Sister Haycock exchanged a glance.

'Hey now, look. I know it may feel like the end of the world right now, but I have to tell you, after what you went through, you are very lucky to be here. Some women who visit places like the one you did, they don't live to tell the tale. So my advice would be to look on the bright side. That young man of yours, he's pacing the corridor outside.'

Dr Mackintosh grinned at Martha, who gave him a weak smile in response.

When Biddy had gone home, Martha, Jake, Emily and Elsie spent over an hour talking.

Martha found it difficult to stop crying, but between her embarrassed, protracted and garbled outpourings they all grasped the gist of what had occurred. She knew there would be repercussions, but there was nothing else she could do now, and to her surprise she felt better, once it was all out in the open. Everything that happened to her now was in the gift of others, and in a way she was grateful. She doubted that she could even dress herself again, the way she felt.

Later, Matron spoke to her.

'Martha, I cannot imagine what you have been through, and there are courses of action open to you. However, if you are concerned for the good name of yourself and your mother, I would like to reassure you. By tomorrow there will be no Mr Scriven at St Angelus. He will be gone. It's up to you to decide whether or not you wish to involve the police. I will not put any pressure on you one way or the other, but rest assured, I will be taking my own action immediately.' She turned to Emily. 'Now, Sister Haycock, if you will come with me, there is a certain Nurse Tanner we need to discuss.'

Martha turned her head towards Jake, who had not spoken a word while she had told her story. Her eyes filled with fresh tears and unspoken questions.

'Martha,' Jake said, sitting down on the edge of her bed and slipping his arm around her shoulders. Matron could not suppress a frown at the sight of a porter's lad sitting on the bed, but her better judgement let it pass.

Elsie kissed her daughter on the forehead and slipped out of the room after Emily and Matron. Martha needed sleep, but for that sleep to be worth anything she needed a few moments with Jake first.

'I hope he does the right thing,' Elsie said as she walked to the door.

'Oh, he will. He will,' said Matron. 'Love conquers all. Or so I hear.'

'Martha, none of this was your fault. You know that, don't you?'

Martha didn't answer, she couldn't. They weren't the words she needed to hear.

'You have to decide what is the best thing to do, but that bastard should be behind bars. Anyway, you don't have to do anything you don't want. You've been through enough, without the police getting involved.'

'I don't know, Jake.' He still hadn't said what she wanted to hear. The only thing she wanted to hear.

A silence fell between them and Martha felt as if it was pushing them apart. As it grew, she panicked.

'Jake,' she said. 'I'll understand if you've decided you don't want to marry me, I will. You won't want used goods, will you?'

Jake rested his head on top of hers. 'I was just listening to your breathing, queen. I was thinking to myself that this is the first time we've been in bed together.' Despite everything, they both laughed. Martha flinched with pain. 'Is it bad? Shall I get them to call the doctor back?'

'No, it's fading now,' she said. 'The doctor said the solution of carbolic the woman used was so strong it has burnt my lining off inside, but he said that he hoped it would repair itself, in time. I've not to get pregnant for a year, though, he said.' She held her breath.

'Well, that's all right, we can wait. Martha, there's something you don't know about and I was keeping it for a surprise, but I reckon you need a bit of good news right now. Last year, I won on the pools. We aren't rich, but we are comfortable. I told you, Dessie's going to promote me to under-porter. So you're going to be marrying a man with a proper job.'

At last, he had said it. Martha had been sure Jake would no longer want to marry her, but he did. She would stay in bed for however long it took. Follow every order. She would recover. She had a future to look forward to. As Jake hugged her to him and rocked her to sleep, Martha vowed she would never forget the little boy she had seen for only a second. No one would want to talk to her about him. No one would want to know. But she would remember him. He came from her. He was part of her, and he would live, in her heart.

CHAPTER 30

Sister Antrobus was the first to arrive. As she sat in front of Matron's desk, complaining about Pammy Tanner, it occurred to Matron that Sister Antrobus had sat in front of her desk and complained in this way about numerous nurses. All of them had gone on to leave St Angelus, often without Matron's encouragement. Matron had defended Sister Antrobus and her capricious relationship with junior nurses, most notably to Sister Haycock, but now she realized that she had committed a dreadful error, one that a woman in her position should never make. She had allowed her judgement to be swayed by her personal feelings.

As she watched Sister Antrobus, squirming and failing to dig herself out of the hole she had found herself in, it was as though a veil suddenly fell from her eyes and everything became clear. Blackie lay in his basket and was silent. Even he could sense that the situation was serious. She had told Elsie not to bring in any tea. A meeting with Matron without tea was in itself an indicator of trouble ahead. As Sister Antrobus dug deeper, Matron felt nothing but contempt for her lack of compassion and her bitterness towards young nurses. It was always the pretty ones she disliked. Matron listened to her tirade for five minutes, then decided enough was enough. It was time to put Sister Antrobus out of her misery.

'Be quiet, Sister Antrobus. I've heard quite enough of your version of events.'

Sister Antrobus stopped, mid-flow. Her mouth flapped open and closed. This had never happened before. She usually had Matron eating out of her hand. For a moment, she was thrown, and fell silent.

'This patient, this young and pretty girl.' Matron loaded the words 'young and pretty' with meaning, pausing to allow them to sink in. 'There were no notes, yet Mr Scriven told you he knew her name. Did this not concern you?'

Sister Antrobus was impressive, thought Matron. She recovered very quickly.

'Why, not at all, Matron. I have nothing but the greatest respect for Mr Scriven. He is a truly great gynaecologist and obstetrician. And we nurses all live by the pledge of Florence Nightingale, to aid the physician at all times, without question.' A look of satisfaction crossed Sister Antrobus's face and this irritated Matron. Her voice was full of sarcasm as she replied.

'I am sure that if Florence Nightingale were alive today, she would be more than grateful for your contribution. Why was this girl's life in danger, Sister?'

'Excuse me, Matron?'

Matron sighed. Sister Antrobus was now deliberately playing dumb. How on earth had she come to rate her relationship with Mr Scriven more highly than her loyalty to the reputation of the hospital itself? How had he achieved that? Matron wondered.

They were disturbed by a heavy knock on the door. 'Ah, that will be Mr Scriven himself, just on cue. I can ask him myself. Would you mind waiting in my dining room please, Sister?'

Matron had chosen the dining room deliberately. Elsie had done a fine job of clearing up that morning, but she hoped the wet stain on the carpet and the faint lingering odour would be enough of a reminder to humble Sister Antrobus.

Matron rose from behind her desk and opened the door to admit Mr Scriven. Gone was his usual arrogant swagger. Matron noticed the look that passed between him and Sister Antrobus before the sister closed the dining-room door. They had sent each other a flurry of silent messages. His look asked plainly, *Does she know?* Hers returned, *It's not good. Hold firm. Not your fault.*

As the door to the dining room clicked shut, Matron wasted no time. She wanted him out as soon as possible.

'Mr Scriven, that baby was your own, was it not? Were you aware of that?'

Mr Scriven was so stunned, he couldn't say a word.

'I shall try another question which may be easier to answer. Does your wife know you raped Martha O'Brien?'

For a moment, Matron thought he was about to turn on his heel and leave, and indeed he began to do so before turning back and placing both his hands on her desk.

'Matron, I am the senior surgeon on ward two, and as you know . . .' He didn't have the chance to continue. Matron was not going to allow him to sidetrack her, or waste her time with weaselly words of bluster.

'Mr Scriven, I think it is best for all concerned if we keep this as brief as possible. I know exactly who you are. Your position at St Angelus is the reason why such high standards are expected both at a professional level and in a personal capacity. You have taken advantage of a member of my staff. A young girl who was trusted to work in the consultants' sitting room.'

She saw the colour drain from his face as he let out a small gasp. She didn't blame Martha. She was all too aware of the arrogant manner in which consultants could behave and of the way in which some of them terrified and intimidated young nurses. Martha wasn't even a nurse. Matron herself had taken Martha on as a maid in acknowledgement of Elsie's service and this made her feel doubly guilty. Martha, the daughter of a war widow, could have stood no chance in the face of advances from a man like Mr Scriven, who was now looking less than suave as the corner of his mouth curled and his eyes narrowed.

She felt no pity for him. Only shame at herself for condoning the treatment of the student nurses on ward two because she had been blinded by her own attraction to Sister Antrobus. Matron knew what it was like to fear the reaction of society, to have to conform at all costs, and now she would back Martha all the way. Mr Scriven, with his god-like arrogance, could have destroyed a young girl's life and as a result all three of them were responsible for the death of a child. How would they live with that? Matron wondered, as she watched the blood rise up Mr Scriven's neck. Thank God I told Dessie to take the baby to the mortuary and not the incinerator.

As she saw his rage change to disbelief, she remembered that she had seen the same expression on the face of every nurse she had taken to task in this office. Always at the personal request of Sister Antrobus, and she wondered now how many of them had suffered advances from the supposedly perfect Mr Scriven.

It all fell into place. A pretty nurse he had tired of could become an embarrassing problem. Far better to bring Sister Antrobus on side, complain about the nurse and suggest that maybe Sister should have a word with Matron. As for Matron, she had been a fool. She had jumped through hoops to accommodate and please; she had wanted Sister Antrobus to like her.

'Mr Scriven, I shall not waste anyone's time here. My suggestion is that you leave this hospital forthwith. I am sure we are both aware that Martha's life was in danger. What you did yesterday was highly illegal. You also administered a harmful drug, oxytocin, in a manner which has yet to receive approval to be used in this way and I am quite sure this was because you wished to leave no surgical trace of your endeavour. Am I right?'

She paused for a moment to gauge his reaction. She was worried that he might put up a fight, prove to be difficult. She was, after all, asking him to walk away from his career, his livelihood and his reputation.

'What other drug did you use, Mr Scriven? We know you used something other than oxytocin. What was it?'

He met her eye. He tried to stare her out. To intimidate and even as he did so, they both knew, he was losing. Her eyes were bright. Her expression bold and her smile challenging.

'I have thought this through, and maybe you need some time to recover from a spell of illness which will mean having to take things easier in the future. Maybe one of your physician friends could help with that?'

He momentarily regained his composure and pulled himself up to his full height.

'I do not think it is your place to tell me what to do, Matron. Martha O'Brien was a very stupid young girl who went to a back-street abortionist.

518

How many times have I had to save the lives of girls who do exactly that?'

She silenced him with one glance.

'I saw Martha last night with her mother, who also works here at the hospital. Martha has told us everything. I can assure you that if you wish to kick up a fuss about this, Mr Scriven, I shall fight you every step of the way. Sister Haycock heard your conversation with Sister Antrobus last night and is happy to provide the police with a statement. If you haven't left my office in thirty seconds, I shall pick up my telephone to call them. I am sure they will be very keen to read your mysterious and elusive notes, when they can be located. Oh, and by the way, when I looked in on Martha this morning, her fiancé Jake was on his way down to Whitechapel police station to do just the same thing. I think you may be in rather a lot of trouble, Mr Scriven.'

This was of course not true. She wanted to scare him. What Martha had done was illegal and Matron knew, if the police were involved poor Martha would suffer. A young hospital maid would not stand chance against an articulate, well educated male.

It was as easy as popping a balloon with a pin. She watched his shoulders drop as he deflated.

'You will pay for this,' he shouted, eyes now bulging in his face, suffused with anger.

'No, Mr Scriven. If you remain in St Angelus a moment longer, you will be the one to pay. Do you really want your peers to see you being interviewed by the police?'

The dining-room door burst open and Sister Antrobus rushed to his side. 'Is everything all right?' His raised voice through the dining-room door had made it impossible for her to remain parted from him. She laid her hand on his arm, entirely ignoring Matron's raised eyebrows.

Mr Scriven, however, was staring at Matron, long and hard. She held his gaze. She was enjoying this. She felt empowered for the first time in years. She was doing something good, and she was winning.

'Darling, are you all right?' The corner of Matron's nose screwed up ever so slightly and her eyes narrowed in a half-mocking manner. No one had ever called anyone darling in her office before today and she found it slightly distasteful.

'Get off me, you stupid woman,' Mr Scriven roared, shaking Sister Antrobus's hand from his arm. 'You make me sick with your fawning. You are an ugly, pathetic woman.' With that, Mr Scriven stormed out of Matron's office.

Matron looked down at her desk for a moment, to allow Sister Antrobus time to regain her composure.

'Was it your idea?' she asked. The answer was important.

'What?' Sister Antrobus was still staring at the door, as though she expected it to reopen and for Mr Scriven to walk back in and apologize. *I'm so sorry, I don't know what came over me.*

Instead, the only sounds were those of his footsteps as he took the stairs two at a time and the slamming of the main door. Blackie sat up in his basket and looked enquiringly at the door before satisfying himself that all was safe and lying back down.

Matron thought that in just those few moments Sister Antrobus had somehow shrunk, both in height and weight. Her cheeks were sunken and her eyes looked haunted.

'No, of course not. He came to me, desperate. He said that it was the son of his friend who had got her pregnant.' Her voice was despondent as his parting words began to sink in, and Matron saw tears begin to fill her eyes. The same tears she had seen fill the eyes of many a student nurse standing in exactly the same place.

'And you believed him?'

Sister Antrobus nodded. 'We all have our secrets, Matron.' She looked directly at Matron, her voice loaded with meaning.

Matron rolled her pen between her fingers. She felt as though she were a child on a seesaw. Which way should she come down? Should she send Sister Antrobus the same way as Mr Scriven? Or should she give her a second chance?

While laying the pen down on her desk with exaggerated care, she made her decision.

'I have decided to allow you to remain in post.' She let the words register before she proceeded. Sister Antrobus stood slightly taller and pushed her shoulders back as she let out a long breath.

'Thank you, Matron.' Her voice was little more than a whisper.

'But there are conditions. Look, sit down, for goodness' sake.' Sister Antrobus pulled out the chair and flopped down as relief washed over her. 'I think we all need to be a little nicer to each other round here and you more than most. When new probationary nurses come on to your ward, try to be a little more encouraging and helpful. I am quite sure that without the influence of Mr Scriven and his unreasonable requests, it may be possible. Do you think you can manage that?'

Sister Antrobus nodded, and sniffed back the tears which threatened to overwhelm her.

'Good, but for heaven's sake don't start being nice to the charge nurses on ward eight. I may be turning soft, but not that soft.' She smiled, and Sister Antrobus smiled back.

'You quoted the Florence Nightingale pledge at me, Sister. I am sure I don't need to remind you of the line in it regarding administering a harmful substance? After today, I think we need to establish a protocol. It is becoming very difficult to keep up with the flood of new drugs, and the BNF is only updated once every three years. I am going to propose to the board that we set up a committee to review and evaluate the procedures used in St Angelus. No nurse should ever be in such a precarious situation again. Doctors are not God, despite the Hippocratic oath. We are also bound by our own code, and yesterday, that code was undermined. I won't have that again. Not in this hospital. Now, return to your ward. Nurse your patient as though she were your own daughter. Make her well again. Tell no one what has occurred. We have a reputation to maintain and the police involvement will be difficult enough to deal with. There is nothing to be done for that poor baby, but we must do what we can for Martha. And, please, make Nurse Tanner welcome. Sister Haycock will be arriving soon and I shall tell her the good news.'

As a relieved Sister Antrobus reached the office door, Matron fired her parting shot.

'Oh, and by the way, Sister, I have no intention of retiring. Not for another ten years at least.'

Sister Haycock decided to call in to the nursing-school kitchen before she made her way over to Lovely Lane. As she suspected, Biddy had all the news. She guessed she would never know how it was that Biddy knew everything before she did.

'Well, you will never guess what. Nurse Tanner is off the hook and Mrs Duffy has just called to tell me that she's running up to the hospital right now, as though she had the devil himself chasing her. Matron rang Mrs Duffy and spoke to Nurse Tanner herself. Couldn't keep the smile from her face she couldn't. You were right about that Nurse

Tanner. She really does have a guardian angel looking after her.'

There wasn't a detail Biddy didn't know and Emily just sat there dumbfounded and listened. Biddy failed to tell her that Elsie had stood behind the door in Matron's kitchen and heard every word, and Sister Haycock knew better than to ask how Biddy knew. The details of knowledge-gathering were the preserve of the domestics and therein lay their power.

On the walk over to Matron's office, Emily had already decided on her next battle. It would be to ask Matron to agree to removing the unmarried-nurses-only rule. It might be much easier now than she had thought at first.

She grinned as she walked and was almost talking to herself while she planned how to strike while the iron was hot and catch Matron on a weak day. She was pleased that Matron had already spoken to Pammy. It must have had far more impact than if Emily had been the one to break the news.

She was spotted by Dessie and Jake from the porters' lodge.

'Well, what do you know,' said Jake, as he gazed out of the window and removed a stump of a cigarette from behind his ear. 'That's the first time I think I have ever seen Sister Haycock smile.'

'God bless her,' said Dessie. 'She has a lot to put up with that one, what with her da in that home.'

'What home?' said Jake.

'Oh, never mind. She doesn't think anyone knows, but we all do. How's your Martha?' Dessie wanted to change the subject. He was cross with himself for even mentioning Alf. Sister Haycock had her own reasons for keeping secrets.

'Thank God you recognized her on the trolley, Des. We would never have known otherwise. Elsie was scouring every bingo hall in Liverpool yesterday, thinking she might have been trying to win a bit of money for the wedding. She noticed money had gone out of her drawer.'

'Look after her, lad,' said Dessie, who was looking forward to being given chapter and verse in Biddy's kitchen over six bottles of stout.

'I will, Dessie. We'll be married soon enough, but first she has to get better. That bastard has gone, which is just as well, because if he hadn't I would not be responsible for what I would have done.' Jake had rolled and passed Dessie a ciggie as he spoke.

'You know what, lad,' said Dessie, 'everyone in this life has secrets. You and Martha have yours now and if there is one bit of advice I can give you, it's this. If you don't want people to talk about yours, you don't talk about anyone else's. I've always found that's the best way.'

Jake looked up sharply and his eyes met Dessie's, searching for a hidden meaning in his words, but finding none he struck his match and lit up.

CHAPTER 31

The only footsteps to be heard pounding the wet tarmac were her own. Aware of the noise echoing in the dead of night, Dana looked up nervously towards the dimly lit windows of ward eight, the male surgical ward, hoping not to wake post-operative patients, sleeping away the combined effects of an anaesthetic and the pain of surgery, or be seen by any nurse who knew her personally. They would wonder where on earth she was going at such a late hour and why she wasn't tucked up in bed in the Lovely Lane home, where her friends and colleagues were fast asleep. She had been a nurse long enough to know that, as she slipped across the hospital grounds, someone, busy or sleepless, curious or just plain nosy, could easily observe her flight as she attempted to slip away into the night unnoticed.

Half an hour earlier, she had crept down the stairs from her first-floor room in the nurses' home and headed towards the back door, one gentle step at a time. She had hesitated outside Pammy's room, half expecting her to cry out, 'Who is it? What time is it?' Pammy was the lightest sleeper of them all and was due back on duty on ward two the following morning.

It had tested Dana's strength to the very limit when only hours earlier Pammy, Victoria, newly returned from Lancashire, and even Beth had bounced up and down on her bed while she feigned toothache as an excuse not to join them that evening.

'Are you sure you aren't coming down to supper?' Pammy had asked, concerned. Dana had hardly been known to miss a meal.

Pammy was one of life's eternal optimists and Dana had known she would not simply accept a toothache as a reason for not wanting to spend her evening with the rest of the girls downstairs.

'Let's get you to Dr Mackintosh right now,' Pammy had continued. 'He will give you some painkillers at the very least. Dana, are you sure you're all right?'

Pammy's words almost brought a smile to Dana's face. But she must not let herself down. She had to keep up the act.

Pammy would not give in. Being the daughter of Maisie and Stan, part of a docker family who had struggled their entire life to make ends meet, Pammy was a fighter who never gave up.

Beth was almost as bad.

'Look here, I've brought you some supplies,' she said, bursting into the room, still wearing her uniform. She slipped a bottle out of her apron pocket. 'Here it is, and there's a couple of aspirin and a gallipot floating around in here, too. My patient didn't want them. Plug your tooth with this.' She tipped the clove tincture on to a cotton wool plug. 'And swallow those,' as she scooped the wayward tablets back together and handed the small glass pot to Dana. 'You'll be as right as rain in no time at all, and you can have a nice bath while they work their magic. No need to bother Dr Mackintosh.'

Dana lay back on her pillows, trying her hardest to look as though she were in pain. The only person who knew her secret was Victoria and she wanted it to stay that way. She had thought she could get this over and done with before the split shift came home from duty, so she would not have to face the indomitable force that was Beth. Tonight was the night. The night of her life. The night when she knew everything would change. Tomorrow could be the day when her life began and she could not wait a moment longer.

She looked at Beth with a woeful expression and tears welled up in her eyes. They were genuine. From the moment Beth had discovered Dana's letter in Celia's room, she had become the group's staunchest ally. They discovered that she had arrived at St Angelus from Germany, where she was based with her army family, and had spent her entire life moving from pillar to post. She claimed that if necessary she could pack up her room and be out of the door in ten minutes. Dana didn't doubt it. Even Beth's cosmetics were lined up like soldiers in a row on her dressing table. The maids knew that there was little to do in her room. Her bed was made so tight each morning, you couldn't have slipped a flat hand between the sheets without ripping off a fingernail, and her clothes were colour coded and stacked as if she were a prisoner, not a student nurse. But as Beth sometimes said, 'What's the difference?'

In the past month, much to Celia Forsyth's chagrin, Beth had planned, made lists and organized the group's daily life. They all wondered how someone so small, with her dark brown hair and upswept glasses, could be as forceful as she was. They all had their orders. Acute short-sightedness was no handicap to Beth. In fact, her spectacles added to the look of bossiness. Not a single patient had ever complained when given an instruction from Beth.

Lovely Beth. So earnest. So indefatigable. She had an answer to every problem. Beth would be cross when she found out what Dana was doing. She would take it personally. She would regard it as her failing not to have been the one Dana confided in or to have seen what was coming, seeing how it was Beth who had played a major role in the whole business by handing over the letter she had found in Celia's room.

'I have news, girls,' said Victoria, unhooking the button on her cape and flinging it over the chair as she flounced down on Dana's bed and blew her a kiss. 'The very young and handsome Oliver

Gaskell came on to my ward today to speak to our consultant and I heard him say to the houseman that he was going to pop into the social club dance, to make sure they were all behaving, but he was only joking. I actually heard him say . . . are you all listening?' The girls gave Victoria their full attention, Dana forgotten.

'Go on,' said Pammy, 'quick, what?'

Victoria almost laughed out loud at the sight of Pammy, waiting with bated breath and open mouth. She had almost never stopped talking about her hero, Oliver Gaskell. The new god on ward two. 'I heard him say that he was hoping to bag a dance with a particular nurse he had his eye on, and he winked at the houseman.'

Pammy lowered herself onto the edge of Dana's bed. 'Oh, my giddy aunt. Do you think that could be me? Do yer?'

'Who else would it be?' said Beth. 'You virtually followed him around ward two and he spoke to you every chance he got. There isn't a nurse in the hospital who doesn't think you have made an impression on Mr Gaskell.'

Pammy dashed over to the dressing table, sat herself on the stool and began rifling through Dana's make-up bag and hair slides. Then she caught sight of Dana in the mirror.

'Oh no, what's the matter? You have such a funny look on yer face, Dana. Is the toothache that bad?'

Dana's look had actually been one of despair. She had realized that her friends were settling in for the night, when she wanted them as far away as possible.

'Get them tablets down her, Beth,' said Pammy, rushing to the sink. Tipping Dana's toothbrush into the basin she filled the glass and handed the warm, disgusting water to Dana. Pammy was as practical as she was unflappable. She often cut corners and didn't always think things through. It wouldn't have taken a second to run the water until it was cold, but that wouldn't have been 'our Pammy', as everyone called her.

'Go on, swallow. Get them down you now. They will kill the pain.'

'That water's almost hot,' said Beth. Pammy drove Beth mad, but in a funny sort of way, although total opposites, they now enjoyed each other's company most of the time.

'So what? Who cares? She just needs to get them tablets down and anyway, some people like hot water.'

Dana took the tablets, and shifting the hot water bottle from the side of her face whispered, 'Could you just leave me now? I really want to sleep. You all go and have a lovely time watching the TV, and tell Mrs Duffy I am fine.'

'Of course you do,' said Victoria, smoothing out the eiderdown. 'Come along, nurses, we must leave our patient to sleep.'

At last, thought Dana as they all began to make for the door.

'All right then, we'll let yer off,' said Pammy,

begrudgingly. 'But if you're no better in the morning, mind, we'll take you in to Dr Mackintosh ourselves. Or Mr Finch has a dental clinic in the morning. If he doesn't know what to do, no one will.'

'Mr Finch is an oral surgeon. This is well below what he is used to dealing with,' said Dana, realizing she was becoming wrapped up in her own tableau of deceit.

'Doesn't matter,' said Pammy. 'We all look after our own at St Angelus.'

She was the last to leave. 'If you need me in the night, if the pain gets too unbearable, wake me. Promise.'

'Don't be daft,' said Dana. 'You have a full day tomorrow. I won't wake you.'

Both girls smiled for a second too long and held each other's eyes. Dana wondered if Pammy was suspicious.

'You sure you are OK?' Pammy asked again, in a tone which could only be described as meaningful.

Dana could hear the fading voices of Victoria and Beth as they moved away down the corridor to their own rooms, already planning what clothes to swap with each other and whose room they would get ready in before the forthcoming doctors' dance on Saturday. Dana heard Victoria, with her lovely, choral-trained singing voice, break into a Doris Day number.

'Yes. Go away,' said Dana gently, turning on to

her side to avoid Pammy's gaze. She heard the door click closed, and then, raising her head, realized that at last she was alone with her secret.

Now, in the dark corridor, from which the excited whispers of the returning girls had long since departed, she hovered outside Pammy's door, the note in her hand. She looked at it long and hard. She was taking a risk.

It was after eleven o'clock, but Pammy was awake. She heard Dana's stealthy steps on the stairs, but she didn't shout out. She had known this was coming, she just hadn't known it was tonight. Pammy, Victoria and Beth had met for coffee in the greasy spoon only last week, and discussed what to do about Dana.

She had talked far too much lately about the fact that she would have to return to Ireland at the end of her training and probably marry a man who was a thug, an oaf and a heartless beast. 'For heaven's sake, why?' Victoria had asked the first time Dana had said it.

'Because that's my lot in life. I'm Irish and it's what my family expects. And sure, why would any man want me?'

They all imagined they had secrets of their own, but Pammy thought, as she stared at the door, no one did, not really. Victoria and Beth had confided in her about the letter Beth had found and Dana's broken heart. It took her a full five minutes to calm her own hurt that Dana hadn't told her.

'I knew something must have gone wrong that night, but she never said a word about it and I didn't like to ask. Didn't she trust me, or what?' she asked Victoria with tears in her eyes.

'Of course she trusts you. I was just in on it because, well, I have a secret too, but I wanted to tell you all together. Anyway, this isn't about me. It's about Dana. Girls, she read a letter from her daddy in Ireland to me yesterday. I used to reckon no one knew more about misguided fathers than I do, but I can promise you, this was on an entirely different level. If we don't rescue Dana from the fate which is surely awaiting her, well, I for one shan't be able to live with myself. She'll be driven back to Ireland to marry a pig of a man for no other reason than guilt and feeling sorry for her mammy, and we have to do something about it. So I've a plan.'

The girls had leant in over the table, eyes wide open and ready to hear Victoria's idea. You are quite bossy yourself, Victoria, thought Beth. But it remained a thought. Saving Dana was far more important.

Pammy fancied she could hear Dana's heartbeat. She listened for her breathing and looked towards the door. In a voice too weak to reach Dana and swallowed by the thickness of the gloom, she whispered, 'Please don't let her down. Please be there, please.'

Pammy knew the sound of every stair. The second to the bottom had a creak that could not be avoided. She counted the steps and right on cue, the last but one creaked. Silence fell. She's nearly there, thought Pammy. Then, she heard stealthy footsteps pass by outside, along the grass border and under her window. She had made it. She was free. Dana was on her way.

Pammy let out the long breath that she hadn't realized she was holding and prayed hard for her friend.

CHAPTER 32

Dana could hear her heart beating as she approached the rear of the theatre block. The note was in her pocket, crumpled and faded by many rereadings. At first, she had ignored it. Pretended to Victoria that she didn't care, but there was no fooling Victoria.

'Look, Dana, Teddy has asked me to pass you this,' she had said. Dana was in her room trying to study for a ward assessment the following morning. Sister Ryan was due to arrive at ten thirty and assess Dana as she removed sutures and re-dressed an appendicectomy wound. As Dana read the letter, the words just swam in front of her and refused to sink in.

'Victoria?' Dana raised her head. 'What have you done? Have you told him about Celia?'

'Yes, I have. I'm sorry to have interfered, but I just didn't think it was fair on him – on either of you – because after all, neither of you has done anything wrong. It was all down to that beastly Celia Forsyth. Anyway, really, Dana, does it matter who plays Cupid here? I'll leave it all to you now, but he's given you a telephone number. The ball's in your court.'

'Don't you dare,' said Dana, jumping up to close her bedroom door. 'You are going to sit here and go over every word with me.' Her eyes were alight. For the first time in months, she felt alive.

Dana kept to the bushes and away from the lamp-posts as she hurried along the same route she used every day. Tonight it felt different. Her heart was beating and her skin prickled as she thought she heard footsteps behind her. She stopped and looked back; there was no one.

She walked faster and there they were again, but still she could see nothing. As she reached the lights at the back gates of the hospital, she saw a dark figure sprint away in the direction of the Old Dock Road and she gave a sigh of relief. She did not have to wait for more than a second. She heard a set of footsteps running down a flight of stairs and then, in a flash, he was standing in front of her.

'Well, what do you know? She came!' He pretended to shout to the sky and threw his arms up in the air. 'I have been on duty since Monday morning and I haven't left since. Liverpool is going crazy. We have done two caesarean sections up there in the past two hours. I'm not off again until Friday night. I've got matchsticks holding my eyelids up.'

He plunged his hands into the pockets of his white coat. 'Look, I'm off on Saturday and it's the doctors' social. I wanted to ask you, but I wanted to ask you to your face. Would you come with me, as my guest? Please. I have no idea why that wretched girl didn't give you the note telling you I wouldn't be here last time, but I can promise you, when I see her next, she will have to come up with a good explanation.'

It was as though a breeze had swept the air away and Dana struggled to breathe. He wanted her to go to the social with him. It was her very first dance in Liverpool and the best-looking doctor at the hospital wanted her to go with him. She blinked in the strong light at the bottom of the theatre-block steps. Much to her embarrassment, she was speechless.

'And before you say no, I'm sorry for asking you to risk getting into trouble by coming out at night again. It's just that if I had arranged to meet you during the day, I would probably have been called away and well, I just didn't want to miss you, not again. That would have been unbearable. At least I know I am stuck here on receiving ward and theatre all night.'

He grinned his ridiculous grin. It was a grin from a man who had a good heart and nothing to hide, and Dana's own heart melted away. 'Well, I wasn't planning on going,' she said.

'That wouldn't have anything to do with you once thinking Victoria and I were an item, would it? When in fact she and my brother are smitten with each other.'

'How dare you?' she spluttered. 'Where would you get that idea, and why would I care in any case?'

He took a step backwards in the face of her mock outrage. They both knew it wasn't real. 'Has she told you yet? They're engaged. He's coming to the dance.'

Now Dana really was speechless.

She took in his flopping fringe and his boyish grin. His shirt collar was slightly crumpled under his white coat and for a fleeting moment the image of Patrick came into her mind. She let her breath escape. This man was not Patrick, she must not concern herself on that score. She must relax. This man was a doctor, healing and saving lives, and had kindness and mischief shining out of his eyes. He was not Patrick.

'I would love to come,' she said and, embarrassed, looked down at her feet. She felt his finger slip under her chin as he slowly tilted her face upwards and made her look at him.

'Well, in that case, roll on Saturday.'

He kissed her gently and she was lost, until they both heard the sound of a voice shouting, 'Dr Davenport, wanted in theatre' through the doors.

'I'll pick you up at half past seven in Lovely Lane,' he said. 'Under the lamp-post, where I first found you,' and then he was gone.

Dana walked back through the hospital grounds and felt as though she were flying. Gone was the cold night breeze which had made her shiver on her way. She had a precious, wonderful secret and it kept her warm.

What Dana didn't know was that in St Angelus, everyone and no one had a secret to hold.

CHAPTER 33

P ammy was in tears. 'How did that happen?' she wailed as she threw the dress she had been trying on on to the floor.

'Well, because you've lost so much weight, queen,' said Maisie, with a worried frown on her face. 'They work you too hard at that hospital.'

Pammy wasn't listening. She was sitting on the edge of her bed, in tears.

'Come on, love, we don't cry about silly things like that,' said Maisie. 'No one has died.'

Pammy felt stupid. She knew the true meaning of those words. Sometimes a neighbour would pop in to have a cuppa with Maisie and if they thought no one was listening, they would start talking about the war and Pammy knew that within minutes they would be in floods of tears, crying over someone they once knew or loved, or both.

'The new lady in number ten has a sewing machine. I'll pin the dress now and run down and borrow it. It will take me an hour at the most.'

'What if she's not in?' Pammy's wail had subsided to a whimper.

'Oh, that's not a problem. She keeps it out on

the kitchen table. If she's not there, I'll just help myself.'

Nothing had changed in Arthur Street for as long as anyone could remember. Back doors were still unlocked and it would remain that way until the new houses and estates were built and the fabric of the dockside community fractured and split apart. Families and relatives who had lived side by side for generations would become isolated and confused, struggling to find a new way to live, to rear children without generations of knowledge, values and expertise at hand.

'I've hung Dana's dress up on a hanger and I've run an old sheet up into a bag to carry them both back to Lovely Lane. Don't you drop them now. And I've turned the hem up on Beth's skirt. That's in the bag too.'

Maisie had become chief dressmaker in preparation for the dance. The only one of the girls who hadn't needed her help was Victoria, and she had come up trumps in her own way.

'Would this dress and cloak be any use, Mrs Tanner?' she had asked. The cloak was full length and made of the most exquisite black velvet. The dress was covered in seed pearls.

Maisie gasped. 'Victoria, I can't cut up good quality clothes like that. Are you out of your mind, love?'

'Oh, yes you can,' said Victoria. 'Look, Mrs Tanner, I have kept all Mummy's dresses and I have as many as you could shake a stick at at Aunt

Minnie's. This dress with the seed pearls was my great-grandmother's. I'm never going to wear it. Look, it is so old-fashioned.' Maisie could barely speak. She ran the dress though her fingers. 'Pammy tells me you're a magician with a needle, so please, turn them into something nice for Pammy and Dana.'

Maisie had worked her magic. Not only had she been able to make two beautiful dresses, but Dana also had a cape to match and Pammy a bolero. Dana preferred the velvet and the original cloak had so many folds there was enough for both dress and cape, with some left over for the bolero. The seed pearl dress was converted for Pammy.

Victoria was to wear a dress of stunning emerald green silk and Maisie had taken up, by over nine inches, a full-length black crepe skirt which Beth wanted to wear with a black silk blouse Victoria was lending her. The excitement was growing as the dance approached.

'Mam, could you do something with this?' Pammy took out a dress she had carefully rolled in her basket.

'Who does that belong to?' asked Maisie, looking confused. 'It's from Goldsmiths. They charge an arm and a leg, they do.' She was checking out the seams. 'Look at that beautiful stitching, Pammy.'

'Mam, I want you to undo it.'

'What? I can't do that. Are you out of your mind, our Pammy?'

'Mam, please, just do as I say. Don't unpick the

543

seams completely; leave it so that each seam is held by a half thread with no close at the ends.'

'Pammy, what are you up to?'

'I'll tell you, Mam, but not until after. But I promise, the girls will love you if you do this for me.'

And, so, with a heavy heart, Maisie unpicked the most beautiful stitching she had ever seen.

CHAPTER 34

Victoria still had told no one any details about Roland. Dana had decided to take matters into her own hands, and had called a meeting in the greasy spoon with Beth and Pammy to reveal and discuss.

'Well I never,' said Pammy. 'When is she going to tell us? We need to buy her a present and get her a card. Something for her bottom drawer.'

'What in God's name do we buy for an engagement present for the daughter of a lord?' asked Dana. 'Anyway, I think we should do something for them at the dance. Teddy told me.'

'Ooh, get you. Teddy told you, did he now,' they all chorused playfully.

Dana blushed. 'Yes, he did. Shut up, will you all. He also told me they have to wait until a respectable time has passed after the funeral before it is announced officially in *The Times* or whatever people like them do.'

'Poor Victoria,' said Pammy. 'She must be heartbroken still, but you wouldn't know it. If it was me and me da had died, I would have cried my leg off by now. It's her breeding, you know, or so me mam says. She hides it well.'

'There isn't anything we can do,' said Beth. 'We have to wait until the day when Victoria wants to tell us about her and Roland being engaged.'

That evening, Pammy called her own meeting in the greasy spoon. This time everyone was invited.

Beth, Victoria and Dana arrived first and had already had their tea, when Pammy sat down next to them. 'Don't you just hate these national issue green cups and saucers?' She leant forward to sip the tea out of her overflowing cup.

'Is that why you have called a meeting?' asked Beth, her voice incredulous.

'No, of course not. Listen, I've just been to the pharmacy to have a word. I've a plan to get Celia back. Who's with me?'

'God, I haven't even heard it yet, but all of us, eh, sisters?' said Beth.

The girls grinned, and Pammy leant in to whisper.

Pammy dropped the clothes off into each girl's wardrobe. She was the only nurse who had the Saturday off. Every other nurse at Lovely Lane was working that day. Lizzie and the older girls were sitting state finals the following week. They were in the library all day, revising. Pammy called in to Celia's room first. She was in and out in a flash. Under no circumstances must she be caught, and she had to return the master key to the kitchen before Mrs Duffy realized it had gone. Celia needed to be taught a lesson and Pammy reckoned she had just made sure it would happen.

They walked up to the hospital in a row. Four girls with arms linked. They were singing Al Martino's 'Here in My Heart' at the tops of their voices. It was the first night they had all taken out together and spirits were high.

'I hope the punch is as good as Teddy reckons it's going to be,' said Dana.

'It had better be,' said Pammy. 'He's the one in charge of making it. You know Sister Haycock is coming too? Isn't that lovely?'

The girls would not hear a word said against Sister Haycock. As far as they were concerned, she was nothing short of a heroine, what with the work she had put into saving Pammy, standing up for the rights of student nurses, and her quest to modernize nursing and life at St Angelus, which was still stuck in a pre-war 1930s rut.

Victoria was quieter than all the others on the way to the dance and Pammy decided to quiz her. 'You all right, Vic?' she asked.

Victoria decided that as they were all looking at her, waiting for a reply, now was as good a time as ever. The street lights illuminated the pavement and bathed the lane in a warm orange glow which lit their faces as they walked.

'Oh, it's no good, I'm going to have to tell you, although it can't be public knowledge yet. I need your help later, and I felt dreadful you girls not knowing, and anyway you will meet him tonight and I can't go on keeping something so important a secret any longer.'

'Victoria, just spit it out will you?'

'Oh all right then, I'm engaged to be married.'

The girls let out a shout of joy as they jumped around Victoria and hugged her, pretending they didn't know.

Mrs Duffy heard them as she put out the rubbish. She tutted as she replaced the bin lid. 'I don't know, one night out and they go mad,' she muttered.

'Married?' squealed Pammy. 'Are you serious?'

'Are you giving up nursing?' asked Beth.

'Go on, tell them,' said Dana. Dana had decided to meet Teddy at the social club. As much as she wanted to see him, she also wanted the excitement of getting ready and walking up with her friends.

Victoria began to laugh so much she had trouble catching her breath. She finished quickly, 'Look, tonight I'm not coming back to Lovely Lane. Roland has booked us into the Grand.'

Three astonished faces looked back at her. Just at that moment a car pulled up alongside and the window wound down.

'Victoria,' said the driver. 'May I offer you ladies a lift?'

'Roland!' Victoria had thought he would be waiting in the social club car park.

As the nurses piled into the car, Pammy whispered to Victoria, 'Why do you need our help, Vic?'

'Because I need you to distract Mrs Duffy, so that she thinks I've gone up to bed, and then tomorrow I'm off, so I want you to tell her I left early.'

Pammy nodded, in deadly earnest. 'Right, I'm your woman.'

Sister Haycock arrived at the dance late. She hadn't really wanted to go, but the nurses had insisted and anyway, Oliver Gaskell had asked her whether she would be attending. His question had been casual, almost throwaway, and she was so long out of the dating game that she had no idea how she should interpret his interest. She felt rather silly, standing in a hall full of her junior doctors and nurses. She was relieved to see some of the younger consultants milling around the punch bowl with one of the sisters from Maternity, and made her way towards them.

He didn't even see them coming. He had waited night after night for her to leave the nurses' home. Most nights he had waited until almost ten p.m. and yet she had never set a foot outside.

Don't come home until she has agreed to be your wife, his father had said.

His wife? He would see her dead before he married her. The stuck-up bitch was too full of herself for him to ever want her in his bed. Country women in Ireland did as they were told, and when they didn't they took the fist. That was the way of it. She would make life far too much trouble. Her own mother had ruined her for any good man. His father must have been mad thinking he would want to marry her. Not now. Now, he would just make her pay for humiliating him.

The hand landed on his shoulder with a thud. There were two of them.

'Oh, a peeping Tom. My favourite,' said one of the policemen. 'Judge Pincher, he loves a peeping Tom. Caught one after his daughter once.'

The other policeman laughed. 'Aye, right, let's be having you down the station, young man, and it's a cell for you. You'll find it very comfortable. Up before Pincher you will be in the morning and then your bed may not be as comfy as the cell.'

Patrick tried to run, but they downed him on the path before he had taken a second step. Handcuffs on. Cold metal digging into his flesh. Soil in his face. From the corner of his eye he saw his flaming cigarette stub on the damp cold grass, slowly fade and die.

Out of the corner of her eye, she saw Dessie, carrying a tray of drinks to the stage for the band, who were playing, 'She Wears Red Feathers'. The dancers on the floor seemed to move as one as the floor vibrated to the sound of tapping feet. And then the tempo altered dramatically as the lead singer of the band picked up the microphone and began to sing his version of 'Here in My Heart'. His voice was deep, melodious and sad, and as the strains of the haunting song caught at her heart, Emily thought he must surely be a professional. She stopped in her tracks, captured by the music.

She was so entranced that she found it difficult to tear her eyes away. How lovely, she thought. What a beautiful song. I need to work less and do things like this more often. She saw Dessie almost drop his tray of drinks as he raised his hand to wave to her. She waved back and took a step forward. She meant to move towards Dessie. To help him to steady the tray. But, instead, she stopped dead. It was the distraction, Dessie waving, that had taken her eye away from the lead singer on to the dance floor and straight on to Pammy, in the arms of Oliver Gaskell. Pammy's head was buried in his chest and the light reflected from the shimmering seed pearls covering her dress.

Did Emily feel her own heart tighten? Did she feel a lump form in her throat when she saw his lips brush against her flowing dark hair, as he whispered something in her ear? No, she did not. What she felt was relief, as Dessie strode across the dance floor towards her, holding out a glass of punch, and rescued her from her lonely place on the edge of the dance floor.

'Come here, will you, and let me hang your coat up for you. You know, I thought they had switched the lights on when you walked in. A ray of sunshine, you are.'

His fingers brushed against her own as she took

the drink and she felt something she had never felt before. She wanted to reach out and wind her fingers around Dessie's. She felt frumpy in her skirt and twinset, but Dessie didn't seem to care what she was wearing. With those few words, he had made her feel as though it was she who was wearing a shimmering dress, covered in pearls. She could have kissed him with gratitude, or at least she thought it was gratitude.

When the band finished, the lead singer announced, 'Time for refreshments, doctors and nurses. We shall return in fifteen minutes.'

As the lights clicked on, they all heard a sound, a little like a mewing cat.

It was Celia Forsyth and she was twisting herself into a dozen different shapes while furiously tearing at her skin, yelling, 'Scratch my back, scratch my back, oh God, my back,' to the girls from the knitting circle who were looking at her in horror.

People gasped as the seams at the back of her dress fell apart, opening from top to bottom, just as a sleeve began to detach itself from a shoulder. It was all over in seconds as a very agitated and humiliated Celia ran from the hall, screaming.

'Were you responsible for that by any chance?' asked Teddy as he led Dana across to the buffet in the corner of the hall.

'I was not. What do you think I am, vengeful? Oh, all right then. I didn't do it, but I know who did and honestly, as God is true, I really wish it had been me. Guess why Pammy was asking the pharmacist for ground rosehip!'

'Ouch! Rosehip.' Teddy flinched.

'More,' shouted a group of doctors to the band, as they picked up their instruments.

'"Here in My Heart", again, please, it was wonderful,' shouted a doctor, hoping to entice a pretty nurse to slip into his arms.

The nurse was Beth, who almost jumped out of her skin when he tapped her on the shoulder. She had been giggling at the sight of Celia as she careered through the exit.

He was six foot four to her five foot two. But she couldn't have cared less. It was her very first dance, and as he took her by the hand and led her on to the dance floor she thought that she might like to join Pammy on the social committee after all and maybe take charge and organize another one of these dances very soon.

The Angels of Lovely Lane

ALSO BY NADINE DORRIES
FROM CLIPPER LARGE PRINT

Hide Her Name
The Ballymara Road
Ruby Flynn